Praise for the Kyle Swanson Sniper Novels

NIGHT OF THE COBRA

"Series fans will find, as usual, that the fight scenes are razor sharp." —*Publishers Weekly*

"Much like Swanson's dispatch of the Cobra, the book's execution is precise." —*Kirkus Reviews*

ON SCOPE

"Fast-moving [and] suspenseful." —*Kirkus Reviews*

"Delivers the goods for fans of high-action military fiction, and they will be pleased to discover that this series is losing none of its energy, even as it ages. Knowledge of the previous installments is not required to enjoy this one." —*Booklist*

TIME TO KILL

"Coughlin and Davis' series only gets better with each installment . . . Kyle Swanson returns for his boldest and best adven~~~~~~~~~~~~ (starred review)

"A definite winner ~~~~~~~~~~~~~~~~ry action thriller." —*Booklist*

be compelled . . . and will look forward to another Swanson adventure." —*Booklist*

KILL ZONE

"Stunning action, excellent tradecraft, insider politics, and the ring of truth. Just about perfect." —Lee Child

"Tight, suspenseful . . . Here's hoping this is the first of many Swanson novels." —*Booklist*

"The action reaches a furious pitch."
—*Publishers Weekly*

SHOOTER: THE AUTOBIOGRAPHY OF THE TOP-RANKED MARINE SNIPER

"One of the best snipers in the Marine Corps, perhaps the very best. When I asked one of his commanders about his skills, the commander smiled and said, 'I'm just glad he's on our side.'" —Peter Maass, war correspondent and bestselling author of *Love Thy Neighbor*

"The combat narratives here recount battlefield action with considerable energy . . . A renowned sniper, Coughlin is less concerned with his tally than with the human values of comradeship and love."
—*The Washington Post*

NIGHT OF THE COBRA

A SNIPER NOVEL

GUNNERY SGT. **JACK COUGHLIN,**
USMC (RET.)

WITH **DONALD A. DAVIS**

St. Martin's Paperbacks

This is a work of fiction. All of the characters, organizations, and events portrayed in this novel are either products of the author's imagination or are used fictitiously.

NIGHT OF THE COBRA

Copyright © 2015 by Jack Coughlin with Donald A. Davis.
Excerpt from *Long Shot* copyright © by Jack Coughlin with Donald A. Davis.

All rights reserved.

For information address St. Martin's Press, 175 Fifth Avenue, New York, NY 10010.

ISBN: 978-1-250-08039-4

Printed in the United States of America

St. Martin's Press hardcover edition / August 2015
St. Martin's Paperbacks edition / May 2016

St. Martin's Paperbacks are published by St. Martin's Press, 175 Fifth Avenue, New York, NY 10010.

10 9 8 7 6 5 4 3 2 1

PROLOGUE

THE EVENING CALL to prayer sounded from the Arba-Rucun Mosque in Mogadishu, Somalia. The temperature was coming down at the end of an early December day, and the first bright stars penetrated the new blackness of the Indian Ocean sky off the eastern coast of Africa. There was no commercial electricity in the destroyed city, so there was no wash of lights to drown that nightly spangle. A few portable generators buzzed as cook fires were stoked, and shadows moved and gunfire barked and people cried. The despondent residents called it the music of the night.

A large man, more than six feet tall and weighing over two hundred pounds, moved like a bad dream through the opaque northern streets and alleyways of Mogadishu, following a path imprinted on his memory. He was a giant among his people and carried an AK-47 with a thirty-round banana clip strapped across his chest, a razor-sharp machete riding in a canvas scabbard on his back. An old Beretta 92 pistol bulged in the rear of his belt. His real name was Omar Jama, but his vicious and deadly work had earned him the nickname "the Cobra." Although young, he was the chief bodyguard and assassin for the most feared warlord in town, General Mohammed Farrah Hassan Aidid.

Omar Jama saw a clump of people on a corner and dodged to avoid being noticed. It was only some displaced family trying to find a safe hole, but he had to be careful, for tonight the Cobra was on the wrong side of the Green Line, a breezy area that once had been the business district where people of the different clans had lived in harmony. Ordinarily, if he had been caught over here alone at night, he would have been given a slow and painful death. This moment was different, and an opportunity had appeared that had to be seized. He moved warily, but with unusual confidence.

Somalia once had been a jewel colony for the Italians, and Mogadishu had maintained a seedy glamour even after World War II, when the Italians surrendered it to the British as a protectorate. The country was given its independence in 1960, the first coup d'état was attempted the very next year, and the nation fell apart as rival tribes emerged to battle for control. The only thing on which they agreed was their religion, Islam, but that alone was not enough to band them together in common cause.

Wars followed, and then came a monster famine that wiped out three hundred thousand people and killed 70 percent of all the livestock in the country. The only true crop left was fear, and vulture warlords and their thugs preyed on the helpless refugees that crowded into camps. Mogadishu became a lawless city in a lawless land.

The rest of the world tried to help and poured food and aid into dying Somalia. The warlords seized the distribution points and looted relief planes as soon as they rolled to a halt. Trucks were ransacked, and everything in them was stolen. The United Nations dispatched some of their Blue Beret peacekeeping troops to protect the humanitarian mission, but it wasn't enough to stop the criminals, and starvation, disease, and the raging civil war gnawed at the decimated survivors.

The big fist was applied on December 4, when the United Nations and the United States agreed to launch a massive American-led military intervention and commit thousands of troops in Operation Restore Hope. At that point, the prime warlords had to move quickly, for whoever was in control when the Americans arrived would likely stay in control.

The Cobra's boss, General Aidid, exchanged smiles and a handshake with his main rival, Ali Mahdi Mohammed, at a photo opportunity that announced both a truce between them and the elimination of the dangerous Green Line. Ten thousand supporters attended the ceremony and waved small leafy branches for peace as reporters, photographers, and television cameras recorded the historic moment. Roadblocks were torn down to demonstrate the new sense of unity. Somalia might be saved after all.

A member of Mahdi's inner circle, a dog named Abdiwel Godah Hamud, had attended the truce ceremony. Hamud was an educated man with a smooth tongue and often made accusations to the press about General Aidid. Following the event, Hamud took advantage of the ceasefire to visit relatives in his old family home, which lay close to the line.

Aidid gave the Cobra an order to carry out an immediate strike, and the young gunman went out alone as darkness fell. The city was full of thieves slinking around in the night, fueled with catatonic khat dreams, stealing and killing at random. Omar did not fear of such trash. He moved with purpose.

He stepped slowly through the charred ruins of the collapsed Cathedral of the Croce del Sud, careful to avoid tiles that might snap beneath his weight. An alley went left, and he edged around the corner, then quickly loped down the short street and hid in a deep doorway, where he waited to be sure he was not being stalked. A noisy truck rumbled toward him, so he turned right and went east for two blocks, then north for another two, and closed in on the bullet-pocked whitewashed walls of his target's home, owned by the Hamud family. It stood in stark, bright relief from the rubble all around. A single guard was at the front gate, and the lights were bright inside, powered by a generator that growled within the compound.

The Cobra had been to this house numerous times in the previous months, scouting the approaches, mentally drawing the layout, and designing three escape routes. There had been no doubt that someday he would have to use that knowledge, and now the time had come for a final visit.

He jumped, grabbed the top of the rear wall, and levered over, then paused as still as a rock until he was certain that he had not been seen. Everything was as he remembered. The house was in relatively good condition. It had two stories that were connected by a set of exterior stairs, and he went up two at a time and carefully opened the unlocked door at the top. It put him in a short hallway. Voices and laughter rose from downstairs, where the Hamud family was enjoying this rare evening together. Omar unlimbered his Kalashnikov and thumbed off the safety.

Four women and five men of varying ages, the eldest being the warlord's adviser, Abdiwel Godah Hamud, were seated on pillows and carpets in the main room, drinking tea and eating from stacks of food on bright trays. The Cobra stepped out, and his first steady sweep of bullets went left to right in a fusillade that killed or wounded most of them. Omar swapped out magazines, went to single shot, and caught one that was trying to crawl away, and another stupidly trying to hide behind a pillow. Then he flipped the selector back to full automatic fire when the front door opened and the guard dashed in, only to be hammered down in the second long, sustained sweep of the room.

In no hurry, the Cobra reloaded again, and then shifted the AK to his left hand while he pulled the big machete from a scabbard on his back. He stepped methodically through the pack of victims and chopped the big blade down on anyone who still seemed alive. Once he was sure that he had them all, he positioned the head of Abdiwel Godah Hamud to expose the long neck and chopped the knife with more than enough power for the decapitation stroke. He sliced out the dead man's tongue and threw it into the pile of food.

Omar knew that neighbors would have been alerted by the gunfire, but he seemed to have a clock in his head that counted off the seconds he had allotted, which included a margin of safety. He still had time enough to go through the pockets of the dead men and found several hundred U.S. dollars and European currency. After that, he had to go. He retreated fast up the stairs and threw an American M67 hand grenade back into the room that was stacked with dead people. The explosion worsened the carnage even more and would give any would-be rescuers a moment of doubt before rushing inside.

Unexpectedly, a thin boy about ten years old appeared in the final doorway of the upper hall. Omar smiled down with a smirk that contained no pity. He kicked the kid hard in the face and stomped his ribs twice, then walked away. He would allow the child to live as a warning to others. *No.* The Cobra changed his mind in midstride, pulled the Beretta, turned slightly, and fired a single shot back at the crumpled boy, who jerked on the impact.

Satisfied and refreshed by the blood of his enemies, the Cobra was not even winded as he climbed back over the compound fence. People were rushing through the front gate and into the house, and screams came when the butchered bodies were seen. The noise faded far behind as Omar Jama vanished into the familiar alleys that would take him safely back across the Green Line. He reported to General Aidid within thirty minutes. It could have been sooner, but he had stopped along the way to buy some banana leaves filled with khat twigs from a late-working vendor. The drug would help him relax.

The truce was over.

There are no clocks in hell, and time was equally meaningless in the chaotic Irish Aid Society clinic on the south edge of 21 October Road. The suffering never stopped in the rickety set of little buildings that huddled behind a head-high wall that had been scoured and chipped by dozens of bullets. Inside, weary doctors, nurses, social workers, and volunteers were trying to run a combination feeding station, medical facility, and school. The building compound suffered as much as the people.

Molly Egan, the clinic administrator, wiped her hands on her blood-smeared smock and rubbed sweat from her face with a dirty towel. She was a tall, slim woman with a tanned face that could have been fashionista pretty in some other city, at some other time, if she wore just a little bit of makeup. *Who had time for that?* A sprinkle of freckles crossed the nose and dappled the cheeks, and her thick red hair was chopped severely to collar length against the heat. Her green eyes had seen too much misery.

She had hoped the agreement between the warlords and the promise of a foreign security force might finally provide a chance for some peace to come to Mogadishu. Now the administrator of the center realized that her thought had been an utterly foolish fantasy. The conveyor belt of misery had not even slowed.

The guard at the front gate shouted, and Molly stepped into the courtyard as a small pickup truck slid to a halt. For a moment, she worried that it might be carrying a bomb, but then two men leaped from the back and lifted out an unconscious child.

"Deqo!" Egan called as she broke into a run. She pronounced the African name as *Deck-oh*. "I need you out here!"

She pointed to a bare plywood table, and the men carefully placed a little boy on it. One man had a rifle on his shoulder, and tears creased his face. They started shouting and waving their arms, but she did not understand a word they said and concentrated her attention on the bleeding child. Suddenly, Deqo Sharif, a dark-skinned Somali nurse, was with her, calming the excited men.

"This child was caught up in a massacre up on the Green Line just a little while ago. The rest of his family was wiped out," Deqo explained to Molly while she did a brief triage examination, probing with gentle, experienced fingers. The boy was in bad shape, his intestines pushing out like sausages. "He has a gunshot wound in the stomach. Superficial head lacerations, but the broken ribs may have punctured a lung."

Molly Egan cringed. Children were not exempt from the savagery of Mogadishu. Between starvation and bullets, they died by the dozens every day. She helped carry the wounded boy inside to a small cluttered operating room as Deqo prepared for the emergency surgery and sent someone to fetch her husband, an overworked Soviet-trained surgeon named Lon Sharif. The gray-haired doctor and Deqo were both in their fifties. As badly hurt as the child may have been, he was just the latest patient to be placed on that bloodstained slab in the operating room.

As the doctor and nurse got to work, Molly Egan turned away and almost collided with another little boy who was struggling to carry in a five-gallon bucket of clean water to help wash away the soiled aftermath. It was his job. At the clinic, everyone worked. The tall and gangly boy was Cawelle Sharif, and he was the eight-year-old grandson of Doctor Lon and Deqo Sharif, his only living relatives. His parents had been killed more than a year ago. Egan took away the bucket, then grabbed Cawelle's hand and pulled him from the room, speaking in a low, soothing voice. "Come along with me now, Lucky. Let's go out and look at some stars. We don't need to watch any more of this tonight."

BOOK
ONE

MOGADISHU

DECEMBER 4, 1992
TWENTY-NINE PALMS, CALIFORNIA

UNDERSTAND THE UNITED States alone cannot right the world's wrongs." President George H. W. Bush was addressing the American people on television, and Marine Corps Sergeant Kyle Swanson listened from his perch on a high stool in a bar in Twenty-Nine Palms, California. An unusual moment of quiet settled throughout the popular watering hole as other strong young men stopped playing pool, clinking beer bottles, and hustling girls. They had all seen the ongoing television reports on the horrors in the faraway African country of Somalia, where life was less than cheap and merciless warlords ruled. A United Nations peacekeeping force had failed to halt the spiral of violence, and talk of possible American intervention had been sweeping through the Palms training areas like a hot desert wind. The president looked anguished, and spoke like he meant business. "But we also know that some crises in the world cannot be resolved without American involvement, that American action is often necessary as a catalyst for broader involvement of the community of nations."

The off-duty marines crowded into the bar cheered.

"Damned right!" one called. "Got that straight!" yelled another, and calls of "hoo-ah!" bounced from the walls like excited echoes.

"He's talking about us, right, Sar'nt Swanson?" asked Corporal David Delshay, a chunky sniper who was finishing off a longneck bottle at the little table. Delshay, a Native American known as the Apache, held a pool cue in his free hand, ready to resume his game against Corporal Mike Mancuso.

"Yep," said Swanson. Everyone on the big sandy base in the Northern California desert had known this was probably coming. Somalia needed help, and from the TV that was clamped high above the bar the president was saying that the United States was going to be the lead dog in this hasty coalition. That meant that the First Battalion, Seventh Marines, would be the lead dogs for a 28,000-man U.S. ground force, and Kyle Swanson and his Scout/Snipers would be the lead dogs for the marines.

Big Mike Mancuso, another one of Swanson's sniper team members, looked a little puzzled. "Hey, this dude just lost the election. So how can he send us off to a war?"

"Bill Clinton doesn't take office for another month, you moron," piped a brunette in tight jeans who was leaning against Swanson's side. "George Bush is still president until then. You guys are going on safari."

Kyle gave her shoulders a gentle squeeze. Chicks loved snipers, and Swanson loved them right back. They came and went like tides, and any relationship could end without so much as a telephone call if Swanson was dispatched on a mission he could not disclose to anyone. Four weekend dates seemed like a lifetime. He was satisfied with that arrangement. Ladies around the bases knew the drill.

"Marines go where they are told, when they are told, and fight who they are told to fight," he said.

It was that time again. By the time Bush had finished announcing Operation Restore Hope, a computer was sending out auto alerts and the beeper on Swanson's belt began to vibrate. He turned it off and saw others in the saloon were also touching their own beepers, finishing up, paying their bills, stealing good-bye kisses, and drifting outside, heading back to the base. The parking lot was almost empty within fifteen minutes.

The One-Seven spent the next week packing its gear, then hauled ass out of the States, with stops in Maine and Germany. Sergeant Kyle Swanson was boots-on-ground in the Horn of Africa on Friday, December 11, 1992, just days before Christmas.

He slapped on his floppy boonie hat as he stepped to the tarmac of the small airport of Mogadishu, Somalia, and shaded his eyes with his polarized Oakley sunglasses to look out over the tumbledown, broken metropolis that was still steaming and stinking after a rainy-season squall. In his mind, the place seemed to be singling him out, glaring directly back at him, reaching out to stake a claim. The sniper immediately felt an internal surge of adrenaline that meant this was where he belonged. This was new territory, but not new ground to him. Swanson had seen plenty of combat in other rotten places, so while Mogadishu promised to be mean, he knew it was nothing he couldn't handle. He was mean, too. In fact, Swanson, all in all, felt pretty good about being out here, back at the sharp point of the spear. Right where he belonged.

Kyle Swanson shouldered his rifle and joined his company as more planes disgorged more marines into the hot sun. Two thousand were coming in as part of the initial contingent of a military buildup that eventually would rise to tens of thousands of troops from the United States and other nations. Swanson was not here to feed people. His unique task was to hide, to observe, and, when necessary, to kill.

Within a few hours of landing, he was about a thousand meters from the airport, concealed in a jumbled pile of rubble that once had been a building with his right cheek resting comfortably against the fiberglass stock of his Remington bolt-action M40A1, which was loaded with 7.62×55 mm rounds and rested on a bipod. He used the sharp Unertl $10\times$ fixed-power scope to visually crawl over the landscape while his spotter, Corporal David Delshay, lay alongside him, doing the same with powerful binoculars. They used a laser range finder to paint distances to fixed objects. It was standard sniper fare. Behind them, more planes landed with the steady rhythm of a metronome, and the anchored ships of the Marine Expeditionary Force off-loaded gear and supplies at the obsolete port. Swanson ignored all of that, for his practiced eyes were pointed the other way, toward the city, and he and Delshay sketched a map of what lay before them. They had only just arrived but were already far out front as a dangerous, but expendable, tripwire. Any offensive move against the airport would have to come through them. Both Swanson and the Apache were cool with that.

The sniper team stayed out all day, immobile while in the scorching sun and drenched by an afternoon deluge. Swanson saw plenty of enemy soldiers running around with guns, but the rules of engagement kept him from firing unless they shot at him first. He prayed that they would, but they didn't. It was hard not to pull the trigger on the thugs that were the reason he was here;

they stole everything they wanted, beat people mercilessly, and used starvation and disease as weapons.

When the sun finally went down on that first day, the two weary snipers returned to the air base, where more marines had arrived. The place was filling up fast. Swanson cleaned his weapons, pulled fresh supplies, had something to eat, washed his face and hands, and immediately fell asleep amid the noise. For now, Somalia was home.

By Monday, the secured area was bursting at the seams, and still more soldiers came in by planes every hour: mean-looking Turks and solid Saudis, laid-back Canadians, chatty Pakis, French soldiers, and Kenyans, and ever more marines, until hundreds of troops were penned like cows at the port and airfield. Swanson and his sniper teams extended their overwatch out to two thousand meters and began providing protection for foot patrols that probed into the built-up areas. The newness of being in a foreign land had already worn off, and they settled in for what had all the markings of being a long haul.

By the end of his first week, Mogadishu had him. The place the marines now called "the Mog" hit him in the face the moment he opened his eyes every morning and rode him like a broken-down horse all day. If he got up to pee at night, it was still there. His morale sank almost with every passing hour as his world became all Mog, all day. When he turned on the radio, the Mog topped the BBC World Service. The feeling of despair was fueled by the heart-rending sights of hunger and deprivation all around, and even that grew stale. There was just too much misery out there for any individual to assimilate. It sapped the energy and soul. Staying sharp and keeping his snipers alert was getting harder to do. There was very little fighting beyond the warlords dealing with each other's forces at night, as if a little secret war was going on right under the nose of a giant.

Political wrangling had staved off open confrontation, and he could see the bad guys; he just couldn't shoot them until they were dumb enough to shoot first. It was frustrating. The obviously outmatched gunmen of the warlords in Mogadishu avoided confrontation in the city and spread like rats to seek weaker prey elsewhere. In response, the operations people of Task Force Mogadishu at the airport fanned troops into the countryside as fast as they could to counter the moving bands of thugs.

The tedium finally broke on Sunday morning, December 20, when Swanson was called to the battalion headquarters tent and told to draw equipment and pick a half dozen of his snipers. An American army unit in the town of Afgoye, twenty-five miles west in the Shabelle Valley, was receiving intermittent gunfire and wanted help. Kyle turned out his marines, and they sailed off in a pair of Humvees, all of them happy to get away from the Mog for a spell, and maybe even find a fight.

They rolled into an oasis of peace, a lush green belt of mature agriculture that followed a river. The army officer in charge told Kyle that shots had come from a stand of trees that walled the western side of the town, so Swanson and his men spread into the area with their weapons hot. Nothing. People were going about their daily routines, and the crowded refugee feeding station was running like a machine. Army troopers were relaxed in the shade with their equipment scattered on the ground. Nobody was shooting at anybody. Swanson went back to the officer in charge.

When the major insisted that there had been an attack, Kyle went up to a rooftop to get a better angle into the jungle. He discovered a half-dozen American women soldiers sunbathing in bras and panties. They were very unhappy that he had invaded their private space on a Sunday morning, and he was equally unhappy that he and his team had rushed twenty-five miles to answer a false alarm. Seeing the near-naked bodies of the G.I. Janes did not impress him at all. Swanson stalked back downstairs, barked a bit at the officer about lax discipline, and took his snipers home, back to the big city.

Mogadishu had waited patiently while Swanson was gone and was ready for another round when he returned.

Swanson met the enemy face-to-face two days later on a dawn patrol that went into the city. By then, the foreign armed forces had grown to become the biggest gang in town, and more marines and U.N. troops were still arriving. They owned Mogadishu.

The marines followed a familiar street to a private compound, and the sergeant leading the patrol winked at Swanson. "You get to do the honors. I did it yesterday. He's getting annoyed." Swanson knocked on a door of hard dark wood. It was exactly seven o'clock in the morning on Tuesday, December 22.

It was opened by a slim man with graying hair and a mustache, sleep still in his eyes. The warlord General Mohammed Farrah Hassan Aidid was consumed with obvious frustration. The marines had come by at this time every single morning for the past week, demonstrating that they could do as they wished in an area that he had supposedly controlled.

"Good morning, General," said Swanson, removing his sunglasses to give the Somali warlord a good look.

He controlled a desire to smirk, and spoke with an even, polite tone. "We are just checking in with you. Is everything okay here today, sir?"

The warlord whined through gritted teeth, "Each morning you people do this to me. Why? Why is it always me and not the others?"

Kyle ignored the comment and touched the brim of his helmet with a mock salute. "You have a good day, sir. Please let us know if we can be of assistance."

The patrol moved out, leaving the warlord standing alone in the doorway. The sun rose to scald the earth, was followed by the usual afternoon rains, then a night of gunplay downtown.

General Aidid was not helpless, although he was being forced by circumstances to bide his time. The morning call by the marines was bothersome, but it was just another part of the greater game.

Intel sources at the airport had been receiving reports that he had been stockpiling weapons within a walled compound during the ceasefire, in violation of the truce agreement. That the warlord had lied surprised no one; the big question was whether he would fight for the arms stash. The marines decided to seize those guns.

The day after he had knocked on the warlord's front door, Kyle Swanson and two of his teams went out before first light on Wednesday, December 23, and wiggled into a watch position at the walled enclosure. They were glassing for threats, and after they reported all was still at the site, a full marine platoon came in, shepherded by helicopter gunships and modified Humvees that bristled with firepower and were known as combined anti-armor teams, or CAATs. The big force that appeared as if out of thin air looked unstoppable to

Swanson as he watched through his scope from a thousand yards away.

Only it did stop—right in the shadow of the front gate. The buck lieutenant leading the patrol was brought up short by the challenge of a single Somali policeman in a light blue shirt and cap, dark slacks, and desert boots. The cop stood there with his hands on his hips, shouting that the area was private property of General Aidid and was therefore off-limits to the marines and everyone else. Swanson couldn't believe it. The momentum had been checked and all the implied power was nullified. The gunships above did figure eights and the CAATs idled on the fringes.

The lieutenant had been a stateside substance abuse counselor and was new to the field, but Swanson believed that was no excuse not to have blown right through this single cop. And the veteran platoon sergeant with him had let it happen!

Swanson erupted out the hide and stormed forward, arriving almost out of breath after running the thousand yards. He ignored the reasonable lieutenant and the temporizing sergeant and yelled for the marine squad leaders to get their men going, to get inside of that walled compound with weapons ready and their eyes up. This was no friendly visit.

A pickup truck rushed through the gate, and General Aidid jumped out and began shouting at the lieutenant while Swanson screamed for the platoon to get inside. Only when the marines started moving again did Kyle turn to where Aidid was snapping at the twenty-two-year-old lieutenant. The platoon sergeant was standing back with his thumb up his butt.

There was a flash of recognition when Aidid saw the face of Swanson, who had awakened him only a few days earlier, and then the sniper snatched the general by the shirtfront and threw him to the dirt.

"Down on the ground! Get your ass down there! Now!!" Swanson bellowed.

Omar Jama, who had driven the pickup truck, had stayed with it as he watched his general screech at the lieutenant, but when the other marine came up and abruptly flopped Aidid onto the ground, the Cobra broke into a run. Swanson saw him coming, dodged with a hip fake, and kicked the Cobra behind the knee as he went by, then shoved with a hard shoulder. Knocked off-balance, Omar Jama felt his collar being yanked, and then he also was chewing dirt. "You get down there, too. Both of you stay down!!" Swanson snarled as he pointed his M-16 rifle at their backs.

Other Somalis in and around the compound watched in disbelief as their leaders sprawled ignominiously in the dirt. They were unused to any challenge, and this was unthinkable. But any idea of doing something brave vanished as the marines stormed into the compound and grabbed them, the big CAATs closing in tight and the helicopters hovering with cannons and rockets at the ready.

The argument was over. The Somali militiamen, their toppled warlord, and his fearsome bodyguard, the Cobra, had their wrists lashed with plastic cuffs.

Swanson took a knee beside Aidid and leaned on his rifle. "You listen to me close now, General," he said. "There is no government in Mogadishu, but there is a new sheriff in town—and it is the United States Marine Corps. Best that you understand that right now."

Aidid exchanged a sharp look with the Cobra. The two powerful men had been disgraced in public, rendered helpless in mere seconds, and that rough handling might have planted seeds of doubt among some of their fighters, who either had seen or would hear about the episode. Such a disgrace could not be tolerated. This man would have to pay.

They had read the black letters stitched to the name tag sewn on the tunic of the marine—SWANSON—and they silently vowed to remember this particular invader. When the chance came, their lost honor would be redeemed in his blood.

Swanson knew they would hate him. He did not care.

THE STADIUM

DECEMBER 24, 1992
SOMALIA

REMAINING APART FROM the human misery in Somalia grew more difficult with each passing day for Kyle Swanson. Every night, there was gunfire deep in the bowels of the city, and each morning Swanson saw new dead bodies. The Mog was very different from real war, and it chewed at his faith in humanity. At least he and his teams were finally busy instead of just moping around for hours on end with nothing to do. The promise of action buoyed them.

The hope to which Swanson clung like a saving rope was that the longer they were in Mogadishu, the better things seemed to get. Some order was being imposed, more kids were getting food, and more old people were receiving medical care; but the scale of the disaster was still incomprehensible.

Another radio call for assistance came in, this one from a refugee-aid center, and Kyle rolled on it with Dave Delshay, Big Mike Mancuso, and Corporal Terry Smith. They were glad to go, since they were missing out on the action to the south, where a marine amphibious force had just pulled off a hot combat landing at the port city of Kismaayo. This was just another baby-sitting job, but it was better than nothing.

The griping was normal, for the One-Seven snipers were war fighters, not policemen, and these fruitless and repetitive assignments were sandpapering away their combat readiness. They were totally unafraid of anything that General Aidid or the other warlords might have, so all four of the marines were cocky, filled with a danger-ous John Wayne bravado. Two CAATs trailed their Hum-vees as backups, making it a sizable force for something that was actually just up the street from the airport.

By the time they curved out of the roundabout, none of them were thinking about shooting anybody, and it had all the signs of another dry run in which the stooges would run as soon as the marines showed up. As usual, this place was also quiet, with no enemy firing any-where. Swanson and his men stepped from their Hum-vee, and he waved for the CAATs to snoop about on their own until it was time to leave. It was so still that Big Mike and Terry Smith scampered up a water tower, and Swanson didn't stop their climb, although it was a dumb war-movie kind of thing to do that would put them in an exposed position. But things were so calm that he judged they were in no real danger, and, besides, it looked sort of cool. They all would be gone in a few minutes anyway. Corporal Delshay had his weapon, so Kyle left his own long sniper rifle and personal M-16 in the seat as he went to the main building with Delshay to check in with whoever was in charge.

The facility was one of the overwhelmed clinics, makeshift hospitals, feeding stations, and refugee camps that dotted the safer areas of Mogadishu. The front wall was pretty chewed up, but the compound seemed safe enough.

He stopped abruptly when a woman stepped into the courtyard to meet them. She was as tall as his 5 foot 9, with high cheekbones and thick, startlingly red hair and a mouth that seemed to want to laugh. He guessed that she was about twenty-five, twenty-six. *Beautiful!*

"Thank you for coming so quickly," she said, her mind still back in the hospital, and she was also caught momentarily off guard when her sea-green eyes caught the visitor's intense gray-greens. She had seen hundreds of military men in uniforms from all over the world, but this man surprised her with his open, confident look. It was as if the rest of Mogadishu evaporated for a micro instant and just the two of them were standing face-to-face in a bright tunnel, and slow smiles creased their tired faces. She extended her hand. "My name is Molly Egan. I'm the administrator here for the Irish Aid Society."

"Hi." He took the soft hand in his own. "Sergeant Kyle Swanson, Marines. Glad to meet you" *Glad? Not the word. Not even close.* He didn't want to let go. "Are you having some trouble?"

Molly pulled her hand away first, and busily wiped it on a towel. "Sorry. I'm all messy from working in there." The red hair bobbed toward the hospital. "Yes. There was some shooting a little while ago." *How can I prolong this?* "Would you like a soda?"

"Sure." He didn't know what else to say. He felt like he was back in high school, afraid to speak to the prettiest girl in the lunchroom. Swanson followed her inside. Her torn jeans and blue cotton smock were speckled with tiny droplets of old blood. "Ah. Then. You guys are okay?"

Egan handed Swanson a Fanta orange drink, tapped out a cigarette for herself, lit it, and blew a line of smoke at the ceiling. "For now," she said. "Those people can be a nuisance. We appreciate your chasing them away for a while."

The soda was warm, but her smile was magic, and he could almost feel little darts of electricity between them. "You have guards here, don't you?" *Damn. What a stupid question. Swanson studied her eyes. They reflected a vast weariness, but she wasn't mad at his comment, which might have been taken as an insult. That was good.*

She nodded. "Yes, of course we do. Bandits show up now and then to try and steal our supplies and drugs, but our guards, local boys we hire, usually are enough to make the gangsters go away just by returning fire. We don't always call for help."

Swanson thought briefly about that. This woman wasn't afraid. *Freckles.* "How are things going here otherwise?"

"Same as always, Sergeant. Any day that we feed more people than we bury is a good one. We've had a lot more of the good days since you guys arrived. Would you like the ten-penny tour?"

He took a final look around. All remained quiet outside. "Sure. So does the 'Irish Aid Society' mean that you're Irish?"

"Indeed I am," she replied. "My people are in County Cork, close to the sea."

Swanson smiled. "I'm Irish, too. Well, American-Irish at least." He blurted it out for no reason other than trying to continue the conversation. He had long ago outgrown any problems of talking with women. *Until now.* "My mother's family came from Shannon. I'm from just north of Boston." He sipped the orange drink to stop himself from babbling.

"Swanson is an English name," Egan said lightly, with a tilt of her head. "Although you do look Irish."

"How long have you been here, Doctor Egan?" he asked.

"Only about two months now," Molly said. Her voice had only a mild accent. "And I'm not a doctor, just a co-ordinator for Irish Aid. Before coming here, I was over in Uganda and, earlier, in the Balkans. There are refugees everywhere, Sergeant." That explained the strain evident in her entire body. Kyle had seen marines get a blank thousand-yard stare after too much combat, and this girl seemed headed that way as she hopped from disaster to disaster. Humanitarian workers got the look after the hopelessness of dealing with too much tragedy. She stopped to tug a ragged red blanket over a child who was sleeping on a piece of cardboard. Her movement was soft, gentle.

Swanson realized they had walked through a whole crowd of black Africans at the clinic, and he had not really seen them before she stopped to cover the child. Mogadishu had rendered them almost invisible to his eyes, like background people in a movie, but his focus snapped to total clarity when she led him into a small operating room where a harried medical team was treating a little patient. A low murmur carried through the hallways where other patients awaited their turns and complained that the child was getting preferential treatment because she belonged to another tribe.

"That's Dr. Sharif at the table. He trained in Moscow," Egan said, pointing to the man performing the procedure. "His wife, Deqo, next to him, is our head of nursing, and she also runs our school." The doctor grunted acknowledgment but did not stop working. Deqo Sharif did not even look up.

Egan tugged at his sleeve and continued the tour as if escorting a four-star general. Military rank meant nothing to her, and this sergeant had come to help. Just touching his uniform had felt immensely personal. He is more than just another soldier, she thought.

Swanson forced himself not to openly gawk at the easy sway of her hips and the confident stride of the long legs.

They really didn't know where they were going, or what was happening to them, but they both understood that something unexpected, warm, sweet, and long un-used was stirring within them like flags catching the first brush of a new breeze.

The moment collapsed with a burst of gunfire.

Kyle ran to the door. Mancuso and Smith were pinned up on the water tower as bullets pinged off the metal around them, unable to do anything more than lie flat and pray. They had not taken their weapons, either. More shots were kicking up the dirt around and even within the compound and pecking at the concrete and mud walls. The firing was coming in at a volume that pre-vented Swanson from running to the Humvee to retrieve his rifles. People at the feeding station milled about like frightened, trapped animals, and the single gate guard was scrunched behind a post.

Swanson lashed himself with a quick curse as he pulled the 9mm pistol from its hip holster. He had let his professionalism be lulled into carelessness, and while he was being treated like a VIP by a pretty girl, strolling around like he was important, he had lowered his situational awareness. *That shit ends right now!* He told the Apache to get to the far side of the building and flank the unseen shooters, then leaned out and began popping at the attackers, firing blindly until the pistol was empty. He reloaded and did it again, moving out of the clinic and into the courtyard, where he burned through another magazine. He slammed in another magazine as he advanced into the open space of the gate, yelling as he fired, so pissed with himself for letting this happen. He clicked on empty, out of ammunition, so he wound up like a baseball pitcher and threw the pistol itself toward the hidden gunmen. It exploded in midair.

Swanson had been so caught up with his internal fury and the noise of the gunfight that he had not heard the CAATs run up and begin pumping a hurricane of bullets and grenades at the target zone. One grenade from the Mark-19 automatic launcher had hit his pistol while it was in flight, and the million-to-one shot blew it up.

Swanson felt an arm wrap around his waist and pull him hard back behind the cover of the mud wall. It was Molly Egan, and she was giggling loudly as they tumbled to the ground. "Got a little temper problem, have we, Sergeant?" she laughed. "Flinging an exploding pistol at them? Really?"

Kyle steadied his breathing as a few more rounds pinged into the compound before the gunmen fled. "I'm sorry about all of this," he said, apologizing for failing at his job. His face was red with the anger he felt with himself. "It never should have happened. I got careless. I'm sorry. It won't happen again." He realized with a start that his team had come to save her, and now things had flipped and she had pulled him to safety.

"No problem," she said, getting to her knees. "This is Mogadishu. Were you hit? Standing out there in the open with all that firing?" *What kind of man does that?* She ran her hands over his scalp, torso, and legs, looking for wounds and blood.

His anger evaporated beneath her touch. "I'm good. Thank you." He jumped up and brushed himself off. "And you?"

"I am fine, Sergeant." She curled into a sitting position

with her back to the wall and smiled up at him while pushing away some loose strands of crimson hair.

"We have some work to do clearing the area," he said, forcing his mind back into the game.

She watched Swanson pick up one of his rifles, get his men together, and sweep the perimeter. The big CAATs rolled in lazy circles. By the time he returned, Swanson had become sullen and quiet.

Molly studied that with some concern. Some after-action response had taken hold.

"I'll get the bosses to put your clinic on the places for regular security patrols," Kyle said.

"Thanks again for your help. Come back anytime," she replied, looking straight into his eyes again with unspoken invitation.

"I will," he said, and had never made a more serious promise in his life.

The return to camp was silent. Every marine in the little firefight had undergone an attitude adjustment. No matter how much the boredom might envelop them, not paying attention to the job could still get them dead. Swanson preached readiness at them all the way back, almost as if talking to himself.

FRIDAY,
DECEMBER 25, 1992
Christmas came the following day, almost as a surprise to Swanson. Some homesick marines had put up and decorated a scraggly tree within the tent, but the other sights and sounds were startlingly absent. To the Muslims of Somalia, it was just another day. To the marines, there was little to celebrate.

Kyle left Mogadishu at dawn to accompany a French Foreign Legion supply convoy to a refugee camp far north of the city, and they drove all day. The place-names changed, but the situation remained about the same everywhere they went. When evening approached, and the afternoon rain stopped, the legionnaires set up camp for the night. They were not about to let a major holiday pass unnoticed, and with cries of "*Joyeux Noël,*" the refrigerated trucks in which they were carrying food for the refugees were thrown open. They unloaded turkeys and geese, seafood, potatoes and other vegetables, and cheese, along with other special ingredients, herbs, and spices chosen just for tonight. Whiskey and wine bottles were uncorked while the cooks created a magnificent Christmas feast, and they sang beside the road, in the middle of the civil war.

Swanson sat cross-legged on a stone and watched them with amusement, with a glass of bourbon in one hand, a half-eaten plate of food beside him, and his M-16 across his knees. Despite the party, the legionnaires had posted tight security. They knew what they were about.

The image of Molly Egan once again swam into his thoughts, just as it had done throughout the trip. He wanted to get back to the clinic and see her before she could forget him, but here he was, stuck beside a dank road in Somalia, having to spend Christmas with the Foreign Legion. Christmas would be long over by the time he got back to Mogadishu. He missed her.

The marines needed to break out of the tight confines of the port and airfield, and the next step was the huge soccer field that dominated Mogadishu like a frontier fort. Control of the sports arena had switched between the warlords while the relief-force commanders had stayed busy protecting their arrival points, sorting out the growing forces, and distributing food and medicine. No Americans had been in the stadium since they had arrived in country, but every night a patrol of M1A1 heavy Abrams tanks left the established perimeter for a run-up to the stadium, where they would turn around and go home again. After a few weeks, the Somalis grew so familiar with the regular trips that they hardly noticed the mechanized monsters that boomed past in the darkness.

The operational planners thought it would be easiest to just bull into the stadium when the time was right, with infantry following the tanks. Swanson thought that was dumb and had let the planners know it before he had headed out with the Legion. Why go blindly into what might easily be a trap? Yes, it might be a walkover, but it might not. Shouldn't they know if the enemy has built hard defensive positions and infested the place with rockets and machine guns? Send in some scout snipers first.

As soon as he got back to the stadium late on December 28, Kyle learned that he had won the debate, but it meant he had to do a fast turnaround instead of hitting his cot. After four days on the road with the Legion, he would go in aboard the tanks tonight and take a look, and if things were clear, the armored column would bring the rest of the regiment in at daybreak. There was no time to see Molly.

There was no moon, and the two tanks went out as usual, but this time with marine sniper-spotter teams clinging to the hulls like leeches, hidden by not only the darkness but also the sheer bulk of the machines and the equipment lashed to them. If anyone looked at the passing sixty-ton tanks, they would see the big cannons and treads, not bumps in the profile.

Swanson breathed slowly through a bandanna wrapped around his face in a futile effort to filter out diesel fumes and the stinking miasma of the Mog. The gagging smell of human waste, decomposing corpses, scorched streets, and uncollected garbage was the city's true signature. He heard the usual chitter of automatic gunfire and the boom of rocket-propelled grenades as rival gangs battled in the tangled streets on the far side of town. The tanks clanked unmolested through the darkness.

He let his fingers roam over his gear to make final checks. His heartbeat ticked like a steady metronome. This was what he had been bred to do, and fear never entered his mind. If anything, he had to fight down any sense of excitement that might start the adrenaline pumping. Swanson wanted to be steady. Usually, the whole time continuum would change for him, and the world would play in slow motion; slow was smooth, and smooth was fast. The tanks crunched along a broad paved street, maneuvering around heaps of trash; old cannon barrels bent at odd angles; and the useless, burned-out carcasses of personnel carriers and other vehicles.

Somewhere back in the warrens of the city, a mortar coughed and the shell climbed high, tilted nose-down, and whistled back to earth to explode inside the bowl of the stadium. No return fire. Another mortar shell hit the concrete building.

Then they were there. The tanks slowed at the front gate of the outer wall, a ten-foot-high barrier darker than the surrounding night. Swanson sucked in a final breath, loosened his grip, and kicked free, hitting the ground with a roll. The tanks heaved away on the familiar pattern that had been established during the previous nights. As their safety line rolled away, the sniper muttered the warrior's affirmation: *Yea, though I walk through the valley of the shadow of death, I will fear no evil, for I am the meanest motherfucker in the valley.*

He gathered his three guys—once again, the team of

Corporals Smith, Mancuso, and Delshay—and checked for broken arms, busted knees, or other damage. They were fine, as were their pair of M-40 sniper rifles and four M-16s, the nine-mil pistols, a bunch of hand grenades, and encrypted radios that could summon a Quick Reaction Force for help in a hurry.

The four men flattened against the rough wall and examined the area through their night-vision goggles. A few souls were moving about on the distant city outskirts, but no one was reacting to their presence. Swanson did a quick radio check to alert headquarters that they were at the broad gate. He stepped into the large entryway, and his team formed around him in a diamond pattern, one of them facing in each direction, including the rear.

In more pleasant times, crowds had thronged through this portal to enter the stadium, which could hold more than thirty thousand sports fans. Now the big structure was more like an abandoned sewer, as if everyone who entered left some waste behind. A concrete apron stretched between the gate and the stadium's inner wall, fifty yards of open space in which the marines would be vulnerable. They hustled across and onto the ramp, then paused again.

They were breathing harder but saw nothing, although there was some scrambling and movement straight ahead. Sticking to the darkest areas, the marines slid forward to where the ramp opened into the seating areas, inclined slopes of concrete benches for spectators. The strange noises were closer and louder, coming from down on the field.

Swanson slithered forward to get a clear view while the others provided a base for protective fire. He raised his head slowly until his eyes came above the concrete rim. A pack of wild dogs, having picked up the scent of the approaching men, stared back from the field, their eyes glowing in the light of his goggles. The pack leader gave a menacing growl, and his fur was standing straight up. The noise had been the grisly sound of the pack devouring the body of a dead man. Kyle eased back down and scooted away.

"Wild dogs," he said. "About thirty of them. They're busy with a meal, so we'll let them have the field for now. That will give us some good rear security." He led his team deeper into the warren of offices and compartments beneath the stands, and they went room by room, any of which might contain a possible threat.

The stadium was a monument to war. Artillery and fire had scourged the seating area, and ragged craters made every step a risk. Down on the field, the dogs snapped and barked around the corpse, and the echo of their primal anger echoed around the emptiness. They suddenly stopped fighting, and Swanson looked back in time to see the animals scatter, fleeing for shelter. Then he hear a mortar round shrieking in.

The other three team members were safe, clearing the interior rooms, but Swanson was standing in the bleachers. He collapsed into a ball, tight against a concrete riser, and instinctively covered his genitals with his hands. It was going to be close. The shell detonated only several layers of seats above him with an explosion that rattled the concrete circle, bounced him hard, and showered him with debris. The major concussion wave had gone up, not down toward him.

"Well, that sucked," he said, rolling over and wiping away the debris.

"What are you doing, just lying there?" Delshay had run back out to help.

"Screw you," said Swanson. He motioned for the

patrol to get back to work. The dogs crept back to finish their dinner.

The four marines found nothing of interest on their first circuit of the wide field and spiraled up to the next level and did another 360 tour. Many rocket-propelled grenades had been fired at the stadium, but they had only bounced off of the hundreds of tons of poured concrete. Mortar rounds splattered with little effectiveness. The place was solid. The marines made their way inexorably toward the highest point in the arena, a section that must have been a press box or a space reserved for VIP spectators. That small rectangular structure was scarred by bullets and scrapes of artillery, but it was also empty. Kyle looked over the edge of a big window and saw the sprawl of downtown Mogadishu not far away. From this vantage point, the snipers would have eyes-on to cover the arriving vehicles when the sun came up.

Swanson radioed the brass back at the airport. Recon mission complete: on site, unseen, not a shot fired. The stadium that dominated the heart of enemy territory was now the property of the U.S. Marine Corps and a pack of wild mutts.

THE WARLORD

DECEMBER 29, 1992
MOGADISHU, SOMALIA

THE PARADE BEGAN at daybreak. A mass of marines left the seaside airport perimeter, curved around the K-4 traffic circle, and headed north on Via Lenin to the 21 October Road, then east to the stadium. The column was led by mighty amphibious assault vehicles, heavy M1A1 tanks, other sorts of armor, boxy Humvees, and both five-ton and seven-ton trucks—all sandwiched by marines marching on foot in full combat gear. The entire regiment was on the move, and the ground shook beneath their tracks, wheels, and boots. A haze of dust rose to match the early yellow sky.

The warlord General Mohammed Farrah Hassan Aidid watched with interest, slouched against a dented Toyota Land Cruiser. In loose khaki slacks and a faded brown shirt, he blended in with the curious crowd that lined the 21 October Road. The marines looked singularly tough, extremely fit and determined, and carried a fantastic array of weaponry. Their unspoken macho professionalism reminded him of how he had been awed by regular Soviet soldiers when he was sent to Moscow as a young cadet to study at the Frunze Academy. He had felt very small and out of place among those men at that time, but that was years ago. He was no longer the one out of place; he was equal to any man on the field, and the game was just getting started.

"Is my Cobra scared of these Americans?" the general enjoyed teasing the bodyguard standing with him. The presence of the Cobra made him feel safer, even in the face of this invading army, for Omar Jama was much more than just a gunman. He had been carefully groomed for this job. His Somali merchant father had taught him English and Italian and the mathematics of business before he was even ten years old. That had drawn the attention of Aidid when the senior Somali army officer decided to recruit a special cadre of boys from his Habar Gidir clan. Omar had proved to be a particularly intelligent student, abnormally strong, and a vicious, natural predator. As he matured and the civil war began, he had proved both loyal and valuable, time and again. Aidid had bestowed the name of "Cobra" on his prized killer.

"What? No, I am not. Of course not!" Omar Jama was sucking on a wad of khat to get a morning buzz after a long night of fighting near the Green Line. His muscled shoulders and arms bulged from a long blue shirt that hid the pistol in the waistband of his jeans. The comment took him by surprise.

The Cobra took a slight step forward and waved at an American as large as himself, who was lugging a big M-249 squad automatic weapon. "Hello, marine! Welcome to Mogadishu!" he called out in good English. The marine did not smile in return, just kept marching along in route step, his eyes on the crowd and his finger near the trigger housing. The machine gun was loaded.

"I am going to get me a SAW like that, General. More

than one hundred rounds a minute and up to eight hundred on sustained fire. I can kill a lot of Americans with that." The Cobra stepped back to his boss.

"Good," Aidid said. "Kill a lot of them. Just make certain that one of them is the Swanson marine. He's in that crowd somewhere."

"We will find him, sir. He cannot continue hiding from us for long, not in our own city."

The four snipers watched the incoming column from the press box atop the stadium, ready to give covering fire, but none was needed. Their position was within an almost solid concrete box with three windows, a large one in the middle and two on each side. All of the glass had been blown out long ago. There was only one door. It was not until daylight arrived that they saw the potential.

"This is a pretty sweet place," said Corporal Smith. "It's ours, right? I mean, we got here first."

"Home is where my helmet is," agreed Corporal Delshay.

They all knew an intramural skirmish was in store once the regiment's rear echelon interlopers started nosing around for the best spaces. Sergeant Kyle Swanson planned to secure ownership immediately. "Let me think about that," he said.

Smitty and Delshay were left in the overlook while Swanson and Mike Mancuso jogged down the bleachers to mingle with the new arrivals. The interior of the stadium was a maze of sunless tunnels, and the two snipers took some time to explore areas they had not had a chance to look over in detail when they had come sneaking in the night before. The wide, flat apron out front was already turning into a parking lot for marine vehicles.

Boom! The bark of a shotgun broke the quiet. *Boom!* A yelp. Swanson and Mancuso walked back toward the soccer field. *Boom* again, followed by the clacks of a shotgun racking in a new round. A reedy staff sergeant wearing glasses was killing the dogs with a Remington 870P. Kyle knew the type: a desk jockey who had volunteered for the dirty little mission and was walking around like king of the jungle, slaughtering animals that had nowhere to run. Just opening a door and chasing them out would have been a lot easier, but less satisfying for this guy.

"Fuckin' pogue," Mancuso sneered. Swanson agreed. They moved on.

The personal gear that the team had left behind was aboard one of the incoming trucks, and it took some hunting to find it. Fellow snipers had made sure that the gear had not been touched, although it was worth its weight in gold: personal cots and cases of ready-to-eat meals (MREs) and crates of bottled water. Those cases would become building blocks for little walls to partition the press box and create the luxury of individual personal spaces. Also buried among the standard supplies was Swanson's personal kit: boxes of Canadian Army rations that were better than the dreaded MREs. It was no contest between the Canadians' chicken carbonara with tortillas and hot sauce versus MRE menu no. 8: ham slice with accessory packet A. Even better was the stash of Johnnie Walker Black Label whiskey and a special bottle of Rémy Martin cognac that Kyle had liberated from the Foreign Legion during the long road trip.

Hauling it all up the stadium stairs was going to be a job, which was why he had chosen Mancuso for the first trip. Big Mike would stand guard at the truck with that dark scowl on his hard face to deter any scavenging jarhead from robbing it, while the other three snipers would work in relays to move into their hideaway.

Within a few hours, it was squared away. They had been awake yesterday, throughout the night, and now well into this new day and were about ready to keel over. Smitty scrounged some paint and posted a SNIPERS IN ACTION sign on the closed door of their private condo. A rotation was set so that two would rest while the other two stayed on watch. Swanson fell asleep as the sun rose in the empty sky, and the sweltering heat beat down.

"We should go back now, General. It is too dangerous for you to remain out here in the open." The Cobra had brought along only three fighters, not enough to repel a determined attack. "Ali Mahdi probably knows by now that you are out here and vulnerable."

Omar was right. Ali Mahdi, the warlord north of the Green Line, was always looking to assassinate him, just as Aidid would someday like to bury his rival in a red-dirt desert grave. The general clapped a hand on his bodyguard's hefty shoulder. The stadium was in the grasp of the marines now, so that show was over. It was time to do some serious thinking about what would happen next. "Let's go," he agreed, and they climbed into the Toyota.

"Did you happen to see him, the Swanson marine, among all of those others?" Aidid looked back at the vanishing stadium as the Cobra drove into the city. The warlord had made a point of having his spies identify the insulting marine as being one Sergeant Kyle Swanson, a veteran sniper with a reputation for toughness.

"No, General. But he's there. I know that. I *know* it!" Omar Jama drove through a crowd without slowing down, and people jumped out of the way.

"I can feel it, too." The general had determined that Swanson must never leave Somalia alive.

There were thousands of marines in his country now, and they had spread like a camouflage cancer. The airport and the port were working, and now they had taken over the stadium. Aidid had decided it would be a losing battle to fight for any of those places, which was why the walled soccer pitch had remained empty. As a result of their presence, the feeding stations, clinics, and refugee camps had gained security, and even the open-air Bakara Market was doing a better business. But the general was a patient man, and he knew all those gains by the crusaders were temporary.

In his opinion, the marines could stay at the stadium as long as they wanted, for entrenched troops hunkered down with machine guns behind sandbags and walls crowned with razor-sharp concertina wire were going to be useless for anything other than protecting a logistics point. The time was near when the Americans would find themselves entangled in the close streets of Mogadishu and their firepower and mobility would be limited. They would not be able to tell friend from foe among tens of thousands of people.

Aidid had studied tactics and strategy in his rise to becoming a major general in the Somali army before war, drought, and famine collapsed the nation. He had come out this morning to personally take the measure of his enemy. Sufficient foreign muscle could reopen and protect the humanitarian missions, but, even numbering in the thousands, the Americans could not stop this war, much less win it. He felt the time was right to move the crisis into a new stage.

Tuesday afternoon, Swanson awoke, rested after a few hours of sleep. The stadium had turned into a marine anthill. Hundreds of sandbags were being filled and stacked, big metal Conex containers were parked to be part of the barrier, wire was strung atop the walls, and men had sighted their weapons. Helicopters whacked through the sky. Throughout the cavernous structure, sergeants barked commands. Setting up a fort in one day was a noisy business. He looked around. Delshay was still asleep, a paperback mystery open across his chest. Smitty and Mancuso were watching the outskirts of Mogadishu through their scopes.

"By God, there are a lot of people downtown today," Smitty declared.

Kyle looked over the parapet. In the daylight, Mogadishu appeared almost alive, squirming with so much life all jammed into one place.

Smith said, "Since I did my bit last night capturing this place, can I go home now, Sar'nt Swanson?"

Swanson stripped and used bottled water for a quick, improvised shower, then put on a clean uniform. He picked up his M-16 and a small box, then clapped the shapeless boonie on his head. "I'm going to take a walk. I'll pass along your request to leave to the commandant. I'm sure he will authorize it."

"Where you going?" Smitty had not removed his eye from the scope while they bantered.

Swanson pointed. "Out there. I'll be back soon. Big Mike is in charge while I'm gone."

THE PATROLS

BY NOON, SWANSON was once again at the Irish Aid Society clinic, rested, clean, and as nervous as a boy on a date. He arrived in a CAAT with a .50 caliber machine gun on top and four marines and found Molly Egan in the hospital, carrying a kid under each arm.

She put the children down as soon as she saw him and came closer. Their eyes met, and they politely shook hands again. "Hello, Sergeant Swanson. Welcome back. Did you bring another exploding pistol?" Her clothes were rumpled, but the deep red hair flashed in the sunlight coming through the window, and her smile made his day.

"Even better. I come bearing gifts. Step outside." He laughed. *God, she is something else.*

The marines were unloading four fifty-pound burlap sacks from the CAAT. "Two hundred pounds of rice for you guys, and something special that no Irish Aid Society center should be without." He reached into the cab and brought out a bottle containing a liquid that had the look of burnished copper. "Rémy Martin cognac, six years old. Consider it a belated Christmas present."

Molly put her fist to her mouth in surprise, and patted Kyle on the arm with her other hand. "Oh, you are a good man, Sergeant Swanson. Where did you get all of this?"

"The French can be a generous people, particularly when they don't know they are being generous. It's for you, Dr. Sharif, and the staff."

"They are Muslim and don't drink alcohol," she said. "Are you Muslim?"

"No, I am not. I can use this. You, too. Come on inside." She walked in, and Swanson followed, after telling his marines to stay sharp. No climbing-the-water-tower bullshit this time.

There was a distinct change of atmosphere in the building, a lessening of the fear and hopelessness that Swanson had seen on the earlier visit. A middle-aged man sat at a small, square table, talking to a woman in a colorful wraparound, and Egan made the introductions. "Do you remember Dr. Lon Sharif, Sergeant Swanson? And his wife, Deqo. This little guy over here is their grandson, Cawelle."

Swanson smiled at the little boy, who stared back with big eyes. He looked to be about eight and was as skinny as a railroad track. Kyle squatted down to be more on the kid's level and extended his hand. "Hello, Cawelle." The kid shied away, then changed his mind and shook.

Molly explained. "His name is the Somali word for 'lucky,' although he hasn't had much of that. His parents died in the fighting about five months ago, so he lives here with his grandparents."

Kyle had a yellow package of chewing gum in his tunic pocket and gave it to the boy. "Can I call you *Lucky*? It's easier for me to say."

The boy understood English, and nodded his permission as he stripped a stick of gum and put it in his mouth. He chewed a few times and, without warning, jumped into Swanson's arms. The marine stood, holding him easily, and turned to the grandparents. "How did the operation on that girl turn out, Doctor?"

"Which one?" The surgeon had a blank look and a furrowed brow, puzzled by the question. "There have been so many."

"From the last time I was here. She had a terrible stomach wound, and I was told that she had been raped and beaten."

"That one died," Deqo Sharif remembered with her confident, but soft, voice. "We save those we can, Sergeant, but we fail too often. Please, sit and join us."

Molly said, "He brought rice for you, and whiskey for me."

"Christmas presents, just a little late. I've been out of town. Next time, I will load up on soft drinks and some other supplies." He accepted the two fingers of cognac that Egan poured into a glass and held it up. "A salute to all of you, for being here and making such a difference."

The Sharifs had just finished their rounds in the hospital and, for a change, had no emergencies demanding their attention. They had cups of tea, but Molly knocked back her own cognac with a practiced ease. Kyle noticed flecks of amber in her eyes.

Kyle gathered his words carefully. "I really came by today to apologize for the last time. I was careless and allowed a bad thing to happen right under my nose. For that, I'm sorry. That's not the way marines do things."

"Nonsense," replied Lon Sharif, brushing aside the apology. "All of those warlord gunmen are unpredictable. You drove them away, Sergeant, and they have not been back since then. That's the point to remember. Without your presence, it might have gotten bad."

Kyle put his empty glass aside. "Nevertheless, it gave me a needed dose of reality. This isn't the Africa of elephants and lions."

The doctor smiled. "It's good that you realize that." His voice was gentle. He smiled at his wife, who nodded approval.

Molly laughed. "I'll always remember you charging out toward them, shooting your big pistol, fighting the war on your own, standing out in the open and then flinging it at them when you ran out of bullets. You were so mad! Want another drink?"

Swanson declined. "And I remember you tackling me. I'll pass on another drink right now because I have to go on a patrol in a few hours. I just wanted to come by and check on you all."

The doctor spoke, almost as if on the edge of sleep. "We are better today than yesterday, which was better than the day before. The supply lines have opened up, and the violence is way down because security has improved. It shows what we might be able to do in this country if we can just have peace. I understand you marines now occupy the stadium?"

"Yes, sir. It gives us a better forward base. And you're right, Doctor Sharif. The logistics are really flowing. I would like for you to make a list of whatever you need here at the clinic—medicine or food or whatever. I can make sure that it finds you."

"That is very kind, Sergeant Swanson. But we get by."

"Sir, mountains of supplies are being off-loaded, and the docks and airports are stacked with crates. The world is pouring in contributions at every port in Somalia. Don't wait for the bureaucrats to assign you a share or for thieves to steal it, Doctor Sharif. Just tell me, and I'll get it."

"Why?" asked Deqo. Her eyes were on him, always wary of any offer that sounded too good to be true.

"I am a sniper, ma'am. I kill our enemies, and I am very good at it. But after seeing what you're doing to keep innocent people alive and feed them, I would like to be a little part of that, too. The only way I can think of, without jeopardizing my mission, is to bring you some of the good stuff, which is already being stolen and sold on the black market. Penicillin? Bandages? Coca-Cola? A portable generator? I can find it all."

Molly pulled out a cigarette, lit, and leaned back. A little trail of smoke weaved toward the door. She studied him. "You're serious." It wasn't a question.

"Yes."

"Very well. Dr. Lon and Deqo may be hesitant, but I will have a list ready for you by tomorrow, if you can get by to see us again." She looked directly at him. It was an invitation.

"Good. I'll see you then," he said, putting Lucky back on his feet. "And please, all of you, call me Kyle."

"Then I am Molly."

Swanson ducked into the new command post of C Company, where the commander was using an old door as a desk. "Request permission to enter, sir."

Captain Harmon Flint said, "Come in, Sar'nt Swanson."

"Your messenger says that you would like for me to join your foot patrol this afternoon, sir."

"Only if you think you're good enough to run with Suicide Charlie." Flint had known Kyle long enough to give him a sharp jab.

"I'll try to keep up, sir." The sniper looked at a flag tacked to the wall, the unique black-and-white skull-and-crossbones emblem that traced its lineage back to a night in 1942 when the company blunted a murderous Japanese attack on Guadalcanal. The survivors painted the image on a white parachute and lifted it high at dawn.

It had bred generations of tough war fighters who took shit from no one. Got a serious mission? Dial up Suicide Charlie. They would take on anything. Flint rubbed his palm across his stubble of hair. In the late afternoon, his shirt was soaked in sweat. "Good. But take a seat first. You want some coffee?"

Swanson shook his head but picked up a bottle of water.

"That was a good job you guys did with the stadium last night, Kyle." He pushed a cross-hatched paper over the desk. "Look at this. We have to make our own maps because an accurate layout of the Mog doesn't exist. A couple of main roads and thousands of little ones." Flint settled back in his chair.

"Sar'nt, I have the statistics from higher up, and my G-2 is on top of things in our area, but I want your opinion, too. You've had your nose in the dirt more than almost anyone. How do you read it?"

Kyle sucked on the water. "Operation Restore Hope has been a walkover so far."

"Yep. Now we hold this stadium on the city's northern flank, we have the airport in the southeast, got the port, and are patrolling deeper into Mogadishu every day. I can't believe this General Aidid character is just giving up."

"That's exactly my estimate, sir. He's not going to quit. I think that's about to change really soon."

Flint squinted. "Why?"

"The warlords decided to avoid any major confrontation when we first came in because they knew we had the firepower to crush them." Then Kyle told the captain about how the situations at both the arms cache and later at the Irish clinic had flopped from nothing happening to deep trouble in a flash. "The Skinnies are losing their fear of us, Captain. Our rules of engagement are pretty benign."

"I read this about the same. Bad news is that battalion got word today that a couple of thousand new troops are not going to be coming to Somalia after all. Also, some are saying we may start to withdraw by the end of January."

"Ouch. That's only a month from now." The sniper finished the water and set it aside. "I don't see the logic in declaring victory when we only really just got here. Probably because I'm just a sergeant."

The commander of Suicide Charlie laughed. "Somalia is a feel-good sideshow, a nice humanitarian gesture, Kyle. The political timing is terrible, with the president being a lame duck until the new administration can take over. Throw in that ethnic cleansing in Bosnia, and that bastard Saddam Hussein in Iraq, and a lot of people back in Washington are feeling that we've done our part here. They want to turn this business over to a coalition and get out."

Swanson stood and gathered his gear. "That's too bad. I can feel trouble coming, Skipper, just as sure as one of these afternoon showers, but this one is going to become a typhoon. When this word gets around, General Aidid will want to have control of Mogadishu by the time we withdraw."

"Yeah. Well, go out with the patrol and see what you can see. Come across anything I might need to know on background, just come see me. Anything else?"

"How about a hundred pounds of rice, sir?"

"That's a lot of rice. Can't you just liberate it from the French?"

"Already done that."

Like every other building in Mogadishu, the spaghetti factory in the northern Yaqshid District had seen better days. The Italian colonizers had stamped their influence on the African city and built a thriving manufacturing plant to turn wheat flour into pasta that blended nicely with the rich tomatoes from the Shabelle Valley. It was now just a ruin, and urban warfare thrived in its rubble. Kyle and his team created a hide from which they could provide support for a recon team picking through the tangled mess.

A light rain had passed through, but the temperature remained warm enough for steam to rise from the rubble. Swanson was seeing things he had not noticed before as they trekked downtown. Every wall was bullet-pocked, and stinking trash and war debris lay around like a lumpy, filthy carpet. Patrols were out probing other sectors, helicopter gunships were overhead, and CAATs scooted around like killer dune buggies. The gangs stayed curled out of sight or hid their weapons and appeared as part of the general population. An old man with a wrinkled face stared impassively at Swanson from a doorway. Children did not play, but begged the Americans for food.

The snipers watched the marine patrol move slowly, exactly nine hundred yards away. Swanson had his big rifle tuned so fine that he would be able to deliver a bullet on target nine football fields away. He concentrated on his breathing, eye to the scope and finger on the trigger. Corporal Delshay was his spotter and glassed the area with a bigger scope.

"Lookathere," the Apache whispered. "Coming in on the flank."

Swanson saw the figure. No more than late teens, skinny, in sandals, shorts, and a T-shirt, with the usual AK-47 in his hands. When the thug spotted the American patrol, he raised his weapon, and Swanson made a snap shot that skipped in front of the gunman and drilled up into his thigh. The target jerked, dropped his weapon, and plopped into a sitting position. With plenty of time to spare now, Swanson made a slight adjustment and brought the crosshairs onto the forehead without ever bothering to look at the face, fired, and flipped him.

"He's done," Apache said. Kyle made a note in his logbook. It was exactly 10:37 P.M., just another night in the Mog.

Having to kill a bad guy wasn't going to ruin his day.

The marines went back to the stadium several hours later, having found nothing but a few targets, misery, and a total lack of hope among the people. As they approached the gate, Swanson saw that some of the inhabitants of Mogadishu were changing addresses and moving closer to the stadium walls, like settlers in the Old West seeking the sanctuary of a military installation. A shantytown was being born under the marine guns.

He slept well, exhausted and dreamless, until the middle of the morning. It was Wednesday, December 30. One more day for the year 1992. Showers had been made operational in the stadium, and he stood beneath the chill water in the canvas tent, working hard with the shampoo and soap to try and scrub away the city's stink. He had a tight window of time before having to attend a mandatory noon briefing, so he rounded up Delshay and a Humvee to rush over to the clinic and get the list from

Molly Egan. He didn't care what was on the list. He just wanted to see her again, if only for a minute. He left Delshay at the wheel and jogged into the dark, muggy anteroom of the hospital.

Molly was alone when he came in. She rushed to him without a word, and Swanson wrapped his arms around her tightly and felt her squeezing him just as hard. His fingers traced her spine and burrowed into her hair as her forearms locked behind his neck.

Their kisses were hungry, and he finally, reluctantly, had to separate. "I gotta go, Molly," he said, then stopped for another long kiss before pushing away. "I wanted to tell you my idea. Tomorrow is New Year's Eve, and there is going to be a party on the rooftop at the press hotel. Meet me there, and we can celebrate in style. There will be a lot of people around. You'll be safe."

"I can be there at ten," she said, and kissed him on the cheek, a light flutter of her lips. She shoved the list in his jacket pocket. She could feel the tense strain in his muscles, although his face remained locked in hard planes that revealed nothing. "You can go for now, but I warn you that you may not be safe from me tomorrow night."

"Ten o'clock it is, then, Molly Egan." He gave her hand a final squeeze, then ran back out to the CAAT, and the big machine thundered away. He made the briefing with three minutes to spare.

THE BOATMAN

KYLE SWANSON WAS as tight as a spring by the time he got back to the sniper's roost in the stadium press box. He knew what was happening to him, and would not let anyone see that Molly had almost shattered his barriers against getting personally involved while on a mission. He shucked the gear, grabbed a bottle of bourbon, and went to the lower level, then out around the edge of the field, where construction units with blades and hoes were tearing out all the overgrowth and garbage and rubble to make the grounds usable.

He discovered a sanctuary on the far side, where a hill of wooden cases surrounded a large shipping container that had been left open and stood yawningly empty and inviting. Swanson made sure no one was near, then dodged inside and pulled the door almost closed behind him, jamming a two-by-four into the opening so it could not lock by accident. The sliver of light did not extend to the back.

His boots walked him to the rear almost automatically, where he tore off his shirt and used it as a towel to mop his face and chest, then threw it aside and sat with his back wedged in the corner. Safe enough. He took a pull of whiskey and welcomed the bite of the liquid, and let the tension go. A tremor ran through his legs, the muscles flashing in spasms, and within a minute, he was curled into a fetal position, shaking hard and gritting his teeth to stop any sound. Swanson sucked fetid air into his lungs and set his mind free to roam and deal with the recurring, hallucinatory dream that haunted him, a subconscious creature that he knew as the Boatman.

"You are doing well here in Somalia." The deep, disembodied voice was familiar to Kyle, and the taste of dust in his mouth was replaced by salty brine and ash. He had been expecting it since he arrived in Somalia. All light in the box had disappeared, and in the blackness he made out the shape of a tall, lean figure approaching from the other side of the container, paddling a long boat. The phantom and the sergeant were not friends.

"Leave me alone," Swanson said in a subconscious voice. "Get the fuck away from me, you maniac!"

The shadow assumed a more solid shape. It was a ghostly presence wrapped in a black cloak that billowed in a wind that could not be felt. A fleshless skull with empty eyes studied the marine, and there was a teasing giggle. "Heh. I was wondering when you would come. Look in my boat."

Kyle kept his eyes clenched tight, not wanting to look, but he saw them anyway. Twelve bodies were aligned in obedient sitting positions, six on each side of the rocking skiff. "I have more waiting to make the trip, but the boat can only hold a dozen at a time. As I said, you have done well."

Swanson had been in country for less than a month, and already his total of confirmed kills had reached double digits when he included the kid at the spaghetti factory. He had killed them all, and now his mind was wrestling with the carnage that his sniper rifle had dealt. The hallucinated figure was only something his brain had concocted by pulling from the morbid writings about hell by Dante, and it was Kyle's subconscious interpretation of the boatman, Charon, who ferried lost souls over the River Styx. Charon appeared only when Kyle had reached a point of mental overload, and served the purpose of scooping out the bad memories and hauling them away to a far, unseen shore where tall flames danced. Dumped over there forever, the souls were unable to haunt him.

The Boatman leaned lazily upon his oar, as if ready for a long conversation. "You seem sad. End your misery now, sniper. Join us in the boat. It would be crowded, but I always have room for you."

"Never."

"Someday you will. Someday soon, perhaps. You will want to kill yourself to atone for all of your murders."

"None of them was murder, you asshole."

"Tell them that." The Boatman waved his skeletal arm over Kyle's victims, and the wind blew the rag of a sleeve. "Sanctioned murder, perhaps, but murder nonetheless."

"Leave me, and never come back."

"I will not promise that, Sniper Swanson. I must go for now, but I will return. I am part of you. And I will keep spaces for you and your friend." Streaks of lightning bolts sizzled on the far horizon, and the Boatman spun his loaded craft around and slid away, back to the other side of the shipping container. He disappeared as Kyle yelled, "What friend? Who? What are you talking about?" There was no response.

Swanson slept for thirty minutes in the hot box, pondering the last words of the dream demon, before he slowly broke from the nightmare. The stripe of brightness coming through the door reappeared like a searchlight beam, and he uncoiled and remained still to get his bearings. He felt better and took another shot of whiskey.

Nobody had discovered him. Almost exactly two years earlier, he had endured his first visit from the Boatman after a hard fight in the Saudi border village of Khafji against an invading Iraqi armored troop. However, in Khafji, a spit-shined major named Bradley Middleton had found Kyle in the throes of the nightmare, and mistook the quaking for cowardice. Middleton had tried to throw Swanson out of the Marine Corps as being mentally unfit, but failed.

Swanson felt there was no shame in this habit. Mental decompression in some form or another was not unusual for combat soldiers, all of whom experienced it sooner or later. He could just as easily have taken a snort of cocaine, beaten his wife if he was married, or tied on an all-night drunk that would have him crawling among the dust bunnies, followed by a healthy puke and a two-day hangover. The few minutes he spent with the Boatman cleansed him and banished the men he killed from his thoughts. It was just his way.

Kyle twitched, stretched, took a final drink, then capped the bottle and put on his shirt again. He felt great. The marine sergeant was back. He plucked away the chunk of wood and kicked the damned door open wide. Time to go back to work.

In this better frame of mind, he would spend New Year's Eve with Molly, and he remembered her hug and kisses, as if her fingerprints were embedded on his skin.

"HEY! Anybody in there?" Swanson turned in his overwatch position when someone pounded on the door of the press box. At least the SNIPER sign had stopped them from barging in unannounced. He found a helmeted captain standing outside.

"Afternoon, sir," Swanson said, stepping out. He did not salute because his hand was full of rifle. Night was almost on them.

"Evening, Sergeant." The captain was a serious and smart guy who had been a combat platoon leader before being plucked out for staff things. "We are going to need this place for the combat operations center."

Ah, our ownership is being challenged, Swanson thought. It was best if the officer did not see the improvements they had made, with walls of water bottles, and whiskey and good food, or all of the good shade from the hot sun that punished the Horn of Africa. Kyle called over his shoulder. "Apache. You get on the window. Watch that rooftop where we saw that guy. If he comes back with a gun, kill him." He walked out, forcing the captain to follow. The door closed.

Corporal Dave Delshay was startled. They hadn't seen any suspicious figures. Then he realized what was happening and dropped his latest book. "Got it covered," he said. *Look busy!*

"I don't think this is a good location for the COC, Captain," Swanson said, intentionally moving toward a jagged crater that had been gouged by a mortar blast sometime back. Chunks of rock and debris stuck out like ruined teeth. "We've been catching sporadic fire from downtown. This is a regular RPG Alley."

"That right?"

"Yes, sir," answered Swanson. "You don't want this. Look at all the damage. It's too exposed for a command center. We've got some sandbags stacked inside, but one RPG through the window and your whole staff would be gone."

"It is kind of beat up and exposed, isn't it?" The officer was nodding agreement.

"Yes, sir. We're only in there to deliver long-distance counterfire."

"An RPG would take your team out just as easily."

"That's why we're paid the big bucks, sir. Did you see that big hole on the front of the place?"

"Yeah. Good. I'll take the word back. Where's your helmet, Sergeant?"

"Snipers aren't required to wear helmets, Captain. They get in our way with our scopes. We wear boonies."

"Well, then, put that on. Stay sharp. Remember Beirut." The officer needed to exert a little authority before closing the conversation and retreating downstairs.

Swanson saluted and ducked back inside. "Close call, boys. Enjoy this place while you can."

NEW YEAR: 1993

DECEMBER 31, 1992
MOGADISHU, SOMALIA

THE SAHAFI HOTEL on Maka Al Mukarama Road at the K-4 traffic circle was about as safe as anywhere in Mogadishu. Every side in the complicated and growing civil war needed it, as did the foreign governments who were fighting both Aidid and Ali Mahdi. An entrepreneur had seen a niche market in the war and opened the place to serve the press. It was neither subtle nor exotic: "Sahafi" meant "press" in Arabic, so it was, literally, the "press hotel." Journalists could plunk down eighty-five bucks cash and get three meals, a bed for the night in an air-conditioned room, and the comfortable comradeship of others of their ilk.

It had five floors, several hundred rooms, and was enclosed within chalky white walls. The rooftop provided an open view of downtown Mogadishu, and the lobby was a handy place for anyone wanting to make a news announcement. The press was propping up the economy of Mogadishu by hiring cars and drivers and interpreters and guards. Every day, the courtyard was the best place in the city for a local to find employment.

Swanson exited the Humvee in the courtyard entry, where the party was already under way in a dozen languages. The guards placidly chewed cuds of khat and impassively watched the foreigners celebrate the end of their year 1992. As Muslims, they observed the Hijri calendar, so to them it was really 1413. They were being paid, so they didn't care.

Kyle found the halls jammed with civilians and men wearing the uniforms of many countries. Beer and booze had been flowing for some time, and nobody paid any attention to the newest marine in their midst. Many doors were open, and people were sprawled in the rooms, drinking and smoking and arguing. There was a hot new rumor of a bloodbath fight somewhere, but that story could wait until tomorrow. Two weird Japanese photographers had gone over to check it out but were not back yet, and who cared; they were crazy anyway.

He spotted her quickly, for Molly had transformed from the blood-dappled aid worker into a beacon who stood out in the crowd atop the hotel. She was not being sensitive to Muslim culture tonight and wore a loose dress of white Egyptian cotton that came just to her knees, with her small waist cinched in a wide green belt that matched her bracelet and her eyes. The red hair was uncovered and shone in lights that were strung on long poles about the parapet. Swanson thought that radiant hair should never, ever be covered. She spied him and gave an impish grin. A German photographer who had been trying to chat her up was summarily dismissed, and she gave Kyle a kiss and a beer from an iced cooler that was kept full by an American contractor.

He popped the tab. "You are beautiful, Ms. Egan."

"Thank you, Sergeant Swanson. You got all dressed up for the occasion, too," she said, tugging the collar of his clean cammies. His .45 was holstered, snug on the web belt. Her skin was soft, and she had light perfume.

"How come you look like you just got out of the shower?"

"Because I have. See that dark-haired Brit girl over there? Her name is Maisie Turner, and she is a reporter with the *Guardian* newspaper, which keeps a room here. We met when she was doing a story on relief work, and she volunteered her facilities tonight."

Turner must have felt the look because she glanced over and gave a little wave. She was petite, had her dark hair tied back in a ponytail, and wore a loose top with tight jeans. Another woman not playing by local rules tonight, Maisie was happily scrunched between a tanned U.N. worker from Norway and an intense Australian freelancer.

"I don't understand these press people," Swanson said, catching the drifting aroma of marijuana. The rooftop was a placid oasis. "Don't they know there is a war going on?"

"War is what they do, Kyle," Molly said. "They move from one hotspot to another and keep bumping into each other in different hotels and clubs. One told me they follow the 'boom-boom,' just like we aid workers follow tragedy and you follow an enemy. They don't want to be anywhere else, at least not this week. Next week, a better story may pop up elsewhere, and they will go chase that one. Now, dance with me, my pretty marine."

Swanson finished his beer and tossed the empty can into a barrel. When he took her hand, the rest of the crowd seemed to disappear. They came together and rocked in place.

Molly whispered, "Maisie gave me her room key." She leaned on his shoulder. "It has air-conditioning, clean sheets, and there's more beer in the refrigerator."

"Then why the hell are we still up here?" He stepped back and gave her a twirl, and her skirt fanned out to show her legs as she spun. She came back to him, even closer now.

"I thought you'd never ask. We can be back up here in time for midnight."

"Why would we want to do that?" Swanson looked at her, and the smile became a serious look. He was realizing the water was deep, and he was ready to drown happily. "I don't want to waste a minute with you, girl."

"I know. I feel the same way, Kyle, and it scares me a little. It is best not to have real feelings in these battered places. But tonight I want you to take me, love me, and tell me everything is going to be all right. I want to still be in bed, naked and next to you, when the sun comes up tomorrow."

JANUARY 1, 1993

The U.S. Secret Service provided a needed break to the daily schedule, which was becoming dangerously routine. President George H. W. Bush, who had ordered the intervention in the Somalian emergency, was in country for a firsthand look at the mission, and Swanson was providing countersniper protection at the airport. While Kyle and Molly had partied at the Sahafi yesterday, Bush had been aboard the USS *Tripoli* after digesting MRE field rations from a lunch with the troops at an airfield sixty miles north of the Mog.

The Secret Service had the job of protecting the president, even in a war zone, and buttoned things up tight for the two-day visit. They automatically turned to Swanson for assistance because he was a known quantity and was already on site—their own snipers trained at the marine scout-sniper school in which Kyle had served as an instructor. However, they didn't totally trust him.

Troops secured the roads into the areas Bush visited, with more marines standing guard on the surrounding rooftops. The president, in a desert camouflage jacket, spent a half hour at a feeding station and an orphanage in Mogadishu. Seven hundred children clapped and welcomed him while the Secret Service sweated it out.

Swanson stood with Corporal Smith in the main guard tower at the front gate of the airport, while other snipers manned other points and glassed the areas both inside and outside the facility at which the big blue and white *Air Force One* waited. With them in the tower was Secret Service agent Mark Deber, a lanky, square-shouldered man wilting in the heat. He had removed his suit coat, but sweat saddlebags puddled his white shirt. Deber knew Swanson from the Quantico training but was in the tower to keep an eye on both of the marines: a guard to guard the guards. Nothing was left to chance where presidential protection was concerned. It was the kind of challenge that Swanson enjoyed.

"Deber, you ought to stick around here in the Mog for a while. You missed a big party last night, and we can take you to the hot joints downtown along the Green Line, catch some jazz." Swanson swept his scope over the open ground beyond the fence, looking for telltale signs of a hide.

"Fuck that. I'm outta here on the next plane after Big Bird. I don't want nothing you got here, like maybe dysentery," Deber said. "How's the duty been?"

"Pretty quiet. The Skinnies don't want to mess with us."

"They just shoot each other," added Smitty, who was examining the edge of the city.

"Sounds like a deal to me," said Deber. "Long as they don't shoot at us."

"Got that right."

The president's armored convoy arrived, and Bush spent some time saying hellos and thanking the people at the airport. Swanson smoothly scanned the exterior of the gate, then the interior area around Bush, tense and watching for potential threats. For the briefest of moments, the Unertl scope on his sniper rifle swept over the president's face, and the twenty-four-inch barrel with its one-in-twelve-inch twist was pointed directly at his ear. It would have been an easy shot. Swanson kept the rifle moving.

"That ain't funny, Swanson. You were somebody else, I'd have taken you down," Deber hissed behind him. The agent wondered if he had screwed up; had he really given the best sniper in the Marine Corps a free shot at the president? Swanson kept a grin buried deep. No harm, no foul.

Then Bush was safely aboard the plane, and it was gone, heading for Moscow, where he was to sign a nuclear-arms-reduction treaty.

The two snipers and the Secret Service agent all relaxed and took deep breaths. The president, the most important man in the world, was somebody else's responsibility now.

"Hey, Deber. Since you were ready to shoot me down like a dog a minute ago, how about giving me a present?"

"What? You want a reward for being your usual asshole self?"

Swanson slid the big rifle into its custom-made bag. "Not for me. I want a souvenir for a kid at a relief clinic. You got something that says WHITE HOUSE on it?"

Deber patted his pockets. "Yeah. Here. They give these things out like candy." It was a white cardboard square with a lapel pin that bore the presidential symbol, an eagle with flared wings and UNITED STATES OF

AMERICA printed in tiny gold letters around the blue edge.

"He doesn't have lapels," Swanson complained.

"Not my problem," Deber said. "I'm gone. You guys watch your asses."

On the way back to the stadium, Swanson considered the presidential trip. The Man had left Somalia, but Swanson and thousands of marines and the troops of other nations were still here, and it seemed that the president had begun to waffle on the planned exit. Originally, the plan was to have it all done before January 20, when Bill Clinton would be sworn in. On this personal trip, President Bush had given it more of an open ending. His spokesman was ambiguous, promising the Somalis would not be abandoned but conceding that some American troops might start handing their duties over to U.N. forces and withdrawing by the end of January. Bottom line was that Swanson knew his days left in Somalia were numbered . . . he just didn't know the number.

Deqo Sharif gave an "I know what you did last night" grin when Kyle Swanson came to the Irish Aid Society relief center. She had been helping Lon with a delicate birth, and her face showed the fatigue. They worked when they needed to work, not according to clock hours, but somehow managed to keep their humanity intact. Sleep was not high on their priority list.

"Molly is not here, Kyle. The agencies are having a conference about how to get more food out into the countryside."

Swanson said, "That's okay, Deqo. Did you get to see President Bush today?"

"No. We were busy here, as always, but it was good

that he came to Somalia at all." Her dark face frowned. "Did you marines hear about a big attack on one of the compounds of Ali Mahdi last night?"

"Yeah. The local cops think it was planned by General Aidid, and was led by the general's pet thug, the Cobra. They are bad news." Swanson was always ready for a tidbit of intelligence to pass along. "What do you think it means?"

"People say that it was an assassination attempt, but Mahdi wasn't there, and he will demand revenge." She adjusted her robe and looked at him with steady dark eyes. "It was also a sign, Kyle, to show everyone in Mogadishu that you marines don't really control the city. You did not know about it in advance and could not stop it." She sighed with frustration. "I think things are going to get bad again."

"You may be right, Deqo. You may be right. I will make sure the patrols continue to come by here." Swanson took out the lapel pin. "Look, the real reason I came by today was to bring this little badge for Lucky."

"He's in class right now. I will give it to him later."

He handed it over and watched her study the shining enameled seal of the president. "Tell him it's a gift from President Bush and will help keep him safe."

"Can it stop a bullet?" Deqo tucked it into the folds of her conservative purple *guntiino,* a long cloth that draped over her shoulder and around the waist. A matching cloth called a *shash* crossed her head.

Kyle rapped lightly on the table and said, "I've got to get back. Please tell Molly I came by, would you?"

"Of course. Thank you. Be careful."

"Don't worry about me, Deqo. I carry the biggest gun out there."

THE FIGHT

THE TENTH MOUNTAIN called for help. Swanson thought they might be running low on suntan lotion, but grudgingly acknowledged the unit was spread thin, with soldiers posted all over Somalia, occupying other cities and keeping roads open. The fact that the Tenth headquarters had been set up in no man's land within Mogadishu seemed to have escaped the attention of the planners.

At the stadium, General Jack Klimp, the marine commander, received intel that the troublemaking warlord General Aidid was up to something, and marine assets were preparing to meet the challenge. The hard-eyed general found Swanson and told him, "Take some snipers over there and scout out what's going on. This might be the fight we have been expecting. Maybe they are going to come out at last. Then get back here with a SITREP."

Kyle and ten of his men piled into Humvees and tore out of the stadium down the 21 October, and were inside the gates of the Tenth HQ compound within minutes. Once again, he found no outward signs of any real gunfight, but the army guys said the usual harassing fire being spat at them had increased.

"Come up here and take a look," said a colonel, who led the sniper up to the flat rooftop of the three-story building, which had been baking in the sun all afternoon. The officer pointed to another compound about six hundred meters away, where a crowd of Skinnies milled about three long warehouses. "That's where Aidid is now storing some of his heavy stuff. We have never seen that many people around those buildings at one time."

As if to emphasize the point, a rifle popped and a bullet ricocheted off of the three-foot-high parapet surrounding the Tenth headquarters' roof. Swanson raised his and played over the area. There was no court-of-law proof of any recent big firefight, but the colonel was right: those warehouses and the large crowd were a real threat, and it was growing. The rules of engagement still mandated that as long as the Somalis did not brandish their weapons, the marines would not open fire. Swanson believed that was about to change in a hurry. With its combat power dispersed elsewhere, the available cooks and clerks of the Tenth Mountain HQ were putting aside their paperwork and suiting up with load-bearing gear and rifles.

"I'll be right back," Kyle said. He left most of his snipers with the army dudes and hauled ass back to the stadium.

Klimp's staff had spread out the biggest map they had, and Kyle pointed out the warehouses and reported the crowd of Somalis there was whipping up its courage. Aidid apparently was ready to do some damage, and although the effort probably was to be directed at his rival warlords, the U.S. troops were in the way.

Klimp wasn't going to give an inch. His plan was to

wrap a bubble around and over the suspicious compound and bring out his own heavy infantry, armor, and air power. If Aidid so much as wiggled, he would be crushed. Kyle dashed back to the Tenth HQ, this time carrying his huge M82A1A special-application scoped rifle with its 10× Unertl scope. On the roof, psyops people with portable loudspeakers were warning the militiamen to surrender by dawn.

When night fell, the darkness came with a rainstorm that slashed in from the Indian Ocean, and heavy winds spun across the ragged city with a discordant, threatening hum. The cold and merciless rain soaked the sniper teams on the rooftop. Visibility fell to zero, blinding Swanson's night-vision goggles. He took them off. The wind was blowing the sheets of rain almost horizontally, right at them, and wiping a hand over his face did not help. No one could see anything in the dirty night, but beneath the storm's roar, he heard the growlings of large engines and a lot of shouting over in the Aidid camp.

Kyle repositioned the M-60 machine guns on the roof and brought up a forward air controller to coordinate the helicopter gunships that might be needed. Newer deep growls of other machines joined the noise as marine armor took stations. The loudspeakers never shut up: "Surrender at dawn!"

The night and the river of rain stretched into an eternity of anxious misery, and Swanson could only wonder what was going on down below where the Skinnies were gathered. He and his spotter, Corporal David Delshay, the Apache, built a ragtag shelter and occasionally took breaks to go inside to dry out and have something hot to drink. His boots were full of water, his clothing was soaked, and he shook like a puppy as the chill seeped into his bones. Sleep was impossible, and battle was certain to come with the daylight.

The African storm tapered away just as the sun began to light the sky, and when the veil of mist lifted, Kyle got his first good look at what had been happening. Tanks and other heavy weapons had been driven out of the Somali buildings and were revving up in the courtyard, and the militiamen were all carrying weapons. Kyle squared into a sitting position between the parapet and a rooftop air-conditioning unit and dialed the scene close with his powerful Unertl scope. The loudspeakers squawked last-chance demands to the Somali warriors to surrender. That wasn't going to happen. The warlord's men, idle for weeks, were spoiling for a fight.

General Klimp watched the brewing situation with real-time imagery back at the stadium. His marines were also weary of the boredom. Klimp got Swanson, his best sniper in the best position, on the circuit.

Kyle had been listening to the increasing radio traffic through an earbud. He had an armor-piercing round in the chamber of his SASR, and five more ready in the clip below. The other snipers and machine gunners along the wall were sighting in on potential targets when the distinctive whopping sound of approaching helicopter gunships joined the morning din.

Beside Kyle, the forward air controller saw something new roll out of the warehouse: a four-cannon ZSU-23/4 called the Zeus, a powerful weapon that could erase the incoming attack birds from the sky as soon as they appeared. "Oh my God," the FAC yelled into his radio. "Abort! Abort! Abort!" The choppers immediately stopped on a dime, just out of range, and hovered behind the headquarters building.

The situation was at the point of no return. None of the Skinnies had yet fired, but neither had they surrendered, and they now were showing off anti-aircraft field guns and tanks. Swanson heard a familiar voice in his earbud; Klimp was asking if the sniper could disable the Zeus without hurting any of the Somali fighters. The big gun was a game changer that could not be allowed to join a fight.

Swanson adjusted his scope to center the evil-looking multiple cannon. The best way to ruin it would be to slam an armor-piercing round through the ammunition canister that fed belts of ammo to the weapon. It was located in the middle of the cannon. Corporal Delshay lasered the range, and Kyle dialed it in while he told the general what he had, adding that there was no guarantee.

"Take the shot," Klimp ordered, and Kyle fired. The powerful .50 caliber bullet punched straight through the metal ammo canister as if it were thin cardboard. Then the round punched straight through the gunner who was seated behind it. The man went over backward, dead, and hell erupted. The battle was on.

Another Zeus answered Swanson's opening shot with thundering blasts from its quadruple guns directly at the sniper's position. Chunks of the rooftop parapet were pulverized with impacting explosions, and Swanson pushed away onto his back as green tracer rounds flew overhead and ate at the protective barrier. The other marines and soldiers opened up in response. The Apache grabbed Swanson's jacket and rolled him back into position. "Get up!" Delshay yelled. "Take that son of a bitch!"

Kyle repositioned and started firing, no longer having to worry about not hitting anyone. His armor-piercing rounds quickly shredded the second Zeus as the world roared in his ears and the militiamen got their first taste of the Marine Corps in full battle cry.

With the anti-aircraft guns dead, the FAC called in the hovering gunships, and the lurking choppers pounced over the rooftop like predatory panthers, their miniguns slashing deadly paths through the Aidid compound. Swanson and Delshay were showered with the falling hot brass of the spent cartridges. It was open season.

Kyle reloaded and began pumping armor-piercing rounds into the gunner and driver positions of the Russian-made tanks while other marines raked the enemy foot soldiers. Firing erupted all around the perimeter, and the big marine tanks crashed forward to add their machine guns and cannons to the scrap. All three warehouses caught fire. Satisfied that the major enemy machinery was dead, Swanson looked to individual fighters who were hiding in buildings that overlooked the battle zone so they could shoot back at the Americans. They died as soon as they appeared. The compound that only minutes before had been the militia's striking power was littered with junk and bodies.

The firing stopped, and Kyle lowered his rifle to reload. As he put in a new clip, a neatly dressed man walked onto a balcony, and the sniper instantly recognized General Aidid. The leader was greeted by cheers from the Somali militiamen, who had just taken a thorough beating. Aidid examined the ruins of the ludicrously one-sided battle, then looked with disdain toward the American positions a few hundred yards away.

A bare-headed marine who was reloading a large rifle was looking back at him. It was the same one who had manhandled him in their earlier confrontation. *The Swanson Marine! Again! Damn him!*

Kyle steadied the mighty SASR so that it pointed directly at the warlord, who realized that his fate rested on the trigger finger of the man he had grown to personally hate.

"I'm locked onto Aidid," Swanson spoke easily into

his radio. An easy three-pound twitch on the trigger would end the warlord's life. A second man who had come onto the balcony also recognized what was about to happen and stepped in front of Aidid. It was the body-guard, the Cobra, and that didn't matter at all to Kyle, who did not adjust his aim. A big SASR round would just burrow through both bodies as easily as it had torn through the armor of the Zeus quad-fifty.

"Cease fire. Stand down," came the voice of General Klimp. The battle was over.

The warlord turned away slowly from the sniper, intentionally ignoring him now, and gingerly left the balcony. The Cobra also backed away, but never took his eyes off Swanson. He raised his empty right hand and pointed an accusing finger at the marine in silent threat. Swanson did not put aside the rifle until the balcony was clear.

"Were you at the Aidid compound yesterday? I hear it was a real battle." They were walking on the beach, holding hands and barefoot in the silver sand. Molly's baggy khaki pants were rolled up to her knees. Swanson wore old cargo shorts and a T-shirt, with his .45 ACP on his hip. Almost every man on the beach carried a weapon.

"Yep. Along with about five hundred other marines. It wasn't much. The whole thing didn't take more than five minutes."

Lucky Sharif was with them, out deeper, but not too deep, for sharks might be about, drawn by the blood of slaughtered camels rendered at a nearby plant that dumped the waste directly in the Indian Ocean. Kyle spun an old football that he had bartered from a corporal, and he tossed it to Lucky. The boy knew soccer, and trying to handle a ball that had points on both ends was unnatural to him, and it knocked him down with a big splash. He came up laughing. "That boy is going to be a fine wide-out for the Pats someday."

"A what for the what? You are *sooooo* American, Kyle. The rest of the world doesn't follow your sports teams, you know."

He pulled her close and they bumped shoulders. "Maybe the world would be a better place if they would, and the sports of other countries are even more weird. I'll bet that even you can't understand cricket."

"You changed the subject. What about that fight?"

"Deqo says you're going down to Kismaayo to do some work. When were you going to tell me that?"

"You're changing the subject again. Some of the other marines told me you were right in the middle of it."

"Nature of the job, Molly. Really, it was not a big thing. We had them from the start. In fact, we picked the fight to teach General Aidid still another lesson. That jerk needs a lot of lessons."

Lucky dashed from the surf and threw the football back to Kyle, using both hands. The boy was having a good time. He had survived dangers bigger than any shark.

"Go long!" Kyle called, pointing, and the boy took off down the beach, his long legs churning. Kyle lofted a tight spiral that fell into Lucky's outstretched arms. The boy juggled it and almost hauled it in, but it bounced away. "He needs some work. What about Kismaayo?"

"It will only be two days to help out with a new U.N. food-distribution point. There is so much matériel pushing into the pipeline these days that the NGOs are having a hard time on the other end." Marine trucks, choppers, and ships could haul the supplies only so far. Then the

NGOs took over because there was no Somali government to handle the distribution.

"Two days and two nights," Kyle said with a glum tone. "That might as well be forever."

"This is nice," she said, and kicked at a small incoming wave. They walked past some bare-chested marines playing beach volleyball over a sagging net, their rifles on nearby towels. Some women in little swimsuits baked in the sun.

Kyle had often scolded young privates who swooned over girls they had just met and wanted to marry as quickly as possible, no matter the situation. Now he had fallen for this Irish girl, and having to swallow his own medicine did not make it taste any better. Stolen hours were all they had, and both were determined to enjoy their remaining time, as long as they had. Kyle had already convinced himself that Somalia, or even forever, would not be long enough. He did not want their love to become a casualty of war. Somalia had brought them together, but it was very weak glue. Either of them could be transferred at a moment's notice.

"Well, I guess that Lucky and I can work on his pass routes while you're gone."

"You realize that he is placing you and me in parental roles, at an age between himself and his grandparents, Lon and Deqo."

"Umm. What are we going to do about that? We're not his parents." Kyle looked at her serious face. "We never will be."

They moved on in silence for a little while, then slowly turned and started walking the other way, back toward the airport.

"I have been thinking about something, Kyle. It's only an idea right now, but maybe we can get all three of them out of this place. I can check out the procedures for Ireland, and you can look into the qualifications for America. Maybe we can pull Lucky, Deqo, and Lon out and safe—all of them."

Swanson felt a wind, and Lucky raced by, football beneath his arm, being chased by another boy. "Doctor Sharif probably won't leave, and Deqo won't leave without him. You know that. Lucky can't go alone."

"It's just something to think about," she said. "Here's something else to think about: suppose we take him back to the clinic and retire up to Maisie's room at the hotel. She flew over to Uganda on a story."

"Things happen when I get you there, Irish. Things of which your mother probably would not approve." He grabbed her by the waist. "Consider yourself warned."

"Words, words, words." She mocked him, then quoted Eliza Doolittle again. "Show me."

She's the one, he decided.

KIA

GENERAL AIDID TUMBLED into a great and furious sulk following the embarrassing defeat of his forces. Ali Mahdi crowed that the Americans had finally taken sides, and everyone in the city was gossiping about how easily the marines had taken down Aidid's forces. The substantial losses in manpower and matériel paled next to the image of being so easily whipped. Weakness was propaganda poison, and Ali Mahdi would use it to the fullest.

Aidid had planned to trap the marines in the urban canyons of Mogadishu and force them into wicked door-to-door battles. His warriors had gotten their guns from the warehouses under the cover of the storm but didn't even get out of the gate to use them. Instead, the marines struck first by leapfrogging out of the stadium and raiding his most important storage site. Seventeen fighters had been killed and twenty-five wounded. Then the marines confiscated hundreds of his rifles and machine guns—sixteen truckloads of valuable weaponry. That was the big picture.

A smaller picture was also seared in his memory: that

of the Marine Swanson positioned on a rooftop and deliberately aiming a huge rifle at the general, grinning while he did so. It was salt that rubbed hot and hard into Aidid's wounded pride.

The general was relaxing on a floor mat in his home, wearing a loose sarong and sandals in the heat as he thought things over, trying to calm himself. He spooned up a ball of spicy rice, vegetables, and camel meat; chewed; swallowed; and made a decision.

"Omar!" the general called, and the Cobra strolled easily into the room, holding a book that he had been reading. "I have a special assignment for you," Aidid said.

"Anything." The face remained expressionless, the eyes unseen behind wraparound sunglasses of the type favored by the Americans. Beads of sweat laced his forehead.

"Thousands of American marines have invaded our country, and thousands of other foreign troops, too." He did not have to finish the thought.

"The Swanson Marine." The Cobra's dour face regained a bit of spark.

"Yes. His time has come. We have spies and a lot of money. Use it. Find him for me."

"And kill him?"

"A simple death would be too easy. I want this sniper to die in spectacular fashion. I want to make an example of him."

"I will have this death, General." Omar also seethed with a desire for revenge.

"Of course. First, we pay him back for being a sniper."

Aidid sprawled back on the mat and covered his tired eyes with folded hands. "You are going back into the Green Line tonight, I hope."

"Yes, sir. I plan to drive out with ten men to raid an

Ali Mahdi storehouse. We need to restock our own armory."

"Be savage tonight, Cobra, and instill fear. I want you to try a new tactic. Take two trusted men who are good with guns and are disciplined. Leave them behind to be a sniper team of our own. They will remain in place until a marine patrol comes near and then shoot one of the Americans. When this killing happens in Ali Mahdi territory, any alliance he is building with the Americans will collapse. They will send more troops in there."

"Ah. And that will help draw the marines into the street fighting we have wanted." The Cobra logged away the information; always learning.

A patrol stepped off into the darkness and was soon beyond the airport checkpoints and into the city itself. An easy rain pelted their faces, much gentler than the recent storm, almost refreshing after the scalding afternoon. The eleven-man column was a coiling snake that would prowl through abandoned buildings, down tight alleys, around blind corners, and into gutted neighborhoods. Out front, on point, was Corporal Jerry Evans, who had been a wrestler in his Iowa high school days and carried his heavy gear with ease. Evans looked up at a tall building and felt a hundred unseen eyes looking back. His night-vision goggles painted things green, and he saw no threats, so he leaned forward into his work, keeping his finger near the trigger.

Evans was not scared. He had lost his combat cherry two years ago in the Desert Shield war that kicked Saddam Hussein out of Kuwait. Mogadishu was just another stop on the marine train. He loved this shit and was going to be a lifer. At the moment, his entire being was concentrated on what he was doing step by step, moving into the heart of the Mog.

It was a repeat of what they had done last night, and by coming back to the same place, they hoped to catch some gunmen who would mistakenly gamble that the marines would not show up twice on the same streets. An hour into the patrol, he had found nothing of interest. The deep cigarette-gritty voice of Sergeant Marty Reyes came through his earpiece and ordered him to change direction and head down an alley to the northeast. Evans stepped out, and the ten other marines followed.

He was on cruise control. Mogadishu was like New York, a city that never slept. There was always something or someone stirring. The big corporal had never been to New York, but he had seen it a lot on television. Lots of clubs and girls. But the Big Apple didn't have the danger factor of the Mog, and that was the rush over here. He stepped around a stack of rocks, paused, listened, and moved again.

Not a single marine had been killed by enemy gunfire since the original unload back on December 6. One civilian contractor died when he ran over a land mine, but that was it. With all the sporadic gunfire that could be heard at almost any hour, it seemed to Corporal Evans that the bad guys should have been able to have hit something by now. He heard the rumble of a vehicle engine and brought the patrol up short, hugged back against a wall as a dirty technical turned the corner, motoring around like it was all king of the night. The marines had the truck surrounded before it could come to a complete halt, and the four gentlemen in it were so surprised that they bailed out, broke, and ran. Their machine gun hung useless on its mount. Sergeant Reyes taped on a block of C-4 explosive to the automatic weapon, and the whole technical went up with a crash.

That would probably do it for the night, Evans

thought. Every goon in town would now know where the marine patrol was. A minute later, headquarters gave the order to come back, and the patrol turned around, being just as careful going back to the airport as they had been on the way out.

A single gunshot cracked from a dark rooftop, and the bullet took Evans in the neck and drilled into his chest, dropping him hard on the stones. The other marines engaged the sniper with a hail of fire as they dove for cover. Sergeant Reyes did a quick head count. Someone was missing.

"Evans?" he called. "Where are you? Anybody got eyes on Evans?"

The marines looked at each other. No Evans. "Let's go find him," said Reyes. He set up a base of covering fire that smothered the building from which the shot had come and then led several of his men back to where Evans had last been seen. He lay facedown on the filthy street, bleeding hard, his head twisted at an awkward angle. They grabbed his web gear and dragged him to cover.

"We have a friendly WIA," Reyes reported over the radio, forcing his voice to remain steady and understandable while a corpsman worked on Evans. "We need an evacuation." He gave the grid coordinates. New rips of AK-47 spattered out of the night, forcing the marines into a tighter defensive perimeter.

Within minutes, three armored vehicles from the Quick Reaction Force trundled into the wasteland. All of the militias were wide awake by now, bringing new guns to the fight. Bullets pinged off hulls, and the armored tracks opened up with their heavier weapons to cover the patrol members, who stuffed Evans into one of the bays, climbed in, and slammed the hatches shut.

A doctor met the little convoy back at the base. He pronounced Corporal Jerry Evans dead on arrival.

Kyle turned to the Central Intelligence Agency for help. They occasionally borrowed him for temporary assignments, and that had built some relationships with their hardened operators. They kept trying to get him to join their secret pack of field spooks, but Swanson was a marine, and would stay one. In marine speak, the CIA acronym stood for "Christians in Action."

One of the rough men was Nicholas Hamilton, a former West Pointer, currently stationed in Somalia. The CIA had a bad habit of making their workplace so secret that it became strikingly obvious. In Mogadishu, the Christians worked in a heavily guarded and separate compound deep within the airport grounds. The place wore a crown of communication antennae and was surrounded by repetitive rows of high fences and coils of spiky concertina wire and bore a wooden placard at the gate that read STAY THE HELL AWAY. Swanson told the sentry to send word into the tent that he wanted to see Hamilton.

In a few minutes, the CIA agent appeared and barked, "Can't you read signs, you fuckin' jarhead?" Hamilton walked to the fence, opened the gate.

Swanson entered. "We lost a guy last night up near the Green Line," he said when they ducked inside and into the cool blast of air-conditioning. Several people gave him a glance but then went back to whatever they were doing.

"Not one of yours, was it? I haven't read the after-action report."

"No. It was a corporal out of the three-eleven. What disturbs me is that it was a clean sniper hit, Ham, not just the usual wild shot in the night. If the Skinnies start good sniper work in that urban terrain, we will have a whole new set of problems."

"A lot of rooftops and rubble," the CIA man agreed. "We have some people out and about, spreading money and asking questions. Who the hell knows? They were bound to nail somebody sooner or later."

"I don't like losing any marine," Swanson responded. A full mug of coffee was put on the table in front of him. "Even if it is just bad luck."

"Neither do I, but the famous Kyle Swanson didn't trot down here because of that incident. What brings you to the land of the supersecret decoder ring? Did somebody call for you? Maybe you want to tell me about your redheaded girlfriend?"

"You know about us?"

"You two are the talk of the town."

Kyle put his face to an air conditioner and let the cool wind blow directly on him. "Passports, Ham. I need three genuine U.S. passports for a Somali family we, meaning the US of A, may want to evacuate in a hurry."

Nick Hamilton laughed. "Every Somali in Somalia wants an American passport, including the warlords. What makes these three so special, out of a couple of million people who would love to leave this godforsaken country?"

"Proper egress papers, too. Visas to pass through Kenya, a smooth entry to the U.S., and some restart cash."

"Why, shit, Kyle! Sure as hell! Anything else? You want me to charter a private jet, too?"

"Not a bad idea, but no." Swanson unfolded a metal chair and sat down, leaning forward, elbows on knees. Drank some coffee. "Ham, these people are nobody, and that makes them special. Just a doctor who will never desert his patients; his wife, who will never leave without him; and their only living relative, an eight-year-old grandson. They live and work at the Irish agency—never stop working, from what I have seen. All three of them speak English. I can get some reference letters from NGO and relief types, but these are not really important people in the grand scheme of things. They are just rocks of resistance who have dedicated their lives to helping other Somalis, which is why we are all here in the first place."

Hamilton leaned back and hooked his thumbs into the waistband of his shorts. "So, there is no real reason other than Kyle Swanson likes them."

"No! Godammit all, Ham. We should do this because we *can*! Because we *should*! Do you want to go back to the real world and have accomplished nothing at all over here? I don't. Someday when we are old, you and I can rock on the porch of your home in New Hampshire and remember back to when we did something more than hand over bricks of cash to warlords."

"We can't save everybody in Somalia, buddy. That's cold, hard fact."

"We can save these. Trust me. They are worth it. They made a difference." Swanson emptied a little envelope from his shirt pocket, and out slid a sheet containing all of the data needed for a passport and regulation-sized photographs.

Nick Hamilton was stunned. He had never seen this Kyle Swanson before, so different from the nerveless shooter who sometimes did black jobs for the CIA. "Idealism doesn't suit you, Kyle," he said.

"You Christians owe me big, Ham. I always come running whenever you crook your finger to tell me to go somewhere and kill somebody. I want a little payback: three passports for a family that would never ask for themselves and probably will refuse to make the jump anyway."

And in the back of his mind: *Out of Somalia, hang up the rifle, quit the Corps, marry Molly, settle down, and help raise Lucky. The family he had never had was within his reach.*

THE SPY

THE COBRA FELT pride about the shot that he had made, which killed the marine. It was another milestone for him in the University of War. He had passed through the cannon-fodder stage of his development long ago, when he had been trained by Aidid's foreign mercenaries to be more than just another black African child with a Kalashnikov. They had schooled him every day in how to kill with a knife and other weapons, and also with his hands and feet. Failure meant a quick shot to the back of the head and eternity in a shallow grave. The Cobra had survived.

So why was the general furious? Omar Jama thought it would be just the opposite, but the man he had sworn to protect was storming around and shouting. "I did not order you to personally make the sniper attack! I told you to pick other men to do it. This was an experiment, nothing more."

"I killed the marine, sir. That was the objective." The Cobra was confused. "It was easier to just do it myself."

"But it was not *my* objective!" The general was in his face, nose to nose. "I never doubt your bravery, Omar, but your eagerness to fight clouds your judgment. You are too valuable for me to lose in a minor skirmish. Do you not understand that?"

"I don't understand, General. I thought I was doing what you wanted." He fondly remembered hiding far back in a darkened room on an upper floor, seeing the marines slowly edge forward, the pleasant stark smell of gun oil and ammunition rising to his nostrils, the care with which he had sighted on the target, and the sensuous, slow squeeze of the trigger. The aim was above the neck to avoid the protective vest, and the single bullet struck perfectly. Omar had repressed the urge to empty the entire clip, but discipline took over, and he withdrew and fled into the neighborhood.

The general calmed. "You are one of my most able officers, Omar, as well as my personal protector. You have a nimble brain, and the strength of a horse, and that elevates you above the others."

The Cobra nodded. While Aidid had arranged for youngsters to learn among the mercenaries out in the bush, he also had furnished the brightest of them, future leaders of elite killing squads, with schoolteachers. Aidid had been educated in Moscow and Rome, and he needed lieutenants who could *think*. The foreign instructors opened the whole big world before their incredulous students, and religious instruction was provided by imams.

"You are the last of your group, Omar. The others have died fighting our enemies. You must assume more of a leadership role. Long after I am dead, you will still be around to carry our movement's legacy forward—my hand beyond the grave. I confide secrets with you, and you perform duties that I would not dare to give anyone else. But you *must* follow my orders to the letter."

"Yes, General Aidid. Whatever you wish."

The general backed away. His prize student was

almost a finished product. "Excellent, my boy. Excellent. Once we are victorious and I become the president of Somalia, I intend to appoint you as an ambassador; you will go to foreign countries and travel widely. We shall practice terrorism without borders, as preached by al Qaeda, and you will carry it worldwide." The older man smiled, remembering his own youthful days wandering the streets of Italy.

"May I make one request, General? Before you make me wear a western suit and tie and polish the asses of diplomats? I still want to kill the Swanson Marine?"

Aidid had been mulling over that very thing and had almost changed his mind. The visceral hatred of a single man was getting in the way of more important tasks. The marines eventually would leave and take Swanson with them, and it would be as if he had never been here at all. But if that particular bit of blood would pacify the Cobra, it was a small price to pay. "Certainly," the general agreed.

Deqo Sharif handed instruments to her husband as Lon calmly operated on another patient, this one a young man with a mangled foot. The patient was stoic, thankful that the physician had magically numbed the limb before starting with his sharp probes. Only a few weeks ago, no such medicine was available. The unfortunate victim would have been lashed to the table to restrain him.

Everybody was starting to believe there was a chance that the tide might be turning. The changes at the Irish Aid Society medical clinic had outpaced many of the others because Kyle Swanson and his sniper teams had unofficially adopted the place. Big Mike Mancuso, Terry Smith, and David Delshay then brought in even more friends to help, for there was precious little else to do in the Mog. The bare-walled compound was cleaned and scrubbed, guys from a construction battalion of Seabees framed new interior walls of plywood, and the exterior was sandbagged. It was painted a gleaming white, inside and out. Visiting navy corpsmen showed up with better medical equipment and hung around to help Dr. Sharif with the patient workload. The battalion surgeon suggested a few more improvements, and better lighting and more potent medicines arrived. Cabinets were refinished to hold clamps, trays, scalpels, and other implements. The Irish place near the K-4 roundabout had been transformed into something resembling an antiseptic infirmary, with Molly Egan running the entire show like a circus ringmaster. Patients who would have died three weeks earlier were being saved. Children were eating.

Sharif determined that the foot was not all that bad, just a series of deep cuts caused by a bad fall onto the rubble, so no broken bones had to be set. He picked out debris, swabbed the wounds liberally with antibacterial lotion—another blessing—and reached for the sharp needle and a length of synthetic polymer fiber, which Deqo had ready. They had done this together so many times that words were unnecessary. The stitches would eventually be absorbed by the body. The doctor wrapped the foot in fresh gauze while she shook a few penicillin pills into a little envelope to fight infection. When the injured man limped away, supported by a friend, Lon pulled his cloth mask beneath his chin, tossed away his rubber gloves, and actually smiled.

Deqo was so proud of him. He had almost worked himself to death to help so many people during the worst of times, back in the famine days when the war raged at its worst and three hundred thousand Somali people were dying. Deqo had not yet mentioned the possibility of leaving Somalia to him. She and Molly and Kyle would make the pitch tonight after a special dinner in their single-room living quarters adjacent to the infirmary.

Hadn't he done enough? Imagine what he could accomplish in a real hospital. This might be the only chance for their grandson, Cawelle, to grow up in peace instead of poverty, someplace where he might have more opportunity. Molly was arranging letters of recommendation from the Irish and United Nations authorities, and Kyle was working on the travel arrangements and U.S. passports. They would gang up on the doctor tonight and try to save Lon from himself. No matter how much her husband might wish to believe differently, Deqo knew that Somalia eventually would kill him, too.

Maryam Ismail was a middle-aged woman whose body was already bent with age, and her dark face was framed with frizzy gray hair. She had lost her husband long ago in the war against Ethiopia in the Ogaden, and, never having been blessed with children, she was on her own. She depended on her Habar Gidir clan for survival, although in Somalia no one received something for nothing.

Omar Jama had discovered the woman had value because foreigners trusted her as a harmless housecleaner. She never stole so much as a cheap ring while dusting and polishing for the infidels, but Maryam listened to gather pieces of information that might be of interest to her clan leaders. At present, she had a job inside the Irish Aid Society. She also was a spy for General Aidid.

"I have something about this man you seek, sir, this United States marine named Kyle Swanson." She spoke softly and with great respect and gave a shy and almost toothless smile when she found Omar Jama at a table in the shade of a sheltered wall in Bakara Market.

"Sit, mother," the Cobra replied politely, pointing her to a mat at his feet. He snapped his fingers, and a stall owner gave her a bowl of warm soup. "Tell me."

"The American is in love with the red-haired whore at the Irish agency, sir. They are together almost every day, and she speaks about him with her coworkers, even in my presence. They never notice me, of course. She is very much in love with him." She had always disapproved of the foreign woman who flaunted herself in front of any man.

Omar straightened his back and bit his lip with anticipation. *Finally, an opportunity.* He nodded for Maryam to continue, weighing a reward that would keep her happy. "Are they always just at that clinic?"

"No, master. They spend many nights at the press hotel."

The Cobra was thinking faster. The Irishwoman with the hair like flame was the key to the Swanson.

Maryam had fallen silent, so Omar handed her some coins and a wrapper filled with khat twigs and leaves. Her face brightened. "They stay in the safe zones, but sometimes wander away from the other marines. He does not want to share this white prostitute with his friends. Will you want me to continue to watch them close, sir?"

"Yes. What else do you know of them?"

Maryam shook her head. Yes. She knew something else that would show her worth. "Perhaps this will be of interest to you, master. They are getting together at the clinic tonight for a private meal with Doctor Sharif and his family. This I know to be true because my cousin, who also works there, was sent to shop in the Bakara for fresh food to cook. We came together."

Had this old woman actually found the answer? He knew of the Sharifs, and hated them for their work, which interfered with his own goals. "Is the clinic heavily guarded?"

"No. They believe things are much safer now, and marines walk by sometimes at night, but no longer stay in shifts at the front gate. There is only one local guard. The Marine Swanson always carries a gun, sir."

The Cobra felt a warm glow in his belly. Here was a chance to catch the Swanson Marine away from the protective security cordons at the airport. As he counted out some more money and more khat, he watched greed grow in the woman's watery eyes. "Mother, a final question. Can you help me enter the clinic tonight during their gathering?"

A cackle erupted from Maryam Ismail as her new treasure mounted. "Oh, yes, sir. I will tell my cousin to expect your visit and to leave a door unlocked."

"She is to tell no one, and you are to tell no one else."

Maryam's shoulders tightened, and she felt a chill. The big man stared down like a snake examining a mouse. She whimpered. "No, sir, of course not."

The Cobra dismissed her and rushed away to report the spy's incredible information. The path to murdering the hated marine was open!

General Aidid listened intently while watching the gleam in the eyes of Omar Jama. A promise was a promise, and it would make Omar content. "Make him suffer," the general said, then flipped away his cigarette and turned to other matters.

THE ATTACK

DOCTOR LON SHARIF called it a day. It had been a long but a good one. A friend had asked him to assist in a late surgery at the Banadir Hospital downtown, and, when that was done, Lon was surprised to find no waiting line of patients when he arrived back at the clinic. The aroma of spicy food welcomed him home, for the women had spent the afternoon preparing an exotic stew. Deqo told him that he even had time for a nap and a bath before evening prayers. The doctor welcomed the respite. There was no doubt that conditions were improving in favor of sanity. It was dark when he awoke, bathed, and wrapped a clean *macawis* sarong in a black and brown pattern around his waist.

Tonight was an occasion that Deqo had planned in mysterious secrecy in some conspiracy with Molly Egan. The only outside guest would be Kyle Swanson. The war would remain far outside for a few hours, and Lon would find the reason.

Kyle was already there, in civilian clothes with a long shirt that concealed the pistol in his rear waistband. He was playing with Lucky, who wore clean blue jeans and a T-shirt with a rock-band emblem. Deqo grunted with effort as she hoisted the heavy cast-iron stewpot onto the table amid the bowls and spoons and cups.

Outside, rain was falling as Omar Jama finished the trek from his downtown lair, immersed in shadows and keeping a keen watch for military patrols. A loaded Glock pistol was in his belt and the razor-edged machete was strapped diagonally across his back.

The mass of the stadium loomed off to the right, bathed in bright lights so that it shined like a wet diamond. It was the safe place in which the boys from America lived. Far to his left was the airport, where more Americans and foreigners were billeted. He padded through the familiar streets to the roundabout without hurry. The city seemed to undulate and breathe around him in the African night. Mud tried to hold his feet. He looked to the left, then the right, and crossed the final road to the Irish clinic.

The compound's stucco walls had been reinforced with stacks of sandbags and tangles of barbed wire, but it was not a military outpost. He slowed, placing each step to avoid ground clutter, and eased up along the outside wall to the wide gap that was a crude gateway through the barricade. The lone guard had taken shelter from the rain and was nowhere to be seen.

He again paused to take his bearings, then crossed into the small courtyard and flattened against an outside wall. There were several doors, and he did not know which led to the living quarters or the clinic's rooms. The western side of the compound contained the medical facilities and the feeding station, which were closed for the night. The quietness disturbed him. Fear was absent here, replaced by the seductive hope of better lives. A thin dog with pale eyes trotted past, gave a sniff, and went along its scavenging way. Then Omar heard a burst of laughter and smelled the scent of food.

A whispered *tssshh* and the cluck of a tongue brought his attention to a woman standing in the darkness. She pointed to a door and then disappeared. From inside that door flowed sounds of happiness.

"Now you all listen to me," the doctor said, looking at them when the meal was done. Swanson had brought along boxes of delicious cream cookies that he swore had fallen from a truck. Sharif nibbled one and relaxed at the low table. "I am an old man, but I am not yet blind. You all have been as thick as conspirators for the last few days, and you set up this feast tonight. I want to know the reason."

Molly looked over at Deqo, who looked at Kyle. His face serious, Kyle reached into a deep pocket of his shirt and pulled out three blue booklets. He placed them side by side like playing cards on the flat surface. The marine felt as if his life was on that table.

"These are legitimate United States passports in the names of Lon, Deqo, and Cawelle Sharif," he said quietly, looking directly at the surgeon. "We want you to take your family to America. The paperwork is all arranged. All that is needed is your permission."

Doctor Sharif was speechless, but Kyle held up a palm. He didn't want Lon to say anything yet. He turned his eyes to Molly. "You are not the only one with a big decision to make tonight, Lon."

He reached into his other pocket and withdrew a small box, changed position, and rose on one knee before Molly. Swanson opened the little box, and a diamond ring glittered in a nest of white silk. "Will you marry me, Irish?"

Molly remained still, and her eyes locked onto him. "Are you serious?"

"Yes, Molly. I am asking you to be my wife. Please?" The warrior had lowered his façade of steel. At that moment, he was just a man who knew he had somehow, against all odds, found the woman of his dreams waiting for him in this hellish country.

Molly had her palms on her cheeks in astonishment, her mouth was in an O, and tears began to leak from her green eyes. Kyle removed the ring from the box and held it out. She had dreamed about such a moment since she was a little girl in Ireland, but had chosen instead to help people in some of the most dangerous places on earth. And it was in just such a place, here in Somalia, that she had found love.

"Yes!" She squealed. "Oh, yesyesyesyes!"

The Sharifs clapped and cheered as Kyle slid the ring onto Molly's finger, and she grabbed him in a big kiss.

Lon was transfixed by the three passports on the table, the unexpected tickets to new lives, and simultaneously was taken aback by the marriage proposal between his friends.

The Cobra wiped his face once he was inside and slid the big knife from its sheath. The heavy handle filled his hand, and he felt the familiar prefight tingle that came when everything was going right. He walked down the narrow passage that remained in a hallway stacked floor to ceiling with boxes of supplies and found the inner doorway to the living spaces, which had been left ajar for him.

He did a quick peek and saw a group sitting around a table. The old man lay on a padded mat about eight feet away. His wife was clapping her hands in delight about something. A little boy bounced like a happy ball.

The white woman was seated cross-legged on the far side, and the Swanson Marine was on one knee, facing her, with his back exposed to attack.

Omar hefted the machete handle up until it was just behind his right ear and the blade pointed back over his shoulder. He screamed a fanfare of triumph for the bloody victory that would be his in only a few moments and rushed inside.

Deqo Sharif screeched in utter horror as the huge intruder swung the long knife down in an overhand cut that razored deeply into the neck of her husband. The blade hit with such force that it almost decapitated him, and a spray of dark arterial blood fountained out wildly. The doctor collapsed full length.

Omar let the swinging blade finish the deadly arc, and his entire arm kept moving until his right bicep pushed against his chin. He ignored the women and the child and stepped past the spewing corpse toward Kyle Swanson, who had only then started his turn around to face the threat.

Lucky had seen the chop come down. Somali children had learned to fight for their lives, even when a loved one lay dying. Doing nothing would be fatal, for the big man would show no mercy. The ninety-pound boy launched himself at the attacker, his arms stretched out as if making an American-style football tackle. He collided hard with the Cobra's left shin and scrabbled for a hold around the ankle. The giant wobbled with the sudden weight that clamped his foot, and then Lucky sank his teeth into the man's meaty calf, trying to bite all the way through, gnawing like a mad dog.

The Cobra snapped the thick wooden handle of the machete down on the boy's head, and clubbed him a second time before the teeth released. Lucky fell off and rolled away from a kick aimed at his ribs. The diversion had cost the Cobra only a few seconds, but he knew those were vital. His forward momentum had been stopped, and he was forced to skip backward to regain his balance.

The Somali woman was still clutching her dying husband. She was not in the fight, and Omar Jama would deal with her, the other woman, and the troublesome little boy later. Swanson was the target, and the American was reaching beneath his shirt, obviously going for a pistol. The Cobra's veins pulsed with blind lust, and he brought the machete back under control, and lunged.

The first indication that Kyle Swanson had that something was terribly wrong was through the reactions of those around him who actually saw Omar Jama burst in. He was still grabbing for the Colt in the holster at the base of his spine when he reached the angle in his turn to see what was happening behind him. He shoved down on his right foot to lever himself into a standing position.

Molly Egan jumped straight through him and knocked him down. She exploded into the danger zone with a terrible primal scream that reached back over the ages to her Gaelic warrior ancestors. She attacked the Cobra with everything she had, her fingers curled like claws and slashing for his eyes.

For the second time, Omar Jama was caught by surprise. The chance to hit the marine was gone, because the berserk Irishwoman had inserted herself between them. The long knife was by his right side, but she had closed too fast for him to bring it up in a full swing. Instead, he thrust the blade straight out and drove the point solidly into Molly Egan's chest, spearing her as she ran into it. Her bright eyes opened wide with pain and shock, but she still pummeled at his nose and scratched at his eyes even as he tried to pull the machete free. The long, wide blade had penetrated vertically into her horizontal rib cage, and its sharpness cut into the bones, which trapped it.

Unable to jerk the blade free, he dropped the girl with the machete still protruding from the chest, and she fell atop the table, mortally wounded. He frantically dug for his pistol to shift back to Swanson.

Kyle came up on all fours, but had lost the grip on the Colt, which skittered away as if trying to hide. For the briefest moment, he wanted to grab the blade and pull it out and make Molly still be alive, but his mind had automatically jerked him into the unseen planes where the pure warrior existed. All he could do right now was to stay alive himself. His emotions froze, the storm went away, and the world slowed down as instinct and training took over.

Once on his feet, he recognized the attacker who was trying to get a pistol up. That gun would make all the difference since Kyle held no weapon of his own, so Swanson smiled and spat at his foe and took a defensive step closer, motioning Omar Jama to come to him. The guy had muscles, but Kyle's body was honed like a precision machine.

"You're the Cobra, right? So come on, you fucking snake. You killed an old man and a helpless girl. Big deal. Time to deal with me now. I'm going to rip your head off." Could he taunt this guy into forgetting about the gun and going hand to hand? Swanson gave a little head feint, and the Cobra twitched, following it.

Despite the setbacks, every advantage was in Omar Jama's favor. Swanson's pistol had disappeared, but why shoot him? He would enjoy beating the marine to a bloody pulp, and it shouldn't take too long. That moment of contemplation slowed his gun hand, and in that instant the little boy was on him again, windmilling with scrawny arms, kicking feet. The teeth now clamped painfully onto an ear.

Swanson kicked the Cobra beneath the exposed right knee on which the big man was resting all of his weight, and the bone broke with a satisfying snap. The Somali fighter tottered and threw a wild punch, which Kyle ducked and countered with a hard pop in the mouth. Teeth splintered, but the pistol was suddenly in the attacker's hand.

Then Swanson moved in close to negate the height and reach disadvantage. He got a hand on the gun and twisted the barrel backward over the trigger finger, as if opening a jar. The pistol slipped free and bounced on the floor.

An ordinary man would have been curled up helpless, but the Cobra's enormous strength kept him going, and he came erect, even on the bad leg. A fist connected on Swanson's forehead and made Kyle see stars. Then the Cobra picked the marine up beneath the arms and flung him against a wall cabinet, which splintered, and the marine fell to the floor amid the debris.

All the Cobra needed to do was keep pushing forward and get the marine's throat in his big hands. Omar Jama knew he was going to win this fight, as surely as the tides rose and fell and night followed day, and he reached out again. First he yanked the boy off his back and threw him cruelly across the room.

Swanson grasped a fallen picture frame and sailed it flat at Omar's face. When the Cobra dodged, Kyle slammed him in the stomach and crunched a knee to the groin, but only managed to hit the inner thigh. It was like fighting a concrete slab. Swanson could not let that monster get on top, so he rolled out of reach and got to his feet. *Don't let him remember the gun.*

Swanson laughed at him, taunted him again. "Are you crying, you tall tub of fat? Get over here and fight me. I am going to kick your ass into next week and nail your balls to General Aidid's door."

Omar Jama scowled and shook his head, trying to clear it. He was having an unusual feeling that he had not experienced since he was a child. Swanson should be dead by now, but was instead dancing just out of reach, crowing and demeaning and dishonoring him once again, still grinning.

"I will kill you!" Omar shouted. One final rush would pin the marine, and Omar would then choke him and break his neck.

Deqo had watched it all unfold like a dreadful stage show. Lon was dead. Molly was badly wounded, and Lucky was sprawled senseless in a corner. Kyle was fighting the madman that was trying to kill them all. Without another thought, she jumped up, grabbed the heavy pot with both hands, and smashed it into the back of the Cobra's skull. The giant wobbled, and Deqo drew back and delivered another strike on the base of the neck, aiming for the spine.

The Cobra was stunned by the first blow and went down with the second. Her third thundered down on the crown of his head and knocked him unconscious. Omar Jama slumped to the floor, redolent with the liquid leftovers of the African crabmeat stew.

Swanson retrieved both pistols, and had one in each hand when he rolled the Cobra onto his back. The man was starting to awaken, despite his beating. Kyle would not let that happen. He began to hit him in the face with the guns—*right, left, right, left*—and each blow ripped a bloody gout in the man's skin. He beat him until he was certain there was nothing left within the Cobra but maybe a tiny spark of life in the back of his bug brain.

Kyle rolled away and crawled over to Molly Egan and brought her up to a sitting position, leaning against him. She was dead, and the machete stuck out like an obscene memorial. Blood had congealed around the blade and soaked her shirt, and more blood smeared her mouth and her nose. He burrowed his face into her hair. He knew that he could never turn this clock back, and tenderly slid his hand down her slender face and closed her eyes. The emotions that he had suppressed before the fight were returning, but he refused to cry and would not pray. If any god allowed a place like Somalia to exist and let Molly be murdered so coldly by a fiend, then what good was he? Swanson softly hummed as he ate his pain. The ring was still on her finger.

Deqo was in the corner, awakening Lucky and checking him for any serious damage. Kyle and Deqo exchanged looks but did not speak. Nothing they could say would change anything.

Other people, drawn by the noise, were rushing in—clinic workers who had been around misery every day—and they immediately set to work, and one covered Lon's body with a sheet. Another ran to get marines from the stadium, and still another bound the hands and feet of the Cobra with lengths of rope. Two women gently peeled Swanson's arms from the body of Molly Egan and removed her to a bed in the surgery, where they would withdraw the machete in private.

Two marines in full battle gear thundered into the room, and others came running to search the area.

"Goddam, Sar'nt Swanson. You okay?" A rough hand shook his shoulder. It was a guy from Suicide Charlie.

Kyle pointed to the Cobra. "Yuh. Call this in, would you? It's going to a political problem. That's the Cobra, General Aidid's personal attack dog."

The marine examined the Somali. "He don't look too good. Did you kill him?"

"I don't know. But you need to get that piece of meat to a secure area right away, before Aidid finds out what happened. He might send more of his goons out."

"Got it." The marine looked around. The room was wrecked, but something was missing. "Hey. Where's Molly?"

"She's dead," Swanson responded in an agonized monotone. He would not crack. From now on, he would be steel. "Molly's dead."

BOOK
TWO

NEW YEAR: 2014

DECEMBER 31, 2013
THE CARIBBEAN

A **GLEAMING WHITE LUXURY** yacht with VAGABOND painted on the stern loafed at anchor in the warm emerald waters near Jamaica. The billionaire businessman Sir Geoffrey Cornwell, who owned the vessel, would go ashore tonight with his stunning wife, Lady Patricia Cornwell, to celebrate the arrival of the new year of 2014 in grand style. Remaining aboard would be their adopted son and sole heir to the Cornwells' holding company, Excalibur Enterprises. He was a slim and solitary man with sharp features and close-cut dishwater-brown hair who was in superb physical condition for someone pushing through his forties. His name was Kyle Swanson, and he was a gunnery sergeant in the United States Marines.

He did not particularly enjoy parties. While others might carry the scents of soap and shampoo, Kyle Swanson preferred the smell of gun oil. This latest New Year's Eve was just another day to him, and he was busy cleaning a new rifle in the ship's armory. Instead of formal wear, he was in a pair of gray cargo shorts, a stained Red Sox T-shirt, and very worn maroon Nike running shoes with no laces.

"You really should come with us tonight," scolded Lady Pat. "The party at the Pegasus is always fun." She was not yet ready and was lounging about in an old blue bathrobe and slippers, with cream on her face and stuff in her hair. She took a drink of single-malt whiskey.

Swanson smiled up at her. "You kiddies go have fun. I'll avoid the loud music and beach orgies and watch the fireworks from here. I plan to shoot this beast a couple of times at midnight to mark the occasion."

"And you will be all alone, as usual. Kyle. I swear you drive me mad."

"Hardly alone, Pat. There are fifteen crew members on this barge. We will eat burgers and drink beer and have a good ole time." He picked at the trigger-housing mechanism with a small brush.

Lady Pat sniffed. "Are you aware what this year is going to be? Two thousand thirteen becomes two thousand fourteen, and that makes me happy. Do you know why?"

Swanson ignored her. He knew why. He bent closer to his work on the latest iteration of the sniper rifle Excalibur, which he and Jeff had invented many years earlier. The original had set a new standard for superior long-range precision shooting that far exceeded all military standards of that time and incorporated state-of-the-art electronics. It was constantly being modified to meet the future. Many companies made sniper rifles; only a few were awarded licenses to hand-craft the Excalibur.

She continued. "Finally, after about twenty-five years, they are going to force you out of the Marine Corps, and don't you pretend that I'm wrong. There will be no more Gunnery Sergeant Swanson. Long overdue."

"Do not count those chickens before they hatch, M'lady. I have been given special exemptions before, and I expect they will give me another one. I will stay in the marines forever."

"Hah! You're going to be out on your arse. Task Force Trident is finished, and you are too old for special operations work. You're a step too slow, and you will be getting no more fruit salad to wear alongside your pretty Congressional Medal of Honor and the two Navy Crosses. This year, you will be all ours, and be the full-time executive vice president of Excalibur Enterprises. I shall find you a nice girl, and the pair of you will produce the wonderful grandchildren that I so richly deserve."

Kyle put the gun down on a clean white cloth that was stretched tight over a long pad. "You sound like a broken record. You throw this at me at least twice a year. Ain't going to happen."

She took another sip of the whiskey and checked the clock on the bulkhead. Plenty of time to finish getting dressed. "I know your problem, Kyle. You're still in love with Coastie, but she went off and married somebody else, so now you just sulk around, pining oh so nobly and silently. Well, she's not coming back." Coastie was Beth Ledford, a Coast Guard sniper who had worked her way into Trident, where she eventually became Kyle's partner. The petite and vivacious little blonde had a savant's ability as a shooter and was as cute as a button and brave as a bull. Last year, she had married Miguel Castillo, a captain in the Mexican marines and an old spec-ops comrade of Kyle's. The two of them were doing the happily-ever-after thing somewhere down in Mexico. He didn't stay in touch.

Swanson blew out a tired breath. One more time. "Coastie and I were never a couple, and there was never any romance, no sex, and not even hand holding on a moonlit lonely night while out on a mission. Why do you refuse to accept that? We were partners and good friends and I trusted her with my life. Anyway, it's none of your business. Also and by the way, the woman is a stone-cold killer."

"Oh, that. I'm a woman. I know all about these things," Pat said, and a little smile tilted the corners of her mouth. "Coastie and I had some conversations. You don't know everything."

"Would you please go away and party with your husband? You look weird with that goop on your face. The helicopter awaits, and the Jamaicans are slobbering with joy, awaiting the arrival of the esteemed Lord and Lady Cornwell and their money. Give me a shot of that booze before you leave."

"Very well. You know I'm right. About everything." She poured the drink and left the room, glad to escape the stink of the gun oil. Still, it never hurt to remind Kyle of his responsibilities.

When the bulkhead hatch closed, Swanson pulled the weapon closer, put on a headset that contained a ring of bright LED lights, and leaned in to touch up the scope mount. What did she know? How many times had she played these cards? True, it had been a bittersweet moment to escort Coastie down the aisle last year and give her away to Mickey; part of him did not want to let go. Ah, well. That was that.

Molly Egan remained anchored in memory as his only true love. Even today, his pulse skipped when he saw a pretty redhead with a short haircut. Why would he ever allow another woman to get so close to him, become that special? It was easy to be an acquaintance, harder to be a friend, almost impossible to be a lover of Kyle Swanson's. Twenty years ago in Mogadishu, his heart had turned into a big block of stone, and it never chipped.

But he had to admit that Pat was right about that other thing—the inexorable march of time. His eyes were still rated as having twenty-twenty vision, which was excellent for a normal man of his age, but not really what he needed as an elite sniper. Other changes were also happening. The long gallops he once did for exercise had become slower runs, not much more than jogs, and he had put on five pounds that exercise and diet had been unable to shed. When visiting Quantico, he admired the effortless workouts of entire platoons of new marines and was glad he did not have to go through that grind anymore.

Swanson had been molded over the past two decades into a one-man weapons system for the marines and his country to use, and in the process he helped create Task Force Trident. The small unit of black operators had carried out missions that were way off the books, some of which had never been acknowledged. Trident reported only to whoever occupied the Oval Office in the White House at the time and had worked out well until a crooked politician had exposed its secret existence and painted Swanson as being the president's private assassin. Trident was shelved, and its members were scattered to the winds.

Swanson landed on his feet. The Pentagon had long ago lent him to Sir Jeff Cornwell to create the futuristic sniper rifle that had spun into a financial empire under Cornwell's hand. Kyle had remained involved because the Pentagon liked having an inside track with Sir Jeff's operations. Now, although still a marine, Kyle also was a senior executive in the privately held corporation. He just rode with it, trained on his own, kept his skill set sharp, and remained an optimist, believing all along that Trident was only resting until the nation needed its special services again. Things would work out just fine. They always did. Trident was too important.

It was nine o'clock. The calendar would change at midnight. *Happy New Year to me.*

JANUARY 1, 2014
MINNEAPOLIS, MINNESOTA
Barlow Hess, huddled on his little yellow tow tractor, asked himself, If there is such a thing as global warming, where the hell is it when I need it? The temperature was minus nine degrees and dropping like a falling anvil in the wind that swept across the Minneapolis–St. Paul International Airport. He didn't want to go back out on the frozen concrete that was iced to the point of looking like a mile of spilled milk. He wore a heavy sweater and a padded jacket over the weatherized coveralls and wool-lined boots, and big mittens protected his hands while a thick hat with flaps was crushed onto his head. Elsewhere in the Minneapolis–St. Paul area, people were going to parties. Not in the little shed at the airport. Hess waited while a private jet taxied to the parking ramp. The snot in his nose was frozen and brittle, and snow and ice had turned his facial hair into a vanilla confection.

Barlow shivered inside his layers of clothing. He might catch a warm blast from the pair of Pratt & Whitney 305 jet engines before they shut down if he approached the Hawker 800XP from behind, right after it parked. His boss would ream him for the safety violation, but it would be worth it. The yellow tug had chains on its tires to minimize slipping on the ice, but there was no cab protection for the driver. In the summer, it was hot. In the winter, it was so miserably cold that baggage handlers stacked meat shipments outside the terminal to keep them frozen.

Hess had checked the flight-arrival schedule and learned that the midsized corporate jet, with a crew of two, had cruised across the country from San Diego tonight. *Why would they do something like that?* It was warm and toasty in California. It was not a trade he would make, but then he was the one sitting on a little tractor on an ice floe that a polar bear would envy. He had never even been to California. What did he know?

The white aircraft coasted to an easy stop with its landing lights still blinking, then sat idle for a moment, as if nobody wanted to be the first out into the bad weather. A black limousine drove up to the side, the side hatch opened, and short steps flexed out and down. Someone got out of the car and held open the rear door. Barlow Hess was already out there on his tractor, waiting for the California fellows to get out of the way so he could move the plane to a hangar.

A large man stepped out first. He had an expensive overcoat and a dark hat pulled low over the forehead, while a thick muffler was wrapped around his neck and most of his face. Barlow caught a glimpse of dark skin around the cheeks and a black patch over the left eye, but that was all. A second man, tall and narrow, followed, and they both ducked into the limo parked at the tip of the left wing. The limo driver closed the door and ran around the car to climb inside, his exhaled breath trailing in little clouds. Within a minute, the vehicle left, and Barlow Hess hustled to get the little bird under cover and out of the bitter weather. It had to be serviced and prepared for another charter tomorrow.

"Welcome to Mogadishu on the Mississippi, sir," the young Somali driver called over his shoulder as he accelerated the stretch limo out of the airport traffic grid and onto Interstate 494. His eyes searched for patches of ice. "And a happy two thousand fourteen!"

From inside his bundle of warm clothing, the large passenger in the rear said, "Turn up the heat! It's freezing in here."

The driver pressed some buttons on the panel, increased the fan speed and temperature, and checked the console lights to be certain the heated seat back there was on maximum. "Is this your first time in Minnesota in the winter, sir?"

"Um." The passenger had never felt such penetrating cold temperatures. It felt like his blood was freezing. Of all the places on earth for the natives from the heat-baked Horn of Africa to resettle, how had tens of thousands washed up here, an arctic sheet where people drilled holes in the ice to fish?

The boy driving laughed. He had no Somali accent. "You'll get used to it, sir. This is an unusually cold night, but the really bad stuff won't hit us until February."

"You like it?" the second passenger asked.

"This is the only place I've ever lived, sir. It is home, so of course I like it. My whole family is here. Where are you gentlemen from?"

"Somalia," the passenger replied.

"Ouch," said the driver. "No wonder you're cold. There are some ninety thousand of us here—the largest Somali community in the U.S."

The big man shifted. It was getting a bit warmer now in the long car, and hot air was blowing on his feet. He asked, "Do you ever think of going back home?"

"Back to Africa? No, sir." The answer was curt and obviously heartfelt. "Parents threaten to send their children back to Somalia if they don't behave. My generation prefers going to Disneyland and Cozumel. Somalia, we can visit through Facebook. Young people there also say good things about Disneyland and Cozumel."

The passengers exchanged a private look. The driver was Americanized beyond hope.

"Are you a Muslim?" asked the thin passenger, pulling off his gloves.

"Of course, sir. Allah be praised."

"Do you defend the faith?"

"Defend it from what, sir? The American Constitution protects our freedom to worship as we choose, and we have plenty of mosques here."

"It was my impression that Americans consider all Muslims to be terrorists."

The boy was relaxed behind the wheel as he steered through the blue-black night. The lights of the city glowed in the cold, and hundreds of automobiles were on the roads. "Most Americans believe that there are fanatics in every religion, sir. We work very hard around here to distance ourselves from extremists. The Christians do the same."

"Hmmm. Good policy." The big man stirred. He did not like what he was hearing. The fervor he expected was not there. He changed the subject.

"Have you been driving limousines for a long time, young man?" he asked. "You don't look old enough."

"I'm twenty," the driver said. "My extended family owns three limos, and we specialize in serving the Somali business community, people like you, sir. I've been around the maintenance shop and driving for years. But I will quit next spring, right after I get my associate's degree in science."

"Then what?"

"I will join the air force, sir."

"You want to be a soldier?" The big man was surprised.

"Hoo-ah, sir. Uncle Sam has already guaranteed to train me in advanced computer technology for a couple of years; then I will come back home, and my family will help me start my own business. My generation is all about computers and the future, sir, and I want to be like Gates and Jobs and Zuckerberg."

The Cobra lowered his chin deeper into the coat. He had no reply to that. This boy was already lost, but no matter. There were already enough soldiers on the ground in Minnesota to carry out the plan. Outside the frosty window, it was very, very cold.

THE DECISION

LIEUTENANT GENERAL BRADLEY Middleton, USMC, left the White House in a four-door sedan with no markings on a clear and brisk day in early January. The recently appointed deputy national security adviser to the president of the United States had been at work since six o'clock, weighing a myriad of global hotspots, but his thoughts were dominated with this upcoming meeting at the Central Intelligence Agency. The final part of a thorny problem had to be resolved.

The three-star general had been the two-star commander of Task Force Trident until it was disestablished and sent into obscurity. Middleton had been as frantic as a teenage girl in a shoe store trying to save it, but there was no chance. Trident had become politically toxic.

The chill Washington wind whistled outside the vehicle as it crossed the Potomac and got into the Mixing Bowl's serpentine highways, following I-95 and branching away on 495. Out here, it did not matter if the shiny vehicle with a driver was carrying a passenger from the White House; every commuter fought for space.

The general mused that he had at least landed good

berths for almost all the former Trident operators. Their impeccable service records guaranteed smooth landings. Middleton himself had emerged unscathed. Instead of being put out to pasture in disgrace, he had been given his third star and a small office in the White House. That was no favor, he thought, because the new job sucked up all of his time, and the unending stress was likely going to make his hair go gray by next week.

The final piece of the Trident puzzle was, as always, the unpredictable Gunnery Sergeant Kyle Swanson. Both of them were marines, and, as such, they never left anyone behind. The bond of the Corps was too strong, and they had known and trusted each other for too many years. From his new office, Middleton knew what was going on all over the world, and he also knew that someday Kyle Swanson would be needed again. The man was too valuable to lose, but the commandant himself had ruled that Swanson must either retire voluntarily or be retired.

The general plugged in the earbuds of his iPad and let Beethoven soothe his busy mind. What to do with the best shooter and operator he had ever seen? The general suddenly gave a deep chuckle that was overheard by the driver, who did not comment. If ever someone did not need rescuing, it was Kyle Swanson.

Sir Jeff and Lady Pat had been trying for the past several years to get him to quit and help run their multibillion-dollar industrial complex, Excalibur Enterprises. The gunny had a boatload of money.

The question on Middleton's plate was how to *keep* the man who had been publicly tagged as a ruthless killer. *Of course he was!* That's what he was supposed to be! Swanson was as smooth as a snake on glass on the battlefield and possessed Sherlock Holmes's investigative streak. He had been a deadly tool that was unleashed only in very special situations, against very special adversaries. *We can't just throw that away.* In the end, the general's decision was easy. All he had to do was convince the sniper to go with it.

The sedan got to the traffic signal in Langley, Virginia; made the turn; and stopped at the security post. Middleton and the driver handed over their ID cards while guards searched the vehicle from its trunk to undercarriage. A few minutes later, Middleton was stalking across the lobby of the CIA, where there was a big seal of the United States embedded on the floor and a wall of stars denoting fallen agents. The stars bore no names.

A young woman in a dark business suit and white blouse introduced herself as Tracy Packard, the administrative assistant of Martin Atkins, the CIA deputy director of clandestine operations. She was slight of build and had deep brown eyes that matched her dark hair, which was pulled back. She smiled. "Deputy Director Atkins is expecting you, General Middleton. Right this way."

"Thank you." They left the public spaces. "Do you know if the third party for the meeting has arrived?"

"Yes, sir. Gunny Swanson got here about ten minutes ago. He and the deputy director are sitting in the office staring at each other and waiting for you. It's kind of spooky." She led Middleton to an elevator, pushed the button, and the door slid open, then hissed closed behind them. "The gunny is somewhat of a legend around here, you know? I'm glad I had an opportunity to meet him."

The general just nodded, but thought, *Therein lies the quandary: There is no such thing as a secret legend.*

Tracy Packard opened the inner door, and the general walked in and threw his overcoat onto a chair and looked at the two seated men. Swanson did not bother to stand in the presence of the three-star, so Middleton got right into the subject. "Jesus Christ, you two. Get over it." He moved to a credenza along a wall and poured hot coffee into a thick mug, welcoming the warmth.

"I don't like this idea, Middleton," said Atkins. Those were the first words he had spoken since Swanson had arrived. "Why should the Marines' problem child be shoved off on us?"

Swanson was casual in jeans and a sweatshirt and winter boots, with a hard tan from the time aboard the *Vagabond* in the Caribbean. He insolently crossed his legs and huffed. "Fuck this. Sir."

Middleton rubbed a hand through his close-cropped hair and drank some of the scalding brew, then plopped down into a cushioned chair. "I feel your pain. I just left the president, who also feels your pain. As of this moment, nobody gives a shit. The decision is final."

"Goddammit, Brad!" Atkins's face was growing red because he was so pissed off. "The CIA is an independent agency. We don't answer to you or anyone else up the military stovepipe."

"And I don't answer to them," Swanson snapped. "I'm a marine."

"Shush," the general said. "Marty, this is the president's decision. It has nothing to do with the Pentagon. You got a problem, go see the Man."

He handed Swanson an envelope that contained two documents. "Gunny, here are the documents that terminate your service with the Corps and transfer you to the CIA. You now belong to Deputy Director Atkins."

"I don't *belong* to anybody." He clipped the usual "sir" at the end of the comment. If he was being kicked out of the marines, screw courtesy.

Middleton drained his cup and clapped it on Atkins's

desk with a firm clunking noise. "This was a tough decision, guys, and a lot of people shaped it. The final call was made in the Oval Office. No matter what you think, it did not just happen, so cut us some slack."

"Clandestine Service already has all the snipers it needs, General," Martin Atkins said with a quieter tone. "Our roster is full."

"Yeah. I taught most of them. I don't want to work here, General. I liked having two hundred thousand marines at my back. If I have to choose between CIA and Excalibur, then I'll take Excalibur."

"Look, Kyle. We have had some differences, but I'm the good guy in this. You cannot just walk out the door. I think when Marty gets used to the idea, he will fit you in to his roster. We have to keep you out of the spotlight but still available when the crap hits the fan, and this may be the only way."

Swanson stood his ground, although his mind wasn't as firm as it had been thirty seconds earlier. Instead of a rejection, he would bargain. "Excalibur is better. Full salary and benefits and a slice of ownership."

"You would be bored within a week out there." Middleton knew the hook was set. "If you want to stay in the game, this is the ticket. You just don't wear the uniform any longer. As for you, Marty, CIA gets an operator with off-the-chart experience and ability. You both know I'm right."

"That's the final word, Brad?" Atkins asked.

"Signed by the president and agreed to by the few people who need to know, Marty. When the moment comes, you will be glad to have this guy as an asset."

The three-star general pulled out a cell phone and tossed it over to Kyle, who caught it in midair with the swipe of his hand. "Make up your mind, Gunny. There's the phone. Call Jeff and Pat and tell them you're coming to work for them . . . or don't. Like it or not, consider this scruffy excuse for a meeting to be your retirement ceremony from the Corps."

Swanson sat still and knew that Middleton was not hustling him. He really had put a lot of thought into this.

The general got to his feet. "Before I left the White House, the Syrians had done something terrible, Vladimir Putin was being Vladimir Putin, and North Korea announced it will send men to the moon, which could mean their crazy prick of a leader might have a booster rocket that can hit America. Closer to home, my dog is sick and my wife is going through menopause. I don't have any more time to give you people. Sorry." He picked up his coat and paused at the door. "Work it out and let me know."

Tracy Packard was waiting outside the door and escorted Middleton back downstairs and out of the building.

"So we have a shotgun marriage, Swanson." Atkins shrugged his shoulders. "Shit rolls downhill, and we are both in the valley."

Kyle needed more coffee. He filled his cup and sat back down. "Marty, we've traded favors over the years. Your field people are good, and I don't want to disrupt them."

"Aww, can the crap, Kyle. I won't send you through basic training."

Swanson laughed. "I will make about a million dollars this year from Excalibur in salary. I really don't need this job, too." He hefted the general's cell phone.

Atkins put one hand flat, palm down across the tips of the fingers of his other hand. *Time out.* "Then how about we try this? The one thing we do best is undercover and clandestine work, right? I mean, that's our *mission*! So let's say you really do go into the private sector, but when we really need your specific help, we can reach out."

"Like an outside consultant?" Swanson thought about it. Maybe he could open an Excalibur office in Washington to stay close to the movers and shakers on this side of the pond. Would Jeff and Pat go along with it? Probably.

Excalibur had always enjoyed a special standing with those who mattered over here in the dark world. Sir Jeff had been a colonel with the Special Air Service before a broken leg forced the transition into private business and had never forgotten his SAS roots.

"I get a CIA cred pack, passport, and ironclad alternate identity, but only a few people know of the arrangement?" Swanson raised his eyebrows.

"Need-to-know basis. I swear. You will have everything before you leave the building today, along with a continuation of your top-secret clearance. Tracy will lead you through the paperwork and run through our drop boxes all over the world if you ever need quick access to a smartphone or new IDs or weapons."

"And when I call here, you answer. Not some middleman."

"I can do that, too. Tracy will set up a special hotline number. We can make this work."

There was a final long pause, and Kyle said, "Deal." He punched a number into the phone in his hand.

A woman answered. "Kyle?"

"You were right. They just kicked me out of the Corps today, Pat. I'm coming home."

Atkins heard the voice shriek with pleasure. When Swanson terminated the brief call, the CIA officer went to the coffeepot himself, then asked, "A fuckin' million a year? Really?"

The tension between them was gone. "Those were the

recession years. Now? Add in the bonuses and stock options that were held in trust while I was in the Corps,
although I used a bit to buy a house in California and
an apartment in Washington."

"You should have quit years ago, you fuckin' moron,
but nobody ever accused marines of being smart."
Atkins extended his hand. "Welcome aboard, Agent
Swanson."

"The Corps has a motto: *Semper Fi*. Do we have one
here in Spookville?"

"Of course," Atkins said. "Blame it on the other guy."

THE STOREFRONT

THE COBRA DID not look in mirrors. The bizarre reflection lurking there reminded him of the night twenty years ago when he had lost the most important fight of his life. His left eye was blinded and was now no more than a milky orb. A deep white scar ran from mouth to jawline, and the badly stitched lip twisted at an awkward angle. Another big scar tracked in front of his right ear, and the hair had never fully regrown over the damaged area of his scalp. The Swanson Marine and the old woman and the kid had beaten the hell out of him, and when the tale of the wild attack followed him onto the operating table, no one in the American emergency medical tent at the Mogadishu airport had been gentle.

They had kept him alive, but barely, and weeks later, under heavy guard, he was thrown into an overcrowded prison hole in Kenya to either rot or heal. There never was a trial.

Every day since he began to recover, he had touched his deformed face; each time he did, his thoughts raced to inflicting revenge on the Swanson Marine. Allah the Most Merciful would not let his loyal follower Omar

Jama become a martyr before that debt was repaid in full. The first weeks and months were a healing hell, but the Cobra overcame his pain and worked toward the day when he would again be free.

Al Qaeda had saved him. The Cobra would never forget that. General Aidid had sent money, but it was al Qaeda that made the difference. It was a relatively new organization that established itself with daring attacks such as a truck bomb that wobbled the giant World Trade Center in New York in 1993, Omar Jama's first year in captivity. He had learned that news when the al Qaeda leader, Osama bin Laden, began sending emissaries into African prisons to recruit men who could help in his war on America. Several of them brought back stories of an exceptional fighter languishing in Kenya. He was known as the Cobra.

Bin Laden was intrigued by the tales. Al Qaeda would need leaders in the future to expand the holy war and keep it going forever. People with money and influence began visiting the special prisoner in Kenya. Doctors tended his body while imams tended his soul, the guards eased up, and his food and living conditions improved.

Omar Jama almost burst with pride on September 11, 2001, when al Qaeda stunned America by hijacking four commercial airliners and crashing into both towers of the World Trade Center in New York and a side of the Pentagon in Washington. With that strike, his patron, bin Laden, changed the world forever. The United States responded to the 9/11 attack by invading Afghanistan, then spun off to invade Iraq.

Eventually, the visitors from al Qaeda deemed him healthy and motivated enough to rejoin the fight. After ten years in Kenya's filthy system, guards were bribed, and the Cobra simply walked away. He arrived in Pakistan in late 2003, a man who had been totally bred for this new kind of war called terrorism, although it was not in the cause he truly wanted. Omar Jama would fight battles all over the Middle East, where he rose to be a leader, an organizer, and a tactician.

In 2005, Osama bin Laden gave Omar Jama a private audience and was pleased with his creation. The Cobra pleaded to go off and fight his own war. Somalia was still aflame, he said, and he would bring it beneath the al Qaeda boot to create a center where Americans would fear to venture. The jihad of bin Laden would conquer an entire nation.

The lean and bearded leader with piercing eyes agreed with the dream, although he stalled: the time was not yet right. The Cobra would be needed in Iraq and Afghanistan for the immediate future. To temper the disappointment, Osama dispatched him on a rest period, during which he would meet the man who had actually supplied the funding during the Cobra's prison years.

Faisal bin Turki bin Naif had proved invaluable in the final development of the Cobra. The extraordinarily rich outcast prince of the House of Saud, which ruled the Kingdom of Saudi Arabia, lived on a Greek island and was delighted when Omar Jama came for their initial visit. The Somali flung broad possibilities for terrorism into the air like strings of firecrackers, idea after idea after idea. It was marvelous entertainment. The renegade Saudi agreed to provide seed money for a new enterprise. A million U.S. dollars up front would tide the Cobra over during his final duties in Iraq and Afghanistan, during which time Faisal would persuade Osama to grant permission to send the man out on his own. Another nine million dollars would be waiting as a line of credit, to be drawn upon so the violent dreams of Omar Jama could become reality.

That changed in 2011, when U.S. SEALs killed bin Laden, and the Cobra decided that all debts to al Qaeda had been paid in full. His attention returned to Somalia, which the United States had left in the hands of the United Nations and other African armies. The U.N. could not handle the job on its own, America was busy elsewhere, and Somalia had dropped into total chaos. The biggest industry was piracy, and a new wave of fighters had emerged to engage the foreign troops. They were overwhelmingly young and vicious and had grown up hearing stories about the famous warrior from the old days, the man called Cobra. But he was not just a historical figure, and when he appeared among them, the youngsters knew their leader had arrived.

He smelled great opportunity. Someone needed to dream big, just as Osama bin Laden had done, and jump over the little wars in the mountains and the sands of the Middle East. The Cobra wanted to leave a historic mark of his own, and nothing would accomplish that goal better than another major strike within the United States. Then he could come back and tame Somalia and spread revolution throughout Africa.

He decided to start his revolution in the unlikely state of Minnesota, a metropolis in the center of the United States. It was not something he did by chance. The largest enclave of Somali refugees in America had located in the twin cities of Minneapolis and St. Paul. His soldiers would be almost invisible there.

Months passed as he laid it out, keeping the details in his head or strictly compartmentalizing them, for the American intelligence services had ears everywhere. As General Aidid had once advised, the Cobra then set out to travel the world and find the right people to help.

He was particularly rigorous in his own intelligence-gathering efforts, for he had a secondary mission that had gnawed at him for many years. When he flew from California to Minnesota, he knew the addresses of the Somali woman from the Irish clinic, of her policeman son, and the places where the Swanson Marine lived. Eventually, he would visit them all, and one by one, he would kill them all.

SUNDAY
MID-JANUARY, 2014
MINNEAPOLIS, MINNESOTA

A lanky Somali man named Hassan Abdi had earned the Cobra's trust in the streets of Mogadishu, when they were both very young militiamen. When Omar was taken prisoner, Hassan's wealthy father stepped in to prevent the same fate from befalling his own son, dispatching Hassan to Europe to be educated. Fate had brought the friends back together once again in Somalia, and although Hassan was the one with a college degree, he fell under the magnetic spell of the rough Omar, the one with the dreams. An agreement was struck to go forward together. Since the Cobra's presence tended to frighten strangers, Hassan would conduct the business conversations. He was the front man.

For a base in Minneapolis, Hassan arranged a one-year rental agreement for office space in a small shopping center, where he established a trading brokerage called Hassan Investments. The name was emblazoned with gold lettering in both English and Arabic on the single wide window, which was darkly tinted. Neat long brown drapes covered the window, and just behind the cloth was a set of vertical blinds that were never opened. That was the front of the building, which one entered through a stubby weatherproof mud room. The office had three cheap plastic chairs and a desk with a computer that was linked to the stock, futures, and commodity markets. Charts flowed across the screen in warm colors.

Behind a separating wall in the rear was an apartment that was a quickie mishmash of Home Depot and Bed Bath & Beyond, a cramped lair that would serve as the Cobra's temporary home and help him remain out of sight. Although it was small, the apartment was much better than the prison cell in Kenya or the mountain camps of Waziristan. Omar Jama would not be staying there long anyway, for it was almost time to launch the operation, and after that there would be plenty of time to warm up and stretch out back in Africa.

For Hassan Abdi to label his front company an investment business was a stretch. Resettled Somalis earned little money. Many still worked in the commercial chicken factories in Marshall and Faribault that had employed the first waves of refugees, while others depended on public welfare and private charities for subsistence. Overall, the resettlement had gone well, and a middle class had emerged. The people who had lost everything already in their lifetimes were not financial risk-takers. Hassan had earned a series 7 broker's license and could talk the arcane language of finance. He was not a pushy salesman, because he did not really care if he sold anything. It was only a cover.

If somebody actually wanted to deal a stock or two, Hassan would make the transaction through an online brokerage in his own account and produce an impressive-looking statement. Like his friend and superior, the Cobra, he was not here to make money as a market trader.

On a Sunday evening, two weeks after they arrived in Minneapolis, a bearded man came to the office, and Hassan ushered him inside, made sure the lock was turned and the curtains were drawn, then took him to the rear.

The Cobra rose to greet the visitor, and, although they had never met, they shared a warm hug and traditional greetings.

"*Allahu Akbar*" (God is the greatest), said Omar Jama.

"*Wa'laikum asalam wa rahmattullah wa barakatuhu*" (Peace and blessings be upon you), replied the visitor.

In the heartland of America, the two terrorists embraced. One was al Qaeda. The other was al Shabaab.

Special Agent Lucky Sharif of the Federal Bureau of Investigation was using four cars to track the dirty little white Chevrolet Malibu driven by Mohammed Ahmed when it left the Islamic Center mosque after *maghrib,* the evening prayers. The four-person FBI team flowed in a diamond formation around the subject vehicle—front, rear, and both sides—and stayed in contact by radio.

Ahmed had been a person of interest to the bureau since the previous year, when Islamic terrorists attacked the Westgate Shopping Mall in Nairobi, Kenya, on September 21, 2013. The bloody assault had lasted several days and left several hundred people dead and wounded. Eventually, three of the attackers were traced back to the Minnesota mosque, and Mohammed Ahmed was the suspected recruiter. With the gigantic Mall USA located in nearby Bloomington, FBI and local police were extremely nervous that the man from the mosque might have similar ambitions for an attack closer to home. They were certain he was al Qaeda.

They knew everything about him, which wasn't much. Ahmed, a resettled Somali, earned a subsistence living as a janitor, wore thrift-store clothes, drove a clunker, was maxed out on a credit card, had less than two hundred dollars to his name, owed money to almost everyone who knew him, and—the only remarkable thing about him—had a long and shaggy gray and white beard. He believed America had failed him, because he could not admit that he had failed himself. The man was steeped in holy words and sacred custom, but too shallow for serious study or organization. The FBI concluded that he was not anyone with real juice but might lead them to a bigger catch.

The trail car slowed when Ahmed arrived at the strip mall, and when he got out, it slid into a parking place at the front of a convenience store on the corner.

"Hard to believe that hairy dude persuaded those boys to go become martyrs," said Special Agent Janna Ecklund from the passenger seat. "I mean, really: 'Come on, boy, we will give you an AK-47 absolutely free if you promise to go get killed.' Keep an eye on the door, and I'll get us a couple of coffees."

"I'll have a Diet Coke instead of coffee," said Sharif. "As a recruiter, he probably framed the pitch better than you, Janna. After all, he did sign them up."

Janna got out of the car. She was six feet tall with a thick mane of white-blonde hair that was covered by a pull-down watch cap. She rolled her shoulders, straightened her down jacket to cover the badge and pistol, then went inside. A coffee urn was on a flat counter in the rear, next to a cabinet of stale and crusty donuts and a rotisserie that was rolling a half-dozen sizzling hot dogs. What was coffee without a donut? She grabbed two of the sugared snacks, pulled a Diet Coke from the cooler for Lucky, fixed the coffee, and paid the young man at the register. He was a good-sized kid with linebacker muscles, pink skin, fair and fine hair, and a zoned-out look on his face due to the tunes chiming in his ears. The head bounced in tempo. An older man sat close by, watching the boy through disapproving eyes. No terrorists in here, thought Janna. Just another immigrant family, old-line Swedes, making a living on the tundra of Minnesota. Her people. Guy looks just like my grandfather. "*Tack så mycket*" (Thanks a lot), Janna said. The old Viking's face lit up.

She balanced his cargo on one palm and walked back to the car. Sharif took the soda can and a donut. "Thanks. I'm trying to keep my blood sugar high."

"So what would have been the right sales pitch for those boys, Lucky? How do you get a kid in America to prance off on a suicide mission?" Ecklund took a good gulp of coffee and looked over to the doorway of Hassan Investments. Nothing but a dim overhead light showed at the entrance.

"You give them something to fight for, not just some undefined injustice to fight against. They already have plenty of martyr volunteers in the refugee camps, so they don't really need to put these out-of-shape kids into the battle at all. They get off on having an American involved. Don't try to apply logic to an illogical situation."

"Too bad they all couldn't turn out like you, Lucky," said Ecklund, chewing a donut and sipping some coffee.

"I had a lot of help. Modern kids here in the States have to survive among urban gangs and dropouts and drug dealers and tweakers and broken dreams and social media. They're really just waiting for someone to tell them what to do. That janitor filled that need."

Janna looked surprised. "Our guy? Mohammed Ahmed? For real?"

Lucky gestured toward the office they were watching. "It's a little late for a janitor with no money to be discussing his portfolio with a financial professional, and on a weekend, yet. Send a text back to the field office, Janna. Let's get all over this new guy on the block, Hassan Investments."

SUNDAY
WASHINGTON, D.C.

General Middleton was wrong. It did not take a full week for Kyle Swanson to become bored with civilian life. A few days were more than enough, and he had an entire lifetime yet to go. Marty Atkins had promised he would not have to endure basic training again, but time had been required to acquaint Kyle with the intricacies of his new employer. It was, after all, the Central Intelligence Agency. Some of it was dull, like the endless briefings. Of more interest were the locations and contents of emergency lockers available to Clandestine Service agents. An operator on the run almost anywhere in the world could access guns, false papers, cash, and safe hideouts if he or she knew where to look. Strongpoints had been established and maintained for almost a half century.

Closing out his marine life had turned out to be just as difficult, for the government demanded completion of paperwork, which would be filed away electronically and in hard copies, too, and never looked at again. The CIA provided private shooting ranges that Kyle used to break the endless paperwork.

"Do you want me to send you some color swatches?" Lady Pat asked during one of her increasingly frequent calls from London. She had hired a designer to prepare the Washington office.

"I don't know from colors. Whatever. Nothing girlie."

"What about the carpet? Any preferences there?"

"No."

"I'll put that down as something basic and utilitarian, with a nice big Persian rug centered before an antique desk. Maybe a Berber, just as we have done in Jeff's office."

"I'm going to hang up before I puke."

"You really must talk to Diana about it. She is just a wonderful interior designer, and she really wants to meet you so she can match up the office to your personality. That reminds me. When you get to London, we shall hand you over to the tailor for some decent suits and shoes." Pat was probably thinking about a basic blue suit in the five-thousand-dollar range. "When *are* you going to get here?"

Kyle was not eager to jump the Atlantic, because he looked at the trip as his unofficial entrance into middle age, and he wasn't ready for that yet. But he did not want to hang around here, either, having already said both his good-byes and hellos. He needed some time. "Pat, I will be over in a few weeks. I have to wrap up a few more things because it is hell to get two government agencies to speak the same language over something as common as a minor personnel matter like me. The marines want to know where to electronically deposit my retirement check, and the agency is giving me the whole series of vaccine shots. It never ends."

She let the conversation fall dead for about fifteen seconds. "I think you're just stalling. You have to leave the marines. You got fired."

"No. I retired, and I'm not looking back. I just need to take a rest, Pat. So before I come over to England, I'm heading up to Minnesota for a few days on the way out. We're working up a surprise party for Deqo Sharif's birthday next Sunday, a week from now. She's turning seventy-five. I talked to Lucky about it last night."

That got Lady Pat centered again. She really enjoyed the company of Deqo, a strong woman who survived the Somali holocaust and raised her grandson alone to become an American FBI agent. "Well. That's good. Let me know the details so Jeff and I can send her some flowers. That should be a fun party. She deserves it."

"Yeah."

"I've almost decided to go with an eggplant drapery treatment, with sheers, of course, for your office. And a subdued hand-painted silk wallpaper. If you don't make a decision, then Diana and I will."

Swanson hung up, wondering how it would be to work in an office the color of an eggplant.

THE COFFEE SHOP

KYLE SWANSON HAD decided to drive to Minnesota, welcoming some time alone on the road behind the wheel of a new car. He let Marty Atkins at the agency know his travel plan, confirmed his encrypted cell-phone number, and then, from his apartment in Georgetown, checked by phone with the couple that rented his custom-built beach house in Malibu, California. She was an artist and he was a retired diplomat, and they reported that things were fine out there. The two real estate investments that Swanson had made when the market was in the crapper had reversed when the economy turned around, and both were now in stratospheric price levels. Sunday night, he packed two travel bags, one black and one olive-green, and was asleep before midnight. He was up at dawn the next day.

Waiting for him in the garage was a light tan 2014 Audi A6 luxury sedan that he had purchased as a birthday present for Deqo Sharif. Understated on the exterior, the sleek car was bathed inside with luxury features that Kyle planned to enjoy during the trip that would take him through Maryland, Pennsylvania, Ohio, Indiana, Illinois, and Wisconsin before he reached Minnesota.

Staying within the speed limit was not in his plans, and a radar-warning device was mounted out of sight, ready to squeak a warning if it detected police radar. He allowed the car's computer to plan the route, and its throaty feminine voice would be his guide.

Swanson had almost convinced himself that making the long drive was the responsible way to break in such a high-performance machine. The car needed an experienced hand at the wheel before it could be handed over to a nice elderly lady. Meanwhile, it was a nice toy for the drive of eleven hundred miles. The engine pounced to life, eager to run. He adjusted seats, mirrors, and temperature controls.

The bland voice said, "Turn left onto L Street Northwest." He would learn that she never said, "Please." He rolled away in the early light and was soon leaving behind the city of monuments.

MONDAY AFTERNOON
MINNEAPOLIS

"I intend to put 'terror' back into the word 'terrorism,'" the Cobra proclaimed to Mohammed Ahmed during their second meeting, which took place in the last row of a darkened motion picture theater. It was a mid-afternoon show that catered to an older crowd, and they had the place almost to themselves. Five other patrons were scattered about, all with gray hair and glasses. Mohammed had been the last customer to enter, and he took a seat halfway down. After ten minutes, when no one else came inside, he retreated to the back row and sat one seat over from the Cobra.

"No American is frightened because some dark-skinned child from the Twin Cities went off to Africa to voluntarily die, for any cause." Omar Jama had a hyp-

notic manner of speech that rode just above the dia-
logue on the screen. Every word seemed to have been
considered in advance and dripped with the honey of
promise.

"I watched the world from inside my prison for ten
years, and then for another ten during my rehabilitation
elsewhere in Africa and the Middle East. It gave me a
unique perspective," he told the al Qaeda man.

Ahmed remained silent, believing the Cobra enjoyed
hearing his own wisdom. He wondered why a Smith &
Wesson pistol was hidden in the large box of popcorn
between them, alongside two magazines of shiny bullets. All of the corn kernels had been poured into a little mound beneath another seat. He felt that he outranked
the Cobra in the local community, for he was the one
who had been recruiting fighters in America.

"It is unfortunate that you are so useless," the Cobra
said, this time with a hiss of menace. "You produced
only a handful of men over such a long period."

"What!" Ahmed cringed at the insult. On the screen,
a romantic scene was in progress.

The Cobra turned the one good eye on him "Al Qaeda is yesterday, my friend. I am with al Shabaab, and
I want more aggressive soldiers. I hope that you can
prove yourself to be more useful." Omar Jama pushed
back in the cramped theater seat, one knee braced on
the seat before him.

Ahmed was glad they had a movie on the big screen
to distract him from that scarred face. "That is not
true. Al Qaeda is stronger than ever! We have evolved
to become a political force that will make lasting
changes."

The Cobra chuckled. "You are old men whose time
has passed and are living on your reputation. Ahmed,

you are more than useless. Where is your financial support? Who are your followers? Who is your new bin Laden? Where are your headlines? In short, where is the terror?"

Ahmed sucked a short breath. "Boston. Our men did the marathon bombing."

"No. That was not al Qaeda. Those two morons were unconnected to any group and just plucked their bomb-making ideas from the Internet. But there was a great lesson there, for their audacity totally shut down a major American city and shook this huge, rich nation. The television audiences were horrified when the police responded with a military-style manhunt that looked like an invasion."

"I work for Allah, praise be unto him, Omar Jama. We must cooperate."

The Cobra shoved the popcorn box and its contents at Ahmed. "Here is the only cooperation I want from you. Prove yourself worthy of my trust. Take this weapon, drive into some small town out in the farmlands tomorrow morning, and find a gathering place. You will shoot everyone in it and create chaos, while praising Islam in the loudest voice. You can martyr yourself with the last bullet, if you choose."

"Kill myself! Why?" The thought of actually being a soldier of the movement had never really occurred to Mohammed Ahmed. Sending others to fight had suited him well.

"It is your duty, old one. For being the one who struck what will be only the first blow of this new revolution, you will be honored by the followers around the world and rewarded in paradise," the Cobra said. "Think of this as a rare opportunity to become someone other than the little man who cleans up the shit of others." The Cobra's voice had grown intense. "By striking the

American middle class in a place they consider safe, you will shatter their confidence. Remember what happened after the 9/11 strikes. You will make America weep."

"And if I refuse? Do not forget that I lead al Qaeda here, not you. I can get someone else for this task."

"You accepted money from me to be a fighter. I will take that gun and shoot you in the head if I think that you will not follow your orders. It is important for you to shoulder this load, my brother. You will give them another day to remember as strongly as they remember 9/11. Stay brave in the battle, and your name will be mentioned alongside that of Osama bin Laden. Our prayers will accompany you."

Ahmed lapsed into silence. Surrendering his leadership to the Cobra was unpleasant, but what difference did the label really make? The new arrival had brutally summed up the failures on the recruiting front and the downward spiral of al Qaeda. Nine-eleven was thirteen years and two wars ago, a very long time. Following the shopping center bloodletting in Nairobi, Mohammed Ahmed was shunned by the younger crowd around the mosque. And the Cobra was right! This grim new offer from al Shabaab would vault him into glorious eternity. He decided. "I will do this thing. Allah be praised!"

"Let blessings flow forever unto you, my brother. Stay here until the end of the film," said Omar Jama, who unfolded from his seat like a giant shadow, gathered his coat, put on a hat, adjusted his scarf, and left. He had purchased tickets for three movies at the multiplex and went out of the one theater and directly into the covering darkness of his second choice. It was a war movie, and he would stay there for several hours before actually leaving.

TUESDAY MORNING

Mohammed Ahmed moved early. He maneuvered on the slick highways and headed east out of the Twin Cities and caught I-94 at the ring road outside of St. Paul. He drove carefully, for the ultimate failure would be for a cop to grab him for some minor traffic violation. It was very cold outside, and the little Chevy's heater was running hard. A bulky blue down jacket kept his torso warm, but his feet were blocks of ice.

Keeping pace, in a loose tail, were the FBI followers, who had no idea where he was going. Ahmed himself didn't really know. Special Agent Janna Ecklund drove a Ford Suburban, while Lucky Sharif worked the radio to coordinate the other three cars, rotating them. One was always ahead of the suspect's grime-encrusted Malibu, which was doggedly pegged at the speed limit. The SUV's big wipers flicked away falling snow.

In less than an hour, the Malibu's rear blinker flashed for a right turn off of exit 41, where the interstate met U.S. 25 at the town of Menomonie, a major intersection for travelers. Motels and services and restaurants dominated the otherwise flat surroundings.

"He's getting off. We will bypass to the next exit and come back. Two takes lead watch," Sharif instructed. "He's been driving almost an hour, so he probably just wants a pee break or some breakfast. Stay sharp anyway, you guys." The black Suburban containing Ecklund and Sharif continued on the interstate, and the surveillance was picked up by the trail car, a battered tan Subaru containing two more agents.

The Chevy curved neatly onto North Broadway. Ahmed was looking for a restaurant. He had not picked out Menomonie in advance, but had no desire to spend extra hours venturing much deeper into the sprawling freezer that was the American Midwest in January. All of the little towns out here were the same to him, and he was to make a random choice anyway. The targets were people. Any people would do.

The .45 pistol was a noticeable weight in his right pocket. Mohammed Ahmed did not have a gun fetish, and he knew only how to load the weapon, turn off the safety, and pull the trigger. Anything else was useless. The wipers slapped the snow away.

GRANDMA'S KITCHEN, read the blue lettering on a white awning. As if by the hand of Allah, there were plenty of parking spaces out front, and Mohammed steered into one of the lanes. He shut down the car and unbuckled. He was not at all nervous, for the prospect of becoming a martyr should not make a fighter sweat. After meeting the Cobra, he had accepted this moment as God's will. He stepped over a thick ribbon of snow piled by the curb and paused beneath the canopy to brush off his coat before pushing open the door.

The FBI watchers coasted to a halt in another space nearby and radioed the location to the other three cars, which closed in to wrap the site in a rectangle of vehicles. The suspect could not possibly leave without being spotted.

A bell tinkled, and the aroma of coffee and pastries assaulted the senses of Mohammed Ahmed. The warmth of the room felt wonderful. He stomped his feet on the mat to kick some feeling back into them. He smiled at the townspeople as his right palm gripped the handle of the .45 while his left hand unsnapped the top of his jacket.

A counter was straight ahead, where two women in gray T-shirts bearing the store logo were busy with orders. A blackboard behind them listed the specials of the morning, and a small swinging gate led into the kitchen. The croissant, egg, and cheese item caught his eye. To his right were a few small tables and a vacant space in which kids could play. A young mother was having coffee while her two-year-old pushed plastic blocks on the rubberized floor.

The entry was the dividing line, and on the left were larger tables, with several people around them. A few glanced his way but immediately discarded his presence. He looked like a guy who needed coffee. The walls were a lemony yellow, decorated with framed art that was for sale, and a rack of coffee urns was at the rear for refills. Next to it was a hallway that led to the bathrooms. *Herd them that way,* he thought.

The teenage girl at the cash register looked up as he reached the counter while unbuttoning his jacket. "Good morning!" she chirped, riding a caffeine high of her own. "Sit anywhere you want. I'll be right with you. Start you with some coffee?"

"I don't drink caffeine. I am Muslim." He withdrew the pistol and lifted it over a tray of muffins and donuts covered with plastic, and he fired the first shot into her chest. The force of the blast threw her backward, her arms spread wide, through the swinging entrance to the kitchen. Mohammed Ahmed shouted: *"Allahu Akbar!!"*

Everyone in the boxy restaurant froze at the dreaded war call used by Islamic maniacs. He shifted his aim and expended four bullets on the mother and her playing child. That cleared his right, and he was turning back when he saw the second gray-shirted server woman try to duck beneath the counter. She was covering her head with both hands. He leaned over and shot her twice in the back.

The customers in the seating room were in motion, and a man in bulky overalls dropped his newspaper and got to his feet. The terrorist hit him twice, and the farmer went down hard. Then he pulled the trigger again and again among the screams, quickly reloaded, and resumed firing at the pond of people that had nowhere to go. A young man in a deep green fleece shirt and jeans picked up a chair to throw, and bullets cut through the light wood to kill the man behind it. An older couple at a laminate-topped table seemed resigned to their fate and were wrapped in a hug with their eyes crushed shut when he got around to shooting them. Gun smoke was filling the area, and his shots were deafening. A young woman in jeans and a flannel shirt, with dark hair that flowed to her shoulders, screamed curses at him and hurled a small rack of grape jelly containers. Two torso shots dropped her.

Was that all of them? He had not counted. He moved around the counter and stepped over the body into the kitchen. A back door was open, indicating that someone had fled, which meant the cops would be on the way. He pulled the door closed and locked it, then stalked to the bathrooms, found a middle-aged woman cowering in the single stall, and killed her, too. Head shot. There was no one else for the executioner to kill. He dropped the magazine and counted his remaining bullets. Only four left. He would spend them wisely.

The FBI agents had not heard the first gunshots because their windows were up, the heater was on, and the traffic noise from the interstate droned in the background. Then the cook came screaming around the corner in a grease-stained apron. The agent driving the Subaru jumped out while his partner yelled for help into his microphone, dropped it, and also broke into a run, two steps behind his partner.

"He's killing everybody inside!" the woman screamed.

"Gun! Gun!" one of the agents called over the radio, even as his partner made a dash for the front door.

Mohammed had anticipated an immediate response

and was behind the counter with his pistol steady and pointing outside. When the shape of a man approached, he pulled the trigger, and the entire plate-glass window shattered in a loud crash of glass as the bullet went through and hit the target. A second bullet knocked the man over. Another figure skidded to a stop and dove for cover.

Ahmed could take a deep breath now, for he knew the police would now become careful, since he had put one down. He wiped the menu blackboard on the wall clean with a swipe of his sleeve, and wrote in pink chalk, "God is great." He used Arabic lettering. Then he roughly hauled the wounded woman server from behind the counter and wrestled her flat onto the top. She was bleeding profusely from her back wounds, and probably didn't have long to live. That made her a compliant and excellent shield.

Finally, he poured himself a cup of hot water and a took bag of tea from a box, picked up a blueberry muffin, and sat behind the counter to await the end. There were a few cries and moans in the big room, so apparently he had not killed them all. He ignored them. When he heard the first sirens, he was not frightened.

THE SHOT

TUESDAY MORNING

SWANSON WAS RIDING on fumes. He had driven all night but wanted to get all the way into Minneapolis without stopping at a motel. East of Eau Claire, Wisconsin, the Audi had other ideas. The calm, slightly agitated voice of the automatic navigator said, "We need fuel," and a warning light snapped to life on the dash panel. "We"—as if there was some relationship between man and machine. It was like a verbal spanking from mission control and actually meant, "You should have filled up one hundred and fifty miles back, you dumbass."

He refused to ask the GPS lady to name the closest gas station. A green mile marker was coming up, and exit 41 was just ahead, a junction with U.S. 25, which meant there would be plenty of service areas in a little town with the peculiar name of Menomonie. He tried to pronounce it several ways, but nothing sounded right.

Kyle put on his blinker and checked the rearview mirror just as a big Ford Taurus from the Wisconsin Highway Patrol came tearing through the traffic behind him with its flashers blazing and the siren on full blast. Kyle punched the accelerator and twisted the wheel to the left to get out of the way of the oncoming cop car that had cut into the breakdown lane. He tapped the brakes slightly, and the patrol car skidded to a stop across the exit ramp, spraying rocks and gravel and rocking on its heavy-duty springs. The ramp was closed.

Swanson had a high enough angle to see why the trooper was in such a rush. Stretched out below was a carpet of blinking blue and red art, a convergence of police, ambulance, and fire department vehicles with their lights slashing crazily across the buildings in the area. There was obviously big trouble down there, and he had a badge in the pocket of his leather jacket and a pistol on his hip, and felt the familiar obligation to pitch in and help. Then he remembered his badge was that of a CIA operative, and that Marty Atkins had warned him to stay out of civilian law enforcement problems. He was not a cop.

He gave the scene a final glance and drove on. The fuel light was still on, and he punched a button that would let him actually talk to the onboard computer person. She would direct him to a gas station where all hell wasn't breaking loose. Then take him to the hotel.

TUESDAY MORNING

Special Agent Lucky Sharif of the Federal Bureau of Investigation had a situation. The terrorism suspect his team had been following had blown through the surveillance net and wreaked havoc inside a roadside café in Wisconsin, and an FBI agent was down from a gunshot wound in front of the place. He did not know if it was a hostage situation because he did not know if anyone other than the shooter was still alive in there. The icy cold stabbed at his exposed skin like needles as he stood in a doorway a block from the scene, working a radio in his gloved hand, deep in thought. His maroon SUV provided cover from the gunman. For the moment, he was a one-man command center.

Sharif did not waste time blaming himself for a tragedy that he could not have prevented. Bad guys never play by the rules, and shit happens. There were things that needed to be done, and the veteran special agent had been trained for just this kind of emergency. Like a test pilot in an out-of-control airplane, he would not let panic take hold. Step by step was the only way to go.

He studied the storefront with a practiced eye. The glass had been blown out of the main window, but jagged points still hung from the top sill. The door just beside it was intact. First responders were still rolling in, and a dozen cops from various agencies were pointing their weapons into the empty space. EMTs had dragged his agent, Burt Loving, away without receiving any more fire and were on their knees working on him.

"Gut shot," reported Janna Ecklund, who had checked the condition. "Not good."

"Hmm." Lucky acknowledged his partner's comment. Must be twenty cops out around. They could lay down some covering fire to keep the terrorist busy, toss in some flash bangs, then enter. One possibility.

A city patrol car edged to a stop, and a stout middle-aged man with more stars on his collar than Eisenhower climbed out. He asked one of his patrol officers where the Fed was who was directing this fuckup. The man pointed to the SUV. Adolf Dixon had been the police chief of Menomonie for three years and knew everybody in town. Murder, even mass murder, was a local matter. He hoped the Feds would not be giving him a lot of trouble about jurisdiction.

He ambled to the doorway, not very impressed by the two special agents standing there talking. One was a tall woman with snowy white hair that fell back over the collar of her heavy jacket, and the other was a black man who was even taller than the woman.

"Who the hell are you?" the chief asked in a sharp voice.

Lucky replied calmly, "This is FBI Special Agent Janna Ecklund, and I'm Lucky Sharif. We are out of the Minneapolis field office." They all nodded, but did not shake hands.

"Chief Adolf Dixon." The cop's forehead wrinkled. "Seems that we have had multiple murders here in my little town, and the bureau shows up before me? Were you all having breakfast together around here?"

Lucky played nice. "It's a national security matter, sir, so I'm in charge right now."

"Maybe not, son. At least not until I know why a bunch of FBIs from Minnesota are over here in Wisconsin at the scene of a crime that just happened."

Sharif dropped the hammer. "We've been following the guy for a few weeks, and we trailed him here this morning. He's al Qaeda."

It landed like a punch, and Dixon coughed. "No shit?"

"No shit."

Dixon looked up at the man. There wasn't any strain showing on the dark face. "Well, that changes things, I guess. Federal matter, huh?"

"Look, Chief Dixon. We all have to stay on the same page here. We all want to get inside and tend to those victims. Hell, we don't even know how many there are. You know everybody in town, so it would be a big help if you organized a command and communications center and keep things under control and quiet. We especially don't want the media on this yet."

"All my people will cooperate, Agent Sharif. The

Dunn County sheriff is sending over his SWAT. What's your play?"

"I'm working on it, sir." He did not share with Dixon that an FBI Hostage Rescue Team had already been scrambled. The HRT would trump the county SWAT. All of that would take time, and Lucky knew he was burning minutes when he needed something fast. He had seen it happen repeatedly: if a reaction didn't happen with speed, the cops would back off and gather their officers, suit up in armored vests, drive up their big armored vehicles, and launch the helicopters. Wait long enough, and lawyers and the press would be involved. With the Hoover Building in Washington now on alert, the bureaucracy would slow things down. Sharif was in charge at the scene and wanted to avoid all of that.

"We're burning minutes," he groused.

Police Chief Dixon had staked out an insurance company's office as a command center, then went to an ambulance to talk to Gertrude Prince, the cook who had witnessed the slaughter. He had known Gert for a long time, and she settled down when he appeared, more comfortable with him than with Special Agent Tim Walz, the FBI man who had been questioning her. She was fixing an omelet with a side of bacon when she heard the first shot, and the new server, Caroline, had come hurtling backward through the doorway and landed with wide, dead eyes and a hole in her chest from which blood bubbled like a fountain. Gert had remained rooted in position with a spatula in her hand and eggs sizzling on the griddle until she heard more shots. Then she bolted out the back.

The FBI man asked if the attacker had been wearing a vest of explosives, but the cook didn't know; she never saw him. The ambulance took her away.

"Say, Special Agent Walz. I got to ask." He nodded toward Lucky and Janna. "Are they up to this? Seem kind of young."

"Chief, they are among the best we have. The woman is highly qualified, and the guy, well, Cawelle Sharif is even more qualified. I can't reveal too much, but he came out of Somalia, soaked up education, got a full scholarship to play basketball for the U of Minnesota, got a law degree, and was snapped up by the FBI. He even served with Hostage Rescue for a few years, did undercover work down in South America, then shifted out here to be a bridge into the Somali refugee community. Lucky Sharif knows what he's doing, Chief. Our job is to stay out of his way."

Lucky was tired of standing around with freezing toes. "I got an idea," he told Janna, and opened the back of the Suburban, then lifted the lid on the emergency equipment box that contained everything an agent might want, from road flares to stun grenades. An AR-15A3 tactical carbine rested snug in its holder, as familiar to Sharif as an old friend. A Colt 4×20 scope was already in place above the sixteen-inch heavy barrel.

"You're going to try to shoot him?" Janna Ecklund's jaw dropped.

"No."

"No! Lucky, wait for our Hostage Rescue guys, understand me? You do not have permission to fire. The Hoover Building will go nuts."

"Is this thing zeroed?" he asked.

"As far as I know, nobody has ever even touched it."

"Okay, then. Factory zero." The rifle wasn't top-of-the-line, but it was more than enough for the job at hand. Sharif would be aiming at a target about a hundred yards distant, so to compensate for the slight drop, the zero would be about one inch up. He checked the load, a magazine of 5.56 NATO rounds, and inserted it, then put one in the chamber. A bullet would spit from the rifle at a muzzle velocity of 3,200 feet per second.

He climbed into the rear seat. "Lower the rear window, Janna? I want to look inside of that restaurant."

"You have no authority to shoot, Lucky. Think about what you're doing."

"Okay. I'll just take a peek. Maybe I can see if he's wearing an exploding vest."

The tinted window hummed down, and Lucky brought the rifle to his cheek and looked through the sharp scope, directly through the destroyed window and into the breakfast place. The carnage swam into dreadful focus. Sprawled atop the counter was the motionless body of a woman in a gray T-shirt that was soaked with blood. The gunman was down behind her, using the body as a macabre sandbag.

He said softly, "I see one body on a long front counter, and in front of it looks like a mother and a child on the floor. Motionless." Dark blood pooled around the downed victims. Details flooded into his mind: the coloring of the walls, debris randomly scattered, and even the menu board, which now proclaimed the chalked message about the greatness of God in familiar Arabic lettering. Pages of a newspaper fluttered in the breeze coming through the window. It was not strong enough to turn the page, so wind was not a factor at this range. "I don't see anyone moving."

Janna climbed into the driver's seat and was watching through the passenger-side window using binoculars. "More victims are in the room to the left, but we don't know how many. Little Ahmed did some damage here today."

While Sharif watched, he saw the top of a head

suddenly rise from behind the counter as the assassin took a quick look out, then ducked back down. Lucky remembered the instructions that Kyle Swanson had given him after Lucky had joined the FBI and was training to be a sniper, and the waiting game began. Normal human behavior made it likely that when the shooter looked up again to see what was happening outside, he would lift up in that exact same spot. Lucky wasn't in Kyle's league as a sniper, but he was good enough. Plus, he had learned more about precise long-range shooting during long talks with Swanson than he had ever picked up while just pumping rounds down a range. Kyle was the reason that Lucky had wanted to be a sniper in the first place.

"Janna," he whispered. "Take a flash bang and pop it in the street. Let's draw his attention." All he needed was a distraction to tickle the curiosity of that cat inside.

Janna hissed, *"YOU DO NOT SHOOT!"*

"Of course not."

Janna Ecklund knew he was lying but fished a flash-bang canister from the equipment box anyway. "HRT and SWAT will be here in fifteen," she warned. "Wait for them, Lucky."

"Do it."

She got out and took two steps forward. Then she called in a loud voice, "Mohammed Ahmed. This is Special Agent Janna Ecklund of the FBI. I want to talk to you. Just talk."

Nothing at first, then a muted voice shouted, "God is great!"

Janna pulled the pin on an M84 stun grenade, flipped away the lever, and underhanded it into the empty street. It bounced and rolled, then exploded with a blinding flash and an enormous roar that jarred everyone who had watched it go off.

Mohammed Ahmed gripped his pistol, then rose slowly until he could just see over the body along the counter. A woman was standing outside, and Mohammed steadied his pistol.

Lucky watched the tableau unfold in slow motion, and the 4×20 scope transformed the actual hundred-yard distance to about twenty-five yards. He had not twitched since coiling into position, and his breathing was slow and steady, with a pulse rate that was only a slow throb that would not jar his aim. The rifle was rock steady, and his world had shrunk to the point of the crosshairs. He eased the slack out of the trigger. The gunman's forehead came into view, then the eyes and nose rose in exactly the same place they had been earlier. Sharif squeezed the trigger, the rifle fired, and the high-velocity bullet smashed into the nose of the terrorist, plowed through his brain stem and spinal cord, and took off the back of the skull. A bright spray of crimson blood painted the yellow wall behind the counter as the medulla oblongata shot blew through.

DEQO

TUESDAY MORNING
MINNEAPOLIS

THE VOICE GUIDED Kyle Swanson to a gas station ten miles away, where he filled the tank, walked around, did some stretches, used the toilet, bought a soda and a bottle of water and a bar of quick-energy chocolate, then drove out again, wondering if the better choice would have been to make this a two-day drive. But the Audi was running perfectly, the computer lady seemed satisfied, and a soft bed was waiting up ahead. He turned on the radio as he scuttled on into Minneapolis on I-94. To stay awake, he skipped around the dial to find a top-of-the-hour newscast. There was a brief report about a multiple shooting in the small Wisconsin town of Menomonie, and Swanson recognized the name of the place back down the road where the cop had cut him off and blocked the exit.

An updated report came ten minutes later, authorities confirming only that there had been several people killed when a gunman opened fire in a coffee shop. The alleged shooter was among the dead. The investigation was continuing. Considering the scant information, Kyle thought that it was probably a domestic quarrel that got out of control and the shooter downed his loved ones and some other people, then committed suicide. It happened all the time.

The voice on the GPS finally guided him off of the interstate and into the web of unfamiliar streets of Minneapolis, taking him right to the door of the Graves 601 Hotel. He handed off the Audi to the valet, along with a fifty-dollar bill and instructions to have the car professionally cleaned and detailed and parked in a covered space. It was to be a gift. He could use taxis in the meantime, or he would walk. Minneapolis had about eleven miles of indoor sidewalks. The Skyway that arched over North First Avenue connected his hotel to the massive Target Center. Or, going the other way, he could cross Hennepin to reach the sprawling Nicollet Mall and major shopping. A blizzard could be watched in comfort.

He had the entire day free before Lucky and Janna were to pick him up, so he clicked on an electric blanket to warm the bed while he took a shower. With the light off, and the heavy curtains drawn to darken the room and maintain its warmth, the hotel noises and sounds from the street were muffled. His cell phone on the table beside the digital clock was silent. Everything was quiet, and as tired as he was, Kyle should have fallen to sleep without problem. Instead, he tossed and turned, wrestling with the uncomfortable feeling that something important was missing. He cocked an eye at both of the timepieces on the table. Hours yet. *Go to sleep!* He rolled onto his left side, punched up the pillow, and finally drifted off.

TUESDAY, MIDDAY
MENOMONIE, WISCONSIN
For half an hour, Chief Dixon, Janna Ecklund, and Lucky stood in a tight group in front of the restaurant, not wanting to track into the crime scene or interfere

with the emergency medical teams. The corpses of men, women, and children lay in the undignified angles of death. An older man was on his back, still clutching a newspaper, as if he had been hiding behind it when two bullets ripped through the newsprint and ended his life. The little boy in the front had managed to crawl closer to his mother after being hit and died at her hip. They had all been ordinary people carrying out a morning routine in a tiny Midwestern town, just starting another day, when off the street had come a man with a dark heart and a gun.

"My God," whispered Janna when she first saw them. A sour taste rose in her throat, and she fought to keep from throwing up.

Lucky was still holding the rifle, less one bullet. He exhaled a balloon of frosty breath, frustrated that he had not taken the fatal shot sooner. Maybe he could have prevented some of this. They could not see the man he had killed, for the target had crumpled back behind the counter when his head exploded.

"That was a nice shot," Dixon said, as if reading the troubled mind of Sharif. "Are you going to be in hot water about not having permission?"

"The guy was a terrorist who had killed people in that restaurant, had downed one of our own, and was pointing a loaded weapon at my partner. That was all the permission I needed. Are you saying that you wouldn't have taken that shot?"

"Not saying that at all, son. Glad you did it, but that's not the point. If someone tries to stomp on you, I'll back you all the way. Everybody here will, although that damn grenade scared the shit out of us."

Janna agreed. Her hands were stuffed deep in her jacket pockets. "Some weenies in the media are going to say that if you had been more patient, we might have taken him alive and gotten him to talk. That he could have given us valuable information."

"No. That guy came here to die, not talk," said Lucky. "What's the butcher's bill going to be in there, Chief? I've got to check in with my boss."

"I'd say eight confirmed dead, and two more about to be. The EMTs don't think they will make it to the hospital. Plus the killer. You know for sure that he was from al Qaeda?"

"Yes," Janna Ecklund said. "He was a low-level recruiter who worked as a janitor at a mosque in Minneapolis. Our surveillance was only to discover his contacts. We never thought he would turn violent himself."

Lucky held up a palm while he answered a new call on his radio. Washington wanted answers, and he drifted back to the SUV for privacy and began his report. Janna joined him, started the engine and the heater, and silently listened while he talked. Sharif suddenly told her to get Chief Dixon, and she fetched him from the crime scene. The veteran officer looked sad.

Lucky hung up his phone and lowered the window to talk. "We're all going to clear out now, Chief, so we are turning it back over to you. Janna and I have to get back and write official reports."

"Okay. Got to do the paperwork. I understand. I'm going over to the command center and issue a statement. The media circus is in town."

"Do NOT use the word 'terrorism' yet. Just paint the big picture: a lunatic with a gun, it's still early, and your investigation is continuing. No mention of al Qaeda, or even the FBI, if you can get away with it. Get them to pay attention to the local angle—names of victims, hospital, that sort of thing. It will fill their notebooks for a while."

"That charade won't last very long, son. Al Qaeda attacking a small American town is a big story. Too many people already know about it."

"Just stall for some time. If the early reports are about common workplace violence, the public won't panic. This incident is over, and there is no credible threat elsewhere, but the investigation is ongoing. Be honest, but the media is not entitled to everything the police know."

"I got it. Nice meeting you two. Now get out of here." He hesitated, then asked, "You think it is really over?"

Lucky shook his head reluctantly. "I don't know, Chief. Let's hope so."

TUESDAY AFTERNOON
MINNEAPOLIS
Deqo Sharif lived alone in a small, neat house on Lake Street in the Cedar-Riverside neighborhood of Minneapolis. She was going to be seventy-five years old in a few days, and looked forward to starting the final quarter of her life. Deqo planned to live to see one hundred, and no one was betting against her. If anyone could reach that impossible number, it was Deqo.

She had left Somalia with not much more than the clothes on her back and her young grandson, with their emergency departure arranged by the U.S. State Department and the Central Intelligence Agency. They were placed beneath the protective umbrella of Lutheran Social Service of Minnesota, where her fluent English and nursing skill led to immediate employment with volunteer organizations. Somali newcomers were arriving by the hundreds with heart-wrenching stories of survival.

She and Lucky started off in a single room, each afraid to let the other one out of sight. Deqo slept in a narrow bed while Lucky slept on a tattered sofa in the same room. They were haunted by nightmares, but they were safe.

The man who had made it happen, Kyle Swanson, had remained with the marines in Mogadishu for several months after the Sharifs emigrated, but he never broke contact. He sent at least one letter a week, uplifting notes about what the future might hold. He never mentioned their beloved Molly Egan or the awful attack by the Cobra. Deqo could almost feel the sadness between the lines.

Then Kyle began coming to visit when he was on leave and spent hours with Lucky. The pair of them would take in movies, play ball, talk about tomorrows, and do Lucky's homework together. As time passed, her teenage grandson grew to worship the marine sniper and wanted to be just like him. Swanson taught him how to shoot and hunt, but he and Deqo agreed that Lucky had already paid his war dues: he should reach for a different star.

Deqo's hair turned silver, and her face today held channels of wrinkles that mapped her seven decades. Some of the back teeth ached, and her bones were giving way, her spine was bending, and she often used a cane for support when she had to walk outside in bitter weather. She accepted that she was simply getting old, but her biggest worry these days was how to properly program her cellular telephone.

She had decided not to move to Florida or Arizona or any of those sunny places. Minnesota was cold for a few months, and the lower the temperature, the sharper the wind and the nastier the pain, but it was home. All of her friends were here, and she could always get a dog or a cat for company.

Deqo had continued to work at the resettlement

center, where it was believed that she knew every Somali in the Twin Cities area. Children who had been terrified little boys and girls when they arrived as refugees had become strong and vibrant teenagers or young adults. At one time or another, all of them seemed to have visited Deqo's home, for she was everybody's surrogate grandmother, and her life had been filled with birthdays, graduations, weddings, school plays, holiday celebrations, and football and basketball games.

And Cawelle—Lucky—had prospered with skills of which even he was unaware. In class, teachers pushed him with more difficult assignments. Outside on the fields, a natural athletic ability astonished the coaches.

By high school, Lucky was the lanky pass-catching wide receiver on the football team and a hotshot point guard in basketball. Scholarship offers came from several big-name universities, but Lucky turned them down, refusing to leave his grandmother, and went all the way through law school at the University of Minnesota. It was almost within walking distance from home. After a year clerking for a federal judge, he joined the FBI, which needed all of the insight into the Muslim world it could get. Deqo was so proud.

She puttered around the house, doing some final cleaning and food preparation. The weather people on television were saying something called a "polar vortex" had gripped the area, but she dismissed the ranting. Minnesota just being Minnesota in the wintertime.

Kyle and Lucky and sweet Janna would be coming for dinner in a little while, and she had to be ready.

THE VISIT

SWANSON WAS WAITING in the hotel bar, watching the television news reports from Menomonie, when Lucky Sharif and Janna Ecklund came in, both still in the hard special agent mode. He got up, hugged Lucky, and got a cheek peck from Janna, whom he had met on several previous visits. From the first look, he realized that his friends had been over there. "You are in need of alcoholic beverages," he said, and called for the bartender to bring glasses, ice, and a bottle of Jack Daniel's bourbon.

They sat silently in the curved banquette, watching the TV, which had gone into high gear and already had talking heads analyzing the event, until the server brought the bourbon and left them alone. There were few other people in the bar, and the booth was in the back, so the conversation could not be overheard. While they waited, Kyle noticed the body language when Janna leaned for a moment against Lucky, and Sharif's tight face relaxed at bit. Kyle thought: *Oh, Jesus. You finally gave in and really have something going with her, don't you? Balancing Deqo and Ecklund and the FBI all at the same time. Is that hard? You poor bastard.*

"So, tell me about it. Are you both okay? Was this dude really al Qaeda?"

"It was pretty grim," said Lucky. "Except for a cook that escaped, the gunman wiped out the entire shop. We had him under surveillance, and he slipped through the net. And, yeah, he's al Qaeda without a doubt."

Swanson raised his glass. "Then here's to good riddance of some bad rubbish. Was he a lone wolf, or was he carrying out an assignment?"

Janna spoke while Lucky took a drink. "One of the many things we don't know yet." She glanced up at the TV. "The media is going to run hard on the al Qaeda angle, so the blame game will start soon."

Swanson looked at her tense face as she glanced over at Lucky. "Blaming exactly who?"

"Him. Lucky took the mutt down." Her ice-blue eyes did not blink. "A hundred-yard shot, right through the face."

Kyle had a quick memory of shooting with Lucky when he was a kid. The boy had the gift, as he had proved with the HRT. "Good. Then you did well, young Skywalker."

"I hope the guys in the Hoover Building think so." He poured another stiff drink and added some new ice.

"Let it go, Lucky. Nobody knows what a crazy man is going to do."

"Damn." Sharif slapped a big fist on the table, making it jump. Janna put her hand on his forearm. "We were all over him, and it still happened. Janna wanted to bring him in for questioning a few days ago."

"But you were right then, too. There was no probable cause, and a lawyer would have sprung him, you would be roasted for religious profiling, and this shit probably still would have happened." She tightened her grip.

"Drop it!" Kyle knew the symptoms. "You did what you had to do, Lucky, and now you have to walk away. Deal with it on your own time. I came up here for some fun, and you seem kind of tightly wound."

Lucky looked at him, surprised at the stern tone, and slowly broke into a smile. He couldn't expect Kyle Swanson to feel sorry for him. Killing an enemy was second nature to the man he admired so much.

"Yeah. Well." He felt the smooth ride of the whiskey kick in, and an attitude adjustment took hold as he downed the second drink. "Grandma's waiting. Let's go and eat and not talk about trouble. There's a basketball game on TV, and that woman loves her Timberwolves."

Kyle agreed. "If they're playing at home, I can get us all tickets for tomorrow night."

"Sweet offer, man, but I don't like her being out at night in this weather. Anyway, Janna and I will probably be busy. You know how it is."

The dinner and reunion with Deqo had provided a great few hours of distraction, and she was unaware of the Wisconsin murders. They let it stay that way. The woman was possessed with an incredible energy that encompassed everyone around her, and her good mood was infectious. Pictures in scrapbooks of Somalis that she had helped find new roots in America were on every available surface, and small boxes were mounded with notes, letters, and little gifts they had sent to mark her seventy-fifth birthday and retirement from the resettlement center. Several newspaper articles mentioned her. The four of them watched the Timberwolves beat the Jazz on television, and Deqo was a merciless critic of the referees.

What a life she had lived, Kyle thought, and hers had been time well spent. The coming celebration would be a special milestone for her. Despite the trials and tribulations, she had made it. Here it was 2014, they were all twenty years from Somalia, and she was still going strong.

He was back in the hotel by ten o'clock, a little bit jealous of Lucky, who would be bunking tonight with the beautiful Janna Ecklund. In the middle of the night, in the middle of Minnesota, in the middle of a snow-storm, Kyle Swanson had nobody.

TUESDAY NIGHT

The Cobra waited until the ten P.M. news was over, then swept through the cable channels before making his next move. He was stretched out back in a comfortable re-cliner in his tiny apartment with a blanket over his feet. The media and the law enforcement officials had fenced for hours about what happened in Wisconsin. The cops were trying to portray the slaughter as being the work of a mentally disturbed individual who had left no note, and the investigation was ongoing. They urged every-one to wait for all the evidence to be gathered before jumping to a conclusion. Leaks, however, helped report-ers obtain the name of the gunman, which led to the connection to the mosque in Minneapolis, and by mid-night the media was flatly declaring the killer was with al Qaeda. The final death toll was ten, plus the attacker, and the story had gone national, which brought in the nonstop chattering social media, which increased the volume of speculation from all points of view.

Omar Jama grunted with satisfaction. He had not been certain that Mohammed Ahmed really had the guts for this attack, but his al Qaeda foil had kept his nerve and done as instructed. Good for him. The ball was rolling. More days of terror would follow.

He tossed aside the blanket and went to bed with the furnace chugging away on a 75-degree setting as he tried to stay warm in this impossible climate. Before turning out the light, he looked at the city map, on which he had located the home of Deqo Sharif. It wasn't time for that quite yet, but it would come soon. Instead, he dialed a number on his cell phone, and when a male voice answered, the Cobra ordered: "Proceed."

LATE TUESDAY NIGHT

Abdifatah Farah understood the message. Outside of his motel room, wind chuckled through the streets and the frigid temperatures fell even lower. He slung on his heavy jacket and a rabbit-fur hat with earflaps, laced up his lined boots, and braced himself before opening the door. He was outside only long enough to turn on the engine of his loyal Toyota RAV4 and crank up the heater and defroster, and then he ran back into the room, shivering.

Middle of the night and it was around zero, with no clouds in the sky. Any warmth from the day had evaporated into the clear canopy of space. He waited ten minutes, then went back outside again and turned the little truck off. There was never a guarantee that frozen pieces of metal would work as designed at this temperature, so letting it run for a little while tonight might help it crank in the morning.

People in Minnesota seemed to be vaccinated against bad weather, and Farah was depending on that. Many would be out and about tomorrow morning, carrying on their normal lives, and traffic would be plentiful around the motel at the junction of I-35 and I-90 near the tiny town of Albert Lea, some ninety miles south of Minneapolis and St. Paul. Motels, restaurants, and service centers were located nearby to care for motorists who braved the cold highways and open spaces.

Farah, finally back inside for the night, opened the gun case that he had stowed beside the radiator of his room to keep the actions of the AR-15 rifle and the Glock 19 pistol from freezing, and checked them both. He had purchased them legally two months ago, under his own name, for he was a naturalized American citizen. He double-checked to be sure they were unloaded, then stuffed the weapons into the bed so his body heat would help keep them toasty and operational.

Before climbing between the covers himself, the young Somali propped a compact disc in a plastic sleeve beside the bathroom mirror, along with a few documents. Police would eventually discover the material and watch the final video message of Abdifatah Farah—a martyr for al Shabaab. "God is great!" was scrawled on the mirror with soap.

His heart leapt with joy as he thought about the panicky, nervous television people who talked about a Muslim terrorist who had raided an establishment in adjoining Wisconsin. *They were afraid!* The entire United States would be talking about it by breakfast tomorrow morning; then they would have something new to talk about. It was the turn of Abdifatah Farah to perform an act that would plant the twin black flags of fear and anger across the entire vast country. He was so keyed up with anticipation that he took two Ambien to help him sleep. He wanted to be fresh.

LOWRY HILL

A **PAIR OF FBI** agents pounded on the door of Hassan Investments in the strip mall at eight o'clock in the morning. Hassan Abdi was already at the desk, in a long-sleeved white shirt and a bland tie under a heavy sweater, and looked up in surprise. He wasn't expecting any customers this morning, or any other morning. Before getting up, he brushed a button beneath the desk to activate a blinking red light in the back rooms and warn the Cobra to remain silent because they had visitors. A video camera in the ceiling would show him what was happening in the front office.

Hassan was met by the badges of Special Agents Janna Ecklund and Cawelle Sharif. Their faces, one dark brown and the other an almost translucent white, gave away nothing.

"Are you Hassan Abdi?" asked the man.

"Yes. Please, come out of that cold." He stood aside as they stomped a crust of moist debris from their boots and walked in. Agent Sharif took a chair, but the woman stayed near the door with her back to the wall. She unzipped her jacket and had a white turtleneck sweater beneath. He glimpsed a pistol holster.

"It is unusual for me to meet FBI agents," said Hassan. "How can I help you?"

Lucky asked, "Do you know a man named Mohammed Ahmed?"

Abdi twisted his brows and flicked his eyes quickly to the ceiling as if in thought. "Has he done something wrong?"

"Do you know him?"

"It is a common name in our culture, as you know."

Lucky handed a photograph to the broker. "This one."

It jarred Hassan. The picture showed Mohammed Ahmed entering the Hassan Investments doorway. They had been watching, so he could not deny the information. "Ah," he said. "Yes. This man. I remember him now. He was a prospective client who walked in off the street. Why are you looking for him?"

"What did you discuss?"

Hassan responded, irked that he only received questions when he asked a question. "I had met him at the mosque, where he works as a janitor. The poor fellow had only nine hundred dollars in savings and desired to invest it into some financial instrument that would magically quadruple in the stock market. I told him that it did not work that way, and advised him to keep his cash in a bank savings account that is insured by the federal government. Frankly, sir, nine hundred dollars was not enough money to interest me, or to help him."

"How did he take that advice?" Lucky watched closely. Hassan was smooth, but seemed bothered by the questioning.

"He was disappointed, of course. I made sure not to give the impression that I was dishonoring him. I promised that when he had saved at least twenty-five hundred dollars, he should come back, and I would help him."

"Was that it?"

"Yes, sir. Then he left. Why are you asking?"

Sharif got to the meat on the bone. "Did you know that he had connections to al Qaeda?"

Hassan's expression turned grave. "No, I most certainly did not, and I find that accusation hard to believe. He appeared to be sickly."

Lucky looked over at Janna Ecklund, whose expression remained blank. He put a business card on the desk. "Okay, Mr. Hassan. Thank you for your cooperation. If you think of anything else, please call me." The two agents zipped up their coats and left, heading for the little shop on the corner of the mall to buy some coffee.

Hassan Abdi remained seated. His heart was in his throat. Only a day after the Wisconsin massacre, the FBI had come knocking. They had been following the al Qaeda contact, and even had a picture of him coming into this very place! Were they still watching now? Did they know the Cobra was here? Hassan pretended to work, but checked the exterior security camera screen beneath his desk. He did not move until he saw the two FBI agents come out with their cups of coffee, climb into a large sports utility vehicle, and drive away. Then he dashed into the back rooms.

The Cobra wasted no time in abandoning the little apartment hideaway behind the Hassan Investments storefront. If the FBI had come once, they would come again, and next time they would probably have search warrants to tear the place apart. The safe-house illusion was over. A phone call from Hassan to an intermediary had been all that was needed to temporarily relocate the Cobra beneath protection of the Somali gang culture.

Within thirty minutes of the moment that the federal agents left, a BMW X5 SUV that was the color of freshly poured champagne arrived behind the financial store with an alert Somali youngster at the wheel and a second youth in the rear acting as an armed guard. The Cobra and his right-hand man, Hassan, got in and were whisked away unseen.

The Somali Outlaws, the Somali Hot Boyz, and a half-dozen other gangs had deep roots within the immigrant community and fought for primacy throughout the urban region. Among the few things that the young thugs had in common was a willingness to use violence and the mutual recognition that the Cobra, the man from al Shabaab, was more violent than them all. While they scrapped for territory, he fought for the homeland, and they were eager to watch over and help him do his work here in America.

Omar Jama was soon settled comfortably in a luxurious home that had the appearance of a small stone castle and was located on two acres of private grounds in the exclusive Lowry Hill enclave of Minneapolis. It spread over eleven thousand square feet, had seven bedrooms, nine baths, and a staff of six. The old mansion was more than a century old and currently was the principal residence of a wealthy and creative entrepreneur who went by the name of E-X. The talented performer had found early success as a rap music star and then traded on his flamboyant style and quick wit to create an empire of entertainment, fashion, and television-production companies. He was extremely wealthy, but was best known and envied for being the husband of Fatima, a tall and exquisite supermodel from Somalia who frequently graced the covers of popular magazines.

Fatima and E-X were not political people. They had fled Minnesota temporarily, not to avoid controversy but to get away from the cold by attending a film festival and cruising in warmer climates. The only full-time resident of the big house on the hill in January 2014 was Fatima's brother, Abdullah, who made up for their political apathy by being an activist with strong connections in the Somali crime world. The Cobra made himself at home.

WEDNESDAY MORNING

The al Shabaab assassin Abdifatah Farah slept late at the motel in the crossroads spiral that twisted about near Albert Lea, Minnesota. But he awoke resolute and eager to go to work, to start his holy mission. Breakfast was cereal and milk and some fruit he had purchased the day before, and he made tea from hot water straight out of the faucet. He felt good and spiritually lifted, as if Allah was guiding him.

Farah wrapped the guns in the bed's blanket, then pulled on his gloves, from which he had snipped off the fingertips. The deep pockets of the down-filled coat would keep his hands warm. Farah doubted that he would live through the day, but he had no intention of freezing to death.

The small SUV roared to life without so much as a groan when he turned the key. That was still another sign that God was with him. The heater had the interior toasty within a few minutes. He arranged the loaded weapons conveniently on the seat beside him. The cell phone had been broken apart and would be scattered from the window along the highway, where it would be hidden by snow and perhaps recovered in the slush next spring. Farah took a deep breath, exhaled, and set out to hunt along the highways.

The roads were not as bad as Abdifatah Farah had feared, and his Toyota RAV4 gripped the pavement with authority. Eighteen-wheelers and people in big cars and pickups went hurtling past, rocking his smaller vehicle.

He let them go. Road rage was not on his agenda this morning.

There! A black Ford F150 with a plow mounted on the front was clearing the parking lot of a box store. The strong truck had scraped much of the snow into mounds along the edges of the lot and was methodically giving final scrapes to the lanes between. He worked alone. A few cars were already parked, and their occupants were inside the building.

Farah turned off the highway and drove into the lot toward the moving snowplow, lowering his window and waving his left arm for attention. The truck driver stopped directly beside him, and the driver also rolled down his window, although somewhat reluctant to let any warm air escape from the cab.

"They ain't open yet, friend," he said. The man wore a purple wool watch cap with a Vikings team insignia. "Doors open in about twenty minutes."

Farah had the Glock in his right hand as he nodded in agreement with the man's comment, then smoothly brought the weapon up and sighted it. He fired three times at the large target no more than four feet away. The truck driver was hit once in the shoulder and twice in the head and slumped back against the seat. The noise from the highway sucked up the gunfire.

Farah put the gun down on the seat, rolled up his window, and drove away. The truck remained where it was, as if the driver were taking a break from pushing the snow around. The Somali decided to drop by a fast-food restaurant a mile back down the road, get a sausage and egg sandwich, and shoot whoever handed it to him at the pickup window. His day was just beginning.

THE BUS

THE CELL PHONE went *ding-dong* in Kyle Swanson's pocket. It did not surprise him. He was up and dressed and was finishing his coffee when he turned on the midmorning television news to catch the updates from the Wisconsin shooting only to find that another slaughter had taken over the airwaves. Another Somali Muslim had killed six people and wounded four in southeastern Minnesota this morning before being shot to death by police after a high-speed chase that ended with a highway wreck and an epic gun battle. Authorities found proof in his motel room that he was a member of al Shabaab

The call was from his new boss, Marty Atkins, the CIA deputy director of Clandestine Service, who sounded flustered. A task force was being assembled to deal with the attacks, which apparently were coordinated strikes, and the involvement of al Qaeda and al Shabaab automatically slopped things onto CIA turf. A conference with representatives of all affected agencies was scheduled at noon at the FBI building in Minneapolis, and Atkins told Swanson to be there.

"You will be the CIA liaison," said Atkins.

"This is no clandestine operation, Marty," Swanson protested. "Surely you have somebody more experienced with agency matters up here."

"Unfortunately, no, Swanson. You are the only CIA agent in Minneapolis on this fine January day. Believe it or not, the agency does not maintain staff in every city in the United States and abroad."

"Shit. Well, what do you want me to do?"

"Just be our eyes and ears for a day. An administrative team will arrive tomorrow and take over. Anyway, the FBI will do the heavy lifting on this one, so you can keep a low profile. Call me if you need anything," said Atkins. "Better yet, don't call me. Call my assistant, Tracy, who can actually get things done that those people might want. I'm going to be running around for some conferences back here. The White House has eyes on it, and Capitol Hill is all atwitter. Obviously, nobody thinks this is just a coincidence."

THURSDAY
WASHINGTON, D.C.

Two mass murders by a Muslim gunman in as many days in the heartland crashed to the front of the news headlines. They could not be ignored or covered up.

At the Hoover Building, the headquarters of the Federal Bureau of Investigation, Director James Hamilton was briefed in detail by the Twin Cities agents, and then he repeated what he knew at a follow-up meeting at the White House. A somber president and his entire national security team listened in silent shock, then asked questions, and finally settled into the frustrated realization that they might be facing a nightmare scenario if these attacks continued.

"There is no doubt, Mr. President, that one of the attackers was connected to al Qaeda and the other was a member of al Shabaab, the newer incarnation of terrorism in Africa. Both gunmen came from the large Somali community in Minnesota," Hamilton said. "I wish I could say otherwise."

"Do you have everything you need to deal with this?" the president asked.

"Yes, sir. We have the manpower and the support and are doing everything in our power. The law enforcement agencies throughout the Midwest are on high alert."

"I will have to issue an official statement, of course, but I don't want to use the *T* word." He passed a meaningful glance at his press secretary. "We don't want to sow panic nationwide."

The president checked around the table. The entire National Security Council remained mute. Terrorism had struck on their watch, despite the billions of dollars that had been spent building an impenetrable security apparatus. Two men with guns had raised the specter of 9/11 all over again by killing average Americans in places thought to be safe.

"Is it over, or are there more of them out there?" asked the chief executive. He was the most powerful man in the world, but felt almost totally helpless. There must be something he could do, but ideas were few at the moment.

"We don't know, sir," Director Hamilton responded, trying to be accurate but not wanting to go too far. His neck was on the political chopping block. "Our people and the local police are trying to find that out."

"Dig harder."

"Yes, sir. One side thing before we move on with the meeting," the director of the Central Intelligence Agency said. "A minor point about the regional task force conference being held in Minnesota."

"What about it? Why bring that to my attention?"

"Sir, the CIA representative there right now is Kyle Swanson. Only man on the scene until a full admin team gets there. He was up there on a personal visit."

The president turned in his chair to face his deputy national security adviser, General Bradley Middleton, who blinked in surprise, and said, "I didn't know about this, Mr. President."

The president gave a little sigh and shook his head. "Be sure to strike his name from all reports and keep him the hell away from the media. We've got enough problems without them catching scent that Swanson is involved. They would drop that whole Task Force Trident private-assassin subject on us again, and there is no telling what the conspiracy crowd will create on the Net. General Middleton, I had hoped that we were through with that, but Swanson seems to stick to me like a patch of hot tar."

"I didn't even know he was up there, Mr. President, but perhaps it is not a bad thing. Kyle Swanson can bring a lot of experience concerning terrorism to that table. Sir, I recommend we keep him there, quietly, of course, until this thing settles down, but under tight rein."

"On a very, very tight leash, General." The president looked over at the CIA chief. "The sooner your support team gets there, the better. Meanwhile, tell Swanson not to kill anybody."

THURSDAY NOON
MINNEAPOLIS

Following lunch of fresh fish and vegetables, the Cobra retired to his bedroom in the big house on Lowry Hill and closed the door. It was much warmer and quieter up here, and he liked being able to look out over the snow-covered grounds of the private estate and not feel cold. He enjoyed having servants. He was quite pleased with the progress being made. If this was a soccer game, the score would be two-nil, against the home team.

There was a light knock, and Hassan entered the room, carrying a sheaf of printouts of news stories that he had downloaded from the Internet. He handed them to Omar Jama. "It is working," he said. "Just as you promised and planned. Congratulations, my friend."

The Cobra leafed through the papers and put them aside. "When do you leave?"

"In about one hour. Is there anything more that I can do before I go?"

"No. We are on schedule."

"I assigned some boys to keep track of the old woman, Deqo Sharif. Do you have any special orders there?"

"No. These other things must come first."

Hassan Ahmed took off his wire-rimmed glasses and polished them. "I don't want to leave. You might need my services here. Police attention is growing all around town."

"Thank you. A few more days, and I will be done here. And we will rendezvous as planned. You need to go and make the final arrangements. It actually is better this way and does not disrupt our plans." The Cobra smiled at his friend. "The sheep are frightened, and we will not slacken the momentum. Anyway, you are known to them, so you must leave. Go."

"The two boys who brought you over will take care of anything you need," said Hassan. "I will see you in Cuba."

"Safe travels," said the Cobra, and Hassan departed.

Omar Jama sat and thought in silence for ten minutes, then used another new, disposable cell phone to dial a number from memory and issue another order. He spent a few minutes to become familiar with the remote control that worked a huge curved-screen television that hung on the wall, for he intended to watch the Timber-wolves game later.

THURSDAY NIGHT

The special task force hammered at the problem all day. Men and women of the various agencies from several states were jammed into a large conference room at the FBI Minneapolis field office in Brooklyn Center, most of them law enforcement types carrying badges and guns, but also some big fish from the political seas and government lawyers. The conference had become a pyramid of concerned voices, people demanding to be heard and put on the record. Kyle Swanson rested against the wall at the rear of the auditorium, and he thought, *Clusterfuck!*

There was little to be done that was not already being done. The routine cop work and forensics analysis was still under way, surveillance was being increased throughout the region, and the usual suspects were being questioned. So far, there were no real leads. To Swanson, the long meeting was akin to rearranging the deck chairs on a torpedoed ship: if the ship foundered, then all of these proper, posturing, and patronizing people would have life jackets. The little people would do the dying.

Hugh Brooks, the FBI's special agent in charge of the office, ran the meeting. He was a middle-aged white man with a wide round face and a slight belly who had conducted many similar conferences and was not bothered by the bureaucrats. He let everyone have their say, within reason.

Swanson was next to Lucky Sharif and Janna Ecklund, both of whom had taken some sharp criticism because the al Qaeda man they had been watching had been the one who stormed the little restaurant in Wisconsin. They just had to sit there and take it. No one had yet been picked to be the sacrificial lamb of blame for the al Shabaab shooter in Albert Lea, but that one certainly did not fall at the feet of Sharif or Ecklund.

It seemed to Swanson that everyone was struggling not to label the incidents terrorism, or even to officially say that they were related. That was absurd. If it was not a coordinated terror attack, he wondered, why were all of these smart people sitting in the FBI headquarters discussing it? Did they think the American people would miss seeing that obvious link?

Another thing that was being raked over in detail was the fact that both of the attackers had come from the local Somali community in Minneapolis. It was an uncomfortable point, for the Twin Cities did not want a valuable community of immigrants torn apart while authorities researched the backgrounds of a few bad apples. A heavy-handed investigation could easily backfire into a wave of xenophobic racism, and the response might be a riot.

Finally, when all the words had been said and all the promises had been made, the meeting ended. Kyle, Lucky, and Janna took a long dinner break. The T-Wolves game was just finishing when they left the restaurant.

Buses were lined in neat lanes outside the Target Center when the basketball game ended, curls of exhaust smoke rising into the night. The drivers were ready to return fans to parking lots outside the city. The Wolves had laid a lopsided victory on the Jazz, and the fans were in great spirits. A young Somali man joined the queue, his bulkiness not an uncommon sight because everyone was huddled in heavy jackets. He paid the three dollars' fare to board, edged down the middle aisle, and found an empty seat at a window halfway to the rear. An old man settled in next to him, and they ignored each other, although the old man thought it a bit strange that the youngster had not unbuttoned his jacket. The bus wasn't all that cold.

The suicide bomber said nothing at all, for offering a prayer might draw attention. He had already made his peace with Allah and had practiced his role a thousand times. His right hand was in his pocket and wrapped around a triggering device for the hidden vest that was crammed with explosives. He took a final look out the window at the milling crowd of passengers, at the sky, then pressed the little plunger to close the circuit.

A spark jumped from a small battery, and the detonation blew out the windows and tore off the roof, evaporating him, his seat mate, and everyone else inside the doomed bus. The thin skin of the large vehicle was instantly transformed into razored shrapnel that preceded a spreading, rolling blast and fire.

Kyle, Janna, and Lucky had returned to the FBI building and gone upstairs to the private office of the special agent in charge. Hugh Brooks was still at it, working the phones. He was the one catching heat from Washington, where important people were demanding answers he did not have. He popped the plastic top on a bottle of antacid pills, gobbled two, and then asked, "Did you see anything we missed out there tonight, Swanson?"

"I think every possible base was touched several times." Kyle scratched his neck as he spoke. "I'm not trained as a crime fighter, but you guys just don't have much hard information yet. I just know that the Wisconsin thing wasn't the fault of these two agents."

"Ah, shit. I know that. The press jumped all over it, so everybody started joining that chorus, not knowing what they were talking about. Janna and Lucky are still running the investigation on this end. You stick with them." Brooks folded his hands behind his head, stretched, and leaned back. "By the way, I was told by my boss to keep you out of range of any reporters."

"No worries there. You guys have a question where the CIA can help, I'll get an answer. Other than that, I'm just an onlooker."

Brooks looked at a note on his desk. "Janna, how'd that search warrant on the investment place turn out? Did it get served this afternoon? Any luck?"

"A team and some locals went over. The guy we were looking for, Hassan, is in the wind. Our forensic people are working on the office. They found a small living quarters right behind it, but we're waiting for the reports."

"Damn. He has to be involved somehow."

"I agree," she said. "He lied to us about only meeting briefly with the al Qaeda shooter, just long enough to turn down some business. That would have taken maybe fifteen minutes at the outside, but the surveillance log shows their meeting went at least forty-five minutes. And why was a little-league financial hustler even open on a Sunday night?"

"Too bad. You track him down. Lucky, you got anything else before we call it a night?" Brooks was out from behind the desk, moving toward his suit coat and jacket, which were on hooks behind the door. Everybody was standing.

"No, sir. Street cops are out in the neighborhoods, staying visible and talking to a lot of people. So far, things seem cordial, but my sources say the Somalis are worried."

"I hear you." He slid an arm into his coat. "Man, this city is on edge. Can't you just feel it?"

His desk phone rang, and Brooks was tempted not to

answer it, but he did. His face paled as he listened, and he hung up the receiver as if it were made of delicate glass, then looked at the three other people in the room. "A bomb just flipped a Metro Transit bus outside the Target Center after the basketball game. All three of you get over there. Move!"

Janna and Lucky were already heading for the door. Kyle fell in with them. Brooks hung his jacket back on the hook. He would be in his office all night long.

CALLS

CLIVE WILCOX WAS up to his ass in alligators at the *Twin Cities Call,* a weekly alternative newspaper. His midnight deadline for the new edition was fast approaching, and the managing editor had everything in place. The *Call* had no mention of the terrorism threat because it could not compete with the big media. Instead, his lead story was about a toxic-chemicals-dumping case. The little newspaper had built its reputation on such material, and the publisher's formula was to surround a few offbeat stories with advertisements for everything from rock bands to yoga classes and columns of extremely personal ads. In the age of electronics, the little weekly was still kicking.

He was alone in the small newsroom on the second floor of a rented building. The place was a mess, and, with the windows closed against the outside cold, it stank. His shirt smelled of cigarette smoke and sweat. His telephone chimed with his *Superman* theme ringtone. "Wilcox," he snapped.

"God is great!" shouted an anonymous voice.

"Whatta you want? I'm right on deadline."

The caller was almost yelling. "We are responsible for the bomb."

Clive automatically grabbed a pen and a piece of scrap paper. He didn't know from any bomb. "What bomb?"

"The bus at the Target Center, ten minutes ago."

Clive had not had either television set on, and his computer and his mind had both been clogged with finishing off the *Call* edition, but he was still a reporter. "Yeah. And?"

"God is great!" the caller shouted even louder.

"You said that already. Who are you? I mean, if you're claiming responsibility, I need to know who you are." Clive tried to force himself to stay calm, but was writing furiously. This might be real, and if it was, then maybe it was his ticket out of the weekly ranks.

"We are al Shabaab! A note that explains everything is in an envelope downstairs in your mail receptacle. God is great!" The phone clicked off.

Man, Wilcox thought, putting down the receiver, this was old-school Woodward and Bernstein stuff. He hurried down to the lobby and found a brown envelope on the tile beneath the mail slot. He ripped the top and slid out a note that had been written on an old typewriter. It announced that a martyr, naming some Arab guy, was a member of al Shabaab and had successfully carried out the attack on America. Several paragraphs followed, gibberish about jihad and freedom fighters.

Wilcox ran upstairs, where the front page of the weekly newspaper was still on his screen, about to be transmitted over to the printer's shop for the overnight run. The weekly probably had been chosen simply as a cutout so the note could not be tracked by the cops. *Was it even true?* Just because the claim was made did not mean someone actually had cooked off a bomb downtown.

He scrambled for the remote under some paper and clicked on the television set. A camera crew that had been covering the basketball game had gotten to the scene and was showing the carnage in graphic detail as some TV guy stood out in the cold with a microphone.

Bomb! The publisher was going to be pissed, but Clive Wilcox could not hold this until next week. He tore out the toxic-dumping report, then pounded a replacement story about how the *Call* was the first to know who set off the explosive and reprinted the content of the note. Once he transmitted the edition, twenty minutes late, he telephoned the police.

FRIDAY MORNING

Omar Jama was at the breakfast table in the big house on the hill, nibbling on fruit and buttered toast and drinking hot tea, feeling like a lord in a castle, better than he had in weeks. Six months ago, his nerves had been stretched, his brain jangled, and worry had plagued his hours, for a hundred thousand things might have gone wrong during the final planning of this intricate operation. Instead, a handful of things had all gone right, and here he sat, safe in a beautiful American home that was so large it even had a special room just for breakfast. He was able to laugh at those past concerns. Everything was working.

The news reports were frantic. Almost twenty Americans had been killed by the bomb blast at the Target Center, and at least fifty were injured. Some of those would die, too. The victims of the multiple attacks were adding up.

Gruesome images were flung across the screen, accompanied by banner crawls and excited proclamations that terrorists were attacking. It was 9/11 all over again!

It was exactly how the Cobra had mapped it out, long before he had even arrived in the United States.

The planning had been carried out in the tightest possible secrecy and with the greatest possible care, for the Cobra was fighting this war on a shoestring. In the heyday of al Qaeda, operational funding came from the very deep pockets of Osama bin Laden and his many admirers. They had found many men willing to die for the cause and had enough cash to spread it around to other terrorist groups. After the United States killed Osama, the easy money dried up, and it was every organization for itself.

The line of credit from Prince Faisal in Greece was the Cobra's only source of income, and he had discovered that a million dollars did not really go very far. He had tried to work with the pirates of Somalia who captured and ransomed cargo ships, but when the world's navies had effectively blocked most of that enterprise, he discovered that the pirates could not be trusted. They were dishonest, and did not fear him.

Years of banking sanctions by America and European nations had similarly crippled terrorist cash flow.

That would all change when he finished his American trip. Then the money would once again roll in, along with the fame and the arms and military power he needed. He would override the chest-thumping usurpers and their ragtag groups that popped up periodically in Syria, Iraq, Afghanistan, and Pakistan and stayed busy killing each other in eternal religious squabbles. Some gained temporary notoriety and promised to attack America, but the Cobra was the only one who had actually done so. He would be the one who would be hailed throughout the Muslim world as the reincarnation of Osama.

The Cobra went to a bathroom and washed his hands and face, avoiding the mirror. He already knew what he looked like. Instead of feeling sorry for himself, he was overjoyed by his train of successes thus far. By his continual pushing and pushing, the Americans were now overreacting, just as he had anticipated, and it was time to unleash the final phase, then flee this humbled country, leaving it much worse than it had been when he first entered.

It was also time for him to begin attending to the secondary goals: the personal business. Unlike the primary mission, these had not been planned in detail because he thought that he could squeeze them into the more important timetable. He had never lost his hatred for the three people who had beaten him in Somalia and put him in that fetid Kenyan prison, and his spies had done good work. If he could not kill them this time, then he would kill them later, but kill them he would.

He stayed in the deep background for the major attacks. His victims and the police did not know who he was. But for the personal hits, he intended to unmask himself before the victims went down. They had to *see* him. They had to *know* who was killing them. First on his private list would be the easiest target, the troublesome woman Deqo Sharif, who had once fractured his skull with an iron pot.

A fresh prepaid mobile phone that Hassan had purchased in California for this one task was in his traveling kit, and he dug it out. The only number was preprogrammed and the call was answered by a producer at a local television station. The Cobra provided an anonymous tip that the terrorist mastermind behind all of this recent terrible violence was being sheltered right here in Minneapolis, at this very moment, in the home of an al Shabaab sympathizer. He recited the address and then terminated the call, which had lasted less than ten seconds, and destroyed the telephone.

FRIDAY MORNING

The bus-blast scene was horrific, although Kyle Swanson had seen worse. Actual war and a relatively small terrorist attack differed on too many levels to count. The one that came to his mind first was the hellish scene on Highway 80 heading north from Kuwait and into Iraq, where convoys of the Iraqi occupation army had been annihilated by air power. His memories of patrolling up that six-lane highway of death, walking among countless dismembered human remains and the carcasses of vehicles, helped keep his reactions in check. Here, one crazy suicide bomber had blown up a bus partially filled with civilians. It was a tragedy, but a poor comparison.

Lucky Sharif carried a similar personal frame of reference from his childhood in Somalia. He had grown up in a place where dead bodies were found in the streets every morning and entire villages were laid to waste, along with all of their inhabitants. Swanson and Sharif looked at the bus-explosion scene through the dispassionate eyes of seasoned professionals.

Both of them, along with Janna Ecklund and much of the available law enforcement apparatus in the city, stayed at the crime scene for hours. An emergency command post had been established inside the Target Center, out of the weather. Swanson hung around, watching, but the CIA had no role in this investigation. He kept in touch with Marty Atkins in Washington, who promised the agency admin team was in the air, heading to Minnesota as fast as possible.

Swanson avoided anyone that might be a member of

the media and did not go near the Friday-morning press conference, where a spokesman announced the note left at the office of a weekly newspaper. The terrorist group known as al Shabaab was claiming responsibility.

Instead, he called to check on Deqo, but there was no answer.

"She's probably out in the neighborhood," said Lucky. He called the resettlement center, but she wasn't there, either. "I'm sure that she's out walking around, keeping a lid on things."

Lucky was stuck at the command center, but Ecklund was free to drive Swanson over to the house and check on her.

As she steered the big sedan through traffic, Kyle asked, "What's with your all-arctic look, Janna? Every other female FBI agent I've ever seen tries to blend in with the male agents. You blend with polar bears."

She gave a look, then laughed. Kyle had no sense of propriety. "Oh, I wore the dark pantsuits and skirts and jackets for a few years. Then I started taking liberties with the dress code. God, I'm a six-foot-tall Scandinavian, so I decided to be distinctive and use it to my advantage. Actually, I blend pretty well with most of the people in this neck of the country." ·

"By scaring the hell out of insecure little men?"

There was a nod and a smile. "That's their problem, not mine." She had perfect white teeth, of course, but the mouth settled into a tight line as she drove. She waited for the inevitable question about whether she and Lucky were a couple, but it didn't come. Kyle had eyes, and nobody was hiding anything.

In the light of day, Minneapolis and St. Paul had assumed the look of cities under siege. It was not martial law, but it was getting close. Security around important buildings was doubled, checkpoints and barricades went up at vital infrastructure facilities, and police roamed in heavy vehicles.

Swanson shifted in his seat, uncomfortable and feeling as if they were driving into a combat zone. He saw cops with sniper rifles and even one manning a .30 caliber machine gun atop a modified military-style Humvee. "I don't like all of the firepower out there," he said.

"No. It looks weird." Something had happened to the peaceful equilibrium of the city. Cops, many wearing helmets, combat boots, and bulky body armor that was festooned with military-style gear, all straps and buckles, were roaming in herds and holding automatic rifles across their chests with slings. Others carried plexiglass shields and riot batons and were ordering—not asking—people to stay in their homes. Some of the vehicles shook the streets as they rolled through on giant bulletproof tires. In all, the picture was one of fear instead of confidence. Two mass shootings and a deadly bomb explosion, with lots of death, had silenced those who would normally speak out against such a show of strength.

The uniformed presence grew stronger as Kyle and Janna neared the Somali neighborhoods, for SWAT and sheriff's-office tactical units were concentrating in the Cedar-Riverside area. Two blocks away from Deqo's house, they hit a dead end.

THE RAID

THE FBI SEDAN was blocked at an intersection where two cop cars nuzzled against a waist-high barrier, and beyond that was parked the hulking goliath of the police arsenal, an eighteen-ton mine-resistant, ambush-protected, military-style chunk of armored vehicle known as a MaxxPro. The MRAP was ten feet tall, and standing in the turret was a scowling policeman in full armor pointing an automatic M-16 rifle toward the gathering crowd and oncoming vehicles. The behemoth war wagon had a new paint job, police decals, and emergency lights but was a terrifying presence, and the camera crew of a television truck gobbled up the scene as a reporter spoke breathlessly of imminent danger.

All the cops were in total camouflage and looked like brown bushes in the urban landscape. One pointed his finger at Janna and signaled a full stop by holding his left hand high. The right palm rested close to his holstered pistol. More cops in battle gear moved to box the car into place. All had AR-15 rifles dangling from load-bearing web harnesses.

"You ready for this shit, Kyle?" she asked, and her voice had steel in it. Swanson nodded that he was.

She tapped her siren and turned on the flashers. That made the cops twitch and the TV producer curse about the noise that drowned out the live reporter. The window hummed down, and Janna badged the cop and said, "What the fuck, Jack?"

Kyle lifted his own creds to show the cops on the other side. *Too tight,* he thought. *Nervous. Bad ju-ju.*

"Sorry, ma'am, but nobody can drive through down there right now." Despite the overwhelming power at his disposal, the cop looked like a mouse who had wandered up to the wrong cat.

"Officer, I'm Special Agent Janna Ecklund of the FBI and I will go anywhere I fucking please. What's so important that you guys are building a fort on a city street and pointing guns at civilians? Who's shooting at you?"

"Ma'am. We received credible information that a terrorist boss is hiding down there. A two-block area has been sealed while we conduct a house-to-house search. Nobody in, nobody out, no exceptions."

Janna's icy eyes flared. "Jesus Christ! And you have the warrants to do that?"

"That's above my pay grade, ma'am. In the meantime, we are asking for cooperation from the residents as we flood the neighborhood with cops. They understand that we are trying to protect them from a killer."

Janna was out of the car now, bigger than the cop and leaning toward him in anger. She had left the siren screaming so the TVs could not overhear them. "And if someone doesn't want to open the door? What, you're kicking it in?"

"I'm following orders, Special Agent Ecklund," the cop said. "Things are critical here."

"I just left the FBI office, and we didn't know anything about this." She pointed to the television people. "And why are those ghouls right up next to you cops, or are you soldiers now? They're broadcasting live."

The policeman stood his ground, tired of being battered by this woman. "You are blocking an operational position. Please get back into your car and move it."

Instead, Janna turned off the engine and pocketed the keys. The siren whimpered off. "Oh, hell no, Bubba. I'm standing right here and calling my boss, who will have an assistant U.S. attorney general on the horn in about thirty seconds. You are way over your head on constitutional issues here, Officer, particularly on Fourth Amendment rights. Whoever ordered this little show has made a monstrous mistake."

"That's bullshit, Agent Ecklund. Our lawyers clear all of that stuff."

She spat the exact words. " 'The right of the people to be secure in their persons, houses, papers, and effects, against unreasonable searches and seizures, shall not be violated, and no warrants shall issue, but upon probable cause, supported by oath or affirmation, and particularly describing the place to be searched, and the persons or things to be seized.' That's the exact wording. You don't have that. So you guys are tromping all over a constitutional guarantee. This isn't Baghdad. Take my advice and back off."

The cop looked across the roof of the car as Swanson pushed open his door, taking in the scene. He yelled, "You! Back in the car! Keep your hands up!"

The closest officer took a step forward and gripped the pistol in his side holster. Kyle stared the kid down and badged him. "I'm with the CIA, and I have legitimate business here. I am going to walk through this barricade, right past your silly fuckin' MRAP, and it would be best for you to quit thinking about trying to stop me."

His voice was hard, and he opened his jacket to show his own heavy Colt .45 that was on his hip. "If you try, I will shoot you. Move aside."

Janna Ecklund called over. "He will do it, too, Officer. After he finishes, I will arrest what's left of you." She turned back to the first cop and lowered her voice to a more reasonable tone. "Somebody issued faulty orders here, Officer, and a legal shit-storm is coming your way as soon as I make that call. Hell, I don't even have to bother, because that television crew has already let the powers that be know what has happened. The scramble has already started. This is your last chance, or I will bring formal charges against you personally for interfering with federal officers in the performance of their duties. Start thinking about ten years in a supermax. Just like my partner, I am not kidding. Stand down."

"No. I will not. I don't take orders from the FBI or the CIA!" replied the cop, but he knew that the situation had been flipped like a flapjack on a griddle. Instead of being the top dog, he had become almost the low man on the totem pole. He holstered his pistol and motioned for the others to do the same. Someone with a higher rank on the other side of the barricade could deal with these two. "Let 'em through," he called, adding beneath his breath, *"Fuckin' Feebs."*

Ecklund got on the radio to Lucky, and a grim Kyle Swanson climbed over the concrete barriers, skirted the MRAP, and broke into a jog.

The little house was in a line of similar small homes, sturdy little shelters that had withstood time and temperature. A snowman built by children silently watched the drama. Police squads were working through the neighborhood in careful, tactical formations. An armored-up cop in camo was arguing loudly on a front porch that the resident had to open up and allow him and his men to come in and search. A terrorist was on the loose! Three other policemen in protective riot gear were stacked behind him, ready to make a forced entry if the guy continued to refuse permission. At the far end of the street, a small group of residents was yelling at the cops and a line of officers with riot shields and batons blocked that route.

Kyle ran hard, hauling in deep breaths of chill air as snow dripped from the colorless sky. Deqo's house loomed into view, the front door yawning open and the entrance empty. The big central window was shattered, and the white curtains inside fluttered like flags of surrender. He leaped up the steps, crossed the porch, and plunged inside, calling her name into the residence that had turned ice-cold. It had been trashed.

"DEQO! DEQO! It's Kyle! Where are you?" He checked the small kitchen and the dining room, where doors had been kicked open and kitchen shelves emptied into piles of broken crockery. The door to the small storage basement had been ripped from its hinges, and her favorite china cabinet was toppled, the contents in pieces. The hunters had not been gentle.

She was in the back bedroom, seated at her dressing table and staring into the mirror, with the remains of a prized ceramic figurine cupped in her hands. Kyle knelt beside her and pulled her close when she turned to him. Tears coursed down the old woman's face, following the deep wrinkles. "Policemen with guns came. Men I have never seen before," she said with a hiccup. "I told them to stay out, but they broke in anyway, screaming awful things and waving their guns. They said I was hiding a terrorist."

He was on fire, but forced himself to stay in control. "Did anyone hurt you?"

"No. They did not hurt my body, no. There are no broken bones. I am okay. What was really hurt was my pride, Kyle. I didn't think such a thing could ever happen here. They said they were going to arrest me."

Kyle said, "Come on. Let's get you over to the bed so you can lie down for a few minutes. I'll bring a washcloth and make some tea. Then I will get Lucky over here." He helped her stretch out and pulled a heavy blanket up to her waist. She looked frail. "I'm here now, Deqo. It's going to be all right. Somebody's not thinking straight, that's all."

"I told them I wanted to see the warrant and just got pushed aside. I fell down."

Swanson knew that well-intentioned operations can spin out of control with only a taste of panic, but this one could have killed Deqo; her heart wasn't strong enough to endure another Somalia, particularly in her own home, which she believed was safe. For now, he bit back his frustration. He closed the front door against the weather and any new intruders, half expecting to hear gunfire somewhere out in the street. The lock was broken. Shouting was growing in volume as more people spilled out to protest the raids. A helicopter came chopping low overhead. Kyle put a kettle of water on the stove for the tea.

He retrieved his cell phone and thumbed a call that bypassed regular command loops and was answered by Lieutenant General Bradley Middleton, the deputy national security adviser at the White House. Times like this, back channels worked best.

"No shit?" Middleton had risen to his feet behind the desk, having trouble believing what Swanson was telling him.

"It's borderline chaos up here," Kyle said. "Cops are forcing their way into private homes, and some very unhappy residents are clustering in the streets. It is only a matter of time before somebody pulls a trigger. The police are quarantining the biggest Somali neighborhood in Minneapolis, and they even brought in some MRAPs, and the television cameras are broadcasting. Nobody is fighting back, but crowds are forming up. It's probably already on your television set in the White House."

Middleton switched on his office TV while he listened. "Got it. Thanks for the heads-up. I need to get this on up the line. Maybe the president will want to chat with the governor, and the governor with the mayor, and the mayor with the police chief. Cops acting like an occupying military force? Ain't gonna happen."

"It already has. The FBI didn't know about it in advance, so maybe just some low-level precinct guy just made a bad choice that has grown out of control."

"I'm on it, Kyle. Call me later."

The front door flew open and an out-of-breath Janna Ecklund rushed inside. "Is she all right?" Ecklund winced as if in pain when saw the damage and called out, "Deqo?"

"She's scared, but okay. In the bedroom." He stuck his head outside and heard a tide of shouting rising down the street.

"I'm back here, Janna." Deqo was on her feet when Ecklund reached the bedroom, and the two women almost collided in a hug, Janna being large enough to make two of Deqo. "Don't you worry," the older woman said, as if gentling a thoroughbred horse and stroking Janna's snow-white hair. "I'm good now, with you and Kyle here."

"Lucky will be here in a minute," Janna said, and guided Deqo back to the bed and made her get back under the covers. "This is so terrible."

"What happened?" Kyle asked, bringing in a cup of steaming tea.

"We stopped it, whatever it was," replied the FBI agent. "The search teams are pulling back and that checkpoint is already being dismantled. Everybody is saying they were just following orders, but that won't stand very long. Some honcho's balls are going to be cut off."

The front door banged open again, and Lucky Sharif stormed in. "Where is everybody?" He was at the bedroom before anyone could respond.

He reached for his grandmother, but Deqo pushed him aside. "I'm getting hugged by too many giants. You're all going to break me. Now calm yourself down, Cawelle Sharif. I just had a bit of a fright, that's all."

Lucky sat beside her. "Did they come in here, too?" His eyes were dark stones.

"Yes," she admitted, looking around her bedroom. "It looks like an army marched through, doesn't it?"

Lucky dug out his radio. Every policeman who had entered a private home was to be segregated and taken to separate holding facilities until they could be questioned individually by federal agents. They were to be kept apart to prevent them from getting their stories straight. The FBI wanted answers. Somebody was going to pay.

The four of them spent a few hours picking up, cleaning the mess, and arranging for a string of repairmen and carpenters. A neighbor donated a sheet of plywood to temporarily seal the broken window. Deqo's mood improved with the work and the feeling that something was being accomplished. The others were still growling, but tried not to show it.

The police net around the Somali neighborhood

evaporated, and regular uniforms replaced the camo outfits. The big guns and riot gear were put away, and normal patrol cars took over from the MRAPs. At three o'clock the assistant chief of police, Paul Gottfried, arrived at the house and was overflowing with apologies. Deqo, the person with the most reason to be outraged, was the only one to be polite to him. She even gave him coffee.

Gottfried was the department's salesman when things got tough. The thick blond hair accented his Nordic features, and his limitless reservoir of energy propelled a gym-fit body and sharp mind. "It was a dreadful mistake," Gottfried said, knowing the admission of guilt could come back to haunt the city if Deqo Sharif filed a lawsuit. Nevertheless, a truthful explanation was the only way to go. Lucky Sharif, Janna Ecklund, and Swanson would nail him on any lies.

Deqo sat with her hands folded in her lap, a kind smile on her face. She asked, "Why me? Why here?"

Gottfried shrugged and let out a long breath, his look solemn. "That's the real question, Mrs. Sharif. We already know how it happened. Shorthand version is that a TV news department received an anonymous tip, and the caller was very specific. He claimed the madman behind all of the terrorist killings was hiding at this address. The source claimed that you were a sympathizer with the group called al Shabaab."

Janna Ecklund rolled her eyes and rested a hand on Deqo's shoulder. "What a crock. Nobody checked this out?"

"Then what?" asked Kyle. "Why the over-the-top reaction by your cops?"

"Without a shred of proof?" added Lucky.

Gottfried paused to get his thoughts straight, then said, "The TV guy called a friend in our department, the deputy chief in charge of the Special Operations Department. That officer, unfortunately, had lost a six-year-old cousin in the Target Center bomb blast, and he went off the deep end without authorization. By the time the chief and I found out, he had already rolled out heavy, wanting to personally take down the terrorist, if not kill him outright. This man, who had an outstanding record, has been relieved of duty, of course. The officers who invaded your home will be reprimanded."

"I see," said Deqo. "That poor man."

Lucky said, "It's too bad about his loss, but he did a lot of damage, Chief Gottfried. This entire neighborhood is angry."

"We're doing what we can to settle things and rectify an error, Agent Sharif, and we could use your help out there."

"Forget it," Lucky shot back.

"Well, I can understand your feelings, but none of us want this community to blow up with a riot when the sun goes down. Think it over, please. Now, back to your original question: why did the caller pinpoint you personally, a woman known to be pillar of the community? We don't know. Do you have any idea who would dislike you this much?"

Deqo's back was ramrod straight. "No! I don't have any enemies at all, as far as I know." Lucky, Kyle, and Janna all agreed. The woman had spent the last twenty years helping people.

"We have to probe this deeply, ma'am. I consider that anonymous call to be another terrorist attack, and this one specifically targeted you. A team of our detectives and FBI special agents is ready to come over now and interview all of you, maybe get a line on this guy. Are you willing to do that?" His eyes locked on hers, then swept around to the others. "Special Agent Sharif cannot be doing the interview because he is personally involved. I think we all just learned a lesson about how personal involvement clouds good judgment."

Lucky agreed, and Deqo said, "Yes. Of course. I just can't think of who might be so angry at me."

Kyle said, "But not here. This place won't be ready again for at least a week. Until then, Mrs. Sharif will be staying in my suite at the Graves 601 downtown, and under our constant protection. Have them meet us there in an hour."

Relief pumped through Gottfried, and he slapped his knees and got up. "Excellent. Again, Mrs. Sharif, I apologize for the shock and the mess our people made. The city will pay for everything, of course, and a general contractor is on his way right now. So, if you will excuse me, I have to get back to work. People are frightened throughout the state, not just here. This whole thing is a nightmare."

They watched him leave, and Deqo allowed that the assistant chief was a true gentleman.

"I wanted to kick his ass." Janna was still furious.

"Take a deep breath instead," Kyle advised. "All of us have to regroup: the cops, you Feebs, and everybody else. We have to stay united and not divide our forces. And Lucky, you really do need to get some Somali leaders into the loop."

He turned to Deqo. "Now, old woman, get some clothes together so I can get you out of here. I've got a suite for you at my hotel, so get some clothes."

Deqo didn't want to leave. "I will be fine right here. I have to straighten things."

"This isn't a debate. Until things shake out, you stay with me so these children can get back to work. Tomorrow, you and I take a break and go over to the Mall USA, do some shopping, get you a manicure, and have us a nice lunch. You still have a birthday coming up. By the time we get back, your house should be looking a lot better. My guess is that this place is high on the priority list."

Thirty minutes later, when Janna drove them all away, the FBI sedan was followed by a dirty red Volvo S40. The driver thumbed his mobile phone as he steered and reported to the Cobra.

BOOK THREE

THE MALL

BY LUNCHTIME, THE city was smothered with cops. It had been staggered by the terrorist attacks and the invasion of the Cedar-Riverside area by the armored vehicles and soldierlike cops, but, although the streets had simmered, there had been no riot. Television reports still carried the taste of a battlefield documentary, and some Somali residents said they actually had feared for their lives, and they hurled accusations that the authorities had overreacted just because they were blacks and Muslim.

How could the Cobra not be happy on such a fine morning? Those shocking reports were the propaganda equivalent of still another attack, for those frightened citizens and the militarized law enforcement reactions would be seen by millions of people all over the world. And all it had cost him was a single telephone call of warning to a television station news department.

Considering the chaos and distrust that he sowed, Omar Jama felt as if he were the captain of a large ship, looking back over its turbulent wake. His daily drumbeat of attacks was wearing down the resolve of the Americans by showing their weaknesses. Everyone out there had but two thoughts: Is it over? What next?

It was the weekend. He was not yet done with his attacks on America. Tomorrow, on Sunday, he would show them what was next and unsheathe the sword! Meanwhile, he had enough spare time to continue his parallel campaign against his other three targets, the first being Deqo Sharif. Omar had laughed aloud when he saw the TV pictures of her wrecked home. That was just the first footfall of an approaching hungry bear, but she did not know that. By tonight, she would be trembling.

He waited in the huge mansion; there were three men watching the luxury hotel where she had taken refuge, but she had to surface sometime. As a bonus, they had identified the suite as being in the name of Kyle Swanson—the Swanson Marine! A pleasant and unexpected bonus.

He intended to make himself personally known to them today and let them recognize him for a brief moment, so they could then live in fear, knowing he was coming to collect them. That meant he would have to go out in the daylight today, so the Cobra assumed the image of a businessman in a dark suit with a blue shirt and subtle tie. The collar of his overcoat would be worn up. A snap-brim hat tilted over his forehead and the eye patch would shield the scars.

The call came in at eleven o'clock. "They're moving."

"Follow them. Stay in contact." He thought perhaps he could just shadow their car for a while, race up alongside and roll down the tinted window and show his face long enough to be recognized, and then escape. Maybe taunt them. Or perhaps have another car hit them. He would just have to wait and see and strike when the opportunity was right, but at least things were moving.

The Cobra watched troubled Minneapolis from the passenger's seat of the stylish BMW X5, escorted by the same quiet and neat youths who had rescued him from the storefront apartment and ferried him to the place on Lowry Hill. Pierre drove, and Clinton was in the rear. Both were polite and neatly dressed and were members of a gang called the Somali Outlaws. He enjoyed their company.

"Do you boys know my name?" he finally asked when they were under way.

"No, sir," answered the driver. "Only that you are important and we are to protect you."

"That is probably best," the Cobra said.

Pierre briefly blinked his eyes from the road and looked over. "Where are we going?"

"Just drive around. I would like to see the area where the trouble took place yesterday."

"Cedar-Riverside?"

"Yes. We can start there."

The new SUV containing the three black males was not pulled over. The plates were traced by several officers, and the police computer spat back that the owners were the famous music star and businessman E-X and his wife, Fatima, two of the wealthiest celebrities in the Twin Cities. That was enough to maintain a bubble of protection and respect around the opulent vehicle.

A video screen on the center console live-streamed the broadcast of a news channel. The Cobra watched, as did Clinton.

"Do you have something to do with that, sir?"

Omar Jama gave an oblique answer. "I work for the glory of the Islam."

"Cool," said Clinton. They rode in silence for a while through the streets of the nervous city, then Clinton asked, "Sir, do you need more people to help? We've got plenty of street boys."

Cobra turned, nodded. "I will keep that in mind, Clinton, and I thank you for the offer. My business is on schedule, and I have manpower equal to the task. Do you follow our Prophet, whose name be praised?"

"You mean are we good Muslims?"

"Exactly."

"No, sir. We are not religious at all. In fact, being a Muslim is an easy way to have the FBI all over you. We are just businessmen, interested only in profits."

The Cobra stiffened, then relaxed. He wasn't here to proselytize. Still, if the faithful were losing the religious grip on the young people, they eventually would drift away. "I know. Well, you shall discover your own path, but please consider resuming your study of the Book. It is part of the culture of our people."

"Okay. Can I ask, not being too personal if you don't want to say, but . . ."

"My face? The scars?" Cobra smiled, glad to move the subject away from religion.

"Yes, sir. I have seen beat-up dudes before, but, damn, it looks like you got run over by a train or something."

Omar Jama trailed his fingers along the misshapen flesh and the patch. "I sustained these a long time ago, in the early days of the war in Mogadishu. War is very dangerous."

"Could plastic surgery fix your face up better?"

"Doubtful. There were no plastic surgeons in the African prisons in which I spent ten long years. I was fortunate to survive at all. Now, I keep my scars as personal reminders of how much I hate this country. America did much worse to thousands of other Somalis. Babies were killed, women were raped, men had their genitals cut off, and whole villages were starved and crushed by the American marines."

Pierre joined the conversation. "I saw that war movie about Mogadishu, but it didn't have anything about the marines. So you come over here for some payback, sir . . . after twenty years?"

"My war will never stop, young man. It knows no boundaries."

In the backseat, Clinton sat in total admiration.

The Cobra's telephone buzzed, and he answered. The driver of the faded red Volvo reported he had followed the man and the woman from the hotel, and they were now eastbound on I-494. He closed the call. Maybe this would be a chance to pull alongside them for the un-veiling of his presence. "Get on Interstate 494 and head east, please. Hurry."

"Yes, sir. Going to the mall?" Pierre knew an inter-state entrance was two blocks over and hurried onto the ramp, then gunned the engine and sped into traffic.

"I just want to find a certain car."

"If they are on I-494, the chances are that they are going to Mall USA over in Bloomington." Clinton crossed his arms. "It's the only thing out there."

"Really?"

"Yes, sir."

This tilted his plan, and he said a quiet prayer of thankfulness for Allah's presenting still another won-derful opportunity. He had known that fact, but had not made the correlation between what was happening at present and what he planned for tomorrow.

The Mall USA was the second-largest shopping mall in North America, and was his target for the final attack. On Sunday, he would dial a single number that would simultaneously burst the attack code word—

"sword"—to eighteen separate telephones, and history would be made. But although he planned to destroy the mall, he had never actually set foot in the huge complex. Today he could track Sharif and Swanson out there and simultaneously do some quiet final surveillance. Perhaps there would be a chance to do even more.

The sleek SUV rode quietly along Interstate 494, and the Cobra noticed the flow of traffic appeared normal. The drivers and passengers apparently believed that bad things only happened to other people. They had not been at the coffee shop in Wisconsin or on the roads around Albert Lea and had not gone to the basketball game, so they were sleepwalking through what could be the most dangerous time of their lives, depending on overwhelmed and ineffective police to protect them from him, an impossibility.

"Do you have weapons?" he asked.

"No, sir. Too dangerous to carry with all those cops running around today."

"No matter. I know where we might find some."

The begrimed red Volvo followed Swanson and Deqo all the way to the mall and parked one row back and five slots down, and its occupants watched the man and woman walk from the parking lot to the east entrance of the mall before checking in with the Cobra. "We're almost there," said Omar Jama. "You go inside but stay near the entrance. The man with her would spot a tail. He is dangerous."

Hugh Brooks, the FBI SAC, looked up as Lucky and Janna entered his office at Brooklyn Center. He brought them up to date. "The forensics and search teams have proven that little apartment behind Hassan Investments was occupied, but by someone other than Mr. Hassan

Abdi. It looks like they all disappeared. There's a BOLO out now, but Hassan smells real gone."

Lucky plopped into a chair. "They had an escape plan because they knew they were going to have to run eventually. Both Hassan and whoever lived behind the shop."

"Just so," Brooks said, wishing he still smoked cigarettes. He could use one right now. "Maybe something will turn up from Interpol. How're things over in Cedar-Riverside, and with your grandmother?"

Lucky adjusted his lanky body in the seat. He was still agitated by the screwup the night before. "Deqo is okay, and the scene is settling down. A tactical team went into her house without a warrant, scared her half to death, broke almost everything, and in the process almost started a riot."

"God almighty. I hear that the mayor got a quasi-impolite call from the governor, wondering if Minneapolis was in need of the National Guard. Apparently the governor had received a similar call from the White House." The strain was telling on the veteran agent. "By raiding Deqo's home, those cops inadvertently got you involved on a personal level."

"They stepped way over the line, Boss, and they knew it while they were doing it. Somebody should lose their badge." Sharif was outwardly at ease, but Brooks saw through the act.

The SAC poured a cup of stamina, returned to his chair, and sipped at the strong, hot, fresh brew. "Nevertheless, your effectiveness with the locals has been impaired until this is all cleared up."

Janna had both hands wrapped around her own mug of coffee. "Pull Lucky off, and we lose our best contact within the Somali community," she said.

"I'm not taking either of you off of the case, Janna, but we do not want Lucky to end up in a confrontation that could get public and nasty and damage the progress he has made over the past few years. The chief promised me a thorough internal investigation."

Sharif kept his face blank. "I won't let it blow up. I came up through the MPD, and I know a lot of them. They're good people. They know a fuckup when they see one and want to clear it as fast as possible." Sharif stopped talking, stretched out his long legs, and crossed his ankles. "On the case, I keep coming back to something Kyle said, that this all has been too much to be accidental. Someone mapped out these moves carefully to sow distrust and get us going after each other. That sidetracks the overall investigation and keeps us from concentrating on who is behind the attacks."

"The guy in the back room."

"Yes. Him."

"Any idea who that might be?"

"No. We went through it all over and over during the interviews. It had to be personal, against Deqo, but she doesn't have enemies like that. Even the gangsters respect her because she knew them as kids."

"Keep thinking about it. Speaking of Swanson, where is he?"

"Taking Deqo over to the Mall USA," said Janna. "Good place for him to cool down, too. He really was ready to shoot a cop at that roadblock. I saw it in his eyes. He didn't give a damn. That is one dangerous guy."

"Well. Whatever. I'm glad you rolled up when you did, Ecklund. You kept a bad situation from getting a lot worse, and this can go back to being handled as a problem for the local police. They get our total support, but it is their ground. You done good."

BLOOMINGTON, MINNESOTA

The gigantic mall reminded Kyle Swanson of Arlo Guthrie's old folk song about a down-home restaurant run by a woman named Alice. You really could get anything that you want here. It measured almost three million square feet and was a commercial city enclosed within the surrounding city of Bloomington.

Kyle smiled as the irrepressible Deqo shed her worries as they mingled through the centerpiece-attraction theme park made for children, who, hollering, loaded onto roller-coasters and thrill rides that dashed amid an actual forest that was rich with trees and bushes. Multiplex movie theaters were open for afternoon shows, and upscale shops were having sales. Sharks and stingrays shared a deep-water aquarium with thousands of other salty sea creatures. Restaurants and food carts were thronged, and the smaller shops on the multiple floors all had plenty of customers. All television sets had been turned off, keeping the news coverage about the terrorist mayhem at bay.

It was life in slow motion, a place where visitors checked their worries at the door, content that they were safe inside, for the mall's twelve thousand workers and a sizable private security force was supported by the Bloomington Police Department. It made Swanson nervous, for that was not the truth in his world. Most of the security personnel were easily identifiable in sharply creased white shirts, dark trousers, and dark hats, with radio mikes on their chests and pepper spray on their belts. They were meant to be obvious. Traditional Minnesota politeness was the rule. He had a tingling feeling that someone other than a security camera was watching him.

He and Deqo followed a map's directions up to the

middle level of the three-story mall, where they found a beauty salon that was shoehorned between a jewelry store and a travel agency. Kyle had reserved an appointment for Deqo, and she was immediately taken beneath the wings of a pair of pretty young Korean women. "You are the birthday girl!" one squealed. "We will have some fun today, and make you even prettier than you already are!"

The other girl put her in the chair and wrapped a slick apron around her neck and got ready to wash her hair while the partner wheeled up a tray of instruments to work on the manicure. Within thirty seconds, they were all chattering away like old pals. It was the same at the other three chairs in the shop. Swanson felt totally out of place.

"I'm going to walk around the mall, Deqo. Call my cell if you need me, but I'll be close and back here in thirty minutes. Then we can have lunch." He wanted her to feel comfortable and safe.

"Go ride the roller-coaster, Kyle," she urged with a big grin. "Play some golf on the computer course."

"When is your birthday, Mother?" asked the beautician working at the sink.

"Tomorrow. I will be seventy-five years old on Sunday." Her response was proud.

"You lie!" the girl laughed. "I would have guessed early sixties."

Swanson had been totally dismissed from their girl world. He would go for a walk, but was too keyed up to be out of sight of the beauty salon, and would not venture to any other level. He was just another weary man waiting for a woman. There were a lot of those in the mall.

Clinton strolled into the mall with a confident stride. His tweed jacket and wool trousers blended with the crowd.

When he saw no threat, he called back to the car, and a few minutes later the Cobra entered, with Pierre fifteen seconds behind him.

Omar was pleased to see that hundreds of black, white, brown, and yellow people were in the crowd so the three of them were not the only Somalis around. He breathed in the atmosphere of the big place. He had never seen anything like this. Allah had indeed blessed him with a perfect target.

At the rich Westgate Shopping Mall in Nairobi, Kenya, al Shabaab had killed 67 people and injured another 175 over three days in September in 2013, and television carried the shocking images worldwide. Westgate would soon be considered child's play compared with the Cobra's "sword" plan. After tomorrow, Mall USA would be remembered in the history books.

He saw Clinton about twenty-five meters ahead, keeping watch all around, and Pierre meandered about the same distance behind him, leaving the Cobra to move on his own. The Volvo driver stayed near the door. They did not stare at the security cameras or at the roving security officers, and were careful to do nothing to attract any attention, although there was nothing he could do about his scars. If people wanted to stare, so be it, but he would not be here very long.

He had operatives among the mall's employees, and they had furnished precise floor plans and other vital data for the Cobra when he was planning the attack. As he walked along, he knew the layout so well that the mall felt like familiar territory. Weapons and ammo were secreted in the storerooms of busy shops and in nooks in the construction and safely stashed in the back corridors used by workers and service personnel. At least a dozen packets of explosives had been prepositioned.

That was for tomorrow. Now, where were the Sharif woman and the Swanson Marine? They had to be here somewhere. He would find them.

He folded his topcoat over an arm, strolled past the aquarium, and paused to watch fish from tropical waters swimming comfortably in a tank that had been built in the middle of a frozen land. His targets were not children, so he could bypass the attractions. They were here for a purpose, which meant the shops because it was a bit too early for the sit-down restaurants. Turning away, he passed in and around some ground-floor stores, then stepped onto an escalator and ascended to the second floor. His protecting angels arranged themselves to accompany him at a distance. The view from higher above the main floor was magnificent, for the mall was a kingdom for the imagination, and he could see more from up there.

The shoppers and tourists seemed untouched by the recent wave of pain. They were not scared. Omar Jama bought a sugary cinnamon bun and nibbled it as he casually walked along a wide aisle that was lined on one side by stores and on the other by a clear protective railing. The place was laid out like a race-course oval, with a middle space that let shoppers on the upper floors see all the way down to the centerpiece attractions on the ground. He moved to the rail to get out of the pedestrian flow and leaned on it with his elbows. It was all quite a sight. Straight across the open space was a parallel corridor where even more stores were open and serving customers. He chewed the sweet bun and looked down on the heads of the crowd below. A weekend crowd of Americans, old and new, were going about their lives. He would change that tomorrow.

He raised his eyes. On the far side was a jewelry store that had gems and polished metal glittering brightly in the artificial bright light and a sign that said the store would buy gold for the highest prices in the mall. A travel agency showed bright posters featuring beaches and bikinis and palm trees: warm locales. Getting on a plane at the nearby Minneapolis–St. Paul International Airport and being in Bermuda or Cancun within a few hours had undeniable allure.

In between those shops was a beauty salon in which women were being pampered. The Cobra froze. In the middle chair was an elderly black lady who was being propped into an upright position after having her hair washed. One attendant was vigorously toweling the wet hair while another picked at the fingernails. It was her. He tossed the rest of the cinnamon bun into a nearby trash receptacle and looked around. The Swanson Marine was not in sight, so he locked his eyes on the woman.

Deqo Sharif had almost fallen asleep in the chair while her hair was shampooed, and she was jarred awake when the chair moved to sit her up straight and a fluffy towel was wrapped around her head. The girls were still chattering around her. Deqo looked straight over the shining black hair of the manicurist and out through the window facing the outer corridor. Across the empty space, staring directly back at her, was the ugly, scarred face of a big man she instantly recognized. The man was smiling, and he slowly raised a hand and pointed his finger at her. Deqo slapped both hands to her chest and screamed, a terrible sound that froze everyone in place for a long moment, then called out in panic: "KYLE! KYLE! IT'S HIM! IT'S THE COBRA!"

THE WARNING

A COVEY OF PRETTY young girls engrossed in texting was strutting past the bench on which Kyle Swanson was resting comfortably with legs crossed and his right arm along the backrest. When he heard the shattering scream from Deqo, he was immediately on his feet, the girls forgotten as he broke into a run. He was about a hundred meters away from the beauty shop and on the same side of the second-floor hallway, and his rubber-soled boots had a tight grip on the nonslip surface floor. *Did she say the Cobra?* His right hand went to the butt of the pistol in the belt holster as he dodged through clusters of startled shoppers and slammed toward the little shop. She stood in the open doorway, a green towel draped over her head and wearing a cream-colored waterproof apron, still calling for him and pointing across the walkway.

"He's over there!" She shook her finger, jabbing across the empty space. "It is Omar Jama! Look right over there! See him? Over there, in the dark suit!"

He followed her gesture while simultaneously grabbing her and pushing her to the floor of the shop, sprawling over her on his hands and knees and pulling the weapon free. The other customers and employees were breaking from their startled silence and were about to erupt.

He saw a husky black man pushing into an overcoat and staring at him. Two young black men closed up on the man's flanks and they all moved away, gaining speed as they disappeared behind a fence of shoppers.

The crowd around the beauty salon came out of its dazed state and milled about like cows in a feed lot, anxious, unsure where to go or what to do. A man with a gun was crouching over a woman on the floor, and she had been screaming and now was crying softly. A woman security officer was fast approaching, radioing the disturbance report to the central security office downstairs, asking for backup and warily watching the position of the pistol. It was pointed up with no finger on the trigger, so she did not break stride. Swanson found his badge and held it toward her.

The Cobra looked back over his shoulder one final time. *Allah be blessed for delivering my enemies unto my hand!* Clinton and Pierre were near, getting him toward the doorway while Omar Jama ran the possibilities in his mind. He had found them, and they knew he was back, something they never dreamed would happen. *Why wait until tomorrow? Why not do it now and roll them both into the inevitable catastrophe?*

The thought arrived with startling clarity. Everything started to make sense. Swanson knew in his bones that this sparkling mall was about to become the target for a major terrorist attack. What other reason could there be for that bastard murderer to be at the Mall USA when he should have been dead many years ago? The Cobra, his old nemesis from Somalia, the killer of Molly Egan and Lon Sharif, had survived and had come to America to orchestrate a tsunami of terrorism. He was the mastermind. It had been him who gave the tip that spawned the police action at Deqo's home, and now he had tracked them to the mall. He wanted to kill them, too. It had been the Cobra all along. To Swanson, the entire mall scenario now was not a matter of *if* but *when*.

But his impulse for a chase was trumped by more urgent needs. He had to protect Deqo. Then he had to alert the mall cops to shut the whole place down to avoid certain disaster.

"What seems to be the trouble here, sir?" The question came from the neat security guard, who held a canister of pepper spray at her side and was watching the pistol. "Is this lady okay? Should I call for medical assistance?"

"She's fine. Get your boss, Officer," Kyle snapped as he held CIA credentials closer for her to read. "It's urgent."

She was in her midthirties and wore a wedding ring and an immaculate uniform with a single polished brass bar on the collar. Her dark hair was pulled back, and her brown eyes were cautious. *Keep the subjects quiet until help can arrive.* "I'm Lieutenant Parker, sir. Suppose you talk to me first, sir. Please put the weapon away."

Kyle's blood was growing hot. He holstered the pistol with practiced ease. "Lieutenant, a terrorist is trying to exit this mall right now. You need to lock it down and pour in the cops."

"Really?" She arched a skeptical eyebrow. "A terrorist?"

Deqo had collected herself and shucked out of the apron and was mopping her hair while gathering her jacket and purse. "Believe us, miss. The man's name is Omar Jama, and he kills without mercy. We have seen his evil work before. He was standing right over there two minutes ago." She pointed to the vacant space on the next corridor.

Swanson had no time to argue. "The description would be for a black male about six feet tall and with a hideously scarred face. Perhaps accompanied by two bodyguards, all of them making for an exit even as we speak. You have to stop them at the doors."

The security officer moved closer and put a gentle touch on Kyle's elbow to steer them out of the doorway of the salon, away from where the curious crowd was gathering. "No offense intended, sir, but was the identification made by this elderly lady wearing thick eyeglasses? A man seen from, what, fifty feet away?"

Swanson was out of patience. "Stop debating and get moving, Lieutenant! Aren't you even aware of the terrorist strikes over the last few days? Or have you just grown stupid in this enclosed little world?"

She remained blank, waiting for backup.

Swanson raised his voice and got in her face. "I AM WITH THE FUCKING CIA. I KNOW WHAT I AM TALKING ABOUT. NOW GET YOUR FUCKING BOSS!"

Two more white shirts hustled up. "The identification is too sketchy," she responded, backing away from his fury as the new guards, two large men, came closer.

Kyle glared at all three of them. "There is nothing wrong with this lady's eyesight. Jesus H. Christ, people. She knows the face of the man who killed her husband right in front of her. She has seen it every night in her dreams for the last twenty years. And it's not only her, because I know him, too, and I saw him! We're the ones who gave him those scars!"

An overweight male officer stepped closer. "Lower your voice, sir. You are frightening people."

"Good. They need to be frightened, and they need to get out of this place."

"Please settle down, sir," said Parker.

"There is no need to panic. We have protocols in place for this sort of thing," said a moon-faced officer. "We get crank calls all the time."

Swanson took Deqo by the arm. His next words were menacingly polite. "This discussion is over. Either you call the cops or you don't, but we are out of here. I suggest one last time that you get everybody on full alert. You don't have much time. You really don't."

"Thank you for your information, sir. We'll take it from here, and I will personally brief the major." Lieutenant Parker actually smiled. "I'll see you to the door."

Deqo turned and spoke in a sad but urgent voice to the two beauty salon employees who had been working on her. "You are good girls, and I don't want anything to happen to you. This is real. Please close up right now and leave. You are all in grave danger. Please." Her eyes rimmed with tears.

"Ma'am. That's enough," said Lieutenant Parker. "Come along."

The patrons of the salon, all in different stages of their hair, skin, and nail treatments, looked beseechingly to the shop workers, waiting for someone to tell them what to do. The chubby male officer winked. "All is well, ladies," he said. "Have a nice day."

"She's seventy-five," said the girl who had been doing Deqo's nails, and she twirled a finger beside her head to indicate the disturbed customer was unbalanced. They could not afford to let a delusional old woman cost them a half day of business and tips.

Deqo moved slowly, her soul twisted by the impending danger. She spoke softly. "Kyle, we can't just leave like this. The Cobra is going to slaughter these people!"

"There is nothing more we can do at the moment, Deqo, because they don't believe us. When I get you clear and safe, I will call Lucky." He looked at the escorting woman. "Tell your major that he will soon be fielding calls from the FBI, the police, Homeland Security, and the governor. Cops will be swarming in here within half an hour. Maybe you'll believe them."

"Yes, sir. I will relay your message."

Kyle had been unable to dent her armor of self-confidence, and she had not changed her placid facial expression by the time they reached the mall's east exit on Twenty-fourth Avenue. He said, "One last thing, Lieutenant Parker. Get a gun, and do it now. I think you're out of time."

The Cobra, breathing hard, was astonished they were not being chased by the Swanson Marine or the police. They reached the parking lot without interference. Pierre had worked the electronic key fob of the SUV, and the engine and heater were on by the time they gratefully scrambled inside.

"What just happened?" Clinton asked from the back-seat, panting only slightly from the run.

"Some people from Somalia recognized me." Omar Jama rubbed his gloved hands together and buried his nose in them for extra warmth while his brain spun in overdrive. "Without a doubt, they are even now raising an alarm. We must leave immediately."

"But no one followed us," Clinton said, scanning around the vast parking lot that was outlined in snow drifts. "We're clear!"

The Cobra was not looking for police or dwelling on

the sighting of the Swanson Marine and old woman. Instead, he was checking the foul weather, which he had to factor in to his next decisions. A chopping cold wind was slashing down from Canada, and although it was not late in the day, a band of darkness seemed to anchor the northern edge of his universe. Low, pregnant gray clouds spat new snow from horizon to horizon. He decided once again that he hated Minnesota. The conditions would make flying dicey for police helicopters, but perhaps a full-throated jet plane could bore through it to the sunshine. Ice and snow would slow down vehicle traffic. He had planned out everything that was to happen tomorrow, but it had all changed with the sightings of his pair of enemies. If he launched now, the attack might not be perfect, but it had the attractive possibility of trapping them inside.

Once they identified him, the Cobra would be hunted by every policeman in the land. Without question, the time was at hand to terminate his visit to this frozen landscape. "Pierre, go ahead and drive us out of here. Be careful and obey all traffic rules. Mix in with other vehicles as soon as possible."

"Back to the house?"

Omar Jama exhaled a long breath as he recalled the road map imprinted on his memory by years of study. "No. Things have changed too much in the past hours. Get on Interstate Thirty-five and head south, toward Des Moines."

"Yes, sir. We are going to Iowa?"

The Cobra motioned for him to drive, and they eased from the parking lot.

Swanson paused at the airlock before leaving the big mall as Deqo wrapped up to encounter the cold. Kyle had his phone to his ear, calling Lucky. It buzzed once, twice, three times. *Pick up, buddy! Answer!*

Cawelle Sharif's voice came on. "Yo, Kyle. How is the mani-pedi going?"

"Hell is about to break loose out here at Mall USA, Lucky. We just spotted none other than the Cobra in the mall."

"Cobra? *Him?* You certain?" That was preposterous. The man was supposed to be either dead or locked in a dirt prison on the far side of the world.

"Hundred percent ID by both of us. He is probably the one behind the whole series of attacks, and I think he is getting ready to hit the mall. I have tried to alert security, but they ignored me; said they could handle it."

"Mutha . . ."

"Yeah. I don't know how much time we have now. This place is a sleeping giant of a target, Lucky. I know that after spotting us, he is already in the countdown."

"Is Deqo safe?"

"We are already clear. Have a cop meet her at the hotel. You start moving, and get these security people to pull their heads out of their butts. The bus and the shootings were diversions to overwhelm the law enforcement system. The mall is what it's all about: something of 9/11 significance."

"Yeah. I buy it. I'm out." Lucky Sharif ended the call and hollered for Janna to get them a car. He headed upstairs to the SAC's office while working his speed-dial directory to begin the impossible task of stopping everything on a dime and then reorienting forces away from the Target Center disaster and the Cedar-Riverside scene and out to the Mall USA. A mall attack by terrorists was the nightmare scenario of law enforcement.

Swanson put away the telephone. "Lucky is in gear,"

he told Deqo. "He will get the cops moving out here. Now let's get you home."

They were at the mall's major ground-transportation hub, and a yellow cab was at the front of the taxi rank. The driver popped its rear door for them. Kyle helped her into the warm interior, then shoved a pair of one-hundred-dollar bills at the driver. "Take this lady to the Graves Hotel in Minneapolis and keep the change. Don't try anything stupid or think you might take a shortcut on this job. Her son is a cop, and so am I. She is to arrive there safe and sound, and you turn her over to a police officer who will meet her there. Got it?"

"Consider her there, buddy," said the cabbie, pocketing the money.

"No, Kyle," Deqo cried. "You have to come, too!"

Swanson looked into the worried face. "I can't do that, Deqo. I have to wait here and work with Lucky. Then we will both be over. It's going to be okay. Love you." Before she could protest further, he closed the door and slapped the top of the cab, calling out to the cab driver, "Go."

The yellow cab moved out, and Kyle jogged to the government sedan he had borrowed back in Minneapolis. The frigid air bit his lungs as he raced through the falling snow, dodging patches of ice, and popped the trunk. FBI cars packed a lot of equipment the normal motorist would never need. He shucked off his heavy jacket and lashed into a bulletproof vest, then lifted out an M-16. The jacket went back on, and he stuffed extra magazines into each pocket.

The Cobra received a brief call from the Volvo tracker, who said the old woman had departed in a taxi but the man was out of sight in the parking lot. Omar Jama thanked the operative and told him to leave the mall.

The job was done, and the final payment would be wired to his bank on Monday.

From his overcoat, the Cobra withdrew a pair of prepaid and preprogrammed cellular telephones, and thumbed the SEND key.

The call bounced along one satellite and two cell towers to activate another telephone hidden in a sealed box of pans behind the gas main of a large stove in a food court restaurant. The signal snapped close the connection on a powerful improvised bomb that had been made from a block of C-4. The device sparked and erupted perfectly to set off a massive gas explosion that created a rolling tower of force and flames. It gobbled up the kitchen, then blew out the thin walls and raked the seating area and swept outward, reaching for the shoppers.

While that explosion was still resounding, the Cobra dialed the second phone, which transmitted a text message simultaneously to a group of eighteen numbers and kept repeating it: SWORD . . . SWORD . . . SWORD.

Two of the numbers came up dry, but Cobra had expected a few failures. The sixteen who did receive the message were expecting it, having just been alerted by the initial explosion and the immediate screech of fire alarms. It was a day early, but that did not matter. They all dropped whatever they were doing and rushed to the hiding places in which they had stockpiled guns, grenades, and rocket-propelled grenades so carefully over the past months.

"So it begins," Cobra said. His face eased into a dreamy look of pleasure. "Now, drive on, Pierre. This is done."

THE BATTLE

MALL USA HAD a security staff of about one hundred officers, although the number on duty at any given moment was much less. Security had to be spread over three shifts a day, seven days a week, plus vacation and sick fill-ins, special details, maternity and paternity leave, and personal requests for time off. The guards covered a massive complex, both inside and out, even in the coldest weather, and scheduling was an ongoing chore for Major Kent Abramson, the security chief. There just was not enough staff to keep the place absolutely tight, and the television monitors were primarily to alert the dispatcher after something had already happened.

He was in his comfortable private office, listening to Lieutenant Fran Parker explain the incident at the beauty salon, where an alleged CIA guy had made wild claims about a terrorist attack. Both of them knew that the last emergency drill at the mall had been turned into a joke.

The merchants hated losing precious store time, so a drill had been scheduled at five minutes before closing time on a specific date, and had been announced well in advance. Even so, it had failed because the storekeepers would not take it seriously. Suddenly a guy flashing CIA credentials was claiming to have personally spotted an infamous terrorist up on the second floor, and his claim was backed up by an excited elderly woman with thick glasses.

The unusual pair had been escorted out of the mall to prevent them from instigating panic, but now Major Abramson and Lieutenant Parker were on the spot. They could do nothing and hope the guy was jumping at shadows to placate the old woman's fear, although, to Parker, he did not seem to be the jittery kind. The badge and cred pack looked real, although neither of them had ever seen CIA credentials. Even if legitimate, the man might be buckling with post-traumatic stress disorder, probably so marinated in terrorism that he saw threats everywhere he looked.

True or false? Mall USA had not been shut down in its seven years of existence. As they weighed what to do, the immense building gave a sudden lurch. The framed grip-and-grin photographs and certificates of accomplishment rattled on the major's walls, and then they heard the muffled *whumph* of the initial explosion, followed by the louder detonation of gas lines in the food court.

They exchanged looks of fear. Abramson grabbed an old-fashioned red telephone on the credenza behind him, which was a direct connection to the Bloomington Police Department. Parker ran into the adjoining communications center and ordered the dispatcher to broadcast an evacuation order over the mall's speakers. She pulled the lever for the fire alarm. Bells and horns blared. Thousands of people began breaking for the exits and safety.

Security Officer Pavel Kadyrov rushed inside the office, his eyes wide with excitement, and Fran Parker tossed him a key ring, yelling for him to open the weapons locker. The big officer with the shaved head fumbled with the keys until he found the correct one, clicked the lock, and pulled apart the twin doors of the cabinet. A selection of handguns, a riot shotgun, and an AR-15 semiautomatic rifle were arranged neatly in a wall rack beside a few boxes of ammunition and a few stun and teargas grenades. The weapons were well oiled and in pristine condition. Kadyrov knew how they worked from previous careers. He loaded a Glock 20 and stuck it into his utility belt, then pulled down the 12-gauge Winchester 870P shotgun and pushed six rounds into the black weapon.

The guard was handy with guns. He had grown up in Chechnya, where he had fought alongside fellow Muslims against the brutal Russians. Four years ago, a visitor with a Frankenstein face came through and recruited him to take his skills abroad, for a special purpose. Entering the United States on a student visa with refugee status, Kadyrov got the job at Mall USA and was studying criminal justice at a Bloomington community college. He was a solid, popular, and conscientious worker who had never missed a shift.

The Chechnyan held the long pump-action shotgun with the familiarity of a long-lost lover, racked one into the tube, brought it up, and fired into the back of Lieutenant Parker. The blast flung her onto the dispatcher at the communications console. Kadyrov cocked in another round and jammed the shotgun against the head of the startled dispatcher. The trigger pull vaporized the skull.

He had mentally practiced this vital opening step hundreds of times. With a third shell loaded, he was ready when Major Abramson opened the door to his private office. The powerful shot tore open the man's gut and kicked him back against the desk, where he slid to the floor with his life spilling away. A second shot tore into the chest.

Kadyrov reloaded the shotgun, then went around the room to kick the plugs from every electrical outlet. The place went dark, and its computers buzzed and flashed and failed. Within four minutes of receiving the "sword" order, the likable big kid from Chechnya had stopped the heart of the mall's security operation.

Other security guards were separated and isolated out on the floors, without comms or leadership, and the arriving police would now have to come in blind because all surveillance feeds had been terminated. Soon, someone would come to the security office, and Pavel Kadyrov would be waiting there with an arsenal that he had barely tapped.

Kadyrov wondered how the assault was going elsewhere in Mall USA, because it had never been practiced with all of the participants. There were others, he knew, and each person had a specific task. The explosions from the food court indicated that his comrades were already at work. Kadyrov concentrated on carrying out his own assignment and thought about the money he was being paid.

Now came the empty time between attack and response, the difference between law enforcement and military, slow versus aggressive defense. The series of explosions was easily heard in the parking lot, and as he approached the east entrance, he also heard the boom of a shotgun not too far away.

With the M-16 in the crook of his arm, he called 911. "A confirmed terrorist attack has begun at Mall USA.

My name is Kyle Swanson, and I work for the Central Intelligence Agency. I am armed and about to enter from the east."

"Sir. We already have help on the way to that location. Don't go in there." The dispatcher was curt and spoke with authority.

"I am five-foot-nine and have long brownish-blond hair. I'm wearing a black armored vest with my shield pinned to it and jeans."

"Sir. Listen to me!"

"I am carrying an M-16 and a sidearm."

"No! Wait for backup and SWAT! You can't do anything alone."

Kyle took a deep breath. "There has been a rolling explosion, and I hear gunfire. People are dying in there. I don't have time to wait." Having given confirmation of the attack and the description of himself, he signed off, unlimbered the rifle, and picked up his pace, heading for the sound of the guns. He would have to first push his way through the thick crowds that were crushing together as they made for the doors.

"Make a hole!" he shouted as he elbowed through, holding his rifle up high. "Make a hole, dammit! Get out of my way!"

From the midst of the panicking throng, a white shirt appeared and a tall security cop stepped into his path. The guard raised his canister of pepper spray, and Kyle butt-stroked him across the face. The man went down. As people surged around, Swanson grabbed him by the shirt and hoisted him back to his feet. "Listen!" Kyle shouted. "I'm a federal agent, and I'm going after the shooters. You guide people out of here and set up a triage area outside. Help is coming."

The skinny young man was wobbly, his bright blue eyes bulged, a purple bruise was forming on his cheek, and his thoughts were scrambled. The lack of training was obvious. "But it's cold out there," he protested in a strangled cry.

Kyle shoved him. "Go!" The *popa-popa-popa-pop* rattle of a machine gun opened up from high overhead, deeper into the mall. He found a stairway but was making only plodding progress because so many people were headed the other way. There must have been at least ten thousand people shopping in the mall when this thing started, he thought. It was a vast free-fire shooting gallery filled with human beings gripped in panic. He could not possibly save them all. His best option was to stop the killing at its source and bring down the people on the guns.

Another automatic weapon opened up deep in the mall, the unique rip of an AK-47. *How the hell did they get automatic weapons in here?* That was a question to ponder later, for bullets were striking and people were falling. Swanson found some free room and raced up the nearest steps two at a time, passing the second floor at a full run, ascending toward the top gallery. Screams filled his ears. Everywhere he looked, people were running for their lives, crouched into hiding places, or lying dead or wounded on the floors and being trampled by others. Glass shop windows crashed into dangerously sharp splinters as bullets sheared them like scissors.

He wanted to reach the uppermost floor, as in any battle: take the high ground and attack from the top down. A stuttering machine gun was close, and Kyle ducked lower as he ended the sprinting climb. Peering to his left, he saw that a man was kneeling and facing the other way, working an RPK light machine gun that was resting on a bipod braced on a solid stone bench. From that position at the end of the hall, the shooter had an unimpeded sight line that covered an axis that prevented anyone from trying to reach the stairs to descend. Bodies were strewn on the floor beyond him and well-dressed store dummies had spilled out from the shattered display windows of the adjacent upscale Cannes Clothing store. The victims looked like broken mannequins. The gunner was doing damage.

Kyle lifted his M-16, steadied up, and did a triple tap that paced up the man's spine, from kidneys to between the shoulders and then between the ears. The pulverized terrorist slammed forward hard against the bench, and the front of his destroyed skull emptied into a flower display. Kyle listened. That takedown had stopped the firing here, but there was more elsewhere. Another explosion as a grenade blew up in the playground far below.

Swanson pushed the body away and took over the well-chosen tactical location himself, gaining a view all the way to the far end of the corridor. From this point, the sniper could reach out and touch someone else. He noticed the dead gunman wore a blue denim shirt that was stamped with the distinctive logo of Cannes Clothing. Obviously an employee. A white strip of cloth was tied around his head.

After a quick scan around, Kyle unloaded the RPK and threw it aside, then phoned Lucky Sharif.

"We're on the way," the FBI special agent barked above the noise of the siren. "Coming in, everything we've got. How bad is it?"

"About as bad is it could be," Kyle answered truthfully. "Terrorists are slaughtering everybody they can. They control the mall. Bunch of bodies already down."

"Where are you?" Sharif recognized that the voice of his friend had tightened. He was in action.

"I just took out a bad guy with a drum-loaded RPK, up on the third floor. A Slavic-looking piece of Eurotrash. Unknown number of shooters are still active. They haven't realized I'm up here with the altitude advantage."

"Roger that. An RPK? How did that get inside?"

"You guys figure that out down the line. Also, I just heard a grenade go off. Talk to you later. I'm busy."

"Good hunting, Kyle. Hold on. I'm coming."

His M-16 was an older A2 model, but it could slam out a 5.56×45mm NATO bullet at a muzzle velocity of 3,050 feet per second, with good accuracy up to 550 meters. Swanson had expended only three rounds, so he had twenty-seven still in the box magazine, with another full thirty-round clip in his pocket. From a kneeling position, he brought the rifle to his shoulder, turned away from the chaos and the dead and the cries of the wounded, and tracked his aim around the third floor: top to bottom, side to side.

At the far end, a swarthy young man with a short beard had leaned over the railing and was showering down wild bursts with an AK-47. He was not aiming, just shooting, almost as if in celebration. Swanson took a line on him and squeezed the trigger with the gentleness born of practice. The first bullet hit the exposed left rib cage, and when he jerked around with the impact, Kyle plunged a second bullet into the soft belly. The terrorist screamed and fell backward with his own trigger still depressed as the AK continued to fire, moving under its own recoil to trace bullets up the nearest wall and into the ceiling.

Swanson realized that one also was wearing a white strip of cloth tied around his head, so it was probably a crude recognition signal. Did they even know each other? He could use that. He snatched the bandanna from his first target and fitted it around his own head. It was stained with blood but still had enough white showing to give a moment's pause to other terrorists, which would be a fatal flaw.

Kyle jumped up and ran into the destroyed Cannes Clothing store. That had been the machine gunner's easiest target because he apparently worked there, and he had shot the hell out of it. Swanson drove hard through the dress racks, leaped over debris and bodies, circled the cashier counter, and charged like a bull through a small storeroom and out the rear exit.

Everything changed as soon as he was through the portal. All of the glitter was gone, and this was the work area, the warren of hallways and storage spaces that made the mall tick. Banks of long fluorescent bulbs provided pale and stark illumination, and the bare floor was unpainted concrete. Wiring and ductwork ran overhead to allow carts and clothing racks and machinery to move about freely. Unfinished drywall was stenciled with signage that told which doors led to which shops.

Kyle stopped and was looking both ways for threats when he noticed a wide chunk of drywall that had been roughly torn away from the back entrance to the Cannes store, a hole made so recently that the bits and pieces still clung to the tape and were scattered on the floor. The hole was ragged around the edges. On the floor, a heavy canvas duffel bag yawned open and empty beside a sheet of plastic that reeked of gun oil. That had been where some weapon, probably the RPK, had been hidden, out of sight until needed. The gunner knew precisely where to find it.

Swanson turned left and moved into a fast jog down the empty hall, noting the locations of the cargo elevators and staircases as he passed. He wanted to reach the far end of the hall before cutting back out into the mall itself and coming in from a new angle, but he had to be cautious. If he could move freely back in this unseen web of corridors, so could the bad guys, who would know exactly where they were. He did not lower his guard. He did not know how many people were on the attack team, but that did not really matter. Two were already off the board, and he would just kill the rest of them one at a time, until there were no more.

THE FIRST HOUR

THE COBRA HAD spent the sheikh's funds wisely, for it was not unlimited. A top priority, even before traveling the world to enlist his assassins, was to set up primary, secondary, and tertiary escape routes from the United States for himself. Becoming a dead martyr was not in his plans.

Within an hour after leaving the mall, Pierre had driven them past Burnsville and Lakeville and was approaching the town of Faribault on I-35 as the radio reported that terrorists were attacking the Mall USA.

Traffic was sparse going south on the broad road, which had been salted and plowed. The BMW's front wheels threw a stutter of grit on the undercarriage, and the wipers stayed busy slashing at the collecting snow. The storm pushed on the car's boxy rear like wind billowing a sail. Minnesota received only about nine hours of sunlight during the day in late January, and by four o'clock, darkness was already clamping down. Headlights brightened the falling snow, and Pierre piloted as much by following the red taillights of other cars as he did by watching the dark ribbon of highway that was bordered on both sides by hefty banks of snow and ice.

There were no roadblocks on the southbound lanes, but law enforcement vehicles blazed up the interstate's northbound corridor beneath flashing halos of red, blue, white, and orange.

Omar Jama was settled and quiet on the open road, for he had no advice to help Pierre drive in such weather. When they saw the illuminated green signs for the town of Faribault, Omar Jama consulted the GPS app on his cell phone and guided Pierre onto the local streets of the small community. They went less than three miles before finding a darkened brick building that housed an enclosed long-term parking garage. The Cobra recited the four-digit entry code, Pierre punched the buttons in a little box, and the folding storm door obediently rolled up. They drove inside, and Pierre was told to park the filthy BMW in a slot adjacent to a clean Lexus.

Omar Jama climbed from the SUV and stretched, pleased to find the temperature in about the sixty-degree range. "This place is winterized, so my car should start, but you may have to give me some help," he said. The garage door, on a timer, automatically lowered itself after forty-five seconds and shut out the noisy wind. Pierre remained in the driver's seat. Clinton stepped out, walked to a steel support post, turned his back, and urinated.

The lights brightened when the door closed, and the Cobra unlocked the Lexus. He adjusted the driver's seat to accommodate his big body, fixed the mirrors, and turned on the heat, spending a few moments to study the controls. Omar was not a car guy, but this vehicle was extremely simple. He got it running, then left it idling in neutral and got out to give it time to warm up and for the oil to circulate.

"I will be changing to this Lexus now and continue on by myself. You both can return to Minneapolis and disappear. I thank you for remaining by my side during the time of crisis. It has been a pleasure to meet you. Would you like to come with me and be my bodyguards? I can promise plenty of money, excitement, girls, and power when we get to Africa."

Clinton shook his head and laughed at the thought. "No, thank you, sir. Africa is too far from home for us. We would melt in that heat."

The Cobra laughed with him. "I understand, but wanted to make the offer. So, good fortune to you both, my friends. May Allah bestow his blessings." He withdrew a Glock 19 pistol from a deep side pocket of his overcoat in a single, smooth motion and shot Clinton in the mouth, then fired twice through the open SUV window and hit Pierre in the neck and head. As the driver collapsed onto the seat, a kill shot was put into Clinton's head. It was unfortunate to have to eliminate such loyal men, but they were all expendable. He had offered them a chance, and they refused, leaving him without a choice. He would not take a chance on either being captured alive.

He put the pistol away, opened the driver's-side door, reached in, and triggered the rear hatch's latch. It was hard work to wrestle the body of Pierre down below window level, then wrestle Clinton's corpse into the wide rear-cargo area without getting his clothes bloody. He shut down the SUV engine and locked it. It should remain undiscovered for hours, probably until late morning at least—maybe days. The Cobra peeled off the overcoat and threw it into the back of the Lexus. The interior was toasty, and he wasted no more time. He backed out of the parking slot and drove to the exit door, then tapped his code into the security box while keeping his other hand over the left side of his face to stymie the surveillance-video camera. When the door was open,

Omar Jama pulled out into the weather. The door closed behind him and the cold, still night consumed the garage.

His escape route was set. Maybe a drive-thru restaurant would be open on Highway 60. The Lexus shouldered bravely into the darkness as he headed west toward Mankato, where a chartered jet was waiting to take him away, boring up above the storm and away from this wasteland of ice, snow, and eternal cold. Within a week, he would be home in Somalia, to be hailed worldwide as the new hero who had struck America a savage blow.

SATURDAY

Swanson made a quick peek around the corner and found the path clear. The door into the rear of a store that sold athletic gear hung open, and he went in with a quick roll that ended with his back to a wall. People whimpered nearby, and he wiggled over and found them huddled behind some cardboard cartons. A man on his knees was bandaging the bleeding shoulder wound of a sales clerk. "Shhhh," Kyle said, finger to his lips. "I'm a friendly. Stay put."

He low-crawled out into the sales area, through the debris, the sharp shattered glass, overturned tables, two dead customers, and another wounded clerk, whose bright yellow golf shirt was smeared with blood. A steady hiccup was popping just outside, and Swanson recognized that it was a pistol. Looking over a display case, he spotted a man with the telltale white bandanna sitting on the floor with his back to a bushy planter, concentrating on reloading a handgun. The shooter was black and slender, built like a Somali, and wearing the gray twill uniform of a maintenance crew member. Swanson had an easy aim with his M-16, waited for the reloading process to be completed, then gave a low whistle. The gunman looked around, and Kyle popped a single round into the heart area, rupturing the vital organ. The body went into the spasms of a death dance. He fell, the body braced against the potted plant.

"Yo! Friendly! Back here! Hold your fire!" A hushed male voice came from the stock room. Quiet and calm with no accent.

Kyle pulled his M-16 around to the sound. "Who's that?"

"I'm a friendly, too. Ernie Harrison. Ex–navy corpsman."

"Come out on your belly, hands first, so I can see you," Kyle growled.

Empty hands appeared in the door, followed by broad shoulders and a square face. It was the guy from the back room. The man had Minnesota-blue eyes, pale skin, and short, sandy hair. He was about thirty years old, and his long-sleeved shirt had dark stains. He squirmed forward, as if he had a lot of practice in staying low under fire. "Can I get in this fight?"

"No, but you can help. Stay here for a second. I'll be right back." Kyle waddled like a duck out of the door and scooped up the fallen pistol, a Smith & Wesson MP9L with a fresh clip of seventeen rounds, then yanked the white cloth from the man's head and replaced the stained one he wore. Returning inside the store, he handed the S & W to Harrison, who had pulled the wounded clerk in the yellow shirt to safety and was probing his wounds. "This pistol has a full clip. You work with the injured, Harrison, and check down the hallway for others. I know there are some back in the Cannes Clothing store. If I find more, I'll send them back. The cops are on the way."

"I can help you. I pulled a tour in Fallujah," Harrison said, expertly checking the clip and putting the safety on.

Kyle ruefully shook his head. "You can help more by staying out of my way and dealing with the injured. The whole mall is a slaughterhouse right now, and there are a ton of casualties out there, Harrison. You may be the only person here with any medical training, so do what you do best. But if anyone with a gun comes around, remember that these tangos all are wearing a white bandanna around their foreheads, so use that as identification and an aim point. Shoot, don't talk."

"Got it. Just out of curiosity, who the hell are you?"

"My name is Kyle Swanson, and I'm a retired marine. I think I have this third level almost under control, so I'm going down to hunt on the second floor. Good luck." Then he was out the door. One moment he was there, and the next he was gone.

Harrison thought: *Kyle Swanson. Why is that name familiar?* He could not recall. He crawled back to the clutch of wounded, pulling the clerk behind him.

The best way to save ammo was to use somebody else's bullets. Using a collapsed aisle for concealment, Swanson found still another shooter on the top level. It was an older guy who walked casually beside the railing, as if strolling in the park, taking single potshots down with an AK. White bandanna.

Swanson put his trust in the flimsy camouflage of his own white bandanna and in the fact that the enemy was not expecting opposition. He stepped out into the open and walked toward the shooter, closing the gap between them with every step. The man glanced over and recognized the white ID cloth. Although the grim eyes were afire, his rifle was still pointed down at the helpless targets. Kyle gave a quick acknowledging wave with his empty left hand to divert the man's attention even more. The puny deception could not last, so he locked into a standing firing position at point-blank range and saw the terrorist flinch upon realizing what was about to happen. Nine shots, and all struck the target: eight torso hits and one in the gun arm. Kyle ran forward, ripped away the AK-47, and snatched up an extra magazine of ammo before firing a make-sure death round into the man's temple.

Swanson slung his M-16 across his back and ejected the magazine of the AK-47 to snap in the fresh one. He would use that weapon until it was dry and then drop it and take another one.

Shoot. Move. Communicate. He had four kills on the top floor and not a shot had come back his way in return. Kyle was in his comfort zone, an elite killing machine, working with precision against an unsuspecting enemy.

Lucky Sharif and Janna Ecklund found mayhem and chaos when they arrived in the sprawling Mall USA parking lot. The bedlam that had surrounded the suicide bomb at the Target Center had spread to the mall, tripled in size, and was still growing. Hundreds of people were trying to escape, and the two FBI agents could hear gunfire ripping inside the shopping center. Moans of despair, sharp curses, low prayers, and keening shrieks rose from the clusters of civilians who scrambled toward the safety of flashing emergency-vehicle lights. Anyone who fell was trampled underfoot.

Janna snaked their car into the tangle and parked against the bumper of a police car to help create a barricade. Another car pulled in immediately behind, and civilians flopped down behind the makeshift barrier, gasping for breath, crying, many of them bleeding.

The spilling tide also pushed against anyone trying to get inside, thwarting cops and first responders. There were too many people in the way, too many people hurting, and the officers and medics and firefighters were unable to get a grip on the scene. Rescuers and victims alike were locked in stalemate, with bullets pecking at those still inside.

Lucky's personal telephone buzzed, and he heard the *bop-bop-bop-bop* of automatic gunfire before Swanson said a word. Then the sniper quickly painted a horrific picture of the shopping center being a free-fire zone, with gunmen on all three levels. The exact size of the attack force was unknown. Kyle estimated at least two hundred civilians were dead, probably many more, and an untold number were wounded. "They aren't taking hostages or negotiating," Swanson said. "They are just trying to kill as many as possible."

The terrorists wore white bandannas as identification, but otherwise looked like ordinary employees and came in all sizes, ages, and colors. Kyle speculated the guns and grenades had been smuggled in over the past months and had been hidden in the walls of the service corridors and other out-of-the-way caches.

"When are the cops coming in?" Swanson asked.

Lucky worked his way forward. "I can't give you a time, Kyle. The first people here were traffic cops, and they have had their hands full at the exits. They won't go inside unprotected. One guy tried to and was ordered to stand down, and he threw his badge in the snow. I see a SWAT team that looks about ready to go."

"Okay. Okay. Tell them to put on the night-vision goggles, then shut off the interior lights. I don't think the bad guys have NVGs. Also, the volume of gunfire seems to be slackening, so it looks like the mass-slaughter phase is done and the terrorists are shifting to find individuals and groups that are hiding. Darkness will help the victims hide."

"If it's dark, you won't be able to see either."

There was a snort that sounded like a laugh. "Don't worry about that, Lucky. They don't know that I'm here. I already bagged four of them, and they still don't know I'm here. Anyway, I like fighting in the dark. I gotta go."

"Kyle, I'm coming in to help."

"Let the SWATs do it, Lucky. We'll force these rats into a kill pocket or help them die in place. You coordinate this mess, and I don't have to explain to Deqo how you got shot right before her birthday. Check with you later." The call ended.

Immediately, Lucky's handheld radio came to life with his SAC, Hugh Brooks, wanting an update. "Imagine trying to evacuate a town of about ten thousand people through a couple of doors. That's about where we are," Sharif answered. "There are about a half-dozen first priorities, and the weather is totally brutal."

"Are the terrorists firing outside the building?"

"Not that we can see. I just got a call from Swanson, who is up on the third floor."

"Tell him to stay out of sight and keep reporting."

Lucky smiled. "Too late for that, Hugh. He has already killed four of the terrorists."

There was a pause on the other end as Brooks made notes. "Order Swanson to stay out of the way. Just report. Washington is flipping out about this," the SAC said.

"They should be concerned," Lucky responded. "It's bad. Kyle estimates minimum of two hundred dead."

Brooks wrapped it up. "The governor has called out

the Minnesota National Guard, so you can expect a lot more manpower and good vehicles soon. Homeland Security is gearing up and has dispatched helicopters. Our own Hostage Rescue Team is five minutes away, and every hospital in the region is preparing for the onslaught of wounded."

Lucky said, "I'm leaving Janna in the command center with the radio. The bad guys knocked out the surveillance cameras, and Kyle is our only set of eyes in there. We need more. I'm going in."

"Permission absolutely denied, Special Agent Sharif. You be clear on that! You stay right where you are and keep things organized. Plenty of guns are coming. I want you and Janna out of the way. Let the locals handle the entry and the fight. We are there to support them."

"Roger that, boss," Lucky said, and signed off.

He gave the operational radio to Janna, who was examining a diagram alongside a state trooper. "Brooks wants me to go in with the SWATs and link up with Kyle. You handle the liaison until I get back."

She flared. "That's bullshit, Lucky. You go, I go."

"Sorry, Janna. SAC's orders." He headed for the SWAT van to join the assault force.

THE HUNTED

FRANJO BOBAN DID not mind this kind of work. The big Serbian had done it before. Back in 1993, when he was a Scorpion with the army of Republika Srpska, the Serbians exterminated thousands of Bosnian Muslims in a valley near the village of Srebrenica. His gun ran hot back in those days, just as his Kalashnikov was steaming after an hour of steady shooting in the mall. He did not know how many men and boys he had murdered back in the valley, and he did not know the score today, either, only that it would be high.

When his side had lost that war, Franjo changed shirts and loyalties, and became a mercenary who specialized in the lucrative trade of helping various African warlords. His real name was on a list of vicious Serbs that the world wanted to arrest and put on trial for being war criminals, so he had purchased a new one. A few years ago, he had been recruited in Libya by a scarred black fellow called the Cobra, who had paid in one-ounce gold coins.

The big man had been working for seven months as a forklift operator at the loading docks of the Mall USA when the "sword" command—the signal to attack—had arrived. Boban drove his forklift to the service area, where it usually was parked, and removed a fake service panel in the rear wall. Inside the wall was the weapon he had hidden there, along with a half-dozen banana-shaped ammo magazines, all of which were wrapped in protective layers of heavy plastic. Also in the plastic roll was a white sweatband that he stretched around his forehead and a canvas bag that he looped around his belt. He ran up to the second floor and came out shooting. This was easier than in Srebrenica, and he was able to take brief breaks in his rampage, for his murders were merely a pathway to theft.

Franjo Boban alternated shooting with plundering cash registers and jewelry stores, where he would stuff money, precious stones, and gold into a simple canvas laundry bag with a tie top. Even the vaults at the high-end jewelry stores yielded to a burst of automatic fire, and then the good stuff was open to him. He planned to hide the loaded carryall in the same place that he had kept his AK, park the big forklift in front of it, and call it a day. Dump the gun and the sweatband, do some small cuts on the face and arms for blood authenticity, and then work his way outside with the crowd seeking protection and help, mingling with the actual victims so he would appear to be just another unfortunate person who had been caught in hell.

Franjo withdrew to one of the broad staircases, for the biggest prize in this section was up on the third floor, an elite shop that specialized in high-end jewelry, loose diamonds, and very expensive wristwatches, from Rolex and Omega to Patek Philippe and Vacheron. He loved merchandise that was easy to carry and even easier to sell at top dollar in Europe. The vaults were waiting for him.

He was starting up the staircase when the lights went

out, and he stubbed the steel toe of his work boot. His rifle was over his shoulder, and the bag was in his right hand, with plenty of room still inside. He caught his balance and came to a stop to allow his eyes to adjust to the darkness, recalling the path he had so often traveled around the Mall USA. After seven months of running around the place, he knew every possible route from any point A to any point B. His vision improved in the ambient light, and he began to make out some details. There was something at the top of the stairs. A person?

Kyle Swanson had kept his eyes closed while anticipating the darkness, and he actually felt a physical change when the lights went out. When he opened them again, he was able to see enough to navigate and instantly made out the shape of a large guy stumbling around on the stairs. The guy had a sack in his hand, a rifle hanging from a strap, and a white sweatband that seemed to glow as he looked up, puzzled. Swanson shouldered his AK-47, clicked the selector lever with his thumb, and, when the off-balance man recovered his footing, opened up on full automatic. He fought down the recoil and didn't bother to count the rounds he fired, because he just kept it up until the magazine was empty. When Kyle padded down the steps, he stepped on paper and objects that had spewed from the bullet-ripped shoulder bag. Money and jewels surrounded the ruthless dead man. All of this murder and a burglar to boot, Kyle thought. He tossed his empty AK and took the one that had been carried by Franjo Boban.

Security guard Pavel Kadyrov had locked the door of the main office after his initial killings, then pushed some desks together for a barricade, unlocking it again and taking a seat in a comfortable rolling chair. Kadyrov laid a pistol on the next desk, where it would be at hand if necessary, and then rested the Winchester 870P shotgun across a stack of telephone books. A white bandanna circled his forehead.

Ten more former friends and coworkers came through the portal one by one, like turkeys to the slaughter. Usually they threw open the door and rushed in to reach some safety and get a weapon and instructions from Major Abramson and Lieutenant Parker. None of the guards had deserted when the melee erupted, but they had no idea how to handle such a situation, and all they carried were cans of pepper spray and radios that no longer worked. When they entered the office and recognized an ambush, it was too late. Pavel blasted each in turn, then closed the door again, shoved the latest body out of the way, and got back into his position to prepare for the next victim. When the lights went out, he knew the easy part was over.

"FBI! Coming in!" A man's deep voice shouted the alert, and there was a loud pounding on the door, but it was not opened. Kadyrov responded with a Winchester blast that tore a huge hole through it. This was the first visitor since the lights had gone out—*no less than the friggin' FBI!*—and someone smart enough not to charge through an unsecured door. The terrorist decided to leave. There was another door in the major's office, so Kadyrov surged to his feet and reached for the pistol on the desk.

Lucky Sharif had donned a set of night-vision goggles before entering the mall, and had dashed straight for the security office on the lower floor to try to get those cameras back online. Then he wanted to organize the uniformed officers, who probably were trapped inside, and turn the office into a solid defensive block so the SWAT teams could leapfrog into action elsewhere.

As he approached the security headquarters, he stopped. A dark stain of blood had pooled beneath the door, and the opposite wall was punctured with bullet holes. Sharif put his back against the wall beside the door, pounded twice on the upper part, and yelled "FBI! Coming in!" He dove flat just as a shotgun blast exploded through the thin door and tore it from the hinges.

Lucky rolled to his stomach, pointed his Glock 22 into the room, and pulled the trigger as fast as he could. Three of the nine .40 caliber rounds caught Pavel Kadyrov in the side and back, and one severed his spine. The killer from Chechnya spun a little pirouette, his arms thrown wide and his feet tangled in the rolling chair. He was dead when he toppled to the floor.

Sharif edged inside and saw the other bodies in the embarrassing postures of death, washed in blood. Lucky moved to the man he had shot and kicked the weapons away. There was no need to check for a pulse. The FBI agent took a quick tour, preaching to himself to ignore the corpses. The comms were shot to shit, the TV screens were shattered, and clumps of wiring had been uprooted by the handful.

He took out his radio and reported back to the command center outside in a controlled whisper. "I am in the security office on the first floor. None of the officers are alive, and the surveillance equipment has been destroyed. I killed one terrorist, who was dressed as if he was one of the officers himself. He assassinated the others, about a dozen."

Janna Ecklund relayed the report to others. With the security office clear, the cops could establish a base of operations inside, Lucky suggested.

"That may still be a little while, Lucky." She hesitated to give him the situation. "We are still somewhat disorganized out here. Battlefield bureaucracy."

"Dammit, Janna. Tell them that civilians are dying every minute in this place. I still hear a lot of gunfire. They need to move!"

"I'll do what I can. You be careful in there. By the way, the SAC is furious with you."

Lucky closed off the call, then swapped to his personal cell and hit Kyle's number on speed dial. "I'm in," he said. "The tangos destroyed the security office, including all comms and surveillance."

Swanson was crouched in a doorway near a dancing pool of water on the second floor. "What about reinforcements?"

"Still gathering outside and blocking off all entrances and exits; secure the area. You know the drill."

Kyle gave a snort. "We need more shooters, Lucky. I get the feeling this is coming to the end game. These terrorists will either go down in a blaze of glory or break off the action and try to escape."

"SWAT will be in soon," Lucky said, hoping he was right. "Meanwhile, let's you and I team up. I will hold my position at the main security office near the east entrance, in the first-floor service corridor. You come to me. We'll make this a strongpoint."

"Don't shoot me."

"I have night goggles."

"Okay. I will be down there in about ninety seconds." Swanson put his phone away, stepped over the body at the bottom of the escalator, tore off the white bandanna, and unslung the M-16 to replace the Kalashnikov. The masquerade, no longer necessary, was too dangerous to continue using. Wearing a white rag on his head was just asking for bullets when the cavalry arrived. He loped over to the narrow steel steps of an escalator that was no longer moving, ran down, and went prone when he got to the first-floor landing.

This was the area that had taken the brunt of the attack, and bodies lay all around. Not individuals, but stacks of helpless and unsuspecting people who had fallen during the opening minutes, when the fusillade fell on them from above. Swanson shut his mind away from the horror, still seeing it but having to continue the fight. *Stay focused!* He came to a knee beside a little motorized railroad engine that hauled shoppers around the mall in miniature boxcars. The half-dozen passengers were dead, as was the engineer. Kyle sprinted into a darkened bookstore and followed the muzzle of his rifle back through the storeroom.

The deal the man from al Shabaab had brokered with Hector Arrado while they drank strong coffee at a Havana sidewalk restaurant the previous year was for fifty thousand dollars, paid up front, for an hour's worth of shooting in the Mall USA and another fifty when it was over. He would not be working alone but was told nothing more about the other raiders.

Just one hour, then each man would be responsible for making his own escape. Each had also been responsible for getting jobs at the mall and for hiding their weapons until needed. Arrado liked the fact that if he didn't know about the others, then the others did not know about him. The only insignia was that each man would wear a white kerchief around his forehead for easy recognition.

The hour was done, and the assault had been an indoor hell. Arrado had aimlessly shot into crowds of Americans and flipped in a couple of flash-bang and teargas grenades to cause even more confusion. This was just a good payday for the old Sandinista fighter from Nicaragua.

The Sandinistas and their former Contra enemies

now lived side by side and continued their war, but with words in the National Assembly instead of with bullets in the jungle. The peace in Nicaragua had put a lot of men out of work, and there was not much in the job market for a onetime Marxist revolutionary such as Hector. Arrado had gone to work after the war doing what he had been trained to do, whenever he could find a willing buyer—except for the drug cartels. The money was better with them, but life was much shorter.

During the mall massacre, he also had looted a few cash drawers, but was not greedy. A bag of money would just slow him down and draw attention, and it was important for him to remain mobile until he was safe outside. Arrado had entered the United States through Texas and had no intention of ever leaving America, the country he once hated with such passion. A hundred thousand dollars was more than a fair wage. A good start.

At first, the shooting had been unopposed, but Arrado had long ago learned the nuances of a battlefield, and the tempo of the attack had changed. He also was hearing a different sort of shooting, a pattern that was more deliberate. A small pistol did not have the crisp and unique sound made by an M-16 rifle. Danger might be headed his way. It was time to go.

Along with his hidden arms cache, Arrado had stowed a medical satchel with a big Red Cross emblazoned on it, and in the bag was the blue scrub uniform of a medic, including a stethoscope. He dumped the rifle and his head cloth and changed clothes. A 9mm pistol was hidden in his belt, and it was not difficult to find fresh blood to smear on his face and shirt.

He was supposed to have yelled "God is great!" a couple of times, too, but had forgotten to do that and discarded the idea of screaming anything at all now as he made his way forward. Along with the new costume, he had one more prop—a little blond boy about six years old, whom Hector had targeted in the opening volley. The child was standing at a popcorn stand that became a handy marker to help Arrado locate the body. He would make his way outside carrying a child.

Cawelle Sharif held his pistol in a two-handed grip as he stood in the darkened doorway of the security office, ignoring the corpses behind him. Kyle would be coming from the far end of the corridor, and the SWATs were expected from the opposite end. He swiveled his gaze back and forth to cover both directions and picked up a distant shadow, coming toward him from the west.

When he recognized that it was not Swanson, Lucky shouted, "Halt! Police! Get on your knees!"

The shape moved closer. It was a man carrying some burden. "Don't shoot! Don't shoot me. Please!" he called in a shaken voice without breaking stride.

Lucky brought the gun square to the approaching target. "I won't tell you again. Stop right now!"

"I'm a paramedic with the mall medical staff. I've got a badly wounded kid here, and we need to get him to safety." Hector Arrado extended his arms and offered the dead child out for inspection while he continued to shuffle closer. "He's going to die if we can't get him to help."

They were only ten paces apart, and Hector Arrado could make out the figure with the gun. It was some kind of cop, wearing goggles.

"I said stop!" Lucky called out, louder. He could clearly see the boy draped in the arms of a man in blood-stained medic scrubs, with a stethoscope hung around his neck.

"Yes. I'm stopping. But I can't put my hands up in the

air." He reached the little body out farther. "Please, Officer. He is hurt bad. I will put him on the floor."

Arrado lowered the child, then thrust his arms forward to hurl the fifty-pound body toward Lucky, who automatically wanted to catch the child. Hands now free, Hector yanked the pistol from his belt.

In the darkness, he never saw the narrow black bulk of the M-16 drop over his head.

Kyle Swanson had one hand on the butt and one on the barrel, and pulled the rifle back with all his strength while simultaneously kicking behind the right knee to drop the guy. Swanson rode the terrorist all the way down, and the built-up rage from the senseless slaughter was transmitted into his muscles. The man clawed at the rifle crushing his throat, making strained gurgling noises as Kyle tightened the grip and pulled back even harder while shoving a knee into the man's back.

The eyes of the old Sandinista bulged, sharp pain swamped his brain, the bones in his neck shattered to seal off his breath, and his spine felt as if it was breaking. His wordless burbling softened to hacking, mewling sounds, like those of a small animal at the mercy of a larger beast.

"Don't kill him, Kyle," Lucky called out. "We need a prisoner."

Swanson gave the rifle a final jerk, and the neck popped with a loud crack. "Then let's go find one," he said, and got to his feet. A sardonic smirk played across his face.

27

THE RIDE

THE LIGHTS SNAPPED back on throughout the mall with
a sudden ferocity. After the period of intense darkness, the bath of brilliant illumination temporarily blinded everyone still alive in the giant shopping
complex. Kyle hit the deck to hide his eyes, and Lucky
shouted in pain because his night goggles amplified the
sudden sun. The loud explosions of flash-bang grenades
added even more shock.

Police SWAT units burst through doors on the east,
west, and south sides, following shimmering clouds of
smoke grenades. The tactical strike forces of several different law enforcement agencies, all armored up in black
coveralls, heavy plate vests, helmets and visors and
goggled gas masks, were carrying an arsenal of weapons when they crashed into Mall USA like long black
ribbons of menacing aliens. Cops with megaphones
yelled for everyone to get down and stay down. Every
exit was blocked.

The heaviest stream of police swarmed in from the
east and fanned into a line across the first floor and advanced step by step, almost inviting a terrorist to take a
shot. The cops' guns were up and ready. The south team

immediately went pounding up the stairs to the second floor, and the west unit sprinted to the third floor, taking the steps two at a time. The former navy corpsman Ernie Harrison, tending the wounded, sprawled onto the floor and laced his hands behind his head, becoming statue-still. When he finally peeped up, Harrison saw the holes at the ends of three AR-15 barrels in his face, seemingly as large as the mouths of battleship cannons. He smiled and extended his wrists to be cuffed.

A lieutenant with the St. Paul SWAT team led another small team directly to the security office, running and shouting for Sharif and Swanson, who shouted back and held their badges high. The officer looked around at the carnage and had to fight back the bile surging into his throat. "Holy shit," he said, then clicked his radio mike and reported slowly, using distinct sounds, to be certain his communication was intelligible. "Comm Six here. Security office clear, and we have linked up with our assets."

The officer waved, and the two men got to their feet. "Are you two guys all right?"

"Why, I'm just skippy," said Kyle.

"We're good," said Lucky. "It's all yours."

"Don't kill the medic up on the third floor," Swanson added.

"We already have Mr. Harrison in hand. He's safe," replied the lieutenant.

A pair of EMT medics entered the bullet-riddled office and stepped from body to body, looking for signs of life but finding none. Fourteen civilian security guards had been shot to death in this one small part of the second-biggest shopping center in the nation.

Lucky pointed to the body of the man in the hallway. "This is one of the bad guys. He was pretending to be a medic. We need to keep his body apart from the others for forensics, and please take special care with the boy. Bastard used his corpse as a shield."

A geek squad arrived with toolboxes and rolls of cable to try and at least slave the surveillance cameras to the command and control center out in the parking lot. Sporadic gunfire echoed from various points of the shopping center as the SWAT officers and snipers engaged the remaining terrorists wherever they could be found.

The techs, firefighters, doctors, and nurses coming into the mall were veterans of emergency rooms and familiar with the dreadful types of injuries that can befall a human body. None had ever encountered destruction at such a catastrophic level. The mall had the look of a butcher shop bombed by aircraft, and dead and wounded were scattered like bloody rags. Streams of crimson blood had congealed into dark puddles. The specialists stepped over the bodies of the dead, some of whom had sustained enough bullet wounds to have been rekilled several times. The stench of death filled the air, and some lunatic terrorist had scrawled "Allahu Akbar!" in blood on the white wall of a shop that sold sunglasses and small gifts.

FBI Special Agent Janna Ecklund gave Lucky an unprofessional hug and a kiss on the mouth. "You are in a world of shit," she told him when she disengaged. He shrugged and sat down to catch a breather.

Janna called for Swanson and the SWAT lieutenant to join them. "You are a priority now, Swanson. The people in Washington want you out of here, and right now, without being identified. The press would have a field day if they find that a CIA agent was involved. So you were never here."

Kyle snapped back, "I shot terrorists!"

"They won't make the distinction. To the media,

it would be the CIA killing people on American soil," she replied. "Lieutenant, can you get him through the cordon?"

"Yeah." He looked at the sniper's lean build. "We'll put a Police Windbreaker and a cap on him and use a marked squad for transport. There are so many vehicles coming and going out of this place on a route that has been secured for emergency vehicles that he won't be noticed."

Kyle glanced at Lucky. "So we go back to Deqo at the hotel?"

"I have to stay here with Janna and deal with the aftermath and let the boss chew my ass for a while. We'll be along soon."

The gunfire in the hallways and corridors had slackened to individual shootouts. Any terrorists still alive were outnumbered and outgunned, and the police fired at them on sight if they saw a weapon. Two-member attack teams cleared the individual shops and hallways and storage areas, calling out "clear" and spray-painting a large X when they were done. It was methodical and thorough and strong. The medical crews followed along.

The lieutenant was listening to the radio in his ear and stepped outside for a minute into the main courtyard to survey the damage. He came back in, muttering, "Impossible. Impossible." His eyes flicked over to Swanson, and the cop nodded approval. "I don't know who you really are, pal, but thanks. Helluva job."

A St. Paul police car ferried Swanson away from the Mall USA slaughter, through curtains of snow and an angry wind that hissed at the windows. Officer Nellie Roper drove him from Bloomington back into Minneapolis. Roper was actually a twenty-year-old police cadet, but the emergency at the mall was of such magnitude that police departments brought in everyone with a uniform and a badge, even those who were not quite yet rookies. Her firm orders were to take this anonymous passenger to the Graves 601 Hotel, keep him away from the media, and not to ask questions; in fact, to say nothing at all. She shelved her natural curiosity and locked her eyes on the tricky cold roads, her hands gripped at ten and two on the steering wheel. The headlights showed a tunnel through the falling snow. It was not hard to keep her mouth shut, for the mystery man was locked up really tight and absolutely oozed danger. Was he even awake? The smell of gun smoke clung to him like a fragrance that she found to be sexy as hell.

Swanson was thankful for the silence. He knew that a case of after-action jitters was approaching, the period in which his body calmed and his mind would relax enough to realize what he had seen and endured at the mall, and what he had done in response. Despite the heater's being on full blast, his hands and feet were numb with cold, and his body so chilled that he pulled his jacket and the Windbreaker tight. He clamped his jaw tight when his teeth started to chatter. He had to just hold off a little bit longer, until he could reach Deqo, who would understand and let him pour it all out. Then, he could be warm again. Swanson yearned for a cup of hot, comforting coffee, and he felt the rhythm of the wheels and each shimmer of the shock absorbers.

There was a lake out there. He could smell it. Of course there was. Minnesota officially was the Land of Ten Thousand Lakes, which was inaccurate because there were really many, many more, from Aaron to Zumbra. When he looked out the side window, streaked by snow, Kyle saw the slick sheen of ice on the lake melting into turbulent water, with small, narrow boats piercing foamy waves. Fire replaced snow along the shoreline. The heat of a blast furnace grabbed him, a heat so real that he flinched. One boat turned and made straight for him. Oh, no. Not now.

"Hello." A reed-thin figure in a long and ragged black cloak spoke, with bright ruby eyes fixed on Swanson. "My entire fleet is busy tonight. We have hundreds of freshly dead to ferry into eternity."

Kyle refused to answer. If he didn't respond, maybe the Boatman nightmare would paddle away. He squeezed his fists tighter in the jacket pockets.

The Boatman continued, unbothered by the silence. He stirred the water slightly with the long oar at the stern. "Look at my boat. The rest are filled to overflowing with new passengers, while I have only these six."

Swanson knew those were the faces of the men he had killed at the mall. They were ghastly. The Boatman always came to haul away Kyle's victims.

"You only killed a handful for me! It was hardly worth the trip. I am very disappointed. Perhaps you have grown too old for our little game, and I should reconsider our relationship. You're not even a marine anymore. Why don't you step into the boat and leave your worries behind. I will allow you to sleep forever."

Swanson jerked his head sharply back and forth. NO!

"Hmm. I could insist," mused the Boatman. "But you are always a good supplier, so once you get the proper feel for your new position, you will again be a reliable harvester. We now won't be leashed by those bothersome Marine Corps regulations and rules of engagement. Actually, I foresee a future of certain slaughter now that you can operate beyond all rules; shining new numbers of souls for me to ferry home." The spectral figure giggled. "You really have no idea of the possibilities. Your new employer will let you shoot first and

ask questions later, but there will never even be ques-
tions. Finally, you will live up to your potential, and
the marine's best sniper will become the world's best
assassin."

Kyle was now sweating heavily, and he unzipped the
jacket and pulled off his gloves. His breath began to
huff to steady his nerves. He was never emotional while
doing his job, but there was always this bitter brew
waiting at the end. Then his post-traumatic stress would
be over—until the next time.

The Boatman gave a final wave and then pushed
on his oar, and the stiletto-thin craft with six dead
men knifed back to join the similar boats going to
and from the mall. *"Only six! You should have done*
better."

Swanson blinked and saw that solid winter had
returned beyond the windshield, with snow dancing
through the lights. Fire had been quenched by ice. The
dream was gone. He snarled, almost to himself, "I gave
you what I could, you bloodthirsty bastard. I, too, wish
I had killed more."

A faint call returned like a fading echo. *"I am not*
the only one disappointed with your work. Because you
did not kill more of your enemies, you allowed them to
slaughter more innocents. Look how full the other boats
are. You failed everybody."

The patrol officer had stopped the car in front of the
Graves 601, more than a bit alarmed at the strange
behavior of her passenger, who was dazed, sweating,
and talking to himself. Perhaps there was a concussion.
"You don't look too good, sir. Let me take you to the
hospital."

Kyle snapped out of it and gave her an almost invisible smile. "No. I'm fine. Thanks for the ride, Officer."
Swanson stepped into the subzero night and breathed in

deeply, then walked into the hotel. Safe at last. Tired to the bone.

SUNDAY MORNING

Lucky and Janna arrived after two o'clock the next morning, having followed a snowplow for the last bumpy mile. Deqo was asleep in her room with two blankets pulled up to her chin. Kyle was asleep in a chair facing the door, with his Colt .45 resting on a side table. Dim light was provided by a single sixty-watt bulb in the entranceway, for he had turned off all the others. It was difficult to keep his eyes open, even with the strong coffee, and he had lost that fight.

Deqo stirred when they entered, then put on a robe and came out to them. Lucky walked across and kissed her on the forehead. "Happy birthday, Grandma," he said.

The old woman smiled. Janna tossed away her heavy jacket and kicked off her boots, sat on the sofa, and put an arm around Deqo. "Birthday girl!"

Deqo Sharif burst into tears. "I saw him. I saw that devil, that evil man," she said. "What happened at the mall, Lucky? Kyle wouldn't let me watch TV after midnight."

Lucky did not sugarcoat the truth. He knelt in front of her and took her hands in his. "The last official count is more than five hundred confirmed dead, with another eight hundred or so wounded. There apparently were at least sixteen terrorists, and most of them are dead, too. Only two were taken prisoner. We don't know how many, if any, escaped."

Kyle gave a low whistle. Thirteen hundred casualties, estimating on the low side! He slipped the pistol back into its shoulder holster. "You guys look a little beat up. Let's have some coffee and slice up that birthday cake."

Deqo struggled to her feet and looked at the three strong but haggard-looking people in the suite: three people she loved, who had just endured a horrible event. "Did you catch the Cobra?"

Janna said, "No. He got away, for now. But we will find him, Deqo. That I can promise. A nationwide manhunt is under way. That's a big net."

"Janna girl, you don't know him. He survived in the slums of Mogadishu for years when he was only a child. He survived the worst prisons in Africa. Now he is back and has spread his poison and has once again escaped. You won't find him."

Kyle had his hands on his hips, and he stretched. His voice was confident. He was with his friends, and they were all safe and warm, at least for the time being. "You're wrong, Deqo. We will find him, and we will kill him. Now, let's go have some cake, and I'll give you your birthday present."

BOOK
FOUR

THE BEACH HOUSE

PRINCE FAISAL BIN Turki bin Naif could not pull himself away from the news shows parading across the big television screen in the entertainment room of his lavish home in Greece. He had never really believed the Cobra could carry out his mad plan of bombing a huge American shopping mall, but here it was, spreading before him in glorious color. Not a bad result for the modest investment made many years ago, the Saudi prince thought. He was barefoot in a dressing gown of black silk, enjoying the soft feel of the fabric against his skin. Beckoning one of his beautiful boy servants, the prince ordered a light lunch to be served poolside.

He laughed with private humor. If only he could see the faces of the old men who ran the kingdom as they learned of the property destruction and huge loss of life. They will be more shocked, he knew, when the Americans identified two of the attackers as being men from Saudi Arabia. It would rekindle the lingering suspicion held by many Americans that the House of Saud itself was tainted by Islamic jihad. Fifteen of the 9/11 hijackers had been Saudis, and that had taken a lot of explaining from Riyadh. Now this! Faisal clapped his hands

with joy and smiled with perfect teeth shining from his
slender face.

The prince had just turned fifty years old and had
been exiled by the royal family when he was only eighteen because he was gay. They could not afford to have
such an embarrassment around the court, for Sharia law
did not permit his chosen lifestyle, although sodomy
was hardly an unknown sexual practice in the Muslim
world. He was allowed to remain one of an entire unim-
portant horde of Saudi princes and would have an eternal
flow of money, if he left the kingdom forever. It was an
easy choice. He had never stood any chance of being king
or holding an important title in the family business, which
was running the entire oil-rich nation of Saudi Arabia.
So the minor prince took what the business world called
a "golden parachute." He set up a new life on a sparkling
island in Greece with the generous income that guaranteed his silence and let him indulge his fantasies.

His hand ran down between his thighs and parted
the silk, sexually aroused by the TV reports. Revenge
was nice.

Although the Islamic hard-liners hated homosexuals,
they still came around to petition him for petro dollars.
The sheikh had proved over the years to be generous
to various causes of Allah. The bearded beggars were
smart enough to never make a rude comment in his
presence, and he privately enjoyed their cowardliness.

A lifetime ago, almost twenty years, a delegation of
such hypocrites had approached him bearing a message
from his fiery old friend Osama bin Laden, who had
never criticized the sheikh. Both were unwanted by their
families. Osama wrote that he had discovered a young
man of great promise who was being held in a Kenyan
prison after being captured by the Americans in the
eternal fighting in Somalia. The boy had merit, Osama

thought, and the al Qaeda mastermind was looking for someone to sponsor him. Faisal agreed to develop the prisoner, whose name was Omar Jama, to become a future jihad leader. His nickname was "the Cobra," which appealed to the sheikh. Money exchanged hands. Wardens and guards were paid to protect and assist the badly damaged young prisoner, and he was trained to discipline his mind, repair his body, and stoke his anti-American fury. A total weapon was constructed.

They finally met some nine years ago, and Prince Faisal had been pleased with the product. The Cobra had come out of ten years in prison a much more mature man than when he went in; being forcibly removed from the battlefield had saved him for something better. The man from Somalia was a burly beast, blacker than anyone the prince had ever seen, with a deeply scarred face and a burning hatred of the United States of America. There was never a doubt about the Somali's bravery. Faisal was not even tempted to try and have sex with his protégé; the man was much too ugly.

The released prisoner had given almost another ten years to the wars in the Middle East to fine-tune his killing skills, before finally striking the United States, just as he had promised. The resulting massacres in Minnesota had been beyond all expectation, and Prince Faisal bin Turki bin Naif had wreaked havoc on the House of Saud, which had shunned him. Omar Jama deserved a fine gift, but the man was already on his way back to Somalia. The prince could think of nothing that would be appropriate for him in that dung pile, certainly not a case of fine champagne. So just some more money then, in that Swiss account.

The storm blew itself out overnight, so dawn allowed a bit of hope to seep through the departing clouds. The sun cast only feeble rays, as if reluctant to expose the Mall USA carnage, and it did little to expel the frigid temperatures. Kyle, Lucky, and Janna had rotated guard shifts in the living room while Deqo slept soundly with the help of an Ambien. Sunday would be better than Saturday, simply because it couldn't be any worse.

Swanson and Lucky were in Washington by noon for a top-level briefing in the White House Situation Room. Every security agency of the government was grinding away on the series of attacks that culminated with the Mall USA bloodbath. The ten men and two women around the table had been studying a river of data throughout the morning; they had a million questions and no answers. The eyewitness accounts of the pair of CIA and FBI agents who had been there jolted them all. The mood worsened even more when Kyle predicted with certainty that the Somali terrorist known as the Cobra was responsible and described the man's pathology and background.

"Is it over, do you think?" asked a worn-looking man in a wrinkled dark suit. It was the vice president of the United States, who had been up for almost thirty hours straight. The current meeting had been going on for more than two hours before the government jet carrying Swanson and Sharif landed at Reagan National, where a waiting black limo had met them for the rush trip across the Potomac River to 1600 Pennsylvania Avenue. There, they had been grilled for almost another full hour.

"Is it over?" Kyle repeated the question. "Who can tell, sir?"

"Give us your best guess, then."

"He knows that we have identified him, sir, and apparently he is on the run. Without him to supervise the operation, and given the increased police presence and alerts throughout the Minnesota area, this particular set of strikes is probably finished. I could very well be wrong, but you wanted my guess."

"Very well. And you are sure it was him? No mistake on that?" That question came from a man he did not know.

Swanson had a brief vision of Molly Egan and a bloody night in Somalia. "It was him."

Lieutenant General Bradley Middleton, at his elbow, knew the background. With a growl, he said, "Swanson can personally recognize the man."

Lucky Sharif interrupted to add, "My grandmother also identified him. There is no doubt whatsoever."

The vice president said, "Well, ladies and gentlemen, let me summarize. The attacks may be over. We know who is responsible and are sparing no effort to find him. For now, we focus on that and plan how to take him down without enlarging the crisis. We cannot allow the wanton and horrible acts of this one mad terrorist to lead us into an even larger disaster, or have the nation panic, and the last thing we want is to get snared in the Somalia quagmire again. There has to be another answer. You people find it."

The meeting ended, and General Middleton, Kyle, and Lucky walked over to the Old Ebbitt Grill on Fifteenth Street Northwest, a half mile from the White House, for lunch. There was a crisp wind, but after the icebox conditions in Minnesota, Swanson and Sharif considered it to be more like a mild breeze.

"So where is this son of a bitch?" Middleton asked as they left the gated grounds, watched by uniformed Secret Service guards.

"Logical thing will be for him to try and get back home to Somalia," Lucky said. "He will be protected there, and he now automatically is in a position to become the ultimate warlord. Cobra does not think small.

I think his primary goal is to take over the government with an al Shabaab revolutionary force."

"If he can pull that off, Islamic fanatics everywhere will start considering him to be the new Osama bin Laden, rally to him, and set Africa afire," Kyle said. "Then he will be in a position to get the other offshoots of Islamic terrorism in the Middle East to deal with him."

Middleton tugged at his gloves and turned up the big collar of his overcoat. "The question is what to do about it."

"You already know the answer, General. Send Lucky and me after him."

Sharif agreed. "The two of us are wasting time sitting in meetings in Washington, General Middleton. This Cobra's level of barbarism is extraordinary, and he is gaining strength by the minute as the world sees what he has done. I was only eight years old when we caught him before, and I could do it better this time. Give us permission and let us cut the head off of this damned snake."

The Cobra, the most wanted criminal in America, strolled in casual comfort along the Venice Beach boardwalk and let the California sun thaw his bones while he took in the extravagant showiness of the busy beachside area. Artists, clowns, muscle builders, girls in bikinis on roller skates, and kids doing tricks on miniature bicycles all existed in their own little bubbles of life. The Pacific Ocean undulated, surfers were out on the waves, sunbathers were on the beach, and a line of tall palm trees lined the sand. The little restaurants were busy. Colorful murals and graffiti decorated the walls. A lone black man wearing a blue Dodgers cap and wraparound shades was not interesting enough to draw the notice of any of the beach denizens. A cop on a bike rode past without a glance.

He had been walking for some time to find an address he had memorized from the intelligence file that he had had gathered over the years by private detectives, whom he hired anonymously. The details of the place were seared into his brain. The only surprise was that it was so easy to locate—right off the boardwalk. An older couple, both with silver hair, were on a second-floor deck that faced the ocean, leaning on the white railing, joking with each other. The man laughed. This was a wealthy piece of real estate. The owner had purchased two adjoining lots, torn down the existing houses, and replaced them with a single modern home.

A block past the building, Cobra veered off the boardwalk, found the frontage road, and doubled back. The house had a formal entrance on that side with a manicured patch of grass, some spiky bushes, and evergreen shrubs. He pushed the bell and a pleasant *ding-dong* echoed through the place. He heard footsteps as someone came downstairs. The woman answered and raised her eyebrows in question. "Yes?" She was an artist and was totally relaxed in his presence.

Omar Jama held a large white envelope and lifted it to read a label. "Mrs. Larisey Walden? I'm a private courier from the Gallery Falcone."

"Yes, that's me." She was excited. Several of her works had been sold by the Falcone. Perhaps this was a new commission. She opened the door, and the Cobra punched her hard in the face. Larisey Walden went reeling back hard into the wall.

He followed the punch inside, shoved the door closed behind him, then kicked the woman in the head. Dropping, he clamped his big right palm over her mouth and pinched her nostrils closed with his left hand. It took less than a minute for the unconscious woman to die.

The Cobra moved quietly through the living room

and into the kitchen, where a rack of cutting tools hung on a wall. He chose a gleaming nine-inch butcher's knife and waited beside the stairs.

The man came down, calling out, "Larisey? Who was that? I heard a noise."

Omar Jama waited until the target stepped clear of the wall, then smashed the man with a punch to the ear that sent him crashing to the floor. The Cobra stabbed the point of the knife into the back of the neck just below the skull and pushed it smoothly through the spinal cord and into the brain. The body struggled, stopped.

The Somali terrorist got up and finished the tour of the house, checking himself for bloodstains. He washed his hands. Then he gathered a propane gas tank from the deck, oily rags and aerosol canisters from the garage, and cans of paint and solvent from the artist's upstairs studio. Most of it went into a neat pile on the king-sized bed, which he soaked with the flammable liquid. The remainder he carried down to the ground floor, splashing the walls and furniture. He lit a set of three candles on the mantelpiece, then went to the kitchen and stripped the gas line from behind the stove. As soon as he heard the hiss and smelled the fumes flowing into the room, he left.

The Cobra closed the front door behind him, adjusted his cap, and returned to the boardwalk, where he found a bench about two hundred meters away and sat to watch the waves. Within minutes, the pretty house detonated in a thunderous fireball that threw debris in a wide circle and then burned to the dirt. He turned to watch, as did everyone else along that section, and eased away in the growing crowd, whistling a tune. The house had been the property of the Marine Swanson.

THE COLONEL

LIEUTENANT GENERAL MIDDLETON was known for his iron courage. Today, flocks of butterflies nervously flapped around in his gut. His bold idea could slide sideways in a hurry, but part of his job as deputy national security adviser was to speak truth to power.

He had been granted ten minutes alone with the president of the United States, who had been catching political hell about the terrorist attacks that had happened on his watch. The most powerful man in the world stood at the paned door of bulletproof glass that overlooked the Rose Garden from the Oval Office, weighted with sorrow and anger. Members of Congress were content to complain on television without offering a solution, whining without responsibility.

With no time to waste, the general started right in. "Mr. President, we have to take this guy down fast."

The president turned slowly. "I totally agree with the first part of your statement. It's the second part—*fast*—that has me stumped. We don't even know where this monster is."

Middleton was standing in the center of the carpeted

office with his big hands folded. "He'll turn up, sir. Sooner or later. Somewhere."

"Tell me something that I don't know, General Middleton."

"I've been mulling this over since you said in your speech last night that all options are on the table."

"And I mean it."

"No doubt in my mind that you do, sir." Middleton shifted his body slightly and glanced over at the fireplace, where a few burning logs were casting unneeded warmth into the climate-controlled room. "Let's say that he surfaces back in Somalia, which I believe is likely. Going after him there is going to be difficult. Full military intervention by the U.S. is out of the question, and any air strike, even a drone attack, will likely result in a lot of collateral damage, meaning that civilians will die."

"That madman killed civilians in our country. He cannot hide behind his own people now and expect us to give a damn. We don't."

"And that is the blank space, isn't it, sir? Somalia did not attack us. One single crazy maniac with a few helpers and a handful of hired guns carried out the murders. Many of the attackers were not from Somalia at all; some were from as far away as Nicaragua and Saudi Arabia. If we bomb the hell out of that lawless dung pile called Somalia, we will lose the sympathy of the world and our allies, while our enemies would have a propaganda field day. If any of the pilots are captured, they will most likely be executed on television. That can't be ruled out."

The president went back to his desk, where piles of material awaited his attention. "You are just stating the obvious, Brad, so I assume it is only a prelude to why you really wanted this time. You have a suggestion?"

"I suggest that before we roll out the big artillery, I be allowed to launch a small operation outside the normal chain of command. If it goes sour, then you can deny any involvement and paint me as the rogue general that did it without authorization."

"You want to put Kyle Swanson into play, don't you?" the chief executive replied without enthusiasm, raising an eyebrow. "The answer is no. You want to replace the big artillery with a loose cannon. Your time's almost up."

"Right. Consider, sir, that not only is Swanson the best we've got, but he has a couple of personal dogs in this fight. He will push it through and kill the Cobra no matter what is required."

The president sat in his big chair. He pressed a button on his desk telephone and said to his appointments secretary, "I'm taking another ten minutes."

"Yes, sir. The chief of staff is waiting, sir," she said.

"Ten more minutes." The response was firm.

The president steepled his fingers as he leaned back and closed his eyes and took a deep breath. He had to admit to himself he had been more comfortable when Gunnery Sergeant Kyle Swanson could be dialed up to carry out a directive. "Personal? How? Have a chair, Brad."

"Absolutely." Middleton quickly touched on how Swanson and the Cobra dated all the way back to Somalia, the murder of his Irish fiancée, the relationship with the family of FBI Special Agent Lucky Sharif, and the fresh news that the Cobra had burned down Kyle's beachfront house in California, killing the man and woman who leased the place. "One reason the Cobra came to America was a desire for personal revenge, sir. He wanted to draw Swanson out. I say we should grant his wish."

"Swanson is with the CIA now, correct? Why not just let the agency handle it with its normal operations? If they can find this guy, I will happily call in the SEALs or shoot a Hellfire missile up his ass. Pardon my language."

"The possibility of leaks, sir. Security clearances no longer guarantee secrecy. Swanson and Special Agent Sharif would be a formidable team on this specific mission. No extra training would be involved. They know the target."

"And you believe we can do this on the quiet?"

"Yes, sir."

The president barked a short, ironic laugh. "We shipped Swanson off to obscurity, and he still ends up in the middle of things. A onetime thing?"

"Then Kyle and Lucky fade back into their regular jobs."

The man behind the big desk thought a long moment. He still wasn't sold.

"Mr. President. Kyle Swanson is going after the Cobra no matter what you or I say. If we don't use him, he will just quit the government and do it anyway. Let's help him succeed."

The president leaned forward and planted his elbows on the big desk. The clock was ticking, and he had to move to other things. "If he fails, you may have to fall on your sword, General, and I don't want to lose you from my national security team."

Middleton brushed his stiff mustache with a finger. "It won't come to that, sir. These are two avenging angels willing to take down a monster, and I will make sure they have whatever they need through the Joint Special Operations Command."

The president lightly knocked the wood on his desk. "Anything else other than give you a green light?"

"Nothing else, sir. Buy us some time while you examine all possibilities. You may even find something better, although I doubt it. In the meantime, Swanson will go after the bastard."

Omar Jama went to Mexico aboard trolley car number 1053, a comfortable fire-engine-red electric people mover that whisked him out of the quiet Santa Fe railroad depot in San Diego for the sixteen-mile trip south. It ran all day. The ticket, which he bought at a vending machine that did not ask questions, cost a dollar and twenty-five cents because he was leaning on a cheap cane and was considered disabled.

At the San Ysidro crossing, he debarked with dozens of tourists. Automobiles driving into Mexico were crowding up along the interstate highway gates, where alert Immigration and Customs Enforcement officers were watching everyone passing their posts. A picture of the Cobra was posted in all of their cubicles. The trolley crowds were unmolested. Smiling and joking with the party people, shopaholics, and other travelers, Omar Jama, the most wanted man in America, left the country by walking casually through a full-length revolving turnstile and stepping across the yellow and black stripe that marked the border. Some twenty-five thousand other people would do the same thing before the day was done.

A stylish straw hat was raked low across his forehead, and he wore dark aviator sunglasses with a pullover shirt and khakis. For the next minute, he stayed with the crowd as it moved through a lightly guarded quarantine corridor staffed by a few Mexican Army soldiers who carried weapons. A young American with a bald head and a helmet of tattoo ink was the center of their attention as they pawed through his bulky backpack, looking for drugs, fruits, guns, or grain. He looked suspicious. The Cobra did not.

No one asked the Cobra for his passport or any identification, and those would only be examined if he came back into the United States, which he did not intend to do. He kept pace with the steadily moving, lighthearted throng, and the quarantine zone ended as quickly and easily as it had begun. He pushed through a second revolving gate and a multitude of taxi drivers called out in English to offer their services. He chose one and got into the little clean vehicle that had a plastic Madonna on the dashboard.

"Avenida Revolución?" asked the driver, a somber man of middle age whose thick black hair was combed straight back.

"No. Take me down to the Rosarito Beach Hotel, please," the Cobra said politely.

"Ah. Okay. Some warm lobster tacos and cold *cerveza* for lunch, eh, my friend?" The car started to move through the heavy traffic.

"Something like that," Omar Jama answered.

Lucky Sharif of the FBI had never been inside the Central Intelligence Agency. He felt like a child who had wandered into a candy factory. No wonder he had almost had to sign an oath in blood to get through the front door. Swanson just slid a plastic card from his wallet, swiped it through a machine, and stepped through. Lucky received a visitor's tag that he clipped to the pocket of his suit jacket.

A quick elevator ride dumped them on the third floor, and Kyle led the way to an unmarked door, which he unlocked with his little card and pushed open to enter a semidarkened room that seemed to glow. "Hello, Marty, everybody," Swanson said conversationally, as if they saw each other daily. "This is Lucky Sharif from the FBI."

There were glances and grunts, but everyone remained in their chairs, watching the six large computer screens on the far wall. An operator was at his console, an organlike contraption with multiple decks of keyboards and towers. The man had a shaved head and big glasses that amplified his vision. Sharif thought that whatever the CIA analyst was doing was eating entire clouds of disk space.

"You find the Cobra yet, Marty?" Kyle asked, taking a rolling chair. Lucky found another and pulled it forward. He noticed they were all in casual civilian clothes, while he was in full FBI dark-suit-and-tie regalia.

"We're not looking for him." Marty Atkins, the deputy director of Clandestine Service, brought them up to date. "The last sighting was at your house in Venice. Odds are, he is already beyond Mexico by now. He'll turn up soon enough. The Behavioral Science people at the FBI agree, don't they, Lucky?" With a single question, Atkins smoothly bestowed CIA legitimacy on the outsider.

Sharif was still going over the busy boards. "Yes. They say that he will want the entire world to know that he is the one who carried out the attacks. He is a megalomaniac, and needs the credit to prove his power and greatness."

"I think he is heading back to his rat hole in Somalia," added the deep voice of a balding, middle-aged man on the far side of the room. "The man who would be king. Show us the big map, Bob."

The operator pulled up a map of northeastern Horn of Africa, then tightened it to just Somalia. The screen sliced, and he added a photograph of a man in military uniform.

The man spoke again. "I'm Paul Graham, by the way, the lead on this project. The Somalis are busy forming a parliamentary system of government, complete with a prime minister and a cabinet and all that malarkey. This is the man with the real power, the commander of the armed forces, General Mohammed Ahmed. Strip away the political trappings, and he is the top-dog warlord in the country right now. The good news, for us, is that General Ahmed is not going to roll over and give up power just because the Cobra would like to take his job."

Lucky shifted his position before he spoke. "I know about him from my work in the Somali community, and it boils down to the same old tribal story. This general is of the Abgal Hawiye clan. Cobra is Habar Gidir, so there is an automatic hatred and distrust. The general has the local guns, but Cobra will now have the mystique: local boy makes good. He has to gather fighters on his own, which will take time."

"Right. That works for us," said Graham. The hum of the secure computers was like background music. "If we move right away, you guys might be in place when the Cobra comes up for air. He has half a world to travel and knows that we might be waiting around every corner."

Marty Atkins spoke. "Let's get out of this dungeon and into the sunlight of my spacious and gilded private chambers and drink some coffee and make a plan. Bob, you stay in here and do whatever the hell it is you do. You will not get sidetracked by playing Mario Kart Five or Call of Duty Twelve."

The operator sneered back. "Right now I'm looking for the money. Always follow the money."

THE MESSAGE

THE TAXI DRIVER in Tijuana had been correct. The lobster tacos from the kitchens of the Rosarito Beach Hotel were delicious and spicy, and a chilled pitcher of sugary fruit juice topped it off. The Cobra ate and drank his fill in a comfortable room on the seventeenth floor. True, he had room service instead of dining in the bright Azteca Restaurant, but at least no one could see him, and he had a view of the beach and the water. Moving around the room behind him, talking on the phone, was Hassan Abdi, who had fled the United States several days earlier and had rented adjoining suites for them under false names. Now the Cobra had travel documents, and all of the requisite bribes had been paid.

"You look tired, brother," Hassan said. "Crossing the border when you are a wanted man required great courage."

Omar Jama finished the glass of sangria. Ice cubes clinked in it. "I am fine. When do we leave?"

Hassan looked in a pocket notebook that he used because he distrusted the security of electronic devices and believed too much information was already out in the e-world. "I have a private car to take us out to the General Abelardo L. Rodríguez International Airport in time for the four-thirty Volaris flight to Mexico City. Since it is an internal trip, there will be no customs or immigration checks."

"Do I have time to rest a little first and take a shower?"

"Yes, sir." Hassan turned a page. "We overnight at the Hilton Hotel at the airport down there, then leave early tomorrow morning at eight forty-five a.m. aboard Cubana. An immigration official and his partner will be around to clear the paperwork and escort us aboard."

The Cobra put down the sweet drink and examined the rich blue passport, which read in gold letters: "Pasaporte" and "República de Cuba." It was a worn document that had passed through many hands and contained the stamps of someone who flew frequently to the countries in Central and South America. An accompanying manila envelope contained a sheaf of supporting documents, business letters, contracts, and receipts. "I am a citizen of Cuba, a weary investor returning home from another successful road trip."

"We will be in Havana shortly after noon. Our friends there will protect us." Hassan closed his notebook and smiled at his brave friend. "We did it."

Kyle Swanson and the team met regularly over the next few days, deep in the CIA building, designing a snare to trap the Cobra. Folders, prisoner interrogations, maps, and electronic data were studied over and over without substantial discovery of his next move or his ultimate intent. Guessing what was in the mind of a mentally unbalanced killer was a roll of the cosmic dice, for Omar Jama himself might be playing it minute by minute.

"This is all yesterday stuff," Kyle said, frustrated with

the lack of progress as he looked through the reports. "Everything in here is dry history. We have to lean forward, not get stuck in paperwork."

Paul Graham rolled his fingernails along the desktop in a staccato that had the rhythm of a horse crossing a bridge. "We've learned some things, Swanson. It's not a waste."

Marty Atkins was relaxed, with his glasses pushed up on his forehead. "We identified one of his bank accounts, although it is under another name, and I could have the State Department get the Swiss to freeze those funds. I decided not to, because it might be a valuable information pipeline. The last deposit was for one hundred thousand dollars from a minor Saudi sheikh who lives in Greece. The House of Saud will slam him hard when we share that news, and he may not live through the experience."

"The Cobra is going to be rolling in terrorist money after these attacks," Kyle complained. "Plus, Iran, Syria, Egypt—you name it; they will all be throwing cash at him."

Swanson leaned back. "We've learned all we can from his tracks, people. We can't stick around here any longer."

"He could be anywhere," warned Graham.

"It will be Somalia," Swanson said with great certainty. "Marty, we need for you to whistle up some air transport to get us over to Jeddah as soon as possible."

"What is in Jeddah?" asked Atkins. The city was a Saudi port on the Red Sea.

Kyle explained. "The *Vagabond,* a private yacht that will take us to Somalia. It was already in the Med on business when the attacks happened in Minnesota, and it immediately changed course. She cleared the Suez Canal last night and will be waiting for us."

Paul Graham blinked. "The *Vagabond*? Is that one of ours, Marty?"

"No." Atkins pointed to Swanson. "It's his."

"Oh." The surprise was minimal. After thirty years in the CIA, very little surprised Graham, but he had never actually known anyone who owned a yacht. He looked at the sweep hand of the clock on the wall. "It will take a little time to nail down a flight. Be at Andrews in the VIP lounge about nineteen hundred."

Kyle looked at his friend. "Consider yourself operational as of now, Lucky. We do not tell Deqo or Janna, and Marty will alert your boss. This is strictly need-to-know."

The long-expected announcement from the Cobra was recorded on a laptop computer that was propped on a beachfront table at a small restaurant on the Bahía de Cochinos, a scuba-diving spot on Cuba's Zapata Peninsula, a resort popular among sportsmen around the world for its warm and crystalline waters. It was also known as the Bay of Pigs.

Viewers saw a husky black man wearing a lightweight shirt and a broad-brimmed straw hat with a thin veil attached to the front brim, both to keep away mosquitoes and disguise his image. The voice was deep and confident.

"My name is Omar Jama, and I planned and carried out the attacks on America in the state of Minnesota. The infidel government of the United States did worse—much worse—to my homeland of Somalia some twenty years ago during a crisis of famine. When we needed food and clean water and medicine and refugee assistance, and while international aid sources responded with kindness and compassion, the United States invaded with tens of thousands of their soldiers

called marines to pillage and punish our poor country solely because of our religious beliefs. We are Muslims. So Washington now dares to call me a terrorist. I call them mass murderers."

With excruciating slowness, he removed the hat and veil and rested it on the table. He removed a dental bridge, used both hands to slide away the large dark sunglasses, then remained motionless, staring into the camera lens. The sharp white scars across his face, the bent nose, the missing teeth, and the white orb of his blind eye.

"The Americans say they do not torture. That is a monstrous lie. My entire family and my friends were slaughtered, and I was given this horrible face by a U.S. marine. Then I was cast into the darkest, most vile prison you can imagine, without charges or a trial. While I rotted in CIA dungeons, my country of Somalia was mercilessly raped and ravaged by the blood-hungry marines." He paused and took time to put his teeth back in, and then the glasses and hat back on. The veil was lowered, and the baritone voice continued.

"For twenty years, I have thought about nothing else but how I must take revenge for what America did to me, to my family, and to my countrymen. The armed forces of the United States slithered away like cowards after my brothers finally were able to rise up on the Day of the Rangers and make the American military atone for their sins. The U.S. took its wars against Muslims elsewhere, but never stopped.

"My dear friend Osama bin Laden struck back with the only weapon we really possess, which is to attack the United States itself without warning. He is dead. Murdered, of course, by Americans." Viewers saw the mouth curve into a smile.

"But I, Omar Jama, am alive, through the mercy of

Allah and his Prophet Mohammed, whose name be praised. My message to my countrymen today is to keep your hearts strong and prepare to rise up and overthrow the tyrants who rule Somalia today. They are nothing but political puppets of the United States. We have suffered for twenty years. That is long enough. I will return home soon and lead the battle for true freedom

"So here is my message to Americans. I am recording at this place, known to them as the Bay of Pigs, where an attempted CIA invasion of Cuba was hurled back into the sea in defeat. Later, the Americans would also run from Vietnam, and are scorned around the world today as being clumsy paper tigers. Even as I make this video, they remain bogged down in Afghanistan in their longest war, unable to even defeat a handful of mountain tribesmen. Soon they will leave there, too. History has shown that, far from being safe, the international adventures have left Americans in greater danger than ever. I proved that last week.

"The citizens of the U.S. share the blood that is on the hands of their soldiers. Your time has come. You may live in a small town or in a big city, be at home with your family or at a shopping mall, or perhaps you are touring abroad. My warning is a prophecy; look over your shoulder. Your armies and police cannot protect you. I am the Cobra. I am coming for you."

Since Cuba did not have the necessary wireless network for a broadcast from the beachside bench, the video was smuggled into Florida, only ninety miles away. From the communications hub in Miami, it was posted to a half-dozen social media sites. It drew millions of hits and was downloaded, shared, and passed around on the Internet as a mega-popular happening. It went everywhere. The laptop from which it was sent was destroyed and the pieces thrown into a canal beside the

Tamiami Trail. By then, the Cobra was no longer in Cuba.

The *Vagabond* swam smoothly through the Arabian Sea after having charged through the pirate-infested Gulf of Aden like a speedboat on steroids, with its pair of 3,240-horsepower engines wide open. Although it showed as a blip on some pirate radars, none could respond fast enough to pose any threat, and the 180-foot-long brilliant white yacht reached the safe channels patrolled by the warships of many nations without incident. Even if one of the little boats of terrorists had somehow managed to stage an attack, it would have discovered this particular pleasure vessel had very sharp teeth, including a pod of ship-killer missiles and a well-supplied armory for a crew made up of a dozen former British special forces operatives.

It belonged to Excalibur Enterprises, the London-based global business of which Kyle Swanson was now in the process of becoming executive vice president. The only passengers aboard were Kyle and Lucky and the quiet CIA communications guy simply known as "Bob," who had been yanked out of Quantico for this mission.

All of them had watched the Cobra's self-serving announcement so many times that they could almost recite it from memory. It disgusted Kyle, and he went on deck to let the fresh air clear the cobwebs. Bob was already at the rail, drinking a cold beer with his sunglasses pushed atop his shaved head, and he spit overboard.

"Don't let that bastard get to you," said the quiet spook. "We were expecting him to sound off."

"It's all such bullshit, like he was just some innocent little guy that was swept up and horribly mistreated by the big, bad American military. Like he didn't do anything to deserve even being arrested."

Lucky Sharif joined them in midconversation. "A lot of people are buying his crap version of history. A terrorist gets a worldwide following with the click of a DOWNLOAD button. That just ain't right."

Bob turned and gathered his thoughts. He was a tall, thin man who was about thirty years old and had been drafted by the CIA out of Silicon Valley, where he had made a lot of money but had become bored. "From what I've seen, this Cobra is a smart dude, Kyle. Best not underestimate him. He has spent a lot of years figuring this out."

Kyle decided to bring Bob in on the background. "Twenty years ago, he murdered the girl I loved by sticking a machete through her chest. He murdered Lucky's grandfather that same night. We took him down hard, and I beat the crap out of him. Now he pops up again like a bad dream with all of these lies."

Swanson had spent a lot of alone time on the voyage thinking about that encounter in the Mog and the terrible death of Molly Egan. It had happened back in 1992. That was ancient history for many people of today, including Bob, who was about ten years old when the savage chapter of the Somalia relief mission was written in blood.

The Cobra was reaching out to the young generations and filling their brains with distortions they would never challenge. The official denials from Washington rang hollow. The Cobra had created a web of fiction about the past, and people were falling for it.

"Social media can be a bitch," agreed Bob. "The bottom line is that he really doesn't like you." Bob tipped back his beer, crushed the can, and tossed it overboard.

Swanson watched the little container sink in the water, and his mind was pulled away from the pit of helpless anger by the distant beat of an approaching helicopter. The white aircraft bearing the golden logo of Excalibur Enterprises was returning. It had left the yacht several hours ago to fetch some supplies and a team of CIA shooters that had been assigned by Marty Atkins. Kyle knew both of them from other assignments— Ingmar Thompson and Bruce Brandt. They had been killing terrorists in the Afghanistan badlands when they were tapped for this temporary assignment.

The helo flared to a stop over the stern helipad, matched up with the moving deck as the vessel crested a rolling wave, and touched down without a bounce. Crewmen immediately tied it down fast, the pilot cut the engine, and the door slid open. Kyle recognized the big frame of Ingmar Thompson as soon as he appeared in the hatch. Thompson jumped easily to the deck, where he dumped his travel packs. Brandt, smooth as a shadow, came out next.

Thompson spotted Kyle and shouted, "Where's the bar?"

31

THE RETURN

IN THE WARPED mind of the Cobra, there remained no doubt that he would soon be hailed as the newest hero for Islam. His recorded manifesto and the startling image of his damaged face would inspire Muslims worldwide to rise up in righteous anger and anoint him as their leader. That he could not now make a move without worrying about being tracked by the United States government did not register as a liability to him. Once he reached Somalia and was back among his own people, the Cobra would no longer be alone but protected by his Habar Gidir clan and also by the ragged army known as al Shabaab. The uprising could begin. He would crush the weak government and execute General Mohammed Ahmed in the middle of Bakara Market, for all to see.

However, he was not back in Somalia yet. Despite the hurrahs pouring in from sympathizers who had viewed his video, Omar Jama had to be slow and cautious in his movements. He had pulled the tail of the tiger, and he could almost feel the hot breath of the deadly beast that was stalking him.

When he read the final list of names of the hundreds of people killed in his Mall USA attack, he did not see the Swanson Marine, nor the woman Deqo Sharif or her policeman relative. Too bad, he thought. *They still lived? So what?* Burning the house in California was the Cobra's final gift, and he had more important issues with which to deal than a washed-up Marine, an old woman, and a single cop.

From Havana, he had fled easily down to Argentina, where getting around the facial-recognition software of the authorities in Rio had been dangerous, but was defeated long ago in the planning. A diamond-and-oil-millionaire relative of the president of Angola had been persuaded to buy a pair of thoroughbred polo ponies, a black and a strawberry roan, from an exclusive criollo breeder outside Buenos Aires. Omar Jama and Hassan were hardly given a glance by airport authorities as they boarded the spacious plane that smelled of grass and hay, invisible among the grooms that tended the celebrity horses all the way from Rio, across the South Atlantic to Luanda.

Upon landing in Luanda, the Cobra was still 2,300 miles from Somalia. His enthusiasm surged. At last he was back in Africa, and Hassan's skills worked wonders in a land where money and bribes provided a common language. Getting through the Congo, Tanzania, and Ethiopia was just a matter of time. Each day, he was one day closer to his destiny. He was impatient.

The Mog was right over there. Swanson could feel the ominous presence of Mogadishu like a weight on his shoulders. He had hoped never to return to Somalia, and memories of Molly Egan swept through his mind—it had been twenty years ago but seemed like only yesterday when he would drive from the stadium to the Irish clinic to be with her. Now Kyle was going back into that place of nightmares.

The thought of killing the Cobra fueled him. If anyone ever deserved to die, it was Omar Jama, for killing Molly and Doctor Sharif with the long, sharp blade of a machete, and forever altering the arc of Swanson's life. Payback was long overdue. He would end it in Somalia.

Kyle needed patience, but he was good at waiting. Snipers could wait forever to let things unfold around them. Bob was belowdecks with his computers linked back to the giant machines of the National Security Agency. Lucky was in the gym, powering through PT programs. The CIA snipers Thompson and Brandt were on the stern, skeet shooting with remarkable accuracy.

Kyle was aboard the Excalibur helicopter, riding with the door open over the Indian Ocean as the outline of Mogadishu clarified into individual structures. The very sight of the long beach made him stomp down hard on his emotions, and he mentally scrubbed them out by remembering that Somalia was a lot different than when he had first served there. Old attitudes and prejudices could not overrule the situation on the ground today. When he was in the dirt on this mission, he would have no time for personal feelings of any sort, because they only complicated things.

The CIA's World Factbook showed that the country actually had developed a functioning government, although outside the cities, lawlessness still prevailed in the form of the Islamic extremist group al Shabaab. Those militants still staged occasional hit-and-run attacks inside the Mog, but the army apparently was a coherent force and held their ground. African Union peacekeepers backed the army up. According to Bob, who had demonstrated a fantastic memory for details, the Mog was going to be a tough nut for the Cobra to crack. Not everyone in Somalia believed he was a hero.

The helo buzzed in from the east over the gently rolling waves, putting Mogadishu on the starboard side. The city wasn't on fire, and from this height and speed, it looked just like a hundred other coastal cities in the third world. Kyle wondered briefly if it was really the same place—the place that had earned a special niche in Marine Corps lore, that had the taste of a job unfinished. A tenuous peace had been in place when the marines pulled out so many years ago and turned the job over to other armed forces, both American and international. Around the clubs and bars for many years thereafter, there was a debate over beers about what would have happened if they had stayed. How long could a thirty-thousand-man footprint be sustained? *Stop doing that.* This was an entirely different mission and an entirely different day, and he brought his mind back to the problem.

The busy port passed beneath the bird, and the chopper danced lower to land at the adjacent airport. A Land Rover with tinted windows drove up close, and the driver, a youngster who looked like he should be in high school, dismounted. "Mr. Swanson?" he asked. The voice was sharp. Not a high school kid.

Kyle nodded. "Let's go."

The Land Rover ran along the side of the airport to a separate compound with a sentry out front and with rolled-out concertina wire but little other protection. The antenna farm on the roof marked it as unique. *Good God, this is the same place the CIA was located back in the day.* The guard opened the door, and Kyle and the driver entered an air-conditioned office complex.

Mark Preston was the chief of station, and the only

other person in the room. His face and forearms were bronzed, the badges of having spent a lot of time in places where the sun shone bright and hot. The sandy hair was cut short but remained long enough to comb. The brown eyes and the lines in the face showed his experience. "Mr. Swanson. I've been expecting you."

They shook hands, and Kyle grinned when he saw a weathered wood placard on the wall. It said, STAY THE HELL AWAY. "That was on the gate outside the last time I was here. Nick Hamilton was the station chief back then."

"It's a reminder of bygone days," said Preston. "Let's do first names. Something to drink?" As if by magic, two beers appeared on the chipped rectangular table, and the driver then left the room.

"I understand Thompson and Brandt are with you on the big white boat? Behaving themselves?"

"Gentlemen and scholars in every way."

Preston took a drink, and his face was unreadable. "We have the whole place to ourselves, Kyle. My instructions are simply to assist you."

"You don't know why?"

"They didn't say, but it ain't hard to figure that you're looking for the Cobra."

"People back in Washington who are smarter than me think he's going to show up here and try to take over."

"My sources around here say the same. We've seen no sign of him."

"We have a guy out on the *Vagabond* who manages our secret comms linkup, and he told me as of fifteen minutes ago that the Cobra is still off the grid."

"Is that Bob?" Now it was Preston's turn to grin.

"Yeah. You know him?"

"Everybody in the agency knows Bob, and nobody

is ever told his last name. He's great at the job, which is the only thing that counts."

"Anyway, Bob says the target is using back routes and taking his time to avoid detection."

Preston leaned back and stretched languidly. "How can we help?"

"I need a name, Mark. Is there an officer in the Somali military structure over here whom you really trust, or is the whole thing still tribal and corrupt?"

Preston thought for a minute. "There are a lot of politics and clan loyalty involved, but there are some up-and-comers who show promise. Best of the bunch, my opinion, is Brigadier General Yusuf Dahir Hamud. He's not afraid to get dust on his boots and is a former commander of the presidential guard. He's pretty plugged in. Father was minister of defense for a while."

"Commander of the presidential guard? Sounds like a pretty job," replied Kyle.

"No. This guy doesn't fuck around. He trained at Fort Bragg, graduated from the U.S. Army's Command and General Staff College and the Army War College. Smart and fearless. If the Cobra wants power, he has to go through General Hamud, and that's not likely. My opinion."

Preston and Kyle finished their beer in silence, giving Swanson some time to think.

"Okay. You say so. He does sound good. Can you set up a private meeting? We have a native Somali with us who is now a special agent with the FBI, and he can be our liaison with the general when the feces hits the fan. Things will move fast."

"I'll try to set it up and get an answer out to Bob for you. You want to stay for dinner? They have some pretty exotic African dishes on the menu this week. Yum."

"Thanks, but I'll pass. Pretty good chow out on the barge, too."

Major Preston took him to the door. The driver was waiting, spinning a ring of keys, and then they were gone.

THE VILLA

THE COBRA STOPPED running. He had made it through all the nets and traps that had been thrown out by the United States hunters, and once again he was in his homeland. Hassan Abdi had arranged an interim rest stop not far outside the city of Kismaayo in the Juba Valley, beside the winding banks of an untamed river. The area was controlled by a two-hundred-man force that soon would be the spearhead for the coming thrust into Mogadishu. However, the revolution would have to wait just a little while longer, for Omar Jama was exhausted. While a contingent of young al Shabaab rebels stood watch, he collapsed onto a wide and comfortable bed and slept for fourteen hours straight.

When he was rested and eager, Omar Jama made the final jump of three hundred miles into Mogadishu, accompanied by a select handful of veteran fighters. The reinforcements would arrive later after picking up more fighters along the way. Many young men wanted to follow the Cobra.

He moved into a well-protected villa off of the 21 October Road, a building that was originally the home of a rich Italian merchant. Perfect. The respectable home of a leader. From this comfortable base, he could launch his campaign of insurrection.

"Gotcha!" Bob, the CIA officer in charge of communications, barely breathed the word, as if saying it aloud might bring bad luck. He rechecked his data once again. No question. Bob called for the rest of the team to join him in the secure *Vagabond* conference cabin that had transformed into a dim electronic wonder-world. His own CIA-tuned computer system blended in real time with the big hog back at the National Security Agency in Virginia, which fed on the world's data. The job consumed him. Since coming aboard, Bob had hardly noticed the difference between day and night, other than that sometimes the sky was dark. The powerful intellect did not shut down when he was on the hunt.

Bob had felt violated by the savagery shown in the Cobra's senseless slaughter at the Mall USA. It could just as easily have been any mall in the States, and his own wife and family could have been out shopping and caught in the trap. Bob had donned a war face after the attacks, using as his weapon the keyboards that plugged him into trillion-dollar computers. It had always been just a matter of time. He knew that the clever Cobra would eventually surface, and then Bob would find him and give him over to the shooters. Kyle, Lucky, Ingmar, and Bruce would take it from there, and the devil would take the bastard's soul.

"I'll start back at the beginning so this will make sense," he said. "The Cobra's entire operation has been relatively inexpensive, but obviously money had to change hands to make it work. We know now from the FBI and police investigation in Minnesota, Lucky, that he paid some of those assassins in gold. Now, nobody carries around heavy sacks of gold coins. The gold was just for flash, perhaps a personal preference of someone he was paying, but this guy needed a more reliable source of funds. And he had a source, because he kept getting what he needed. With me so far?"

"Where is he?" asked Swanson.

"Soon enough, Kyle. Soon enough. Stick with me." Bob hit a key, and the picture of a skinny, well-dressed black man slid onto the big screen mounted on the bulkhead.

"Hassan Abdi," Lucky Sharif said, with instant identification. "He ran the Hassan Investments storefront in Minneapolis, then ran before we could bust him."

"Right. Who better to handle the Cobra's money than someone who understands money? So instead of following each of Omar Jama's footprints, I concentrated on Hassan."

Ingmar spoke up. "Even looks like a bag man. Do you have proof?"

Bob replaced the picture with a screen of numbers. "Hassan was not a passive observer; he was a player. He was the advance man for the Cobra, and I discovered some of his transactions through the Society for Worldwide Interbank Financial Telecommunication. That organization is headquartered in Brussels and is used by more than seven thousand banks in some two hundred countries and promises secrecy. All of those SWIFT banks got very upset when that asshole Edward Snowden leaked that the NSA was stealing their data."

Brandt said, "My tax dollars at work. Where's this going, Bob?"

The electronics analyst held up a palm for patience. "Using that encrypted data, I constructed a virtual fingerprint of Hassan and dug out more information through the Terrorist Finance Tracking Program. Enough of the nerd stuff. In plain English, Mr. Abdi washed his money back and forth between Banque Suisse Kanton Group in Switzerland and a bank in Singapore that is owned by investors from nations all over the Middle East, and it boasts a substantial reserve of available cash and credit. Both of these banks pride themselves on having impenetrable walls of secrecy. It ain't exactly true, but their depositors and customers don't know that."

"Again, Bob. Where is he?" Swanson was on the edge of his chair.

"Almost there, Kyle. With these financial connections in place, Hassan could sweep in donations and deposits and order legitimate money transfers and establish lines of credit with other banks, which would then gladly hand over whatever was requested." He changed the screen again, and a glowing map came up with a highlighted dot glowing in yellow. As Bob narrated, the dot moved and trailed behind a yellow line that expanded steadily to show the movements of Hassan Abdi, based on hard facts and banking data. It started in San Diego and extended to Minnesota. There, he paused. "Hassan Investments hired a charter jet that brought them from California to Minneapolis. Police found a witness who saw them get off the plane together."

The date changed on the dot, moving it ahead in time, and the line reversed and headed back to California. "That marks when Hassan Abdi escaped," Bob said, letting the story unfold. "The money trail shows San Diego to Tijuana, Mexico, and on to Havana, Cuba, where the Cobra broke his silence. Then Hassan drew down a substantial sum, and it was off to Rio. One of his wire transfers went to an operation in Brazil that breeds polo ponies, two of which were purchased by a rich sportsman in Angola and flown across the Atlantic by private jet. I have four sources that indicate that

Hassan and Cobra bought their way aboard the plane." The glowing line swam steadily over the South Atlantic.

The cabin was absolutely silent except for Bob's quiet, persuasive voice. "Hassan made large cash withdrawals in Angola, so he has a full wallet now. So it is pretty obvious that the Cobra followed his advance man to Mexico, and they have been traveling together since then. Hassan was the front to keep the Cobra off the books."

"Damn. So he's finally made it back." The words came softly from Ingmar Thompson as the yellow dot on the map traced over the eastern border of Kenya and entered Somalia.

"Three months ago, Hassan Abdi signed a year's lease on a large farm down near Kismaayo, deep in al Shabaab territory." Bob splashed up an overhead sat view of the big place. Yesterday's date on it. He turned to the others, and a smile creased his face. "He also leased another place at the same time."

The dot advanced steadily across three hundred miles of jungles and clearings, and Bob replaced the picture of Kismaayo with a tight satellite shot of Mogadishu that made Swanson's stomach clench. He knew exactly what he was looking at. There was the oval stadium, and the familiar network of streets, the K-4 roundabout, and the spaghetti factory. The dot stopped there.

Then Bob shifted to a red laser pointer and rested the crimson speck on a specific rooftop. "So, Hassan called the bank in Singapore from that location. He has been so intent on covering the trail of the Cobra that he forgot to cover his own. I can ask our head of station over in the Mog to authorize drone surveillance to get some pictures. Omar Jama is right there, right now."

Everyone in the cabin felt as if a jolt of electricity was sizzling from the bulkheads. This time, there would be no years-long clandestine hunt for another Osama bin Laden hiding beneath layers and layers of protection. Bob had carefully pieced together an electronic trail from points all over the globe, and it led to an exact address. They had guessed right about the maniac returning to his original lair.

Swanson now wanted to pounce before higher-ups could start having second thoughts. "Great work, Bob. For now, hold on the drones request and do not pass this up the chain of command. Keep it tight. In this room. We are an autonomous unit, so our best opportunity for a strike is to remain independent and not allow too many fingers in this pie. Better to seek forgiveness than seek permission."

Lucky Sharif was thinking if this worked, no one would question the decision to keep Washington in the dark prior to the strike. If not, he could kiss his FBI career good-bye. "Good," he said. "Let's do it."

Bruce Brandt checked the time. "It's almost fourteen hundred hours. If we want to expedite this thing, we can use the rest of today and tonight, and all of tomorrow and tomorrow night to gather more intel, lay our plans and line up assets."

Bob scratched his chin, thinking about what was needed for even a limited raid. He had organized this sort of operation before. "A window of forty-eight to seventy-two hours is pretty tight, boys. There are lots of moving pieces involved for entry and egress protection, diplomatic notification, weapons, medical, comms, local support. Remember that we are dealing here not only with a foreign government within its own borders but also the African Union troops. They need to be in on it."

Swanson snapped, "I'm not waiting around two days just to get close. We go in tonight."

"You're out of your mind," said Bob.

"Flippin' impossible," agreed Brandt. "We know nothing about his protective umbrella."

"I kind of like it," said Ingmar.

Kyle slowed down to consider their concerns. "If anyone can make this happen in a hurry, it's us. You are some of the best operators around, and we don't have to be tactically perfect, just better than the bad guys."

"Have you already forgotten your marine training; how hard it is to get the military machine moving?" Bob protested. "We can't just snap our fingers and reposition hundreds of troops and machines. Putting boots on the ground and rounds on an exact target is a complicated business."

"No. I haven't forgotten, but this is not a totally strange environment. I know Mogadishu like the back of my hand, and Lucky knows it even better." He would not allow doubt to enter the room. "I can see how it comes down right now. It is a minimalist action, and actually all we have to do is work out a few details. Okay?"

"No. Not okay." Bob was suddenly edgy. "You and Special Agent Sharif have personal scores to settle with the Cobra, and a lust for revenge could lead to sloppy decision making. We just found the bastard a few minutes ago, Kyle! You have to slow down. Think in terms of military necessity and go by the book, because if you go too fast, all of you may be killed, and the Cobra might get away again."

Swanson understood that he was cornering his friends. "Look. If we wait too long, the Cobra might disappear anyway. He's home now and can just put on an old shirt and khakis, then vanish in a crowd. There is no question that he already has alliances in place, and no matter how many fighters he already has, tomorrow he will have even more, and next week, more than that. To do this job, we have to move now. I want your help, guys. Goddammit, I *need* your help."

"The CIA is not going to allow you to go off on a suicide mission, Kyle. Just wait a few hours and let us make sure that when we go in, we do it right."

"I'm going in tonight. Lucky and I can do what we want."

"And I can stop you in a heartbeat with a telephone call."

"You can, but you won't. Bob, you're no keyboard warrior; you love this shit. We already have all of the authority we need to bend some rules and stage a lightning raid. I want to be looking at that house when the sun comes up tomorrow."

Bob was near his boiling point. Swanson was not bluffing. He would swim ashore if he had to, and Lucky Sharif would follow him through the gates of hell. If he couldn't talk them out of it, at least he could try to make this work. He could always go back to Silicon Valley. "Okay. You win. Let's get to work. We have about twelve hours."

Bruce and Ingmar did a high-five palm slap. Lucky felt his shoulders ease, as if a weight had been lifted.

Kyle read the disappointment in the face of the senior CIA officer. "One last point, Bob. You're coming in with us. We'll have some fun."

"I don't know if I can shoot a rifle." The seriousness faded. *A gunfight instead of keyboard!*

Swanson reached out for a fist-bump. "If we die, I will admit being wrong."

THE HIGHWAY

BRIGADIER GENERAL YUSUF Dahir Hamud, the commander of army special forces within the Somali Ministry of Defense, had granted this unusual meeting at the request of friends in the U.S. Central Intelligence Agency. It was five o'clock in the afternoon, and the sky and the ocean both wore the glow of liquid gold. Every day was a full day for the intense and thoughtful officer, because al Shabaab never stopped, but this was a special favor asked by his friend Mark Preston over at the airport. Fifteen minutes with one individual. A favor done for the CIA was a valuable thing. Keeping it off the record and out of official channels, as Preston also wanted, only increased the value.

The general's khaki uniform with the red tabs on the collar and pips on the epaulettes looked fresh off the hanger, which it was, and the shirt was crisp, as if wrinkles were enemies. Appearances were important, particularly when doing a favor. His hair and mustache were turning gray, unusual for such a young officer, but they were a telltale barometer of the constant stress under which he lived. Undisturbed sleep was a luxury.

The general had been surprised when the guest

arrived through a secluded entrance. Preston had not said that the man was a Somali. In fact, he was not even with the CIA. Settled in a chair on the other side of the desk was Special Agent Cawelle Sharif of the Federal Bureau of Investigation. Another thoughtful and serious man.

"My sympathies for those attacks in Minnesota," said General Hamud. "I never got up to that part of America, but those people certainly helped a lot of our refugees back during the troubles." His English carried only a slight accent. "I assume you were one of them."

Lucky Sharif agreed. "That is why I am here, to ask your help."

A polite question followed, although the general already was feeling a connection of common cause. "Do you want to arrest this terrorist, this Cobra fellow, Special Agent Sharif?"

Lucky shifted in his seat. Tilted his head. "It would be good to put him on trial in a federal court. We have convicted a lot of terrorists, and this one even confessed his crime on the Internet. He would be put away forever in a prison from which escape is impossible."

"You did not answer my question."

"I don't think that a trial is really the best resolution in this particular situation, sir."

Hamud leaned forward and slowly tore a piece of paper in half, then tore those pieces in half again before speaking. "No arrest and trial. Not if you want my help. I consider him a monster. I want him dead. As long as he draws breath, he will be a potential rallying point for al Shabaab. Not only that, he has this wild dream of taking over Somalia with his terror group. We won't let that happen."

Lucky smiled. "Then here it is."

He had laid out the entire plan that was hatched earlier in the day, including the fresh news that the Cobra was already in Mogadishu, in a villa over by the spaghetti factory. The general's last intelligence report had the man still down in the al Shabaab stronghold of Kismaayo. "We want him badly, General Hamud, but our team will act in support of your troops. Absolutely."

The general was wondering why he should not slam an immediate cordon around the neighborhood and go in and personally put a bullet in the head of Omar Jama. "Agent Sharif, I can handle this threat without you."

Lucky disagreed. "Our president needs absolute proof of his death, General. We want DNA and photographs, which is why we have not just dropped a bigass bomb on that house. It has to be our people—me, actually—collecting it, to establish a solid chain of custody. There can be no hope left behind for his followers."

Hamud understood that process. It made sense, and the value of the favor would increase. "But why use these others, the CIA shooters? I truly don't need them. You can come along to establish the validity."

"Why pass up this opportunity? Having our sniper in an overwatch position not only guarantees success, but he would provide your troops extra protection. Two other operators would be on the scene only to cover him."

"You don't think my own snipers can do that job, Agent Sharif? It isn't all that complicated, and they are very well trained—as good as any."

Lucky hesitated. "There's something else. You want him dead. I want him dead. And so does my sniper."

He then unveiled the chilling story of what happened in a room at the Irish clinic twenty years ago. General Hamud had heard many horrible stories about the hell of those old days, when life was cheap and killers roamed the streets of Mogadishu like hungry dogs. This was one of the worst.

"The Cobra killed your own grandfather and this Kyle Swanson's girlfriend right in front of you both?" Two decades, and the wounds on the soul of Lucky Sharif were as fresh as the night they were made.

"Yes, General, and he tried to get the rest of us, too. We eventually stopped him, and now we are all back at this same place. It's time to finish the job. Kyle and I both deserve to be in on the kill."

The general put his palms flat on his desk. "Very well. Swanson can do the overwatch. We all want the same thing, and although your proposed timetable is tight, I agree with it. We must not give the Cobra time to build a viable strike force. Just be clear that everyone understands that I am in overall command, not the CIA, not the FBI, and not the U.S., nor the U.N. Me."

Lucky picked up the tone. "This is personal for you, too, isn't it?"

The general pulled back on the emotion. "Yeah. He murdered my grandfather about the same time. You take the word back to your team and get things moving, then come back to be my liaison during the raid. No miscommunication."

"Good. One last thing you should know. Your snipers may be good, but they aren't better than Kyle."

General Hamud responded. "Really?"

"No, sir. Nobody is."

Swanson worked in the armory to prep Excalibur. Spread before him was a clean blue plastic sheet on which lay the parts of the big .50 caliber sniper rifle, a weapon that was much more than the sum of its various components. Its sole reason for existence was its ability to kill a human being at very long range, almost on its own. He used a voltmeter to check the power packs, both the primary and secondary, and other specific lab instruments to tune the miniaturized circuits of the on-board microcomputer—all of the readings were within their proper range. Swanson had helped design the original Excalibur, and it became the cornerstone of Sir Geoffrey Cornwell's empire. Then they steadily improved it. This was the fifth generation of the light-weight rifle, and the eighth version for the magical scope that brought pinpoint accuracy under any conditions. When firing with a unique rocket-propelled load, the fearsome weapons system was good for up to about 3,200 meters: two miles. Everything was patented, and the technology was out there earning money for Excalibur Enterprises.

"That's some gun. Is that what I'm going to use on this job?" The analyst Bob was at an adjacent table, cleaning and prepping a black Sony video camera with a long-lens combat camera from Nikon.

"You're coming along to take pictures. That's all. We do the shooting." Swanson slid the various parts home.

"Well, I still need a gun. Something more than a Glock pea shooter."

Bruce Brandt was at another table, finishing with an M-16A4. He worked on the bolt carrier group with careful efficiency and a practiced eye: firing pin, firing-pin retaining pin, bolt-cam pin, bolt, bolt carrier, and the charging handle. "This one is yours, Bob. Kyle won't even let me or Ingmar use the Excalibur."

"I'm rated as an expert. Shot a forty-two on the KD Course, and he's worried that I might break his toy." Thompson was wiping down his own gear. He was about ready to suit up and get on with this.

"Get the CIA to buy you one. We'll give them a good deal. This one is built to match my grip and my eye."

He slid the pieces of Excalibur back together, turning the screws to precise settings, and rubbed it down a final time. It was ready.

"I'm done over here," said Brandt, snapping the rifle back together. "Bob No Last Name is good to go. Let's shove some food down our throats. It's going to be a long night."

Omar Jama felt uneasy, although he remained outwardly calm. The sleep had helped. The trip was over, and the tensions had eased. He was concentrating on the present and the future.

He stood on the verandah of his villa and took stock. There were about twenty-five young al Shabaab fighters inside the house and in defensive positions around the grounds. More volunteers were drifting in as the word spread among the rebels that the Cobra had returned. In truth, they were not grizzled veterans of many battles but much younger men, most with stars of idealism and religious fervor in their eyes, and their brains scrambled by khat. They were cannon fodder, not leaders around whom he could build an army. They would keep him safe until the force of some two hundred veteran fighters arrived from Kismaayo tomorrow morning.

The sun was leaving the sky, and Mogadishu was quiet. He breathed it in. Gone was the steady beat of gunfire that he remembered, and from this distance on the outskirts of downtown, he could see people moving through the city as if nothing extraordinary was happening. A police car even drove by, slowed momentarily, then went away.

This was not the Mogadishu he had dreamed about for so many years, the wild place of his youth, where guns and daring and the willingness to kill could take a young man far. It was too quiet. He had expected more of a welcome, although he had entered the metropolis quietly.

"You must give this some time, brother. You have only just arrived." Hassan Abdi shared the evening meal following their observance of the familiar call to prayer from the mosque. "It would not surprise me if you were visited tomorrow by a delegation of government officials who will want to broker a deal in order to keep their skins. You can offer a peaceful transition of power."

The scent of warm rice and lamb and fresh vegetables surrounded them. Hassan had hired a wonderful cook, and there was a woman housekeeper and a man who worked the grounds, which had grass and shrubs and was not rubble-strewn. Electric light bathed the freshly painted interior of the spacious home. Electricity! Plumbing that worked! Peace in the streets! He chewed a mouthful of food as he considered these magical events.

"You are right, Hassan. Of course, you are right. I have arrived amongst them suddenly, like a mighty bomb that is ready to explode," said the Cobra. "They were not expecting me, but now they will know my standing with al Shabaab and my deeds. Our following will increase by the hour. If an enemy tries to touch me, the city will explode in fury, and there will be civil war again. They don't want that. They have grown soft under this so-called federal government."

Hassan stared at his friend for a long few seconds. He did not want the Cobra to get angry, for then he would be uncontrollable. This was more about symbolism, the appearance of control and inevitable power, than it was about actual military strength. Another twenty-four hours, and the Cobra might be sleeping in the presidential palace, but the boss needed to remain in control of his temper. He just had to hold on. "There have been many changes since you were last in our homeland, brother. This is true. The people yearn to overthrow their foreign puppets, and you have given them reason to again be proud of being Somalis. Your attack on the United States has had a profound effect below the surface. You will be the leader."

The Cobra felt that the situation was workable. "After I am in power, the Americans will not dare come assassinate me. Tomorrow the troops arrive. It will truly be the start of a new day for Somalia!"

Shortly after dark, road flares and racks of construction lights slowed drivers to a crawl along the broad coastal road from Kismaayo to Mogadishu. Those heading northwest were channeled into a single lane over a space of three miles as road crews in bright reflective vests and hard hats ran loaders and heavy equipment to lay a new stretch of blacktop. Such stoppages were routine during the dry season. Tonight was particularly slow.

After three miles, more orange cones loomed along the road, and more bright lights edged drivers onto a dirt-road detour. Bulldozers growled up on the highway. Cars and trucks were barely moving over unfamiliar rough ground when they came around a broad curve and saw the roadblocks.

Five hundred seasoned soldiers of the Burundi National Defense Force were in an ambush configuration at the barrier and out of sight in the darkness all along the detour route. Machine guns and cannon were pointed at the approaching vehicles, which were stopped one by one, the passengers and drivers ordered out and held at gunpoint while searches were made. Men were arrested, and weapons were confiscated.

Captain Beck White watched from a Humvee, talk-

ing by radio with some CIA officer who went only by
the code name "Bob." The tall, dark-haired captain
was a Force Recon warfighter with SP-MAG TF-13, a
special-purpose marine air-ground task force, and he
had been helping train the Burundi contingent of the African Union mission. It was a peacekeeping force that
had seen a lot of action. He liked these guys. Poor as
mice, they were fine soldiers.

"We bagged a bunch of al Shabaabs in the first hour
and only had to kill six. More than fifty prisoners, and
lots of weaponry has been confiscated," the marine captain reported. "Word is getting back to Kismaayo that
the highway is closed, so traffic is getting scarce."

"Outstanding, Captain. Any friendly casualties?"
Bob made notes on a legal pad aboard the *Vagabond*.

"Not among my boys. There's no love lost between
the Burundi military and al Shabaab. The terrorists
know we tend to shoot first and ask questions later."

"And your roadblock will be up all night?"

"We ain't going nowhere until I hear from you. This
road is closed."

Bob switched off and looked over to Lucky Sharif.
"You can let General Hamud know that the al Shabaab
reinforcements from Kismaayo have been indefinitely
delayed." They stepped onto the deck, where Kyle Swanson, Ingmar Thompson, and Bruce Brandt were waiting near the fantail, menacing, ghostly figures, all in
black overalls.

THE COBRA

SWANSON HAD BEEN here before, back in the Mog, back on a rooftop, waiting in the dark of the night with a long rifle in his arms. The former Irish clinic was less than two klicks to the south, and memories of Molly chewed at his concentration. The man who had murdered her was asleep in a nice villa two hundred meters straight ahead. Swanson intended to balance the scale, but he swept the uneasy thoughts with iron self-control.

They had taken the helo in from the yacht to the air base, where a few battered Land Rovers met them, along with some Somali commandos who would be their guides. The CIA station head, Mark Preston, was there for a final radio check so he could stay in touch with all the moving parts, just in case.

It was almost three o'clock in the morning. Lucky Sharif had gone in earlier and was already embedded with General Hamud. Thompson and Brandt piled into the lead vehicle, and Kyle and Bob boarded the other, with Bob in the backseat so he could stretch out his long legs. Kyle rode shotgun, half expecting to see the landscape as scarred as it had been when he rode through on the back of a tank that took him to the stadium in the final dreary days of December, 1992. Back in the day, there was nothing but chaos and hopelessness. This was different, and the two-SUV convoy sailed along the roads as smoothly as if they were on a Sunday drive.

"This sure isn't like the 'Stans and Iraq. Like this war is over, or almost." Bob had never been to Somalia before.

The driver was a sergeant named Hussein Kedeyi, and he answered, "Al Shabaab has not been defeated, sir. They remain a huge threat, but we are winning the overall battle and slowly pushing them out. They have been reduced to doing hit-and-run raids because they do not have organization and training. Give us a few more years, and they will not bother us."

Swanson saw bright lights throughout the city, even at this early hour, and the people on the street were not armed mobs. Business was being done, and entrepreneurs were making money. No one bothered them. Nobody shot at them. Jobs were replacing poverty. Everything needed for a functioning society seemed to be coming together, including the formal government. At least the opposing sides were not killing each other on the streets. The pleasant smell of the ocean was no longer overwhelmed by rot and decay. He smiled to himself. *Molly would have been proud. She sacrificed her life to help turn this place around.*

The sergeant was young but had grown strong and gave off the confident sense that he knew what he was doing. After all, Kyle reflected, he was special ops. The Land Rovers doused their lights as they neared the K-4 in northern Mogadishu and pulled out of sight beside the old spaghetti factory and shut down. The large building had been a landmark battleground for many years and showed its scars. Hundreds of militia bullets pocked the dirty white walls, the windows were empty holes, and the roof had been blown away by bombs. Urban renewal had not yet reached this centrally located pile of rubble, but the sergeant told them that a new pasta manufacturer had opened elsewhere.

"That's good news," said Bob as he climbed from the SUV. "You cannot really have true civilization without spaghetti." He slapped Sergeant Kedeyi on the shoulder. "Lead the way, son."

Swanson followed, only slightly nervous that they were not clearing the old building room by room until he saw two other Somali soldiers were already positioned inside. The place was safe. Kedeyi and the other driver joined them, and suddenly the ground floor was as secure as Kyle could have wanted it; a friendly was at all four corners, weapons up and pointed out.

Ingmar and Brandt took the stairs and looked around, then called down for Swanson and Bob to come on up. The CIA sniper team would hold the second floor.

The top floor was a wasteland. Little remained other than a ragged concrete-block surface and piles of junk. Kyle and Bob slid through the litter on the northwest side. They stacked rubble and debris and old concrete to improve the hide, then went in on hands and knees and adjusted the space to fit them both.

Bob pulled his jacket open, took off the gloves, rolled up the black beanie, and removed the video cam and a still camera that had a snout of a long lens. The M-16 was placed at his right side.

Swanson peeled Excalibur from its carrying case, looked it over quickly, and loaded a sleek and heavy .50 caliber bullet in the chamber. The magazine held only three more, which he considered to be more than enough for tonight's job. He opened the bipod and pointed the rifle just behind the hide opening so it could not be seen. The power source for the scope was activated. His position was the highest spot in the neighborhood and provided a good view across the fences and low walls, all the way to the villa in which the Cobra slept. The scope automatically painted the place with an invisible electronic beam and recorded the ranges, its sensors sniffed the weather, and the computer did the complex math for a solution that would allow the sniper to make a hit.

"Big place," said Bob, focusing the viewfinder of his video cam, which also had night vision. "I can see two static guard posts."

"Yuh. That's what I see. No guards are roving around. That's sloppy. He feels safe."

"Not a good idea for him."

"No."

Bob radioed the SITREP in to the CIA station at the airport and received confirmation; then they settled down to wait. There was no live feed relayed to Washington. Kyle had not wanted anyone getting cold feet at the last minute.

For almost an hour, they didn't exchange a word, and the silence lay heavy between them. One would watch while the other rested. Kyle was almost in an easy trance, breathing smoothly, keeping the blood pressure and heartbeat in low gear, thinking of nothing in particular. The big gun seemed a comfortable extension of his body. This would be an easy shot, if and when it came.

The plan was for the Somali special ops people to encircle the house and hit it hard from the rear just before dawn, driving anyone inside out the front door. If the Cobra lived through that initial attack, Kyle would take him down when he appeared.

Swanson exhaled a long breath but never wavered from his sight line. The weight of the big rifle was evenly distributed. Almost time. It felt good.

His mind was steeled with professional detachment now, and nothing would break his concentration. No memories could intrude to rattle him. Still, time passed slowly. "You watch for a while," he told Bob.

Kyle rolled onto his back, squinting his eyes closed, and a drop of water came down his cheek. He had been staring through the scope for too long; just normal eye strain. He knew better. Thirty minutes was max, and he had stretched it. He doused a cloth and wiped his eyes and there was clarity.

Bob rolled into position and let the lens of his camera magnify the scene. "I got it," he said. "We've got plenty of time."

Lucky Sharif had nothing to do but stand quietly beside the Humvee with a radio in his hand. He could connect to Bob and Kyle with a single click, but he had nothing to report. General Hamud was studying an area map. An entire company of his men had stolen out of the city during the darkest hours and had thrown a net around the villa.

"My grandfather was an educated man," the general said, breaking the quiet. His eyes were focused in the middle distance, which was only a deep emptiness. "His name was Abdiwel Godah Hamud, and he became a spokesman for our clan during the years of horror. Do you remember his name?"

Lucky didn't. "No, sir. I was just a kid."

The general resumed. "Well, he helped negotiate a treaty to stop the fighting. Then he made a terrible mistake by thinking that General Aidid, the worst of the warlords, would honor the peace agreement that he had just signed. So my grandfather went to the home of a family member to celebrate. A few hours later, the Cobra broke in and killed them all."

The soldier put his attention back on the map and was satisfied that everyone was in place. "He broke a couple of my ribs, shot me, and left me for dead. I learned only later that the Cobra murdered my grandfather, with a machete, just as he did yours. I think this man has lived long enough, don't you?"

"Yes, General. I do." A recollection swam to his mind. "By any chance did they take you to the Irish clinic for treatment?"

"I don't remember anything after being shot."

"I was raised at the clinic. I saw a lot of kids go through there. You may have been one of them."

Hamud and Lucky exchanged knowing looks. Then the general read the glowing hands on the face of a clock in the Humvee's front panel. "It is six o'clock. The sun rises in ten minutes." He motioned to a nearby colonel and said, "Go."

Lucky passed the word to the sniper and climbed aboard the Humvee.

A storm of gunfire at the villa shattered the early-morning stillness of Mogadishu—an old, familiar, dreaded song for Somali citizens. General Hamud's commando unit took down the pair of guard posts with a combination of machine-gun fire and rocket-propelled grenades, then closed the net, firing disciplined bursts and aiming before pulling triggers. Smoke grenades boiled up in a covering screen, pushed by the morning breeze.

The Cobra had been in bed, relying on his fearsome al Shabaab bodyguards to protect him overnight and hold the place safe until the reinforcements arrived from Kismaayo in a few hours. The gunshots alerted him that it wasn't happening that way at all. By the time he was dressed, his defenders were crumbling in the path of a trained force. He screamed with fury and grabbed a pistol, stalking through the building and yelling at the men to fight to the death. "The entire city will rise up and protect us," he screamed. "Hold tight! Do not abandon your positions! God is great!"

The young bullies specialized in random raids on easy targets and were not used to the fierce attack of the commandos. The boys usually melted away when the army brought its strength to bear, but this time there was nowhere to run. They heard the Cobra's words, but those empty promises and exhortations floated away like balloons. One by one, the al Shabaab boys went down beneath the unrelenting, ferocious assault.

The main attacking force was pushing from the back of the villa, and the rooms were being cleared one by one. The only route out was in the front, where machine guns were raking the open ground. After only five intense minutes, General Hamud ordered his troops to stop shooting. A tense silence gripped the villa. He clicked the loudspeaker mounted on his vehicle.

"You boys of al Shabaab! This is Brigadier General Hamud of the Somali National Security Forces. You know who I am. There is no escape route open, and the column of reinforcements that you were expecting has been obliterated. In one minute, I will resume killing you all. Your only hope for survival is to give me the coward named Omar Jama, who calls himself Cobra. Turn him out, and we will take you prisoner. One minute!"

Inside the villa, Hassan Abdi was crouched beside a wall, bleeding from a shoulder wound. He looked up when he saw his hero and friend approach, noting that the scarred face was twisted in hatred and anger. For the first time, Hassan recognized the true madness that possessed the man. He had spent twenty years chasing a dream that did not exist. The Cobra was no great warrior who would lead Somalia and Islam to a new day. The only people who followed him did so because he had money to pay them. Hassan finally understood that he had made a terrible mistake by attaching himself to such a false and wicked man.

"You failed me," the Cobra shouted. He spat on his old friend, then shot him twice in the head. The remaining al Shabaab gunmen scuttled into other rooms to hide from both the soldiers outside and the crazed man inside. The Cobra knew it would be only a few seconds before they turned their weapons on him and tossed him out. With a final defiant yell, he burst into a run and crashed through the destroyed front door and into the hazy dawn, intent on killing anyone he could. Whoever it was did not matter. He just had to kill somebody. He ran toward a parked Humvee, firing his pistol as fast as he could.

Kyle Swanson took the shot. The .50 caliber thundered, and the mammoth bullet caught the Cobra on the right knee, tearing the leg away in a gout of blood, flesh, stringy muscle, and bone.

The Cobra spun and fell with a yowl of hatred, still gripping the pistol and finding the strength to fire it again. Swanson adjusted, then took away the gun hand. The sniper watched the Cobra writhe on the ground, wreathed in gore. One more shot, and this would be done. He jacked in another round to put one in the head.

"Cease fire, Kyle! Don't shoot!" The voice of Lucky Sharif was shouting in his ear. "We've got him."

Swanson had a history of disobeying orders, but Lucky sounded like he meant it. His trigger finger froze halfway through the pull. "Roger that."

"Bob, turn off the cameras." Sharif was insistent, urgent.

"Done," he replied, then turned to Kyle and asked, "WTF?"

Swanson kept his eye glued to the scope. Bob went back to the big camera and pushed the magnification to its max to get the closest image on the 3×5 screen. The body of Omar Jama bled and shook, the face twisted and the body in spasms. A ring of soldiers had closed around the villa and were herding out the remaining al Shabaab fighters, their weapons thrown into a pile.

General Hamud stepped from his Humvee, and Lucky Sharif came from the other side. Both were carrying machetes with long, sharp edges that glinted in the morning sun. Lucky kicked the Cobra over onto his back so he could watch.

"For our families," the general said.

"For everyone from Mogadishu to Minnesota," added Lucky.

The Cobra saw the big knives rise and then come slashing down, and he cried out as waves of agonizing pain ripped his body with each new cut. There was no mercy.

Bob pushed the cameras away. Swanson watched until the very end.

EPILOGUE

THE WALLS OF the new Washington office of Excalibur Enterprises were painted a muted basic white, with plenty of hardwood and glass throughout the suite. Kyle Swanson had a corner office the size of a small bungalow. An adjacent conference room of equal proportion shared a connecting door. The rest of the space was given over to a receptionist and three staff cubicles for sales and office management. Such a layout was common in the building, where lobbyists and corporations nested in the nation's capital.

A full model of the original Excalibur sniper rifle rested in a cabinet in the reception area, below the name and elegant logo of the firm. The big rifle and the smiling receptionist would be the first things a visitor saw on entering.

Excalibur was the only piece of hardware on display. On one wall of Kyle's private office hung a framed print of Jasper Johns's *Flag*, while the iconic photo of the marines raising the flag on Iwo Jima was opposite. His desk faced outward because he liked the view of the Capitol dome, and a silver laptop computer was on it. Behind it was a built-in credenza bearing the eternally brewing coffeepot and white ceramic mugs, with a sink. A little refrigerator was hidden underneath. The sand-colored wall-to-wall carpet was dominated by a starred Azerbaijani rug, on which rested a few tables and chairs.

Lady Patricia was pleased with the way it had all come together, although she had considered it still rather too masculine and lacking charm. She solved that problem by hiring a willowy, snow-haired, and very attractive former FBI special agent named Janna Ecklund, who would act as both the receptionist and on-site security officer with a weapon beneath her desk. Her boyfriend, Lucky Sharif, had been promoted to the Washington FBI headquarters.

Janna wore a black dress that reached her knees and some neat jewelry, and her almost-white hair was fresh. Young men experienced in the ways of Washington were surprised when she coolly avoided their invitations— seemingly unaware of the fact that they were very important men.

Kyle was in a two-button gray herringbone Canali suit that had set him back almost four thousand dollars and an olive-green tie. He would have preferred to be in jeans and a Red Sox sweatshirt, but Lady Pat had insisted, so that was that.

Sir Jeff Cornwell and his wife had flown over for the official opening party, which was attended by Washington movers and shakers and the professional hangers-on who were always hunting free food and drink on the D.C. cocktail circuit. Lieutenant General Middleton represented the White House, and the three stars on his shoulders added weight to the affair. He was surprisingly comfortable mingling in the relaxed setting and was particularly attentive to Deqo Sharif, who was seated, almost dwarfed, in Kyle's high-backed desk chair. She told him that she would be living with Lucky and Janna in a house on the Maryland shore, finally escaping the cold of Minnesota. She had baked a plate of cookies for Kyle's party, and Middleton said they were delicious.

There was a firm five-to-eight lid on the evening event, because it would otherwise go all night. The visitors came in waves, nibbled, and checked out the place and its people, then moved on to other pastures. As it grew near to the shut-down time, a young man who had made great use of the open bar introduced himself to Kyle as the administrative aide for a rookie congressman. "You were in the army or something, weren't you?" the aide asked.

Kyle gave a half smile and replied, "Umm. Something like that. Now out in the private sector." He tried to recall what role, if any, the congressman had in military or budget affairs but drew a blank. Obviously this one had no seniority: yet.

"You know, I was a captain in the field artillery, with a tour in Afghanistan." The man looked at Kyle, who was shorter and older.

"Well, everyone at Excalibur thanks you for your service. Enjoy the party."

"Hella party," the visitor said, leaning in closer and nodding toward Janna. "But I've struck out so far with the chicks, and it's getting late. What can you tell me about that Nordic queen before I make a move?"

Kyle almost laughed but whispered and answered. "My new receptionist. I just hired her. She's new in the city from Minnesota, is pretty lonely. She likes her men and her coffee strong. I think that with a subtle pat on the butt, she'll follow you anywhere. Be assertive. Show her you mean business."

The guy juked his shoulders and brushed his thick hair with his hand, transforming into a Capitol Hill player before making his run. Within a minute, a loud slap to the face sent him reeling sideways and onto the floor, and Janna stood above him, looking down with a smirk of contempt. Lucky laughed to himself as the young man slinked away to the door like a whipped puppy. Kyle allowed himself a laugh.

It was not an unusual way for a Washington reception to end, and the other guests took it as the cue to finish their drinks and depart. The Spanish embassy party would still be going strong along Embassy Row because the Spaniards always dined late.

The doors closed and locked, and it was time to get comfortable. Janna kicked off her three-inch heels and became noticeably shorter, but she was still above six feet. Kyle and the other men ditched their jackets and coats, and everyone refilled their glasses.

"To the new life," Sir Jeff said from his wheelchair, raising a toast to Kyle. "You are going to make us a lot of money in this town."

Lieutenant General Middleton knocked back his bourbon. "Well, I bring the best wishes of the White House, plus some news. The president will be making a state visit over to Somalia in about a month to demonstrate our support for the federal government in Mogadishu. That's a big step forward."

Everyone had heard the president's speech to the nation a week earlier, in which he reported that the terrorist known as the Cobra had been killed in Mogadishu in a combined action by American and Somali Special Forces. DNA, photographic evidence, and personal recognition had determined the right man had died. The body was burned in accordance with local customs. General Hamud was reporting that the terrorist group al Shabaab had been staggered by the loss of its new hero. America had buried its own dead with honor and was rebuilding again, too strong to ever yield to terrorism. The tracking and the death of Omar Jama proved once again that there was no place where terrorists who strike America could hide—nowhere in the entire world.

Lucky Sharif was not mentioned, and the FBI returned him to duty after official reviews of the takedown film showed no wrongdoing on his part. A camera glitch at the decisive moment had prevented a total analysis of Sharif's actions, but he had a letter from Brigadier General Hamud saying that Agent Sharif had wanted to arrest the suspect and return him to New York for trial. Lucky received a letter of appreciation from the Somali government and a commendation and the transfer to the Hoover Building from the FBI.

"So you guys are all in the clear. Good job. Finishing that job quickly was the right move," Middleton said. "Off the record, I can tell you that the man in the White House is very pleased that Excalibur Enterprises has established a Washington office. I promise you that the Pentagon is also pleased."

He said good-bye, then left. The Cornwells departed a short time later, with Lady Pat giving both Janna and Deqo cheek pecks. It meant they were in cahoots to keep the men under control. The Sharifs and Janna followed in ten minutes.

The cleaning crew would not arrive until midnight. Swanson took his drink over to the broad window. Traffic was busy, even long after normal quitting time—the vehicles of people who made the government work. Kyle was one of them now. It was a special kind of freedom that he had never before experienced.

"Can you handle this?" The question came from the other person in the room, Marty Atkins, the deputy director of CIA Clandestine Service. He had hovered around the edges of the party like an anonymous nobody, identifying himself as a venture capitalist from McKinney, Texas, just outside Plano, and asking if the questioner had ever spent much time down in Plano. Now he had ditched the cover and was back to being one of the top men at the CIA.

"This first mission was difficult, but it was really a good test. You blended seamlessly with the support units operating outside of the military. You see how that works now. You will use them as extra assets when needed, but much of the time you will be on your own."

"I didn't have a problem not being military. Is that a double negative?" Kyle said, looking deep into his drink.

Marty Atkins waved his hand to sweep the expensive new offices. "And this is your day job. Pretty sweet. Hide in plain sight as a high-flying business type until you get a call from me. Then you go. Can you handle that?"

Kyle remained silent for a few moments, still taking it all in. His new life. He had enjoyed the actual independence of command more than he expected. Although a civilian, he would always have the U.S. military backing him up when he needed big boots. Lucky Sharif and Janna Ecklund would be direct hooks into the FBI. He turned to face his CIA boss, and he smiled.

"Yeah. I can handle it."

Read on for an excerpt from the next book by
Gunnery Sgt. Jack Coughlin with Donald A. Davis

LONG SHOT

A
S N I P E R
N O V E L

Coming soon from St. Martin's Press

ROME, ITALY

THIS HAD TO be a head shot. Under normal circumstances, a sniper goes for the chest, which not only provides a larger area and is thus an easier target, but the chest also is the gateway to the vital organs of the body. A big bullet in there goes spinning and bouncing around, breaking bones and shearing veins and pulping muscles, and collapsing the frail human machine that made life possible. Kyle Swanson knew that as he ignored the easy shot and instead dialed in on the head of Roland Lewis Martin from Bellwood, Indiana. The CIA sniper knew a lot of other things, the total of which meant that young Mister Martin had richly earned the .50 caliber bullet that would soon tear off his entire skull and leave his quivering body with a bloody stump of a neck.

Martin was a nice-looking young man, at least as seen through the powerful scope mounted on the Excalibur sniper rifle. Only twenty-nine years old, he still had the muscular build of his days being an offensive tackle on the Bellwood High Blue Jackets football team. The continued physical conditioning was a testament to the exercise he had received in his years of fighting for ISIS, the murderous Islamic State jihadists. His hair was black and cut short, and his cheeks wore a stubble of beard. The broad nose had been broken twice, healed a bit crookedly, and his teeth gleamed plastic and bright after so many caps and root-canals. His white cotton shirt was open at the neck, showing the deep tan. The sleeves were rolled up, exposing the blue tattoo of a snake that coiled from his wrist to his elbow on the right arm. Martin had picked that up in Yokohama during his short career in the U.S. Navy, which had taught him computer science. The black slacks were clean and pressed, with matching socks and leather loafers. A tiny earring twinkled on the left lobe. The tip of his left little finger was missing due to a childhood tractor accident. In all, he looked pretty good; a capable poster boy for ISIS, a former cold-blooded killer turned recruiter.

Swanson had decided to use the new clear polymer-encased M33 ball ammunition for the job instead of the standard brass, primarily for the lighter weight. The 687-grain bullet was a shade under five and a half inches in length, would leave the muzzle at a velocity of 11,091 foot-pounds of energy to cover the 200 yards to the head of young Mister Martin in only two-tenths of a second, actually.231 seconds. It would strike with enough power to take down a tree. The plastic covering on the bullet interested Swanson. Trying out new things was part of his day job.

Rain was on the way and the air seemed heavy, even apprehensive, as if the weather knew something was going to happen and wanted to serve up an appropriate background of thunder and lightning. The skies would burst and the dark clouds would empty and the Eternal City of Rome would be cleansed once again. So far, not a drop. That was a good thing. The three young people at the table of the sidewalk café could remain outside, talking, as the ISIS recruiter slowly reeled in his catches in the sunlight. The sniper watched as a girl with long brown hair leaned close to Martin. She appeared to be in her mid-teens. Her friend, a brunette only a couple of years older, snapped their smiling picture on her cell phone, then showed it to them. They all laughed. Martin topped off the wine glasses of his American visitors. An unfolded street map of Rome lay on the table.

From his prone position on the third-floor of a rather common yellow neoclassical villa on Quirinal Hill, Kyle Swanson could see an edge of the elegant Trevi Fountain, into which the girls and Martin had tossed a few coins and wishes before they all settled in at the corner café a few blocks away. It was hard to find a place from where you could not see any monuments or splendid ruins in Rome, for they were everywhere, old stones with stories to tell. The three million people in the city passed through the historic paths with a leisurely pace that was bred into them. Nothing ever happened fast in Italy. The brothers Romulus and Remus probably took their time while being suckled by the she-wolf in the founding legend. The *dolce vita* was the city's charm, and it was practiced from the Vatican to the Coliseum. Of course, Romulus murdered his brother later on. Brutus assassinated his good buddy Julius Caesar. Various Popes were poisoned, strangled, stabbed and one was thrown into the sea with an anchor tied around his neck. Life was not the most expensive thing in Italy.

"One minute," said the spotter beside Kyle. A dark-haired Oklahoman with the eating-disorder build of a marathon runner, Dan Laird had been with the CIA Directorate of Clandestine Operations for almost five years after leaving the Delta Force, and was no stranger to pressure. He was busy handling the spotting scope, the cameras and the communications. "Everything in the green."

"Umm." Swanson hummed in reply. He breathed with his mouth open slightly, feeding measurable amounts of oxygen into lungs that had been conditioned by years of aerobic training. His heart rate was under control, with his pulse steady at 45 beats per minute. His mind was clear, focused as much as his eyes. A lot of things could go wrong in a minute, or even in a second. The fleshy tip of his right index finger rested light on the trigger of the long rifle, and the world before him was in slow motion. The target was right where he was supposed to be, his back to the street, unmoving in his chair, nothing beyond him but a meticulously parked truck that would eat the big bullet. The wanted terrorist filled his scope, but Swanson ignored that fact, for to dwell on the madness of this evil man might have stirred the sniper's emotion, and that might alter the target picture; this was no time for buck fever.

Young Mister Martin had been dug out by the intelligence analysts of the Central Intelligence Agency some months ago, and at first they did not realize who they had found. He had been posting in chatrooms and using his American idiom to woo impressionable girls in the United States into coming to visit him. *Don't believe all of that crap in the media. All Muslims aren't evil just because there are a few crazies. Look at me! Do I look crazy or scary? Come on over for a visit and we'll have some fun in Rome.* His accompanying picture showed a handsome guy leaning against a white Mercedes convertible beside a beautiful beach. The man was a hashtag Romeo, and several American girls who had bought his Twitter act never returned home again. Once ensnared abroad, it was simple enough to drug them and smuggle them straight across the Tyrrhenian Sea to Tunisia and into lost lives they would never have imagined in their most horrible nightmares.

But as the ISIS trolls reached out for new brides and potential turncoat agents in the United States, the terrorist group was itself being trolled by even better hackers who were on the payrolls of many governments, and those were the bleary-eyed wizards who had hooked Roland Lewis Martin. When his picture beside the luxury car was studied, it was determined to be a Photoshop digital stage set. That aroused enough suspicion to wash it through multiple facial recognition and other identification databases, which pointed up the blue snake tattoo, the missing fingertip and the pierced ear, matched his height, erased the beard, fixed the proper eye color by erasing the contact lenses, chalked in personality traits, and discovered that this target was really Abdul Ansari Mohammad, the *jihadi* American who had decapitated a captured U.S. journalist in Iraq on live video.

Washington moved to set the trap, and tagged Swanson to do the hit. For many years, he had been the deadliest sniper in the U.S. Marine Corps, where he was the trigger-puller for a top-secret special ops team known as Task Force Trident and won the Congressional Medal of Honor and a salad of other decorations. That was all in the past, and while his current day job was vice president of the multinational defense industrial company called Excalibur Enterprises, he had another job, too. Like Laird, he performed special missions for the CIA.

With the cover of being a businessman, it was easy for him to arrange a business trip to Rome without arousing suspicion. The rest of the team was waiting for him there, including the two women operatives who would act as the bait. They were made up to appear to be in their late teens, although both were college graduates.

The girls rendezvoused with Martin at the famous Trevi, a magnet for tourists, and guided him to the nearby sidewalk café. He planned to get them out later for dinner and a sightseeing trip around Rome by night. It had worked before, and he had a confident swagger as they reached the table, which had been set aside by the cooperating Italian police, the *Agenzia Informazioni e Sicurezza Interna*, one of whom became their waiter. Martin took the chair beside the street so his guests could watch the passing throng. The opening chit-chat was friendly.

"Thirty seconds." Dan Laird pressed a button on his cell phone, and the phone in the back pocket of one of the girls vibrated silently. Swanson watched the agent casually dab her lips with a white napkin, then say something to her girlfriend. She never looked up to locate the sniper. Her friend asked Martin where the bathrooms were located. He pointed inside, the two women smiled, promised to be right back, and pushed out of their chairs. The waiter also vanished. There were no other customers, and police a block away were quietly detouring tourists around the site. Martin, confident of his quarry and very pleased with himself, did not realize that he was alone on the street. He took a drink, fished his own phone from a pocket to send a coded message that once again, the kidnap operation was going very well.

"Area is clear. He is all yours." Laird's words were businesslike, but Kyle could sense the tension and his peripheral vision caught the agent's hands moving to cover his ears. Kyle preferred not to wear ear coverings, balancing the need to hear what was going on around him against the unconscious anticipation of a loud explosion.

Swanson had no further adjustments to make. The head was as big as a Halloween pumpkin in the scope, and steady. He slowly brought the trigger straight back with no lateral pressure, felt the slack disappear, and then came the explosion as the sniper rifle boomed. A .50-cal shot in the tight confines of an urban center sounded like a cannon blast, and the first thoughts of unaware people who heard it was that a terrorist bomb had been detonated. Pedestrians and tourists scattered, and pigeons soared away in flapping panic. Sirens began to whoop. Kyle soaked up the mighty recoil and brought the glass back on target.

The body of Roland Martin had been jerked almost out of the chair, but was still in it, canted sideways over the strong metal arm. The head was gone and the debris of the skull and brains had spewed in a long trail toward the parked truck.

"Done," he said.

"Done," agreed his spotter. Laird kept the camera recording as police vehicles wailed up to the curb, uniformed cops set up a perimeter and as soon as the two women came out, they were roughly arrested and cuffed and put into a marked van. That was part of the show in case ISIS also had a watcher. The pair of agents was released as soon as they were out of sight.

"Strange," said Dan Laird, looking at his cell phone as Kyle packed away the rifle. A police car was waiting for them downstairs.

"The boss is in town."

"Marty?" Martin Atkins was the deputy director of clandestine operations was long past his days as a field officer but ran the secretive clandestine operations department with meticulous planning, including the care and protection for agents at the sharp end of the dark

CIA spear. From the Agency headquarters in Langley, Virginia, Atkins was like a spider in his web, controlling everything, and seldom left it.

"Yeah. Probably wants a first-hand briefing on this op."

Swanson had the Excalibur safely in its case, and was straightening his clothes as Laird finished packing. "Maybe he wants to post that video on the Net. The op was symbolic and intended to remind those ISIS crazies that we can and will reach out and touch them whenever we please."

Laird gave a deep laugh. "It would go viral in ten minutes. Let the social media pass the word for us."

They took their time getting downstairs. Nobody was hunting them because the cops were in on the action, although they had not been told any more than they needed to know. The small unmarked car that met them had another agent at the wheel, and Swanson and Laird climbed into the rear seat. Kyle started thinking about dinner tonight, wanting something special before he and Laird left off tomorrow to take out another ISIS recruiter, a British predator operating out of Cairo whose game was convincing gullible American kids to come visit the Pyramids in Egypt.

The Agency safe house was west of the Tiber River in the working class neighborhood of Trastevere, far from the grandeur of the Vatican, but equally a part of Rome, a city that was saddled with a Madonna-whore complex. The people who served the upper crust Italians and rich tourists had to live somewhere, too, and the squalid apartments along the tangled medieval streets of the Trastevere had housed them for generations. The CIA had a multistory building with a middle-aged Italian couple living on the street level, where the stew was always warm in the little kitchen and the floor tiles were always chilly. Marty Atkins was waiting on the upper floor in a soundproofed room that had bullet-proof glass in the window and was examined for electronic eavesdropping equipment daily.

His gray hair had grown out since the last time Kyle had met him several months ago, and the new style gave him a more distinguished look, and an obvious loss of some weight had sharpened his features. Laser surgery on his brown eyes meant he no longer wore steel-rimmed glasses. Atkins had figured out that further advancement in government required that he moderate his former hell-for-leather lifestyle and look like a gentleman when meeting politicians. His temper still needed work.

He was reading briefing papers when they entered, and put them aside to greet both of his visitors warmly. There was a tenseness about him, and a sense of apprehension. "Dan, hate to seem rude here, but I need some private time with Kyle. If you go on over to the hotel, I'll spring for drinks for everybody in about thirty minutes."

Laird shrugged. "Free drinks sound good. Can I ask if this concerns tomorrow's mission?"

Atkins exhaled and shook his head. "Yes. That job is not going to happen."

Dan Laird had been around the Agency long enough to know when he was a supernumerary. Only two people were to be part of this conversation, and Laird made three. Counterintelligence was a fluid, ever-changing game. Nothing personal. Just part of the job. He winked and left without another word. They would tell him what he needed, when necessary.

Atkins motioned Swanson to an awkward, overstuffed chair beside the table near the window, and picked up one of the briefing papers he had been reading. He studied the sniper. "Do you know a Russian by the name of Strakov? Ivan Strakov?"

Swanson did not recall the name immediately, but slowly an image swam into shape. Long ago, there was an intense, skinny enlisted man on an exchange training program between Russian naval infantry and the U.S. Marines. He wanted to be an elite sniper. Kyle, as the instructor, washed him out of the program because of poor shooting scores and had ordered him to undergo a thorough medical examination. The Russian had been hiding the fact that his vision was failing, but the scores spoke for themselves. He was a lousy shot. Strakov could no longer hack it, which meant the end of his career in the Russian marines.

"Yeah. I remember him, vaguely. Very intelligent and great with numbers, but so bad with a long gun that we called him Ivan the Terrible."

"This is beyond top secret, Kyle," Marty Atkins said as he handed over the one-page memo of a few short paragraphs.

Kyle read it, then slid the paper back onto the table. "When do I leave?"

"Go back to the hotel and shit, shine, shower and shave, then you're outta here."

"Where am I going?"

"You don't need to know that yet. Call me when you get there."